"In repayment of your debt, I would like you to marry me."

Grant stared at the diminutive redhead, certain he must have misunderstood. "You'd like . . . what?"

"For you to marry me," Dina repeated, with perfect calm.

"Why should you wish for such a thing, Miss Moore?"

"I'm not a fortune hunter, if that's what you're thinking, Mr. Turpin. Rather the reverse, in fact."

She leaned forward, keeping her voice low. "First, I want to assure you that if you marry me, I will not interfere in your life in any way. If you have mistresses, you may keep them. Whatever routines you have, you may continue to follow. My only concern is to safeguard my inheritance."

"A wonderful and talented author."
Under the Covers

"[Brenda Hiatt] swirls the reader into passion and danger."
Jo Beverley

Other **AVON ROMANCES**

BRENDA HIATT

The Runaway Heiress

AVON BOOKS
An Imprint of HarperCollinsPublishers

This is a work of fiction. Names, characters, places, and incidents are products of the author's imagination or are used fictitiously and are not to be construed as real. Any resemblance to actual events, locales, organizations, or persons, living or dead, is entirely coincidental.

AVON BOOKS
An Imprint of HarperCollins*Publishers*
10 East 53rd Street
New York, New York 10022-5299

Copyright © 2005 by Brenda Hiatt Barber
ISBN: 0-06-072379-3
www.avonromance.com

First Avon Books paperback printing: June 2005

Avon Trademark Reg. U.S. Pat. Off. and in Other Countries, Marca Registrada, Hecho en U.S.A.
HarperCollins® is a registered trademark of HarperCollins Publishers Inc.

Printed in the U.S.A.

10 9 8 7 6 5 4 3 2 1

In memory of Monique Ellis,
gifted author, tireless teacher,
and my dear friend

Chapter 1

Staffordshire, England
December 1, 1816

The horses stamped with impatience on the dark, deserted road north. A cold rain fell impartially on the sturdy traveling coach, the huddled postboy on the box, and the couple who faced each other at the edge of the road, several yards away.

Undine Moore stared at her would-be bridegroom in blank disbelief, shivering as icy water wound along the once jaunty ribbons of her bonnet and found its way inside her cloak and down her bodice, where it added to the chill his words had given her.

"Not going? What do you mean we're not going?" Anxiety—and anger—made her normally low voice shrill. "We've been planning this for a month."

Diggory Tallow appeared paler and thinner than ever in the flickering lights of the coach lamps. "I know we have, Dina, but I've realized an elopement will not serve. Think of the gossip, the scandal . . . of your brother's anger. A more conventional wedding—"

"There's no time and you know it," Dina protested. "My birthday is in four days. If we wait for a license—which Silas will doubtless attempt to prevent us from procuring in any case—my share of the estate will become his."

Diggory stared at the ground, making patterns in the mud with the toe of his boot, and shrugged. "It's . . . it's not as though I'm marrying you for your money, Dina."

"Of course not." Indeed, Diggory's fortune was three or four times greater than her own. "But why should Silas have what is rightfully mine—what should be ours?"

She lowered her voice persuasively. "Come, Diggory, I've gone through the difficulty of slipping out of the house and walking all the way here in the rain. The carriage is already hired. And there's no knowing when Silas may return to Ashcombe, making another attempt impossible. Let's head for Scotland as we've planned. We'll be married before Silas can stop us."

Though he still did not meet her eye, Diggory spoke firmly—more firmly than she'd ever heard him speak before. "I'm sorry, Dina. I can't."

"But why not? What has changed?" It was unlike the normally malleable Diggory to resist her leadership. His docility had been one reason she'd set her cap at him in the first place—that and his availability, as he lived only two miles from Ashcombe and visited Silas frequently.

Of course, he had always dragged his heels when it had come to actually planning a wedding. She assumed it was fear of her brother, who admittedly was almost twice Diggory's size, and had clearly established his dominance over the smaller man during his years as Diggory's upperclassman at Cambridge.

Finally, after repeated excuses to delay their nuptials, Dina had realized the only course that would guarantee her absolutely necessary marriage before her twenty-fifth birthday was an elopement. Rather to her surprise, Diggory had seemed perfectly amenable—until now.

"Do you no longer care for me?" she asked when he did not answer, trying to ignore the water soaking through her thick wool cloak as well as the guilt that assailed her at asking such a question. She quieted it by telling herself—again—that though she did not love Diggory, she would be a good wife to him.

"It's . . . it's not that," he stammered, flicking a quick glance at her before staring at his feet again.

Hoping that denoted a softening of his inexplicable stance, Dina shivered visibly. "I'm freezing. Let's at least get into the chaise to discuss it, shall we?"

Diggory bit his lip. "I, ah, I don't think we'd better. I can't stay long."

Dina wondered with a spurt of amusement whether he feared she might try to kidnap him, to force him to elope with her after all. Then, as he shifted uncomfortably, she wondered if she shouldn't do just that.

No, it would take at least two days to reach Scotland. She could never compel him to remain with her if he was truly unwilling. Perhaps if she had brought along a pistol . . .

"You promised to help me safeguard my inheritance," she said, not bothering to hide her irritation. "This is the only way."

"Yes, well, I've been thinking." He spoke quickly, as though he'd rehearsed his words in advance. "Surely you can trust your brother to do that? You can't really think he'll refuse you your dowry, once you do marry?"

Dina let out a hiss of exasperation, for she'd been over this with Diggory before. "No, I can't trust Silas in this, not with his gambling debts mounting. His own fortune is gone. I've no desire to see mine go the same way, nor can I believe you would wish for that, either."

"No, but I . . . well, that is . . ."

"You're afraid of him, I understand that," she persisted.

"Not . . . not afraid, exactly . . ."

Her brother had always held a great deal of influence over Diggory. No doubt Silas had tyrannized him—along with the other underclassmen—at school. Her brother had always been a bully, as Dina herself knew from long experience. Though now they were adults he rarely threatened her physically, he still occasionally vented his temper by restricting her to the house. She didn't care to think what he might do if she went back there now, if he discovered where she'd gone and why.

"Silas likes you," Dina told Diggory firmly. "He might be angry at first, but he actually told me recently that he'd like to have you as a brother-in-law."

She'd nearly told Silas about her betrothal when he'd said that, but caution had prevented her. She knew that Silas was not eager for her to marry. He'd used one excuse after another to prevent her London come-out, until he could honestly claim he couldn't afford it. And on the two or three occasions that local gentlemen had shown interest in her, Silas had "convinced" them to look elsewhere.

"He's told me that, too," Diggory said now. "That's why I'm sure he'll do right by us, if we just wait."

Dina frowned at him in the darkness. "Silas told you . . . Did you tell him I had agreed to marry you?"

A long silence greeted her question, then, "I, ah, may have mentioned it once." His sudden nervousness was palpable.

Vague suspicions that had played at the edges of her mind off and on for months suddenly crystallized. "Silas knows all about our plan, doesn't he? He's persuaded you to play along, to pretend to go through with this elopement, only to renege at the last minute."

When it would be far too late for her to find another willing bridegroom.

The frightened glance Diggory sent her was all the answer she needed, belying his stammered denial.

"But don't you see that by marrying me, you will have control of my fortune instead of Silas?" she said with growing urgency. She must convince him, persuade him back to her side. "How could he convince you to give that up, even assuming you care nothing for me?"

"It's not that I don't—that is—I told you it's not about the money. Silas has made it clear I'll be sorry if I marry you before your birthday. On the other hand, if we wait, he has promised to do well by us and . . . and not to hurt me."

"Then he's been in it from the first?" she demanded, aghast. That meant they had both been stringing her along for most of the past year, keeping her secure in the belief that she'd found a way out of her dilemma—and so keeping her from seeking another solution.

"I . . . I'd better go," he said, turning toward the carriage.

Dina's heart pounded as she watched her last hope disappear. How could she have been so stupid? She'd thought she was the one pulling Diggory's strings, when all the time it had been Silas pulling both Diggory's and her own. And now—was she to tamely return home and admit defeat?

"No," she said sharply. Diggory stopped, his hand on the door of the hired chaise, to glance back at her curiously.

Dina took two quick steps toward him, pulled back her arm, and drove her fist into his jaw with all her might. With a single grunt of surprise, Diggory collapsed into a heap on the muddy road.

" 'Ere, now!" exclaimed the startled postboy, who had been discreetly ignoring the entire exchange until then. "What'd ye do to him, miss?"

"He, ah, had too much to drink," Dina improvised, looking down at Diggory's awkwardly sprawled form with only the smallest bit of regret. Should she ask the postboy to help her get him into the carriage? No, already he was beginning to stir— and groan.

She stepped around to the front of the coach. "I assume you've already been paid for the first stage?" she asked.

"That's the funny thing. He told me to get the rig up for a trip all the way to Scotland, then tonight he just give me half a crown to bring 'im here, then back to 'is house."

Dina bit back an unladylike curse. She'd given Diggory enough money last week to transport them all the way to the border. "A minute," she said, bending down to search his pockets before he came fully to himself. In a moment she found the twenty pounds she'd given him in his breast pocket.

Standing, she showed the postboy the money. "This should get me to Gretna Green. Will you take me the first stage?"

Slowly the fellow nodded. "Just you? What about the bloke?" he asked, pointing.

"He'll be all right," she assured him—and herself. "It seems he didn't wish to go to Scotland after all . . . but I do."

Picking up her satchel from the side of the road, she opened the door to the coach and climbed inside just as Diggory managed to sit up, confusedly rubbing his jaw. She tapped on the roof, and with a lurch, the carriage headed north.

Dina had intended to elope, and elope she would—though what good doing so alone would do her, she wasn't sure. Still, it was preferable to returning home, where Silas would make certain she couldn't escape again before her fateful birthday. Perhaps by the time she reached the border, she would come up with a plan.

* * *

"Quite a run, eh?" asked Lord Rushford with a grin as the members of the Odd Sock Hunt Club returned to Ivy Lodge, where they resided during fox-hunting season.

"One of the best this year," agreed Grant Turpin, better known to his intimates as Thor because of his imposing stature. "The Quorn can always be counted on for an excellent day's sport. Superb pack, that. Which reminds me, I need to check on Princess. She's near to whelping."

Thor planned to build a foxhound pack of his own one day, and had been breeding some superior bloodlines toward that end. With a nod to his cronies, he headed in the direction of the stables, one corner of which he'd set up as a kennel block for the season, where he could supervise a few of his more promising pairings.

A chorus of tiny whimperings greeted him as he neared the stall where he'd left Princess. His groom, who also helped with the hounds, met him with a grin. "Six pups, sir," he announced. "Three dogs and three bitches. All healthy."

"Good man, Farrell," Thor exclaimed, entering the stall to kneel next to Princess. She looked tired but contented, greeting him with a thump of her tail as she nursed her new brood. Thor examined each perfect pup in turn, humming with satisfaction.

It was early for a whelping, as most pups were born in February or March, but he'd had a chance to put Belvoir's Rounder to Princess, so had bred her on an early heat. Besides, the early whelping might give these pups an advantage over smaller, younger ones when they were walked out to farmers in May.

Thor stood, smiling. "They seem off to an excellent start," he said to Farrell. "Mind you keep plenty of fresh straw in here, as it's like to be cold tonight." Turning, he headed back to wash up for dinner, ducking his head slightly, as the stall door barely accommodated his height, which was some inches over six feet.

He was halfway across the stable yard when he heard rapid footsteps. Looking up, he was startled to see Jonas, a footman from his parents' house in Lincolnshire, hurrying toward him.

"Thank heaven you're here, sir!" the man exclaimed, quickening his pace further. "I set out this morning, soon as we found out, and only just arrived. The roads were a fright."

"Found out what?" Thor asked, alarmed. "Are my parents—?"

"They're . . . they're fine." Jonas panted. "That is, Lord and Lady Rumble are in good health, or were when I left. It's Miss Turpin that, well, here." He pulled a sealed envelope from his pocket and handed it to Thor.

Quickly he broke the seal and unfolded it, to read what his father had written in his precise, scholarly hand.

My Dear Son,

I hope this finds you well. I regret to inform you that your sister, Violet, has done something your

mother believes most unwise, in eloping with a cer-
tain Mr. Plunkett, a young man she met at one of
the local assemblies. The house is in an uproar since
the event and your mother in decline, so I trust you
will write speedily to assure her that you will do all
in your power to recover your sister and protect
both her virtue and her dowry—for your mother be-
lieves this Mr. Plunkett to be a fortune hunter. For
my part, I can't help thinking that if Violet truly
cares for the fellow, little harm can come from their
marriage, but your mother is of another mind. In
hopes you will respond accordingly,

                 Your affectionate father, etc.

Thor was already striding toward the house as he
finished reading. He'd have thought that if anything
could bestir his phlegmatic, unflappable father to action, it would be the elopement of his only daughter,
but it appeared he was wrong. No doubt his father's
easygoing attitude had been added encouragement
to this Plunkett fellow, in fact.

He cursed under his breath, not only over the
likely loss of his sister, but at the knowledge that he
would doubtless miss the next week of hunting. Of
course, there was nothing else for it but to go after
Violet and do what he could, as it was clear his father
meant to do nothing himself.

Heaven only knew what agonies his more emotional mother was suffering. There was a degree of
irony in her opposition to Violet's marriage, considering how she'd been mercilessly badgering Thor

himself to wed, to the point that he had begun to avoid going home. Still, he would not be so uncharitable as to mention that to her. At least not unless this current matter was resolved happily, against all odds.

On entering Ivy Lodge, he went at once to the writing desk in the parlor. "Rush, I need to leave at once and will be gone some days—perhaps a week or more," he said to Lord Rushford, the lone other occupant of the parlor. Thor pulled out a sheet of paper, dipped a pen, and began writing.

"What is it, old fellow?" Rush asked in obvious concern. "Anything I can help with?"

Thor shook his head, his instinct to keep the matter secret as long as possible. "It's a family matter."

His friend frowned, then nodded. "Of course."

Finishing the brief note to his parents, Thor sanded and sealed it, then handed it to Jonas. "Get something to eat in the kitchen before you start back," he told the man.

Once the footman was gone, Thor turned back to Rush with a sigh. "Now that I think on it, you might be able to advise me. I've never—that is—devil it. Violet has eloped."

Rush blinked. "But she's just a child. How—?"

"Actually, she was twenty in August." The surprise on his friend's face would have made Thor laugh if the situation hadn't been so grave. "My mother believes this"—he glanced down at his father's letter—"Plunkett is a fortune hunter, and she's likely right, or they'd have had no need to elope."

"Clearly it's been longer than I realized since I last saw Miss Turpin. But Lady Rumble is undoubtedly right. In fact, I recall a Plunkett from Lincolnshire, never promoted past ensign—a plausible rogue and a gamester as well. If it's the same fellow, you'd do well to prevent the marriage, if possible."

This was unwelcome news to Thor, if not particularly shocking. Violet had always been a hopeless romantic, often abetting his mother's incessant attempts to interest him in some girl or other. Unfortunately, that would make Violet easy prey for a "plausible rogue."

"I'll do my best," he said, "though if she spends a night on the road with him, we may not have much choice in the matter."

Rush frowned thoughtfully. "Assuming they're headed for Scotland, they'll not likely make it past Yorkshire by tonight. How much of a start do they have?"

"I'm not sure. Apparently her disappearance wasn't discovered until this morning." Which meant it was probably too late already to salvage poor Violet's reputation.

"Don't look so glum, man," said Rush bracingly. "If you head north at once, there's a chance you'll catch them before they reach the border. Word can't have gotten 'round yet. We'll manage to hush things up, you'll see."

"I hope so," Thor replied without much hope. "At any rate, I'd best be off. Pity Othello is already tired." His smoky black hunter was the fastest horse Thor owned, but would have little speed left in him after today's hunt.

"Take Pilot." Rush owned three hunters, and had ridden Comrade today. "He should be spoiling for a run, and he's big enough to bear you. Change horses at Grantham, and I'll go fetch him tomorrow. Go on up and pack a few things, and I'll have Mrs. Sykes put together a few pies and a flask of something. We'll have you off in ten minutes. With any luck, you can make it to Wetherby by midnight. And who knows? They may stop for the night there themselves, and your chase will be over."

Thor nodded, somewhat cheered by his friend's positive attitude. "Thank you, Rush. I know I don't need to caution you—"

"Not a word, on my honor. Now, go."

Ten minutes later, Thor was mounted on Rush's burly chestnut, provisions in a bag tied to the saddle. With a last salute to his friend and wartime commander, he spurred Pilot to a canter and headed north. Whether he would hug his sister or turn her over his knee when he caught her, he didn't know— but first, he had to catch her.

Dina felt a mixture of relief and anxiety when the coach finally lumbered to a halt, her journey at an end. Relief that the longest trip she'd ever taken was over—who would have guessed that travel would be so tiring?—and anxiety because she was no nearer a solution to her problem than she'd been when she'd left.

She pulled her satchel from the coach, thanked the driver, and headed wearily toward the Gretna Hall Hotel, which had become infamous in recent years for its clandestine marriages.

After two nights and two days on the road, she was feeling the lack of the regular exercise and physical training she subjected herself to at home. Why sitting in a coach should leave her more exhausted than a two-hour walk or a vigorous bout of shadow-boxing or weight lifting, she had no idea. She was also feeling out of sorts—and desperate.

At the various coaching stops, she'd discreetly examined any man who looked unattached, with some vague idea of explaining her plight and relying on gallantry—or, at least, greed. However, none had appeared at all promising: colliers blackened with coal dust, wizened farmers, brash tradesmen.

She'd even struck up a conversation with one of her drivers, for all he looked twenty years her senior, only to discover that he had a wife and four children at home. That she'd even asked showed her how hopeless her situation had become.

Hopelessness led to rationalization. Perhaps it would not be so terrible for her inheritance to come under Silas's control. His luck at the tables might turn, or she might convince him to keep her money separate. She knew the odds were small, but with her birthday only two days away and no potential groom in sight, rationalization was all she had.

Entering the hotel, she bespoke a room, a private parlor, and dinner, which the clearly curious innkeeper promised would be served within half an hour. She was just settling herself into a chair near the parlor fire to wait, when the clatter of another carriage arriving drew her attention.

Rising to look out of the window, she saw a slim, dark-haired lady being handed down by a rather sullen-looking young man with obvious aspirations to dandyism. As they entered the Hall and approached her parlor, she could overhear their conversation.

"I haven't the money, and you've spent all yours," the man was saying, clearly continuing an argument that had been going on in the coach. "Can't think why you bought that bonnet in Halifax."

"I wanted something special to wear for my wedding day, since I haven't a veil or new slippers," the lady replied.

The gentleman snorted. "Now we're in Scotland, let's just tie the knot. Especially since you won't—"

"A nice dinner in a private parlor and a few hothouse flowers isn't so much to ask," the lady retorted with a pout. "And you'll have money enough when we return to Lincolnshire. What of all those poems you wrote me, so full of romance? A girl has a few expectations of what her special day will be like, you know."

Her interest caught, Dina moved to the door of the parlor. The lady appeared to be no more than eighteen, her pretty, animated face framed by a cloud of dark curls. The gentleman was older, probably nearing thirty, and handsome in a dark, flamboyant sort of way. Or would have been, had his expression been less peevish. Even as Dina examined him, he smoothed his features into a cajoling smile.

"Come, now, Vi, we had all this out before. You'll have all the hothouse flowers you could ever want, once we're properly wed. We'll throw a ball and invite all of our friends to celebrate our marriage. You'll like that, won't you?"

"Yes, I should like a grand ball," she conceded. "But it's not the same. This will be my actual wedding. I want it to be special. Something I can remember forever."

The gentleman sighed but clung to his charming smile. "Please, Vi—" he began again.

Realizing that this might be the very solution she'd been hoping for, Dina stepped forward.

Chapter 2

"Hello," Dina called from the parlor door. The arguing couple turned to face her, just as the innkeeper approached to see to the newcomers. "I'm Dina Moore. I realize we've never met, but I wonder if I might not impose upon you to be my guests for dinner, to spare me the tedium of dining alone."

The man frowned suspiciously and started to shake his head, but Dina sent him her most bewitching smile—the one she'd practiced all those months on the traitorous Diggory—and his brow cleared. "I, ah, I suppose——" he began.

"Yes, let's do, Gregory," his partner pleaded prettily. "I'm famished, and Mrs. Moore seems a respectable lady."

Dina nodded to the innkeeper, who bustled off. "Actually, it's Miss," she said, with another smiling glance at the gentleman. "But I am respectable, I assure you."

"Gregory Plunkett," he said with a smart bow. "And this is Violet, er, Plunkett, my wife."

"Fiancée," the girl retorted, flashing him an irritated glance before turning back to Dina. "I'm still Violet Turpin. Gregory and I have come to Gretna Green to get married. Isn't that romantic?"

"Exceedingly so," Dina agreed, carefully keeping cynicism from her voice. "Is there an angry father in pursuit, to make the adventure complete?" She was determined to keep the conversation away from her own situation—for now.

Though a trace of alarm showed in Mr. Plunkett's eyes, Miss Turpin grinned engagingly. "Unlikely, knowing my father. I can't imagine he'd bestir himself, though my brother would likely come after me if he knew I'd eloped. But he's hunting in the Shires, miles away from our home, so there's little risk of that."

"Still, to be safe, we probably ought not delay the wedding." Mr. Plunkett glanced toward the windows. "I'll just pop out and ask the innkeeper to send for the parson, and to prepare us a room for the night—a proper bridal chamber, m'love."

Something about his manner irritated Dina—perhaps because it reminded her of Diggory's placating promises, all of which had proved false. Her nebulous plan to steal Mr. Plunkett from Miss Turpin solidified into resolve. Aside from her own situation, she couldn't allow this innocent girl to marry such an insincere fortune hunter—for such she assumed him to be.

"A moment, Mr. Plunkett," she said now, as he made to rise. Then, to Miss Turpin, "Surely it would be far more romantic to be married in the morning, by which time you would be able to procure flowers and other traditional trappings?"

The girl nodded, clearly unaware that Dina had overheard her earlier. "Just what I have been telling Gregory. This hurried declaration between dinner and bed is not at all what I had in mind."

"But, sweetheart." The syrup in Mr. Plunkett's voice was enough to make Dina retch. "That would mean separate rooms yet again, and you know we can't afford that—not if I'm to pay the parson."

"Miss Turpin is welcome to share my room," Dina said quickly. "As it appears neither of us brought a maid along, that should serve nicely. I had worried about the appropriateness of sleeping alone at an inn, I confess. In light of that, I would be willing to pay for your room as well, Mr. Plunkett. I can well afford it." She definitely didn't mistake the speculative gleam in Mr. Plunkett's eyes at her addendum.

Miss Turpin didn't appear to notice, however. "May I, Miss Moore? That would be lovely. I would rather wait, if you don't mind too much, Gregory."

"Very well, if that will make you happy, my dear," he said, though he still looked at Dina.

Their dinner arrived then, and during the course of it, Dina discovered that Miss Turpin had known Mr. Plunkett less than a month, and that their engagement had preceded their elopement by only two days.

"Gregory made it sound so romantic," Miss Turpin explained. "But I confess, had I known how tedious the journey would be, I'd have chosen a more conventional wedding."

Mr. Plunkett quickly commented on the excellence of the cheese, which told Dina he didn't care to pursue the topic. No matter. She would get the details from Miss Turpin once they retired to their shared bedchamber. In the meantime, she behaved as charmingly as she knew how, given her limited practice, hoping both to win Miss Turpin's confidence and heighten Mr. Plunkett's interest in herself.

As all were tired from traveling, they agreed to retire directly after dinner. Preceding Miss Turpin into their room, Dina was relieved to note that it seemed clean, if small, and that the bed was easily large enough to share.

"You never did say, Miss Moore, how you come to be here in Gretna Green all alone," Miss Turpin commented, following her into the room and closing the door.

"Please, call me Dina. All my friends do, and if we're to share a bedchamber, it seems you should follow suit."

"And you must call me Violet," the other girl said readily, but she was not so easily deflected as that. "So why are you here?" she persisted. "Have you a bridegroom of your own on his way to meet you? Perhaps we can have a double wedding tomorrow."

Dina had to smile at Violet's unquenchable optimism. For a moment she debated how much to tell her, but the temptation to pour out her troubles to a sympathetic ear was too strong to resist, and soon she was relating her entire story.

"How dreadful," Violet exclaimed when she had

finished. "Your brother and his friend have treated you most infamously. And your birthday is but two days off?"

Dina nodded glumly. "December fifth."

"Really, though, I can't think you'd have been happy married to a man such as that. You would be better off poor than trapped in a loveless marriage."

At that, Dina managed a wry smile. "You are very young, Violet."

"Twenty. Not so very young. I guessed you to be no older, truth be told, for I am half a head taller than you."

That wasn't exactly what Dina had meant, but she nodded. "Yes, I've always been rather small, I fear. I've done my best to compensate for it, however."

Violet grinned her engaging grin. "Indeed, no one could overlook you, with such bright red hair. I've never seen such a lovely color."

Now Dina's smile was genuine. "That's very kind of you, though I must tell you that as a child, I endured quite a bit of teasing over it."

She saw no point in telling Violet that her way of dealing with her insecurities over her hair color and small stature had been to wheedle a favorite uncle into giving her boxing and fencing lessons on the sly. She'd also learned to handle a pistol quite handily. She hadn't practiced in the two or three years since her uncle had left for America, but she still followed a private regimen of calisthenics and weights, so that her strength and flexibility far exceeded those of most gently bred ladies.

Instead, she turned the conversation away from herself by asking, "Are you quite certain you wish to marry Mr. Plunkett in the morning? You've known each other such a short time."

She expected an ardent declaration of love, but instead Violet frowned. "I thought I did. An elopement seemed wildly exciting—and romantic—when he first proposed it. But now . . ."

"Now, perhaps, you wonder why he didn't dare to approach your father? There must be a reason, you know."

"Yes, that's the bother of a long journey. It gives one entirely too much time to think."

Dina nearly laughed, though in fact she'd discovered the same thing herself. "Surely that's a good thing in such a situation as this? A marriage is forever, after all, while infatuation can disappear overnight."

"My fortune will not, however," Violet replied with more cynicism than Dina had expected from the girl. "And that, I begin to suspect, is what primarily matters to Gregory. He does write such beautiful poetry, though." She sighed. "Would you care to see a bit of it?"

At Dina's nod, Violet pulled a few sheets from the side pocket of her valise. Dina read the first poem, then the next, with a growing sense of outraged disbelief.

"Are not his verses fine?"

Setting the papers aside, she met Violet's expectant gaze with a sympathetic one of her own. "I should think so, considering that they were written by none other than Shakespeare himself."

"What?" The younger girl snatched up the pages

and stared at them. "Oh, surely not! Why, here, he calls me his muse—the tenth muse. He even named the poem after me: Violet. 'How can my muse want subject to invent, While thou doest breathe, that pour'st into my verse—'"

"'—thine own sweet argument, too excellent for every vulgar paper to rehearse,'" Dina continued from memory. "My mother was a great lover of Shakespeare, particularly his sonnets, and insisted I learn them all. At her direction, my governess had me commit nearly half of them to memory."

Violet sat back, deflated. Before Dina could find the words to comfort her, however, the girl gave a little laugh. "I begin to realize it's a very good thing I happened upon you, Dina. Otherwise I would have married Gregory for his poetry, when it isn't even his. It seems he has been insincere on all fronts."

"I'm sorry," Dina said gently. "But, as you said to me about Diggory, it's better that you discovered it now, before binding yourself for life, hard as it may seem at present."

"Yes. Yes, you're right, of course. In the morning, I'll break it off." Suddenly she smiled—a genuine-seeming smile. "I think you must be my guardian angel, Dina. I'll do my best to dream up a solution to your problem while I sleep, to return the favor."

Dina thanked her, feeling more than a little bit guilty. Convincing Violet not to marry Mr. Plunkett had been far easier than she'd anticipated, which meant there couldn't have been much affection involved, but the girl would still likely see Dina's marrying him herself as a betrayal. However, it seemed to be the only answer.

Somehow, she suspected she'd have no trouble getting Mr. Plunkett to agree to allow her to live her own life as she chose, with a generous allowance, in return for control of her fortune. Especially once he realized Miss Turpin was lost to him. On that encouraging thought, Dina was able to fall quickly asleep.

Thor was in the devil's own temper. The farther north he rode, the nastier the weather became—and his hope of saving his sister from a disastrous marriage faded at each change of horses. As Rush had suggested, he had indeed found evidence of the fleeing couple at Wetherby, but had also discovered that they were at least ten hours ahead of him. As he neared the Scottish border just after daybreak after a second night on the road, he feared his chance of preventing the wedding was nonexistent.

Spurring his latest mount to a canter, he squinted into the icy wind, hoping against hope that some miracle might have delayed them. For if the worst had happened and Violet was indeed married to a dastard, it would be his duty as a brother to kill the fellow. Even in wartime, Thor had abhorred killing, though he'd been forced to it on occasion, just as they all had.

This, however, would be different. This would be murder. Much as the idea revolted him, however, he would not shirk his responsibility for Violet's future. Sleet began to sting his face, but he refused to slow. Better to get it over.

* * *

"How shall I tell Gregory that I won't marry him after all?" Violet asked worriedly as she and Dina helped each other dress. "Suppose he is driven to despair—or becomes angry with me?"

Dina seized this perfect opening. "Let me tell him for you," she suggested. "I can make you sound both regretful and reasonable, and you will be spared any entreaties to change your mind—or any outbursts of temper."

Violet looked vastly relieved for a moment, but then shook her head. "No, I cannot ask you to do that for me, Dina. Suppose he takes his anger out on you?"

That was the least of Dina's worries. "I can handle him, I'm certain. And if I can't," she added, as Violet still looked concerned, "I will simply call the innkeeper. I can't imagine he will attempt violence, in any event."

"If you're sure . . ." The relief was back in Violet's eyes.

"I am. I'll return once it is done." Thrusting down another surge of guilt, Dina smoothed the skirts of her travel-creased gown and went down. Mr. Plunkett was waiting at the foot of the stairs, resplendent in an impeccably tailored blue coat, a gold waistcoat, and a voluminous, intricately tied cravat.

"Ah, Miss Moore," he exclaimed, his gaze straying past her up toward the second floor. "I trust Miss Turpin will be down directly? I'd thought to send for the parson as soon as we've breakfasted."

Dina took a deep breath, pinned her most charming smile to her face, and moved toward him. "Good morning, Mr. Plunkett. My, but that coat becomes you well! Please, join me in the parlor. I have something rather important to discuss with you."

Frowning curiously, he followed her into the room where they'd dined last night. "Important? Violet, er, Miss Turpin is not ill, is she?"

"No, no, she is fine. Please, sir, take a seat, do." Dina gestured to a chair, taking the one opposite it. She waited until he settled himself before continuing. "I fear Miss Turpin has had a . . . change of heart. However," she said quickly, as he made to rise again, an exclamation on his lips, "I have an alternative to offer you."

"An alternative?" he echoed suspiciously. "What do you mean? Did you talk Violet out of marrying me?"

Dina bit back the retort that nearly escaped her, schooling her expression to one of calm sympathy. "I did, for your sake as well as hers. I believe you can do better—as can she."

His face darkened. "Better? What do you—?"

"I mean that my own fortune is greater than Miss Turpin's." She did not actually know that to be the case, but it was clear she had Mr. Plunkett's attention. "Nor do I have a father with the authority to disinherit me should he disapprove of the man I marry."

His brows rose. "You . . . you are offering to marry me in Miss Turpin's stead? Why?"

Perhaps he wasn't quite as dull as she'd assumed. Still, Dina felt fairly certain that her will was stronger than his. "My father left my inheritance in such a way that if I do not marry within two days, it will revert to my brother. To prevent that, I am willing to strike a bargain with you, Mr. Plunkett."

"What sort of bargain?" he asked, leaning forward, his former fiancée apparently forgotten.

"If you marry me, you will have control of my fortune and the freedom to pursue your own life as you will. All I ask in return is the guarantee of a generous allowance that will permit me to live in independence. I am no romantic, Mr. Plunkett. I merely wish to safeguard my future."

An incredulous smile broke across his face. Dina noted dispassionately that while it made him appear more handsome, it also emphasized his weakness—but that was all to the good, for her purposes. Yes, she could control this man, she thought.

"Miss Moore, I believe you have yourself a bargain. Shall I call the parson, or would you prefer we commit our agreement to writing first?"

Triumph welled up in Dina's breast. But before she could answer, a commotion arose outside. She heard raised voices, and then a hurried knock came at the parlor door.

"Yes, what is it?" Mr. Plunkett called out impatiently.

"A gentleman has just arrived, shouting for his sister," came the innkeeper's voice through the door. "A great big fellow, he is. I thought I should warn you."

Dina stifled an unladylike curse. A great big fellow? Silas must have followed her after all. She turned back to Mr. Plunkett, who had jumped to his feet, suddenly pale.

"Tell him—" she began, only to be interrupted when the door flew open with a crash.

The man who entered was a stranger, though he was certainly large—larger even than Silas. He moved menacingly forward. "Plunkett?" he all but roared.

Dina sat as though glued to her chair, all notion of intervening gone. This man was terrifying.

It appeared Mr. Plunkett shared her view. "Y-yes?" he gasped.

Without another word, the giant swung a huge fist and sent Dina's would-be bridegroom crashing to the floor. "Name your seconds," he growled at the heap of tailored blue, gold, and white.

"But . . . but I—" Mr. Plunkett stammered, looking to Dina for support.

Following his glance, the giant noticed Dina for the first time. She drew back as far as her chair would allow. "My apologies, madam," he said stiffly. "I—"

"Grant?" Violet's voice came from the open doorway. He turned to face her, to Dina's relief. Then she felt a twinge of guilt for that relief, for surely she was better equipped to face this angry colossus than young Violet could be.

She rose, ready to leap to her new friend's defense if necessary. Certainly he still looked angry enough to commit further violence as he strode toward her.

"Vi! Thank God I found you. What on earth were you thinking?" he fairly shouted. "Have you any idea how frantic Mother has been?" He gripped his sister by the shoulders and gave her a shake.

Dina quickly stepped forward. "Mr. Turpin, I presume?" she said, mainly to divert his attention until the worst of his anger passed. In her experience with Silas, those first few minutes were always the most dangerous.

The large man frowned down at her in pardonable confusion. Dina couldn't help noticing—quite irrelevantly—that he was actually rather handsome, with waving golden-brown hair and brilliant blue eyes blazing from beneath dark brows.

"Who the devil are you?" he demanded, his voice still angry.

Before she could answer, a crash recalled the momentarily forgotten Mr. Plunkett. They all turned in time to see him disappearing through the parlor window, which he had apparently forced open with a poker from the fireplace.

"The blackguard!" Mr. Turpin exclaimed, starting after him, though there was no way he would fit through that window. "He won't escape me so easily. I'll be back once I've made a widow of you, Vi. You'll be happier that way, believe me."

Dina took a step back at such bloodthirstiness, but Violet only laughed. "How very medieval of you, Grant. But I haven't married him yet, so there's no need for such extreme measures—though I had a few choice things to tell him myself."

His glance swiveled back to Dina, making her cringe. "And who—?"

Violet put an arm around Dina's shoulders. "This is Miss Moore, Grant, and you mustn't shout at her. She has been exceedingly kind to me." She didn't seem the least bit afraid of her imposing brother.

"Has she?" Mr. Turpin raked Dina with a glance before turning back to his sister.

Feeling suddenly out of place in this interview, and seeing that Violet was in no apparent danger from her brother, Dina excused herself and hurried out to the inn yard. Mr. Plunkett was her last—her only—hope. Perhaps there was still a chance that she could intercept him and induce him to marry her. Maybe if they went to another inn . . .

She saw no sign of him, however, so went back inside to find the innkeeper. Violet and her brother emerged from the parlor as she was questioning the man.

"Gone," the inkeeper said with a shrug. "Hired a horse and headed south. He paid his shot, so I had no cause to stop him," he concluded defensively, for Mr. Turpin was again frowning thunderously.

Despair hit Dina like a wall. She had been so close—so close!—only to have this bullying giant ruin everything. Now her last chance of saving her fortune was gone beyond recall.

"Perhaps it's just as well," Violet said, making her blink, before she realized that the girl wasn't talking about her situation. "I'd have liked to think he'd have fought for me, but I suppose I'm not surprised. And now you've no need to kill him, Grant, and end up in prison, or worse."

Still struggling to understand this unexpected turn of events, Thor continued to frown at his sister. "How is it you didn't marry him?" he asked. "You must have reached Gretna Green sometime yesterday."

"Yes, late yesterday afternoon. Gregory wanted to marry at once, but I insisted on dinner first. And then I met Dina—Miss Moore. She allowed me to share her room last night, then opened my eyes to Gregory's true nature, before it was too late."

He turned to examine the other woman more closely. At first he'd assumed that Miss Moore was somehow attached to the inn, but now he realized it was not so. Her gown, though creased with travel and at least two years out of style, was well made, and there was a certain intelligence in her green eyes.

She lifted her chin to meet his gaze, but did not smile. No, definitely not a servant.

"It seems I have cause to be exceedingly grateful to you, Miss Moore." As he relaxed, it finally penetrated that none of his worst fears had—or would—come to pass.

"Yes, we should repay her somehow, don't you think, Grant?" Violet asked, her natural exuberance reasserting itself.

The sudden rush of relief made him smile. "Indeed we should. What can we do for you, Miss Moore? Like King Ahasuerus, I feel I should offer you anything, up to half my kingdom—not that I have a kingdom, of course." He paused, realizing he was on the verge of babbling. "Seriously, though, Miss Moore, name your reward."

She regarded him speculatively for a moment, then gave a small nod, as though coming to a sudden decision. "Very well, Mr. Turpin," she said. "In repayment of your debt, I would like you to marry me."

Chapter 3

Thor stared at the diminutive redhead, certain he must have misunderstood. "You'd like . . . what?"

"For you to marry me," she repeated, with perfect calm.

"I, ah . . ." He groped for an appropriate response and came up completely empty-handed.

Violet, at his side, suddenly clapped her hands. "Why, what a perfect idea, Dina! That will solve your problem admirably, and give me a sister into the bargain. Oh, do, Grant. Indeed, in honor you must, for you did tell her to name her reward. We owe her a great debt of gratitude, do we not?"

"Yes, but that was—I didn't—" He shook his head in an effort to clear his thoughts and unblock his tongue. If what Violet said was true, this woman had

saved his sister from a most imprudent marriage—
and had likely saved him from a murder charge, as
well, which meant he owed her for both their lives.
Still—

"Why should you wish for such a thing, Miss
Moore?" True, he stood to inherit a fair fortune
along with the barony someday, but she couldn't
know that. Could she?

"I'm not a fortune hunter, if that's what you're thinking, Mr. Turpin," she said, startling him with her at-
tunement to his thoughts. "Rather the reverse, in fact."

"But—"

"Why do we not have the innkeeper bring us
breakfast, and I'll explain while we eat? Perhaps, after hearing my story, you will be willing to honor
your offer."

"Offer? But I—" He subsided, for he *had* obliquely
promised to grant whatever she requested. "Breakfast seems an excellent idea." Not only was he hungry, but it would give him time to think. And to hear
whatever story she might have to account for such an
outlandish request.

"I'll tell the innkeeper," Violet said, fairly bounc-
ing from the room. The moment he had her alone,
Thor intended to give his sister a thorough scolding.
She wasn't treating this situation with nearly the
gravity it deserved.

"Won't you have a seat, Miss Moore?" he said, mo-
tioning toward the table and chairs in front of the
fire. "As it appears my sister has already heard your
story, feel free to begin in her absence." He knew he
sounded stiff, but this was all quite outside his realm
of experience.

With a nervous glance from those brilliant green eyes, she moved past him and seated herself at the small, square table. He moved to do the same, sitting opposite her. "Well?" he prompted.

She leaned forward, keeping her voice low. "First," she said, "I want to assure you that if you marry me, I will not interfere in your life in any way. If you have mistresses, you may keep them. Whatever activities you enjoy, you may continue. My only concern is to safeguard my inheritance."

Before he could ask for clarification of that remarkable promise, light footsteps approached, and she sat back. Thor stared at her with surprise and a great deal of curiosity.

"Our breakfast is on the way," Violet announced, seating herself between them, on Thor's left. "Have you begun yet, Dina?"

Miss Moore shook her head, avoiding his eye. "Since I'd thought to give your brother more background than I told you last night, I waited for your return." She paused for a moment as though marshalling her thoughts, then began.

"My father was Ezekiel Moore, second son of Viscount Mendenthorp. My mother was born Rose Weymount, only child of Baron Weymount. As his estate was unentailed, my mother inherited everything but his title when he died."

Thor was startled. How could a woman of such impeccable lineage have found herself in such an unusual situation, with no one to look after her interests?

"That inheritance stipulated that my father will his estate equally to my brother and myself," she continued. "My father did so, but with the caveat that if I remained unmarried by the age of five and twenty, my portion would revert to my brother, so that he could use it to care for his spinster sister— women, as he believed, being ill-equipped to manage their own affairs."

Violet snorted and seemed about to say something to that, but just then a servant came in, bearing their breakfasts on a tray.

"That seems a reasonable compromise with respect to your inheritance," Thor commented when the man was gone, with a quelling glance at his sister.

"Yes, most would agree. I thought so myself when I discovered the terms, on my parents' deaths five years ago. They died of a fever, within days of each other," she explained in answer to his questioning glance. "But that was before I discovered my brother's penchant for gaming."

"I take it your brother has not been particularly lucky at the tables?" he prompted when she paused.

"Quite the reverse, I fear. In fact, his losses have been so heavy that I suspect he has already pledged a portion of my inheritance to his creditors."

Thor nodded, though he still had questions. "I see your problem. But why have you not solved it by marrying before now? As you are of age, your brother could not prevent you, and I can't imagine you'd have difficulty finding a willing gentleman, given your fortune and your appearance." There was no point in denying that she was an attractive woman, if not in his usual style.

Pinkening slightly, Miss Moore managed a small smile. "I thought to do just that, but it turns out that the gentleman in question was under my brother's control. He made what I assumed was an honorable offer, only to renege at the last possible moment, with my twenty-fifth birthday just days away. Thus, my current dilemma."

Thor involuntarily clenched his teeth at the thought of such a heartless deception, but only asked, "But how does that bring you to Scotland just now?"

She pinkened further. "Diggory—Mr. Tallow— and I were to elope, as he had put off our wedding for so long that time was growing short. He kept saying he wanted to tell Silas first—" She broke off and shook her head fiercely.

"The carriage was already hired when Mr. Tallow refused to accompany me to Scotland," she continued, "so I, ah, decided to come alone, in hopes that some solution might present itself."

"And now it has," Violet broke in excitedly. "Don't you see, Grant? You *must* marry her, or her wicked brother will win the day. We can't have that, can we?"

Though sympathetic, Thor was not so easily swayed. "You can't actually know that your brother intends to use your inheritance to pay gaming debts."

"When Silas returned from London in October, a flurry of letters followed him. Suspicious, I read a few when he was out, and discovered them to be from creditors. Then I overheard him telling his secretary that they only needed to be put off for six weeks—which would exactly correspond with my birthday. That's when I realized that a quick marriage would be my only hope of safeguarding my fortune."

"Circumstantial, but still rather damning," he agreed. "What of the estate itself?"

"Mortgaged—and many of the valuables have mysteriously disappeared over the past year or two. Sold to pay earlier debts, I imagine."

He was silent for a long moment, mulling over everything she'd said. As it happened, he had met Silas Moore on one or two occasions in Town and had been less than impressed. The fellow frequented some of the worst gaming hells, using his charm— and his size—to attract women and intimidate men. Needless to say, Thor had not been intimidated.

If he refused to marry Miss Moore, it would be tantamount to giving her inheritance to her brother or, rather, to his cardsharp creditors—a distasteful prospect. Acceding to her request, however, meant binding himself for life to a woman he didn't even know—also a distasteful prospect.

"Given your brother's apparent perfidy," he said, "why should you trust me? You know nothing about me. I could be a gamester as well, or have other, even worse vices."

"You could," she agreed. "But desperate circumstances call for desperate measures. I am willing to take that chance."

"And he doesn't," Violet assured her. "Have any terrible vices, that is. I'm sure I'd know, if he did."

Thor sent his sister an exasperated glance, but Miss Moore smiled. "That is all the surety I need. I believe that my future would be safer in your hands than in my brother's, Mr. Turpin. I therefore await your decision."

"Oh, do agree, Grant," Violet urged. "Mother keeps saying you must marry, and I know you've no prospects. Think how happy this would make her."

Yes, his mother would no doubt be ecstatic—and would cease flinging debutantes and neighbors' daughters at his head. He had to admit *that* was an attractive prospect. Miss Moore's lineage was impeccable, and she apparently had a sizable dowry, as well. He could no doubt do worse.

Then there was the matter of Miss Moore's startling promise not to interfere in his life—something most men of his acquaintance would envy. He could leave her in the country and go hunting, or to Town, as he pleased. His life would scarcely change at all by marrying her. And she was a pretty little thing . . .

He glanced across the table at her again, appraisingly. Little. Definitely little. That detail, as much as any other, made Thor balk.

He'd never cared for petite, delicate women. Had, in fact, been almost afraid of them. They seemed too . . . breakable, given his own size and strength. For that reason, he'd avoided the usual bits of muslin when it came to mistresses, preferring instead to dally with the occasional strong, strapping country lass. Bedding Miss Moore would be rather like mating a bull mastiff to a foxhound like Bluebell—both cruel and implausible.

Not that she would have any desire for the physical aspects of marriage, of course. And he was sure he could keep his own passions in check. But there was the matter of the succession . . . No, it was out of the question.

"Violet, I'd like to speak privately with Miss Moore." Refusing her request would be easier for him—and less embarrassing for Miss Moore— without his sister in the room.

"Oh! Certainly. I'll, ah, go upstairs and pack up my things. Then I'll be ready should you wish to head home right after the wedding." Flashing them both a grin over her shoulder, she left the room.

"That girl has no sense of shame," he murmured, shaking his head. "She likes you, however, Miss Moore, which is a point in your favor."

"Then your sister normally exhibits better judgment than she did in the matter of her elopement?"

He nodded. "She has always had a tendency to romanticism, but in all else, she has a remarkably level head for her age."

That was good to know, as Dina was relying on Violet's commendation of her brother as much as Mr. Turpin was apparently relying on her good opinion of Dina herself. Still, Dina was more than half inclined to withdraw her suggestion that they marry.

Though Mr. Plunkett had also been a stranger to her, she had been able to take his measure and use it to her advantage. He was a man who put greed above reason, so she'd been reasonably sure that she could arrange their marriage to her liking: a percentage of her fortune in exchange for a guarantee of her independence.

Mr. Turpin, she knew instinctively, would not be

so easily manipulated—and that thought frightened her more than she cared to admit.

Even so, she forced herself to meet his gaze squarely and say, with a confidence she couldn't feel, "Then we're agreed?"

But to her surprise, he shook his head. "I'm sorry, Miss Moore, but a marriage between us really won't do. Surely there is another way to solve your problem?"

She let out the breath she hadn't realized she'd been holding, feeling an unexpected surge of relief. Yes, perhaps he *could* help her in another, less frightening way. "I can't blame you for refusing, Mr. Turpin. You can have no more desire to bind yourself to a stranger than I have."

He blinked, clearly startled by her calm response.

"I, however, am driven by necessity," she continued before he could speak. "I *must* marry, or resign myself to poverty. There are no doubt worse fates, but it is still one I prefer to avoid. Unfortunately, your arrival here ruined my last chance of doing so, which is why I made such a bold suggestion."

"My arrival?" he asked in obvious confusion. "But—"

"Mr. Plunkett," she clarified. "I had just prevailed upon him to marry me, instead of your sister, when you burst into the room and knocked him down, causing him to flee."

"Then I'm doubly glad I did so," he declared, the same fierce frown he'd worn on his initial entrance again descending upon his brow. "Damned fickle blackguard."

She hid a shudder at her narrow escape from marrying this big, overbearing brute. "Mr. Plunkett can't have gone far yet," she said. "If you can find him, explain the mistake, and bring him back here, I'm quite willing to marry him instead of yourself. That will solve both my problem and yours, wouldn't you say?"

Dina sat back in her chair with a smile, but to her surprise, Mr. Turpin didn't seem nearly as pleased with her solution as she had expected.

"Solve your problem? By marrying a man you *know* is a fortune hunter and a wastrel? He's a gamester as well—like your brother."

"How can you know that?" she asked uneasily.

"A friend of mine knew Plunkett during the war. I doubt he's changed, given his recent behavior."

That seemed likely, but she still saw Mr. Plunkett as the lesser evil. There was something so . . . forceful about Mr. Turpin. It was more than just his unusual size, which was intimidating enough. He dominated the room by his very presence.

"Men do change." Surely that was true? "In any event, my options are limited. If you will fetch Mr. Plunkett back for me, I will consider your debt to me discharged."

"I'll do no such thing." His brow reminded her of a thundercloud. "Apart from . . . How do you suppose Violet would feel to know Mr. Plunkett would so easily jilt her?"

"But Violet had already decided against marrying Mr. Plunkett before he agreed to marry me," she explained. "I'm sure he wouldn't have considered my offer otherwise." In fact, she suspected he would have, but she had no more desire for Violet to discover that than Mr. Turpin did.

"And such constancy recommends itself to you, does it?" he said sarcastically.

She flinched at his words, but tried to conceal it. "As I said, I had—and have—little choice, particularly as you refuse to offer yourself in his stead."

For a long moment he glowered at her—for so long that it was all she could do not to fidget. Suddenly he let out a gusty sigh. "Oh, very well."

"You'll go after him, then?" Marriage to Mr. Plunkett would not be so bad. He had been willing to put their financial agreement in writing, after all. Perhaps—

"No. I'll marry you myself."

Dina's mouth fell open, but she did not notice for several seconds. She closed it, then opened it again to say weakly, "You? But I thought—"

"I know what you thought—what I said. But I asked you to name your reward, and you did so. I will abide by my original bargain."

"It . . . it wasn't precisely a bargain," she stammered, confused by her conflicting feelings. She supposed she should be grateful, but—

Without warning, he stood, startling her again with his sheer size. "I feel I must honor it as such," he said firmly, pacing to the window and back. "Still, there are one or two particulars I wish to have clear before we take that irrevocable step."

He continued to pace, not looking at her.

"Particulars?" she prompted when the silence stretched into awkwardness.

"Yes." He stopped, looming over her. "You made a rather, ah, unorthodox promise earlier. I wanted to determine just what you meant by it."

Dina swallowed. She would not be afraid of this man. He had done nothing—yet—to directly threaten her.

"I meant exactly what I said. All I require is a legally binding marriage certificate that I can show to the trustees, to prevent my brother from claiming my inheritance. Nothing more."

"So we call the parson, marry over the anvil, then—what? Go our separate ways?"

She breathed easier at this evidence that he was willing to be reasonable. "Surely that would be easiest for both of us."

Frowning, he again seated himself opposite her. "Then you wish to simply go home and continue living on your brother's mortgaged estate after we marry?"

"That was my intention, yes. Is it not what you would prefer, as well?"

He raised one thick brow. "I was merely asking if that's what *you* would prefer. Personally, I think it would look dashed odd—unless you intend to keep our marriage a secret?"

"No, I must inform my brother and the trustees, to secure my inheritance. In any event, secrecy would be difficult to maintain, would it not?" She was thinking of Violet.

"It would. Nor would it serve my own purpose. For one thing, it would require me to lie to my parents, which I will not do."

She found his uncompromising attitude oddly admirable. Such integrity was outside her experience.

"What do you suggest, then?" she asked nervously. Silas, at least, was a known quantity, however unpleasant.

He knit his brows thoughtfully for a moment. "I should like to take you home to meet my parents. From there, we can contact your trustees, and your brother, by letter. By now I'm sure your brother is greatly concerned about you, however dishonest his intentions may have been."

Dina wasn't sure of that at all, though she supposed it was possible. At least she liked to think so. But there was a definite flaw in Mr. Turpin's plan, apart from that.

"I really must return home first, even if only briefly," she said. "I brought only the barest necessities with me, for one thing. In addition, I dare not let Silas—or the trustees—assume that I was still unwed on my birthday. He might well spend a large portion of my inheritance before realizing his error."

"Your birthday is when?"

"Tomorrow. I realize that I can't reach Ashcombe by then, but the sooner I do, with proof of my marriage in hand, the sooner I can prevent Silas from doing any damage to my inheritance."

He shrugged. "We can send a letter."

"Yes, we should probably do so as soon as we are wed," she agreed. "But that won't solve my other problem."

In addition to her clothes and other effects, she would prefer to retrieve what was left of her mother's jewels before Silas found them—and sold them. Of course, her brother would be furious when she returned with the news that she had successfully thwarted his plans, she realized with a shudder. He was perfectly capable of violence when angered. Still, she had learned to defend herself fairly well.

"You don't really wish to go alone, do you?" His blue eyes were disturbingly perceptive.

She blinked. "You will want to take Violet home as soon as possible, will you not? Your mother is worried, you said—"

"I can send a letter to allay her fears. If you feel you must return to your brother's house before coming to mine, I will escort you. As your husband, I can scarcely do less."

"If . . . if you feel it would be best." She couldn't deny a certain degree of relief at the idea of having him with her when she confronted Silas. "But what about Violet?"

"She will have to come with us. If she finds the journey tedious, it is her own fault. Besides, her presence may reduce the . . . awkwardness we might face in traveling together alone."

She had to agree that much was true. But then another thought occurred to her. "What on earth will your parents have to say about such an unexpected development?"

"I suspect they will be delighted." He smiled wryly. "As Violet intimated, my mother has been quite anxious for me to marry. However, that brings us to a more . . . delicate matter."

To her surprise, his face reddened slightly. When

she suddenly realized why, she felt her own face pinkening in turn.

"The, ah, nature of our marriage, you mean?" She couldn't think of a more delicate way to put it. "As I said, all I require is a marriage certificate."

"Yes, and I'm to continue my own life however I see fit—in return, I presume, for making no, ah, physical demands upon you?"

His question was gentle, but she suddenly found herself unable to meet his gaze. Though acutely embarrassed, she nodded.

"Fine. I just wanted to have that clear," he said, his voice now brisk. Clearly he was relieved to have that matter resolved.

So was she, Dina told herself. Exceedingly relieved. Still, she couldn't deny a prick to her feminine pride. Diggory had lied about his attraction to her, and this man apparently felt none, either. It seemed she was simply not the sort of woman who affected men in that way.

Which was just as well, she told herself firmly. Mr. Turpin was so very large—larger even than Silas. In the throes of passion, he would surely be terrifying. Quite unexpectedly, her mind conjured a picture of him, shirtless, passionate. The emotion that accompanied the vision, however, was definitely not fear.

Quickly she set the vision—and the emotion—aside. The last thing she needed was any sort of emotional entanglement with this man, as she had given him carte blanche to continue his life unfettered. Should she grow to care for him, that would only lead to heartbreak and humiliation. No, platonic friendship was definitely best—for both of them.

"I do require your cooperation in one area, however," he said then.

She braced herself for some mention of his need to get an heir eventually. She could hardly refuse, though—

"Keeping my sister's elopement quiet. Perhaps we can say that you and I eloped, that she came along as your chaperone?"

"Oh. Yes. That . . . that should serve. Once we are wed, you can trust me not to say anything that might sully Miss Turpin's reputation."

"Thank you—again." His eyes held hers for a long moment, making her insides flutter.

She stood, hiding her confusion under a businesslike manner. "Then we are agreed, Mr. Turpin. Now we merely have the formality of the wedding to get through."

Chapter 4

~~~~~~~~~~~~~~~

Half an hour later, Thor found himself exchanging marriage vows in the same parlor where he and Miss Moore had negotiated their agreement. Mr. Elliot, the parson brought in by the innkeeper, offered to read them a longer, more traditional service for a higher fee. To Violet's evident disappointment, both of them declined.

Having taken down their names and places of residence for the register and establishing that neither was already married, Mr. Elliot then asked, "Have you both come to this place of your own free will and accord?"

"I have." Miss Moore's voice, though soft, was firm.

"Mr. Turpin?"

The absurdity of the situation struck Thor, and for

an instant he was tempted to comment on it, but he mastered the urge and answered, as she had done, "I have."

"Mr. Turpin, do you take this woman to be your lawful wedded wife, forsaking all others, keeping only to her as long as you both shall live?"

With a distinct sense of unreality, Thor replied, "I do."

He turned to Miss Moore and repeated the question. Thor half expected her to hesitate, but she spoke her assent as steadily as he had done.

"Is there a ring?"

Thor started, for he hadn't considered such a detail at all, but Miss Moore nodded. "I have one."

Mr. Elliot held out his hand for the plain gold circlet, then handed it to Thor. "Place it on her finger."

Thor took her small hand—it was less than half the size of his—and slid the ring onto her fourth finger.

"Now, Mr. Turpin, repeat after me. With this ring, I thee wed; with my body, I thee worship; with all my worldly goods I thee endow; in the name of the Father, Son, and Holy Ghost. Amen."

Feeling as though he were playing a part on stage, Thor repeated the words, vaguely wondering if it was blasphemy to do so under the circumstances.

Even as that thought crossed his mind, Mr. Elliot placed her hand in his again and asked her to say, "What God has joined together, let no man put asunder."

This time she did hesitate, but only for a moment, before haltingly repeating the words. Her voice seemed higher than before, and rather breathless—not that Thor blamed her.

He remembered her expression when he'd agreed to make no physical demands on her. Stung by her obvious relief—even though he was relieved as well—he had cravenly neglected to mention the succession. Now, too late, he wondered whether that had been fair to either of them.

"Forasmuch as this man and this woman have consented to go together by giving and receiving a ring," Mr. Elliot intoned, "I therefore declare them to be man and wife before God and these witnesses in the name of the Father, Son, and Holy Ghost. Amen. Now," he continued in a much less formal voice, "if you will each sign the register and this certificate, I'll be on my way."

They did so, and it was over. Thor was married—to a woman he had met only two hours before. As the parson and innkeeper left the parlor with perfunctory congratulations, he commented, "Undine. That's an unusual name." What an inane thing to say at such a time.

"I was named for my maternal grandmother," she said. "I suspect my father would have objected, had he known it was mythological, rather than biblical."

"A water sprite, as I recall." He smiled down at her, wanting to ease her obvious discomfort. "Oddly fitting."

She glanced up at him in surprise. "Fitting? How so?"

Before he could answer, Violet piped up. "He probably means because you are so small—spritelike, you know."

"Of course," Dina said, feeling less womanly than

ever. "I suppose it's rather ironic that I've never even seen the sea."

"We can remedy that. Plumrose Park is near Alford, only a dozen miles or so from the coast." Her new husband—how odd to think of this imposing stranger in that way!—was still smiling. He was almost disturbingly handsome when he smiled.

"Well, Mrs. Turpin, shall we go?" he asked, compounding her feeling of disorientation. She would never be Dina Moore again.

"Go?" she almost squeaked, thinking of the bedchamber upstairs. But he had promised—

"Back to England," he clarified. "It is not yet noon, so if we start directly, we can be in Staffordshire tomorrow night."

Feeling foolish for the turn her thoughts had taken, Dina nodded. "My valise is already packed. Perhaps we can have the inn prepare us a luncheon of sorts that can be eaten along the way?"

This idea was praised as most clever by the others, though to Dina it seemed merely prudent, if they wished to make good time. Violet accompanied her upstairs to fetch her satchel while Mr. Turpin went to settle accounts with the innkeeper.

On the landing, Violet startled Dina by stopping to give her a hug. "I cannot believe that I suddenly have a sister," she exclaimed. "We shall have such lovely times, once we're home. I'll introduce you around, Grant will take you to all of the local assemblies—it will be famous!"

But Dina was not quite ready to think that far ahead. "Yes, no doubt," she murmured.

"Oh! And when I go to London for the Season, you can be my chaperone, instead of prickly Aunt Philomena. I hadn't even thought of that advantage before." She linked her arm through Dina's and continued on up the stairs.

"Chaperone?" Dina echoed weakly. "But I . . . I have never had a Season in London myself."

Violet turned to stare at her in dismay. "Never had a Season! I know your brother has not behaved well toward you, but to allow you to reach four-and-twenty without a proper debut? That's . . . why, it's almost barbaric."

At that, Dina couldn't help but laugh. "Not quite that. I was presented at Court when I was eighteen, while my parents were still alive. But Father hated London, so we only stayed a week."

"Well, that's something, I suppose." Violet seemed partially mollified. "But never to have been to any of the parties, or balls—they're much grander than any of your neighborhood dances, I assure you."

Dina remembered the last local dance she'd attended, more than a year ago. Held at the vicar's house, it had consisted of seven ladies, most of them past forty, and five gentlemen, all but one of them married. "No doubt you are right," she said.

While Violet put the finishing touches on her packing, Dina penned a brief letter to her brother, informing him of her changed status. Though she worded it as diplomatically as possible, not wanting to alienate him before she could retrieve her things, she was just as glad she would not be there when he received it.

When she and Violet came downstairs a few minutes later, Mr. Turpin was waiting by the front door.

"I have our luncheon." He held up a cloth-covered basket. "Now we won't have to stop until we change horses this afternoon. I have also written two letters, and have arranged for them to be sent by special messenger—one to my parents and one to your trustees."

"And I have written one for my brother," she said, handing him the sealed paper. He disappeared for a moment to intercept the messenger to Staffordshire, then returned to them.

"Where is your trunk?" he asked Dina as a servant carried Violet's downstairs.

She held up her valise. "This is all I brought, as I escaped my home on foot."

"A woman who can pack lightly is a treasure indeed." His blue eyes twinkled, almost as though he was enjoying himself.

Dina looked up at him curiously. "How can you be so . . . so cheerful? I actively sought my change in circumstances, but yours was rather thrust upon you."

He shrugged, still smiling. "Life is full of unexpected changes, I've found. All one can do is to make the best of them."

As the hired coach rumbled along on its journey south, Dina thought about that glib response. It made sense, she supposed—but did he mean it? And just what would "making the best of it" entail?

She glanced surreptitiously at the man next to her; Violet had insisted on taking the backward-facing seat so that the "newlyweds," as she called them, could sit side by side. Large as he was, there didn't appear to be an ounce of excess fat on him. Her new husband was fit, powerful . . . and very, very male.

They had passed the first hour or two by eating the luncheon they'd brought along from the inn, and with general conversation about the food, the weather, and the condition of the roads. Now, however, silence reigned in the coach, giving Dina a not necessarily welcome opportunity to think about the future.

"It occurs to me that we should use this time to become better acquainted." Mr. Turpin's deep voice startled her after the long silence. "What are your interests, Miss, er, Mrs.—devil it, what am I to call you?"

"Call her Dina, as I do, Grant." Violet smiled across from one to the other.

He looked down at Dina questioningly, and she felt herself blushing. After an embarrassed moment, she nodded. "Dina will be fine. It is what family and close friends have always called me."

"You do have close friends, then?" His voice was gentle, sympathetic, causing an unbidden lump in her throat.

"I . . . I did, when I was younger. They have all married and moved away now, however, after having their Seasons in London." She realized anew how lonely her life had been of late. Was that why she'd been so easily duped by Diggory and her brother?

"Then, Dina, I ask again—what are your interests? What do you do for enjoyment?"

She looked up at him blankly. "Enjoyment?

Why . . . I read, I suppose. Sometimes I help the vicar's wife to prepare baskets for the poor in our parish."

The last activities she'd truly enjoyed had been her lessons in fencing and boxing, and her practice at shooting, but those had been years ago. Her calisthenics and weights brought her satisfaction, but she could not precisely say she enjoyed them. In any event, she felt it might not be prudent to mention such unorthodox pursuits so early in her acquaintance with the Turpins.

"A lonely existence," he said, echoing her earlier thought. "But I'm sure Vi will have you in the thick of the social whirl in no time. No doubt you'll become positively nostalgic for your quiet, isolated life."

Smiling, he held her gaze, as though trying to divine her feelings. Dina doubted he was able to see much, as she wasn't sure herself how she felt about such a prospect.

"Do you attend so many entertainments at home, then?" She directed the question to Violet, relieved at the excuse to draw her gaze away from Mr. Turpin's too-perceptive one.

"Not so many as Grant implies," her new sister-in-law replied with a glance at her brother. "Mother and I dine with neighboring families two or three times a week, or have them to dine with us. Then there are the weekly assemblies in the village, and the occasional card party or rout, of course. I should say I am engaged no more than four or five nights a week, however, except when everyone is in the country during the summer."

Dina blinked at such an excess of activity. "I . . . see." Then a detail struck her. "You and your mother, you said. What of your father?"

"He rarely goes out," Mr. Turpin said before Violet could answer. "Our father prefers to socialize with his books."

"Yes, he is a great scholar," Violet agreed. "It drives poor Mother to distraction sometimes, but she dotes on him nonetheless. She is unwilling to leave him to take me to London—which has left me to Aunt Philomena's tender mercies. But this year will be different, of course, with you there, Dina."

But Dina still didn't care to look that far ahead. "What town are we likely to reach today?" she asked, mainly to change the subject. "I confess I paid little attention to the names of the stops on my way north."

"We will attempt to make it to Kendal," he replied, "though this mud is making for such slow going, we may only reach Penrith by nightfall. I'd have thought the roads would be frozen by now, this far north. It would have made for a quicker journey."

"At least it's not snowing," Violet said. "Besides, I am in no hurry. Mother will read me a terrific scold when we return, and I'd as soon delay that as long as possible."

"Oh? But I'd thought to pass the time on this journey by scolding you myself—for hours on end."

He frowned ferociously, but Dina thought she detected a twinkle in his blue eyes. Still, it surprised her when Violet laughed, for she had no experience with the sort of relationship this brother and sister enjoyed.

"I am far more afraid of Mother than I am of you, Grant, but you may attempt your worst, if you feel you must."

He shook his head with a sigh. "If I thought it would do any good, I would. But no words of mine are likely to instill sense in that romantical head of yours. You must realize by now how foolishly you behaved, Violet."

"Yes. Mr. Plunkett would have been no bargain, and I'm glad I did not marry him. I can't be sorry that I eloped, however, for if I hadn't, we should never have met Dina. Surely you can't regret that, can you, Grant?"

Dina tensed, wishing that Violet had not reminded him of their awkward situation just when the atmosphere in the carriage had been so relaxed. She stole a glance up at him, to find him regarding her speculatively.

"Not yet," he said. "What of you, Dina? Any regrets, now that you've had time to reflect on what we've done?"

She had several, in fact, but her situation was surely better now than it had been yesterday. Remembering her hopelessness then, she shook her head. "Not yet," she said, just as he had done.

"But the day is young, eh?" His cajoling tone made her realize how grudging her own must have been.

"If I discover regrets, I will have only myself to blame." She tried to convey an apology of sorts with her eyes.

He shifted slightly and his thigh brushed hers, though she was almost certain that was not intentional. Still, it sent an alarming thrill of awareness through her. Yes, she might very well come to regret what she'd done today.

Or not . . .

"Oh, pooh." Violet broke into her nervous thoughts. "What is this talk of blame and regrets? It is your wedding day! You should both be full of happy hopes and dreams for the future. What a pity that I am here to spoil what should be a romantic tête-à-tête between you."

Dina waited for Mr. Turpin to take his sister to task, to explain to her the difference between a marriage of necessity and a love match, but he only shook his head.

"Still the incurable romantic, after your own near-disastrous experience? You are incorrigible, Vi."

"Completely," she agreed, grinning across at him. "Life is more fun this way, I assure you."

Dina wished she could share the girl's optimism, but at least the embarrassing moment was past—for now. With Violet along, there were sure to be many others before they reached Plumrose Park.

"It is already beginning to get darker," she commented, staring out the window—more to avoid Mr. Turpin's gaze than because of any fascination with the view.

"Yes, the days are short in December, this far north." She felt his movement as he turned to look out his own window. "It will be full night before we even reach Penrith, at this rate."

"Or perhaps we shall be stuck in the mud and have to make our way on foot," said Violet. "Or be accosted by a handsome highwayman, who will be smitten by my beauty and carry me away to his secluded cottage."

Dina had to laugh. "Really, you should write romantic novels, Violet, with such an imagination."

The younger woman tossed her dark curls. "Perhaps I will. Then, when I become fabulously rich, Grant will no longer be able to tease me for my romantic fancies."

Mr. Turpin—somehow Dina couldn't yet think of him as Grant—leaned down to rummage in his bag. "I wish I had paper and pen in here, so that you could start now. That would at least silence your impertinence for an hour or two."

Their lighthearted banter caused Dina another pang of something like envy. Silas had rarely paid any attention to Dina at all, except to bully her when they were younger. How different her life might have been had she enjoyed this sort of relationship with her brother. She could not imagine Mr. Turpin ever plotting any sort of harm to Violet for his own gain.

Not that Silas had exactly planned to *harm* her, of course. No doubt he'd convinced himself that he would use her money to take care of her, as well as to support his gaming habit. Still, the very fact that he would put his own comfort ahead of Dina's welfare made him a different sort of man from Mr. Turpin.

She hoped.

The carriage gave a sudden jolt, causing Violet to exclaim and brace herself against the side of the vehicle, while Dina was thrown against the immovable force that was Mr. Turpin. Caught unawares, she found herself half across his lap, her head against his broad chest.

"Oh! My . . . my apologies," Dina stammered, struggling to extricate herself from such a horrifyingly undignified position.

Mr. Turpin grasped her by the shoulders and set her back on the seat beside him as though she were a child—or a doll. "No harm done," he said gruffly, though she noticed he didn't meet her eye. He seemed almost as embarrassed as she was.

A moment later the carriage lurched again, but this time Dina was better prepared, so that her hip merely grazed his—and only for an instant. Even that brief contact was both intimate and unsettling, however. Or perhaps unsettling because it seemed intimate. Not that—

"Goodness!" Violet exclaimed as the carriage gave an even more violent jolt, nearly unseating them all, before rocking to a halt. "What has happened?"

"I'll step out and see." Suiting action to words, Mr. Turpin opened the carriage door and climbed down, only to utter a loud curse, quickly muffled. "Apologies, ladies, but the road is nearly a foot deep in mud—well above my ankles. What ho, driver? Are we stuck?"

He closed the carriage door against the chill wind, preventing the women from hearing the man's reply, but it appeared that was the case. They heard some shouting, after which the coach lurched forward again, but only for a few seconds before shuddering to another stop.

A moment later, their escort stuck his head back into the coach. "The coachman says there is an inn of sorts less than half a mile ahead. I believe we would reach it more quickly on foot than by sitting here, and the walk would keep us all warmer, as well. Have either of you any footwear suitable for such an enterprise?"

"I left home on foot, so I was obliged to wear these," Dina said, displaying her sturdy half boots.

"Good girl." His tone was approving. "Violet?"

His sister grimaced. "Not really, though I can always bring along spare shoes and stockings to change into once we reach the inn."

"That will have to do, I suppose. Here, let me lift you over the worst of the mud." Grasping his sister about the waist, he swung her over to the grassy verge, which was soaking wet but not particularly muddy. He turned back to Dina. "Your turn."

She swallowed. "There's no need for such heroics on my behalf, as my shoes are up to the task."

"Nonsense. No need to get them muddier than necessary. It's over your ankles here by the coach, I assure you."

Without waiting for her reply, he reached in and seized her as he had Violet, easily lifting her over the mud and depositing her on her feet next to his sister. Dina felt a thrill laced with alarm at the man's sheer strength.

Retrieving a few necessities for each of them, he informed the driver that he would send someone from the inn to help with the coach, then turned to the women. "Well, ladies, shall we?"

The wet grass was slippery, and several times both Dina and Violet had to clutch at Mr. Turpin to keep from falling. He appeared to have no such difficulty, tramping stolidly along, keeping his pace to one the two females could match.

In about twenty minutes' time, they reached a village consisting of a dozen or so cottages around a market square and a slightly larger house that declared itself the Spotted Dog.

"Our inn, I presume," Thor commented, regarding the building dubiously.

His sister and his new bride had acquitted themselves remarkably well so far, but he suspected that there were more challenges ahead. This place could not possibly boast more than one or two guest rooms—if any. No doubt it primarily served as a pub and gathering spot for the village's inhabitants.

Pushing open the front door, they found themselves in a taproom, occupied by some four or five sturdy farmers engaged in conversation and mugs of ale. He was beginning to regret his decision to come here when a portly, jovial-looking man came through a door at the rear of the room and hurried toward them.

"Welcome to the Spotted Dog," he exclaimed in a thick Cumberland accent. "Here for a spot of dinner, are you? We've a nice dining parlor right through here, if the ladies would prefer not to eat here in the common room."

Thor moved toward the indicated door, for he didn't at all care for the idea of the ladies waiting in the taproom until the carriage could be shifted.

"Thank you," he said, "but I fear we need more than a meal. Our coach is stuck in the mud half a mile north of here. Is there anyone you can send to help get it out?"

"Oh, aye, I'll send Bob and Blinker right away. You

and the ladies wait in the parlor, and I'll have my Sue bring you summat."

Thor had thought to go back to the coach himself to offer what help he could, but he could scarcely leave the ladies here on their own, so he nodded and ushered them into what turned out to be a small but perfectly clean and cozy parlor.

"I suppose it could be worse," he said as soon as the innkeeper was out of earshot.

"Worse?" Violet echoed. "I think it's simply charming! What an adorable little village this is, don't you think, Dina?"

Before Dina could answer, however, a buxom young woman bustled into the room bearing a tray with bread, cheese, and three mugs of ale. "I'm Sue," she announced with a friendly smile. "Me dad wanted me to ask if you'll be needing a room for the night?"

"Do you have any available?" Thor tried not to sound skeptical.

"Just the one, but one of the ladies is welcome to share my room, as well." She beamed, as though this unorthodox arrangement was perfectly normal—and perhaps it was, in such a remote corner of England.

"If our coach can be freed, we'll doubtless continue our journey after we eat," he said. "If not, the ladies may have the room. I can sleep in any corner you can provide." He'd put up with far worse during the war, after all.

"You'll do no such thing," Violet exclaimed then, surprising him. "Why, this is your and Dina's wedding night! Of course the two of you must have the room. I don't mind sharing with Sue here in the least."

Young Sue exclaimed with delight. "Wedding night? My congratulations to you both. I must go tell Mother—she'll want to fix you a special dinner to celebrate, I'm sure." She bustled out again, and they could hear her shouting the news to the farmers in the taproom.

Thor frowned at his sister. "Was it really necessary to share our private concerns with the whole village?" Dina, he noticed, was looking acutely embarrassed.

"Private? A wedding should not be kept private," Violet protested. "I should think you would both want to celebrate."

"Why must you persist in treating this like a love match?" he snapped, before realizing how that might sound to Dina. Not that either of them had pretended the least bit of fondness for each other, of course. Still, he sent her an apologetic glance.

She did not meet his eye, however, only saying to Violet, "Your brother is right. Given the unusual circumstances of our marriage, the fact that we did not even know each other yesterday, I can't help feeling that the less said to strangers, the better."

"Hmph. No matter how it began, you'll be spending your lives together now. Why not eke as much romance—as much fun—from the situation as you can? That is what I would do, in your place."

"No doubt," said Thor acidly. He hoped more than ever that they would be able to travel farther that day.

Unfortunately, when the driver and other men returned to the inn half an hour later, it was to report that one of the wheels had been damaged in their efforts to free the coach from the mud.

"They already have the village wheelwright working to replace the broken spoke, but it won't be ready before morning," the postboy informed them.

"Early morning," the innkeeper chimed in. "Mr. DiMartino is very good at his craft, for all he's a furriner and a newcomer to our village."

"A newcomer?" Thor wondered that anyone would intentionally settle in such a remote place.

"Aye, he's only lived here some twenty years or so, when he come as apprentice to old Mr. Noseworthy what died a few seasons back. But Mr. DiMartino, he's starting to take to our ways now, and he's a bang-up blacksmith and wheelwright. Now, let me see about your dinner—and your bedchamber. I hear it's a special night for you two." He waggled his thick eyebrows at Thor and Dina.

They exchanged alarmed glances, then Thor shrugged slightly. "Er, yes," he said to the innkeeper. "Thank you."

It was likely to be an interesting night, at the very least.

Chapter 5

Though the dinner was excellent, simple country fare that it was, Dina could scarcely eat, she was so nervous about what lay ahead. Why had Mr. Turpin not insisted on his original suggestion that she and Violet share the inn's one guest chamber? It would have led to awkward questions, true, but surely no more awkward than the situation they would face once they retired.

It was as well that Violet carried on the bulk of the conversation over the meal, for Dina was almost too preoccupied to talk.

"What is Staffordshire like, Dina?" she asked at one point. "I have never been there, though it is but two counties away. Do they hunt foxes there?" She gave her brother a sly grin.

"Why, yes, I believe so," Dina replied, jarred from her disturbing thoughts. "I seem to recall—"

"The Atherstone hunts there," Mr. Turpin put in. "A fair-sized hunt, I understand, though I've never ridden with them."

"Perhaps now you will have a chance," Violet suggested. "We could stay there until Christmas, could we not?"

Dina tried to imagine what it would be like to live at Ashcombe Hall with her new husband and his sister, as well as Silas. Strange, at the very least. But he was shaking his head.

"I promised in my letter to Mother to bring you home as soon as may be—much as I know you would like to tarry."

Violet grimaced, then shrugged. "That's just as well, I suppose, for our neighbors will have all manner of parties in the coming weeks, and I should not wish to miss them."

"You will be lucky if Mother allows you to attend any of them, after the way you have behaved," he cautioned his sister, but she merely tossed her head.

"She will scold and threaten, but I'll talk her 'round—I always do." She went on to speculate on the various entertainments likely to occur and who was likely to attend each one, allowing Dina to lapse back into her thoughts until dinner was over.

Violet yawned as the plates were cleared away. "Goodness, I'm tired."

"Poor thing," said Sue sympathetically, balancing the empty dishes and mugs on a tray. "Soon as I dump these in the kitchen, I'll show you to our room—and you two to yours, as well," she added, with a saucy wink that made Dina blush.

A moment later, she led them up to the second floor. "This here's the guest room—or, I should say, the bridal chamber." She giggled. "Me mum and dad are across the hall if you need anything. You and me are upstairs," she said to Violet.

"Good night," Violet said. "See you in the morning." With a mischievous wink, she followed Sue up the next flight of stairs.

Dina watched her go, her heart thundering in her chest. Behind her, she heard Mr. Turpin turn the handle to their chamber.

"We can't very well stand about in the hallway all night," he said softly, "much as we might wish to." His addendum reassured her that he was no more eager to spend the night alone together than she was.

Nodding, she walked through the door he held open. A small but cheerful fire burned in a tiny grate, helping two candles to illuminate the chamber. The room itself was even smaller than she had expected, barely accommodating the bed, a three-legged stool near the door, and a narrow washstand.

He followed her in and closed the door. "Hm. If there were a proper chair, I would offer to sleep in it, but I can't quite see myself balancing on that stool all night. I suppose it will have to be the floor."

Dina eyed the narrow strip of bare boards visible between bed and wall. "The bed is much bigger than the available floor space. It would make more sense for you to have it, given our relative sizes."

"Don't be absurd. I would never be able to call myself a gentleman again if I agreed to that."

A hurried glance revealed the glimmer of a smile, but then she quickly looked away. This situation was far too intimate for comfort—and likely to become more so.

"I presume we will both sleep in our clothes?" She felt a pang of regret for the only gown she had with her, already showing the ravages of several days' continuous wear.

"I'd prefer not," he surprised her by saying. "I've been wearing these things for three full days now already. I can't imagine you would prefer to sleep in a corset, either."

That much was true, though she was slightly shocked that he would mention such an indelicate item. "But—"

"I'll just step downstairs, say we want more hot water or some such thing, and give you a chance to change. You can be safely under the covers before I return."

And then? she thought, but only nodded. She could turn her face to the wall while he stripped off his boots and . . . other things, she supposed. The moment he was gone, she unbuttoned her gown and draped it over the stool. Her corset took a bit more time, making her worry that he might return before she was finished. Nervousness made her fumble-fingered, so that it took even longer to unlace than usual.

Finally she had it off, however, and tucked it under her dress. Then, listening for returning footsteps, she gave her face a quick splash from the basin, quickly unlaced her boots, peeled off her stockings, and climbed into the bed, pulling the covers up to her chin. A moment later the door opened.

"Sorry to take so long." He set a small pot of hot water on the washstand. "The innkeeper's wife wanted to add her congratulations to the others we've received."

A mercy, Dina thought, for if he'd returned a moment earlier, he'd have caught her standing in her shift.

"I must say, I'm looking forward to a real bath, once we arrive at your brother's house," he said then. "Since the privations of war, I've grown inordinately fond of cleanliness."

Dina thrust away the image that arose at his words. She was looking forward to being clean again herself, of course. And their respective baths would have nothing to do with each other.

"It must have been very difficult, serving in the war." That was a much safer topic. "The marching, the camping, the fighting." Had he ever killed anyone? she wondered. Most likely, since he had been a soldier. The thought sent a chill through her.

"I didn't have to do much marching, as I was cavalry, but it was nothing like living in Town—or even the country," he admitted. "Our camps were generally of the most primitive sort, and it was common to go weeks at a time without a proper bed or bath. And I won't even mention the food."

She tried to imagine such a rugged, dangerous existence, one so many men had endured. Not Silas. There had been some talk of a commission, she recalled, but nothing had come of it. "What of the fighting? Did . . . did you have to do much of that?"

"My fair share, I suppose. That's the worst of war, of course. The rest could be regarded as an adventure, but getting shot at, and being forced to kill—that changes a man. But why are we discussing such an unpleasant topic? The war is over, and I, for one, am very glad of it."

So he *had* killed. Not only that, he was able to speak of it almost flippantly. And she was married to this man.

"I . . . I suppose we had best get to sleep. We will want to get an early start in the morning."

"I suppose so." He stripped off his coat and draped it over her things on the stool, revealing a white cambric shirt underneath. "I'll, um, have to sit on the bed to remove my boots, if you don't mind."

Dina swallowed, staring at the broad expanse of his chest, seeming even more massive without the coat, and at the V of skin revealed by his open collar. She shook her head. "No, of course not."

"After that, well, I suppose you'll just have to promise not to watch while I change. Unless you want to, of course," he added with a grin that made her whole body flame with embarrassment.

Instead of replying, she turned onto her side, away from him, and pulled the covers over her head.

Behind her, she heard him chuckle. "It would appear not. I'll try not to take offense."

She tried to relax, but it was impossible. Every nerve in her body seemed as taut as piano wire, her senses preternaturally sharpened. The bed shifted as he sat on the edge, but she had been expecting that. Even so, she tensed further at his proximity, given her own state of undress.

First one boot, then the other hit the floor, then the bed leveled again as he stood. She breathed a bit easier, but an instant later she heard splashing. Screwing her eyes tightly shut, she tried not to imagine him bending over the basin, his big hands moving over his face, his strong jaw, his neck. Would he have taken his shirt off entirely by now? A part of her longed to peek, to find out.

No! She had no desire for that sort of relationship; she'd made that clear. And so had he. His teasing just now only underscored it. She was a woman grown, not a silly schoolgirl to be undone by a man's mere proximity.

Without warning, the bed shifted again, and for a wild moment she thought she would roll toward him. Frantically she clutched the edge of the mattress, bracing herself against the sudden slope. What was he doing? She twitched at the covers, half tempted to peek, to make sure he wasn't actually climbing into bed with her, when she heard a slithering sound.

His stockings. He must be removing his stockings. The bed shifted back, and she heard louder slithering that she realized with a shock must be his trousers. She swallowed convulsively, unable to completely rein in her wayward imagination.

"If you've no more need for the candle, I'm going to blow it out now," he said softly, as though he didn't want to wake her if she was sleeping.

At first she didn't answer, thinking to pretend just that, but then decided that was cowardly. "All right," she said. "Good night."

"Good night, Dina."

Though she still had the covers over her head, she

knew when each candle went out from the soft puffs of his breath, almost like sighs. That would be the one on the washstand . . . and the one on the mantel. She risked a peep now. Yes, the room was lit only by the dim glow of the coal fire.

She took a deep breath of the cooler, fresher air of the room, a relief after the stuffiness under the covers. There was no real need to hide her eyes now that the candles were out. But then a shape loomed up in the darkness, almost making her gasp. As she watched between nearly closed lids, his large form disappeared into the narrow space between the bed and the window.

Dina began to relax at last, only regretting that she hadn't waited a minute or two longer to pull back the covers, as that would have spared her that disturbing silhouette of his near-naked torso. A bump made her tense again. Then came another.

"Damnation." The curse was a mere whisper, followed by two more bumps in quick succession.

With a start, Dina realized that poor Mr. Turpin had nothing to lie on save his cloak, and nothing to use as a blanket. How could she have been so selfish?

For a long moment punctuated by more bumping, she struggled with the conflicting demands of decency and courtesy, then said, "You may have the blanket, if you like. It seems only fair, as I have the bed."

From beneath the edge of the bed, he asked, "Is there more than one?"

"No, but it is quite thick and should cushion you from the hard floor."

"I can't take the only blanket. You'll freeze."

She was warmed by his concern, but of course could not say that. "I would still have the linens. Or we could ask the innkeeper for an extra blanket."

"That would mean getting dressed and undressed again, with all the attendant awkwardness. Not to mention the speculation it would cause, that a newlywed couple should need more than each other to stay warm," he added with a chuckle.

Dina felt her face prickling in the darkness and was glad he could not see her. Already his bumping about on the floor had likely been noticed by those downstairs. What would they think was going on? Poor man, it was her fault he was in such uncomfortable straits. If not for her, he'd have been safely on his way back to Lincolnshire with his sister.

She bit her lip, struggling with her conscience as well as her nervousness. "Please allow me to take the floor, then," she finally said. "I can fit in that space with no trouble, and will wrap myself in the blanket. That way, you can sleep under the linens as well as your cloak, and we should both be warm enough."

"Very well," he replied. "I suppose there's little gallantry in keeping you awake half the night with my tossing and turning down here." With a few more bumps as well as a grunt or two, he heaved himself to his feet. Dina was relieved to see that he'd wrapped his cloak about his body.

Following his example, she attempted to wrap the blanket about hers, only to discover that was trickier than she'd expected. First she had to extricate herself from the linens—and the blanket was tucked in at the foot of the bed.

"Drat it!" she exclaimed under her breath, tugging at the blanket. Should she ask him to help her? Even as she thought it, he moved to the foot of the bed and deftly released the blanket.

"Thank you."

"I should warn you that floor is harder than it looks."

"I . . . I'm sure I will be fine." It simply wasn't fair to make him sleep in that awkward little crack.

"You know, this bed is quite large—large enough that two could sleep in it quite comfortably without touching."

Dina froze, the blanket half wrapped about her. She opened her mouth to reject the scandalous suggestion, before realizing that in truth it wasn't scandalous at all. They were husband and wife, married in the eyes of the law and the world. And it wasn't as though he was suggesting any actual intimacy.

Still, it was a frightening prospect, sharing a bed with a virtual stranger for an entire night. What if he—

"I give you my word, I will not take advantage of the situation," he said when she did not answer.

Suddenly Dina felt foolish. He had already made it perfectly clear that he did not desire her as a woman. Why should she deny them both a good night's sleep over some sort of misplaced modesty? To him, it would no doubt be much the same as sharing a bed with a comrade—or a sister. As it would be for her, of course.

"Very well. That does seem to make the most sense, given our situation." Her voice, she was pleased to note, held more confidence than she felt.

Scrambling back under the linens, she let him re-arrange the blanket, which she had pulled askew in her attempt to wrap herself in it. Surreptitiously, not wanting him to think she was afraid of him, she inched away, to the very farthest edge of the bed.

In a moment he'd righted the blanket and moved back to the side of the bed. "I can sleep on top of the linens, if that will make you feel better."

Yes, that would make her feel much better, she realized, but only said, "If . . . if you'd like." Where was that confidence now?

The shifting of the bed when he'd sat on it before was nothing to what it did when he put his full weight on the mattress. Though she'd thought she was braced, Dina found herself rolling helplessly toward him, fetching up against his broad back.

What a mercy he was atop the linens—and facing away from her!

"I'm sorry," she gasped, scrambling backward under the covers. "The . . . the bed—"

"—isn't as stable as I'd thought," he finished. "The fault is mine. I should have lain down more gradually."

Thor was pleased to note that he was able to keep his tone brisk and impersonal. The unexpected contact had been by no means unpleasurable—or particularly unwelcome. He did regret her embarrassment, however.

He fought against instinctive arousal at her soft sounds and the little bounces of the bed as she moved back to the opposite side. He wouldn't be male if he wasn't affected by such close proximity to a pretty woman in a state of undress, he told himself. It didn't signify any *particular* attraction or affection.

Still, it probably hadn't been wise of him to suggest sharing the bed. The rational part of his mind said that it was the only realistic solution to their problem, but he couldn't seem to keep the wayward part of his mind from imagining the possibilities their current situation offered. Once asleep, they might well both roll toward the center of the bed, then—

No. He had made Dina a promise. He would not break it at the very first opportunity. She had made it abundantly clear that she had not the least desire for any of the physical aspects of marriage, and he was very nearly certain he felt the same. It was only the darkness and his sleep-fogged mind that suggested anything else.

He'd only had about four hours' sleep over the past forty-eight hours. That was enough to make any man's thinking fuzzy. A good night's sleep would put everything back into its proper perspective, he was sure.

Dina shifted slightly and let out a soft sigh—and immediately he was aroused again. Shouldn't exhaustion keep that from happening? Disgusted at himself, he punched his pillow. It made almost no sound, but a moment later he felt something soft touch his face. Was she—? No, there was another touch, then another.

He put a hand to his face and felt small bits of softness on his cheek. Feathers! Behind him, Dina sneezed. "What on earth—?" she mumbled.

"I, ah, seem to have damaged my pillow." He felt

like an idiot. "It appears to have been no more stable than the bed."

"Oh. That is . . . ah . . ." Her voice trailed off into a sort of choking sound.

He sat up in alarm. He'd heard of people who had adverse reactions to feathers, who could even be incapacitated by them. "Dina, are you all right?"

"I'm . . . I'm fine. Oh, bother." She made another odd noise. Even more worried, he reached for her, but before he made contact, she suddenly let loose with a peal of laughter. "Oh, I'm sorry. It's just, after all that has happened today . . . your poor pillow!"

Thor felt his own lips twitching, the humor in their situation striking him as well. Perhaps exhaustion was making him giddy, but the whole thing suddenly seemed hilarious—the capping absurdity of a bizarre day. His chuckle turned into a full-throated laugh as feathers continued to drift down on them both.

"It has been rather a trying day," he was finally able to gasp, "but that's no excuse for my assaulting a defenseless pillow."

She giggled in the darkness, an oddly appealing sound. "I'm glad to hear that you don't regard your outburst of violence as justified, as I can't help feeling the poor pillow was my proxy."

Her words sobered him at once. "I hope you don't think for a moment that I've contemplated the slightest violence against you, Dina—or that I would ever do so."

"Well . . . I have rather disrupted your life, have I not? It would not be remarkable if you felt a desire to retaliate for such interference. Not to mention that I nearly let you spend the night on a little strip of bare boards." She chuckled again, but Thor was frowning into the darkness.

"I agreed to marry you of my own free will, as I swore to Mr. Elliot in Gretna. To retaliate against you now, particularly physically, would be a despicable act, and one of which I'd like to think I'm incapable." What sort of men had she been around, that she might expect such a thing?

She was silent for a moment, his seriousness apparently having subdued her laughter. "I . . . I was jesting," she said in a small voice. "But thank you."

"We'd better get to sleep." He couldn't bring himself to acknowledge her thanks, unnecessary as it was. Folding the split end of his pillow shut, he carefully lay down on it again.

When she'd exhibited fear of him that morning—quickly concealed, he had to admit—he had attributed it to his size and the towering temper he'd been in. Surely that would have frightened anyone, at least momentarily. But what if there was more to Dina's fear than that? Had her father or brother ever lashed out at her physically?

The thought made him vaguely ill. She was so tiny, so defenseless, so . . . fragile. But perhaps he was wrong. It was late, and he was beyond tired. He could be reading things into her behavior that were not actually there.

Still, when they reached Ashcombe, he would keep a close eye on Silas Moore, and particularly on his treatment of his sister.

With that resolve settled in his mind, Thor finally fell into a deep, dreamless sleep that lasted until Violet knocked on the door, well after daybreak.

*　*　*

Dina sat up with a start, then snatched the covers to her chest as she realized just how compromising her situation was. No, not compromising, since Mr. Turpin was her lawful husband, but definitely . . . vulnerable.

"Are you two awake?" came Violet's voice through the door. "I thought we wanted to get an early start."

"Just a moment," Mr. Turpin called back. While Dina averted her eyes, he pulled on his trousers, stockings, and shirt, then padded across to the door. The moment he turned the handle, Violet poked her head in.

"Happy birthday, Dina," she began, then broke off with a giggle. "My goodness! Look at all those feathers. Dare I ask—?"

Dina felt her face flaming, though she tried for an unconcerned smile. It must be obvious, at the very least, that they had shared the bed.

"No, you may not," Mr. Turpin interrupted his sister dampeningly. "Is there a report from the wheelwright yet?"

"I don't know. I was just on my way downstairs," Violet replied, her eyes still dancing.

"Give me half a moment and I'll join you." Sitting on the foot of the bed, he pulled on his boots, then donned his jacket. "Breakfast should be ready by the time you come down," he said to Dina in a tone that was almost tender—or did she imagine that?

Violet looked from one to the other. "Are you sure you wouldn't rather—?"

"Let's go." He cut her off again. With one last, backward glance at Dina, he closed the door behind them, but not before Violet sent her a saucy wink that had her face flaming again.

The moment she was alone, Dina scrambled into her clothes, dusting feathers off her gown as she buttoned it up the front. If not for those tiny white reminders, she might almost have believed the laughter of the night before was a dream. Would it have been better if it were? She wasn't sure.

It had shown her another side of Mr. Turpin, a softer side, despite his small outburst of violence against the pillow. After laughing with him and then talking with him afterward, she didn't think she would ever feel afraid of him again. That was a good thing, of course, but it had also softened her feelings toward him, which could be dangerous—to her own peace of mind, at least.

"Don't be absurd," she said aloud to the empty room. Simply because he was proving to be a kind man didn't mean she was going to develop tender feelings for him. That would be the height of stupidity, since she'd promised to make no wifely demands upon him—a promise he had readily accepted.

It simply meant that they might deal comfortably with each other, she told herself, like civilized people. That should make life far more pleasant than she'd been used to with first her father's and then Silas's unpredictable temper.

Taking what satisfaction she could from this reflection, she finished lacing her boots and went downstairs.

As they went in to breakfast, Mr. DiMartino arrived to inform them that he had indeed managed to repair the carriage wheel. Dina couldn't help noticing the flirtatious looks young Sue kept sending toward the dapper Italian wheelwright as she set their dishes on the table. She had no doubt Violet noticed as well, though for once she held her tongue.

In addition, Mr. DiMartino told them, there had been a hard freeze in the night, which should make the roads easier to travel.

"We should start directly, then," said Mr. Turpin, picking up another of the excellent muffins and spreading it with thick country butter. "We'll want to get as far as we can before a thaw can set in and soften the roads to mud again."

To this they all agreed, and in half an hour they were again on their way. Violet still had a tendency to smirk, so to prevent her asking any more awkward questions, Dina said, "How far behind schedule do you suppose this has put us?"

Mr. Turpin shrugged. "We are making far better time now, with the roads frozen. If we can continue so, we may be able to make up for what we lost yesterday and still reach Ashcombe by late tonight. I'm sure you'd prefer that to spending another night on the road."

Dina glanced at him, then away, having caught the rueful look in his eyes. Clearly he would prefer that as well—for the very reason he attributed to her. Ignoring the pinprick of hurt that thought caused her, Dina turned her thoughts to the coming confrontation with her brother instead.

Chapter 6

❦

Silas Moore rode up the drive to Ashcombe Hall feeling as though a great weight were being lifted from his shoulders. Today, finally, all his problems would be solved. The past ten days spent hiding from his creditors in a friend's old shooting cottage had been hellish. The fireplace had smoked, and the furniture was threadbare. Why Deever had thought he'd appreciate such a ramshackle place was beyond him.

Still, it had served his purpose, and once he settled things with the trustees today, he would never again be driven to such exigencies.

Halting before the front steps, he dismounted and handed his reins to the waiting groom, then hurried into the house. He needed to freshen up and have a bite to eat before heading out to Litchfield to sign whatever was needed to secure the remainder of Ashcombe's assets in his name. It would probably be prudent to bring Dina along, just in case her signature was required on anything—not that it was likely.

"Ah, Mrs. Macready," he greeted the housekeeper as she emerged from the back of the house. "Where is my sister? Upstairs? Send someone to tell her to be ready to leave within the hour."

Instead of the quick, quiet answer and instant obedience he expected, the plump, iron-haired woman twisted her apron between her hands, her lips pressed together.

"Did you not hear me?" Silas prompted testily. "Fetch Miss Moore at once. I am in a hurry."

Mrs. Macready took a step backward before speaking. "I'm afraid I can't, sir, begging your pardon."

Silas scowled, but then remembered what would have transpired earlier in the week. No doubt Dina had been upset when Diggory Tallow backed out of their supposed elopement. She'd had enough time to get over it by now, though.

"Been refusing to come out of her room, has she? Well, I've no time for her sulks. Tell her I'm home and that I need to speak with her. Immediately."

But still the housekeeper did not move. He began to wonder if perhaps she did not have the wits for such a responsible post, for all she'd held it for six years.

"Are you gone deaf?" he demanded. "I told you I was in a hurry. Oh, bloody hell. I'll tell her myself." He started toward the stairs, then glanced back to see Mrs. Macready still frozen in place, her eyes wide with fear.

The first prickle of foreboding crept up Silas's spine. "What? Is there some sort of problem? What has happened?"

"It's . . . it's Miss Moore, sir. She's . . . she's . . ."

"Out with it!" he fairly shouted, restraining himself with difficulty from shaking the halting words from her mouth. If Dina had gone into a real decline, she might not be able to accompany him—not that it should make any real difference.

"She's not been seen since Sunday night." The words came in such a breathless rush that at first Silas did not understand them—but then their import sank in.

"Sunday night, say you?"

The housekeeper gave a quick, frightened nod. She took another step backward, but in one long stride, Silas closed the distance between them and seized her by the shoulders.

"Are you certain?" Could Tallow have betrayed him and eloped with her after all? He'd thought the fellow thoroughly cowed, but the lure of Dina's fortune might have—

"Yes, sir," Mrs. Macready gasped, bringing him back to the moment at hand. "Her maid said that she took a small valise with her, but nothing else. We didn't know how to contact you, or—"

Silas released her so suddenly that she stumbled slightly. "No. No, you didn't." Tallow did, however. There was no point taking out his anger on a servant instead of the proper target. He turned toward a shrinking footman, hovering near the front door.

"Have my horse brought back 'round. And I want

a meal prepared," he added to the housekeeper. "Have it ready when I return."

A few minutes later, he was galloping his tired horse in the direction of Diggory Tallow's manor house, though he scarcely expected to find his old school chum at home. By the time he arrived, he had devised all manner of fitting punishments for his supposed ally's perfidy, but the exercise did little to assuage the knot of dread in his stomach.

Surely, even if Diggory had married Dina and now had control of her fortune, Silas held enough influence over the man to regain enough of it to pay of his debts. He hoped.

"Is Mr. Tallow in?" he demanded of the butler who answered his pounding on the door.

To his surprise and vast relief, the servant nodded. "If you'll follow me, Mr. Moore."

Silas found Diggory at table, finishing what appeared to have been a sumptuous luncheon. At Silas's entrance, however, his fork clattered onto his plate and he jumped to his feet. "Silas! What . . . what a surprise," he stammered.

A glance proved that no one else had been dining with him, but still Silas had to ask. "Is my sister here?"

"Dina?" Diggory seemed honestly surprised. "Of course not. Is . . . is she not at home?"

For a moment Silas regarded his erstwhile friend through narrowed eyes, then pulled out a chair and seated himself across the table from him. "No. She's not been home since Sunday night. You can imagine what I thought when I discovered that."

Diggory paled visibly. "You thought I had—but I promised you I wouldn't go through with it. Nor did

I, as you can see. Would . . . would you like something to eat? To drink?"

Silas nodded, the knot in his stomach unclenching as his friend rang for a servant. No matter where Dina was, she hadn't married Diggory, so Silas's fortune should be secure.

"So what did happen Sunday night?" he asked, once the servant had gone again.

His friend still looked uncomfortable. "I, ah, hired a post chaise and met your sister on the road, as planned. It was raining," he added irrelevantly. "Once . . . once she arrived, I told her I wanted to wait. Until we had your blessing."

Again, Silas nodded. That was just how he and Diggory had planned it, not wanting to wound Dina's feelings or make her suspicious of their true motives. Silas saw no point in adding insult to injury, given that he planned to use much of her dowry to pay his gaming debts—though of course he would repay her once his luck changed.

"And then?"

Diggory swallowed visibly. "She . . . she was quite insistent on going ahead with the elopement. Tried to tempt me with her fortune, though of course I was not to be shaken in my resolve." He sent Silas a shaky smile, seeking approval.

Silas did not give it to him. "So . . . what? You came back here?"

"Ah . . . yes." Clearly there was more to the story.

"What aren't you telling me?"

At his tone, Diggory blanched again. "If you must know, she . . . she hit me. Hard. She really was quite upset."

"Yes, Dina can throw an impressive punch for her size," Silas said with a degree of pride. "Our uncle taught her a bit of boxing when we were young. But that does not tell me where she is now."

"I . . . I don't know," Diggory confessed. "While I was, er, incapacitated, she spoke with the postboy and drove off. I assumed she had him take her home. It was raining, as I said."

"Incapacitated? Do you mean she actually knocked you down?"

Diggory nodded shamefacedly. "I, er, wasn't expecting—"

"Never mind. She didn't go home, so we must figure out where she did go." Not that it mattered for purposes of Silas securing the money he needed, but she was his sister. He supposed he had an obligation to discover what had happened to her.

"You don't suppose the driver kidnapped her? For ransom?"

"I shouldn't think so," Diggory said. "How would he have known she had any sort of fortune?"

"Still, it's a possibility." The servant returned with a plate of sandwiches, and Silas grabbed a couple of them. "I'll go home and see if any message has arrived." The idiot housekeeper might have forgotten to mention it. "If you remember anything else, let me know."

"Of . . . of course."

He still had a niggling suspicion that Diggory was hiding something, but as long as it wasn't Dina herself, it didn't much signify. Snatching up one more sandwich, he headed for the door, munching as he went.

No matter what ransom was demanded, Silas himself would still come out ahead—even presuming he agreed to pay it. He was only mildly worried about Dina, for if she'd been kidnapped, her captors would not harm her as long as they hoped for money. And if she had not, then no doubt she was hiding somewhere, pouting over Diggory's inconstancy, and would come home when she felt better.

Now that he thought on it, her absence might prove to be a blessing in disguise, affording him the opportunity to search her rooms for their mother's jewel chest.

A month or two ago, she'd moved the chest out of the library safe, no doubt upon discovering certain items missing—items Silas had sold to satisfy one particularly insistent creditor. He hadn't commented on it at the time, secure in the knowledge that he would soon have her entire inheritance at his disposal. Now, however, it seemed prudent to hedge his bets. Besides, he reasoned, it wasn't as though Dina was likely ever to have need of those baubles.

"Have there been any letters for me?" he asked Purseglove, the butler, the moment he returned to Ashcombe Hall. Mrs. Macready was nowhere to be seen.

"Why, yes, sir. A messenger arrived only half an hour ago," the butler replied, plucking an envelope from the tray on the hall table.

Though surprised that the ransom note—if that's what it was—had not come days before, Silas opened the message with more relief than dread. At least it would mean that Dina was safe, along with her—soon to be his—fortune.

He received a second surprise when he saw that the message was written in Dina's hand—and then he felt the color leaving his face as he read it through. "It's not possible!" he exploded.

"Sir?" Purseglove asked in apparent concern, though not before moving a prudent distance away.

Silas brought a fist crashing down on the hall table, shattering the porcelain correspondence tray. He barely noticed the butler disappearing into the library. How in hell had the little jade managed this on such short notice? And who was this Turpin fellow?

The name seemed vaguely familiar, but he couldn't put a face to it just now, his mind was in such chaos. Some fortune hunter she had met along the North Road, no doubt. Silas had kept Dina so sheltered, she'd no doubt been easy prey, falling for the fellow's blandishments. He glanced over Dina's letter again, then crushed it in his fist.

So they were on their way here, were they? That didn't give him much time. It was suddenly imperative that he find that jewel case—and come up with a plan to separate as much of Dina's fortune from this upstart as possible, before his creditors got wind of her marriage.

He smiled to himself. Perhaps this Turpin fellow could be . . . *persuaded* to forget that the wedding ever took place. Then it would be a simple matter to cow Dina as well and destroy whatever documentation they might have.

First, though, the jewels, as insurance.

It was after midnight when the post chaise finally rolled through the sleeping village of Ashcombe.

Dina watched with bleary eyes as they passed the market square and the little parish church before continuing on up the road to Ashcombe Hall.

"We're finally here," she whispered, touching Violet to wake her. At her side, Mr. Turpin stirred as well.

They had traveled the last two hours in near silence, as first one then another of them dozed, while the others stayed quiet to avoid waking whichever one was sleeping. Now they all blinked at one another in the dim light from the coach lanterns outside and began to gather up their belongings.

The house was dark, but when Dina and the others walked up the front steps, the door opened to reveal old Purseglove, holding a candle.

"Good evening, Miss Moore," he said, his glance straying to the others. "Your brother asked me to watch for you, in case you arrived late. He, I fear, has already retired for the night."

That was just as well, Dina thought. She would far rather face Silas in the morning, after a good night's rest in her own bed. "Thank you, Purseglove. This is Miss Turpin and this is my husband, Mr. Turpin."

The retainer's eyes widened. "Your—? Ah, very good, Miss . . . Mrs. . . . Er, shall I show you upstairs?"

"Yes, please. And have Thomas—or whoever is awake—fetch our things from the coach." So it seemed that Silas had indeed received her letter, but had declined to mention her changed status to even the upper servants. Interesting.

Once upstairs, Mr. Turpin was shown to a room at the end of the hall, which put Silas's rooms between Dina's and his, while Miss Turpin was given the guest chamber across the hall. Dina was too tired to puzzle through the possible ramifications of Silas's choices, however, and it was with relief that she finally entered her own bedchamber for the first time in nearly a week.

Her maid hurried forward to divest her of her cloak. "Oh, miss, I am so glad you are returned home safe! We were that worried about you."

"Thank you, Francine. I'm sorry to have caused anxiety. We can talk in the morning, however. Just now I want nothing more than my bed."

With a nod, the maid hurried through her ministrations, then left Dina alone. She turned toward her familiar four-poster with a weary sigh, but then paused, noticing that the nightstand was farther from the bed than usual—as was the chair beyond it. A quick survey of the room revealed that nearly all the furniture was slightly out of position.

Frowning, she went to her dressing table and opened the top drawer. Here, too, things had been moved from the way she normally kept them, her powder box pushed all the way to the back of the drawer. This had not been a matter of the carpets being cleaned, as she'd first thought. No, someone had searched her room.

The jewel chest, she realized. Silas must already be searching for it. No doubt it was the first thing he'd done after reading her letter—after the inevitable outburst of temper. Quickly she crossed to the fireplace and knelt down.

Clumsy in her weariness, she took a moment to find the loose stone and pry it out of its place. With trembling fingers, she reached into the hole revealed, cringing, as she always did, at the thought of spiders. When her fingers encountered a hard, rectangular object, she gave a sigh of relief.

Still, just to be sure, she pulled it out—with difficulty, as it was nearly the size of the opening—and opened it. Yes, everything Silas had not already taken was still there: the diamond parure, the emerald ear drops, and the sapphire set.

Satisfied, she replaced the chest and the stone, then checked to make certain she'd left no evidence, even sprinking a tiny bit of soot across the stone so that it would exactly match the others. Finally she wiped her fingers on a scrap of paper, threw the paper into the fire, then dragged herself into bed.

The next morning she was up early despite her late night, determined to speak with Silas before he saw either of the Turpins. Francine, her instincts apparently not dulled by Dina's brief absence, appeared the moment she stepped out of bed, bearing two coppers of hot water.

"Oh, bless you," Dina exclaimed. "I'm dying for a bath—though it will have to be a quick one, alas."

It was heavenly to be clean again, and to dress in a different gown from the one she'd been wearing for days. This blue one had always been one of her favorites, even though it, like the rest of her wardrobe, was woefully out of fashion. Still, both cut and color flattered her, she thought.

Finally, her hair washed, dried, and arranged, she headed downstairs, trying to focus only on the interview ahead and not what Mr. Turpin might think of her improved appearance—and smell.

"Ah, there you are," Silas greeted her when she

entered the dining room. Rather to her surprise, he was smiling, though the smile seemed strained. "Purseglove told me you all arrived in the wee hours. Sleep well, did you?"

"Exceedingly. Travel is far more tiring than I'd realized." She seated herself across from him. Even though he seemed surprisingly calm, given the circumstances, she felt it wise to keep the width of the table between them.

Now he leaned forward with what appeared to be genuine concern, though she thought she caught a flicker of anger in his eyes. "Perhaps you should have considered that before embarking on such an ill-advised journey. Dina, what on earth were you thinking? And who is this Turpin fellow, anyway? I was worried sick about you, imagining the worst. When your message came, I more than half expected it would prove to be a ransom note."

"I never meant to alarm anyone, Silas," she replied calmly, "but I saw no other way to safeguard my future."

"Your future?" He sat back in apparent surprise. "Why could you not trust your future to me? I am your brother, after all, and your nearest living kin. Who better to safeguard it than I?"

Though loath to shatter this fragile civility between them, Dina knew it would be best to get the worst over before the others came down. "Perhaps someone who does not intend to spend my inheritance on gaming debts? Or who has not conspired to keep me from marrying before that inheritance could become his?"

As she'd expected, her brother's already florid complexion darkened further. "Gambling . . . conspired . . . What the devil are you talking about?"

"You know quite well what I'm talking about, Silas, so you need not dissemble. Diggory all but admitted that you and he plotted together to delay my marriage. And I've read some of the letters from your creditors. I am fully aware of what you intended to do."

Both of his large hands came crashing down onto the table, on either side of his plate, and he heaved himself to his feet. "The devil, you say! You had no right to read my correspondence, and Tallow had no business—"

He broke off and took several deep breaths before continuing. "If Diggory told you that, he was lying. If either of you had but asked my consent to your marriage, I'd have given it. As for my debts, it's true that I have a few—what gentleman doesn't? But all I needed was a portion of your inheritance, and I fully intended to repay it."

"And Mother's jewels? I know you have already sold some of them, and would have taken the rest, given the chance. Would you have returned those to me as well? I'm well aware that you searched my room for them while I was away."

Only a brief clenching of his jaw betrayed that her words had struck home before he widened his eyes in a surprisingly convincing show of innocence. "I have no idea what you're talking about. I must say, it hurts to think you would believe such a thing of me, Dina."

"I have no wish to hurt you, Silas." She kept her voice low and soothing, knowing that his mood might shift and explode into violence at any moment. "But you cannot claim to have acted honorably toward me in this matter, whatever intentions you now profess."

"And this fortune hunter you've married, this Turpin fellow? Has he acted honorably? I think not," he continued before she could answer. "And he'll answer to me for it, mark my words."

That was just the sort of reaction she'd come downstairs to head off. "Our marriage was my idea, Silas, because I could see no other way to keep my fortune out of your creditors' hands. Had I left my future to you, I've no doubt we would both have ended in poverty. Now, at least, I am in a position to help you somewhat."

Silas's face reddened. "Help me?" he exclaimed. "By paupering me? By turning to a complete stranger instead of to your own flesh and blood? It only proves how crafty this Turpin is, that he was able to convince you this marriage was your idea instead of his. Call the bastard down and I'll tell him so to his face."

"You'll do no such thing," she exclaimed. "Mr. Turpin has in fact behaved most honorably, marrying me as a favor, after I rendered a service to his sister. I'll not have you insult him because of it."

Her brother snorted. "Sister? You're such an innocent, Dina. I'll lay any odds the woman he was traveling with is his doxy, not his sister. Perhaps I've kept you too sheltered after all."

Dina would have laughed if she hadn't been so angry. "You know nothing of it, Silas, so pray don't embarrass yourself with such insinuations."

"I'll do as I please. It's not as though you can stop me. Let's call this Turpin fellow down and see what he has to say for himself, shall we?" He was smiling again, but the smile was most unpleasant.

She opened her mouth to respond, but from behind her came a voice like a drawn sword. "There's no need to call the Turpin fellow down, Mr. Moore. However, I strongly suggest you retract what I just overheard you saying about my sister."

Chapter 7

~~~⚬⚬~~~

Dina watched with surprise and some relief as Silas's expression shifted from smugly triumphant to openly hostile, and then to guardedly respectful as he took Mr. Turpin's considerable measure. She should have known that her brother would not be able to bully this man.

"Mr. Turpin." Ever so slightly, Silas inclined his head. "My sister and I were just, ah, discussing you."

"So I heard." Mr. Turpin kept his voice low and level, giving nothing away by his expression. "I wish I could say that I'm pleased to make your acquaintance at last. As I recall, however, we encountered one another briefly in Town last summer."

Dina saw a dawning recognition in Silas's eyes. It appeared that he did indeed remember a previous meeting—and not particularly pleasantly. Of course, Mr. Turpin would be rather difficult to forget.

"Ah, yes. You're the fellow known to his intimates as Thor, are you not? Heir to Lord Rumble? I thought the name Turpin seemed familiar. My apologies for not making the connection sooner." A belated smile lifted the corners of his lips.

Thor? It was the first time Dina had heard the nickname, but she couldn't deny it fit, with his Viking build, his fair but powerful good looks, and a voice that could sound like thunder when he was angry. Thor. Yes, it definitely fit him better than the name Grant.

Mr. Turpin—Thor—did not return Silas's attempt at a smile. "Perhaps now you will acquit me of marrying your sister for her fortune, and recant your aspersions against my own sister."

"Er, yes, yes, of course. Pray have a seat, Mr. Turpin, while I call for more food. Dina, you'll want your breakfast as well, I don't doubt, as will Miss Turpin when she awakes. Shall I have a tray sent up to her?"

His manner was now positively ingratiating, but though that relieved Dina's immediate fears, it did not engender any more confidence in her brother's actual motives. She'd seen him pretend one thing while plotting another too often over the years.

"No need. My sister said that she would be down directly." Thor glanced over his shoulder. "In fact, here she is now."

Light steps heralded Violet's entrance. She was dressed, Thor noted with faint disapproval, in a form-fitting morning gown of bright pink that served to emphasize the womanliness of her figure. He'd have preferred to see her in something more modest and subdued, under the circumstances.

"Good morning," she said breezily, moving toward a seat next to Dina. "I hope you have not all been waiting on me. I confess I insisted on a proper bath before coming down, after so many days of travel."

Dina, who had been both still and silent since Thor's entrance, now came to life. "Good morning, Violet, and no, we've not been waiting. Pray do not apologize, as I felt the same need of a bath myself." Then she turned to her brother. "Silas, pray let me present Miss Violet Turpin. Violet, my brother, Silas Moore."

Mr. Moore stepped around the table to take Violet's extended hand. "Your servant, of course, Miss Turpin," he said with a chaste kiss of her fingertips. "I am delighted to welcome you into my home."

Violet glanced in apparent confusion from him to Dina to Thor, then back at her host. "Why, thank you, Mr. Moore, that is most gracious of you. I'm pleased to make your acquaintance."

Thor moved to pull out his sister's chair, but Moore was quicker. "I must thank you, Miss Turpin, for befriending my sister in what must have been a most awkward situation. Believe me, I am most grateful."

She smiled up at him, a hint of flirtatiousness in her manner that made Thor clench his teeth. "It is I who has reason to be grateful to Dina, Mr. Moore. Your sister is quite the heroine, in my opinion, for she saved me from a most imprudent step."

"Indeed?" He moved back to his seat across the table, his gaze never leaving Violet's. "I have yet to hear the details of how you all came to meet—and how my sister came to marry so, ah, unexpectedly. Perhaps you would care to enlighten me, Miss Turpin?"

Thor glanced at Dina to find her frowning. Catching her eye, he raised a questioning brow, and she responded with a slight shrug, though she did not seem best pleased. Violet, oblivious to the interchange, chattered on.

"Oh, certainly. It's rather appropriate that I do so, actually, since it was my own folly which precipitated everything. You see, I had quite unwisely agreed to elope with a man who turned out to be more in love with my fortune than with me. Why, even the poetry he sent me turned out not to be of his own composing! I have Dina to thank for that knowledge, as well."

Thor could wish Violet had not been so candid. He didn't think he'd imagined the gleam in Moore's eyes at the word "fortune," but the fellow only said, "Indeed? Then it sounds as though you made the right choice when you declined to marry him, though I can't imagine any man being truly unmoved by your charms, Miss Turpin."

She dimpled at the compliment. "You are very kind, sir."

"Not at all, for it is the simple truth. But how did my sister—and your brother—come into the mix?"

"Oh, yes. Dina had arrived in Gretna Green a short time before we did, and invited us to dine with her, then allowed me to share her room at the inn. It was through conversation with her that my eyes were opened to Mr. Plunkett's true character. By morning I had decided against marrying him. My brother arrived a short time after that, having pursued me there from Lincolnshire."

"I see. But how—?"

"One thing I don't understand," Violet interrupted him, frowning. "Dina told us that she needed to marry at once because, well, because you were going to steal her inheritance. But now I meet you, you seem such a nice, gentlemanly sort of man. Surely you wouldn't really have behaved so infamously toward your sister?"

There was an awkward silence, with all eyes on Mr. Moore. For a moment he seemed nonplussed, but then he smiled again. Thor narrowed his eyes, wondering how the rascal meant to wriggle out of this.

"Of course not," Moore said smoothly. "It was all a most unfortunate misunderstanding. She misinterpreted something she overheard and behaved somewhat impulsively as a result. Had she but asked, I would not have hesitated to tell her all. Dina and I were just sorting out the facts when your brother came downstairs, and all is well between us now."

Violet smiled in obvious relief. "I am glad to hear it, Mr. Moore, for I should hate to think so ill of you—or for Dina to have reason to be estranged from her only brother. Perhaps the misunderstanding was for the best, however, since it has resulted in her marriage to Grant, which I cannot help but see as a happy outcome indeed."

"The workings of fate are always a mystery." Moore's smile seemed only the slightest bit strained. "But though it occurred under a misapprehension, if Dina is now happy in her marriage, I could not be more delighted for her. I presume you married her out of gallantry, Mr. Turpin?"

Thor did not bother to hide any skepticism that might show in his expression. "I suppose you could say that. It seemed the decent thing to do, under the circumstances, particularly given the favor she had done my sister—and our family—by preventing Violet's marriage to Mr. Plunkett."

Their breakfast arrived then, which served to partially smooth over the awkward moment. Thor was determined, however, that they would spend no more time at Ashcombe than was absolutely necessary. The less opportunity Mr. Moore had to speak with Dina—or Violet—privately, the better.

Accordingly, after breakfast, he suggested that they all drive into Litchfield so that he, Dina, and Mr. Moore could speak with the trustees and take care of whatever legalities Dina's new status required. Moore had no choice but to agree.

The drive to Litchfield took nearly an hour, and Mr. Moore spent much of that time in conversation with Violet. He continued to play the part of charming host, pointing out sights along the way. There was nothing in his manner to indicate that he was dreading the coming interview, even though it was likely to beggar him, if Dina's story was true.

If? Thor felt a pang of guilt over doubting her, even for a moment. So far, everything he had seen of her brother only added to her credibility. Still, he couldn't quite silence a faint voice that asked whether their marriage had really been necessary.

That question was answered during their conversation with the trustees a short time later. After a brief interview with all three gentlemen, the head trustee, Mr. Pickering, ushered Dina and Thor into his office to sign a few documents.

"We will take care of the transfer of funds to Mr. Turpin's name, of course," he said, after examining the marriage certificate, "but I must confess to some curiosity, madam, as to why you chose to marry in Scotland rather than England. That will slow the procedures somewhat."

Dina glanced at the closed door that separated them from her brother and Violet in the outer office. "It was a question of expediency, sir. I knew that my inheritance would revert to Silas if I were unmarried on my birthday, and I feared there was not time to procure a proper license in England."

Mr. Pickering furrowed his graying brows. "I see. Then you had reason to believe your brother would not be a proper steward of your funds?"

"Er, yes. At least I thought I did." She seemed unwilling to voice her suspicions openly, perhaps out of familial loyalty.

"Then you should have come to us, madam. As you were of age, you could have requested that your funds remain under our supervision, rather than Mr. Moore's."

Dina's mouth fell open, and Thor had to make an effort to prevent his own doing the same. "I . . . I could have?" she stammered. "But I thought . . . My father's will . . ."

"Yes, I know that the default was for your brother to take over the administration of your inheritance should you reach your twenty-fifth birthday unmarried, but the law generally makes exceptions for good cause in cases such as this. Were any question to arise as to your brother's intent to preserve your funds for your own use, we would have been empowered to delay or even prevent his gaining control of them."

"Oh," she said faintly. Then, "Did . . . did Silas know this?"

Mr. Pickering shrugged. "I have no idea. Perhaps not. To my knowledge, he never asked."

"I see. Well, ah, thank you, Mr. Pickering."

Though numb with shock, Thor forced himself to speak. "Yes sir, thank you. Please have word sent to us at Plumrose in Lincolnshire when the paperwork is complete."

"Of course, sir. And now, if both of you will sign here . . . and here . . ."

Thor signed mechanically, his mind a morass of conflicting emotions. Dina seemed as surprised by this news as he was, but still he could not help blaming her somewhat. Why had she never taken the simple step of speaking with the trustees? Then she would never have had to go to Scotland . . .

And Violet would undoubtedly be married to Plunkett.

Was it fate, as Violet had said? He didn't know. All he could seem to grasp at the moment was that he was married and that there had been no real need for it.

"All done?" Violet greeted them as they gained the outer office. "Good. Silas was just telling me about some picturesque ruins that I was hoping we might be able to see on our way back to Ashcombe."

"You two are on a Christian name basis already, are you?" Thor knew he sounded peevish, but his temper was not the best at the moment.

Violet nodded, apparently oblivious to her brother's mood. "We are family, are we not? Oh, do say we may visit the ruins."

But Thor shook his head. "With our business here concluded, I believe we had best impose no longer on Mr. Moore's hospitality, but head back to Lincolnshire as soon as possible. Our parents, I know, will be anxious to have you back in their care, Violet."

"Silas," Dina said then, "Mr. Pickering needs your signature on a paper or two as well. He asked us to send you in."

Once he was gone, she turned to Thor, her eyes shadowed with something that might have been guilt. "Do you still mean to take me to Lincolnshire as well?"

Thor frowned down at her, startled by her question. "Of course. The reasons I mentioned before still stand."

"Still?" Violet echoed. "Has something unexpected occurred?"

While he hesitated, unsure how much to tell his sister, Dina responded. "It . . . seems that I need not have married to secure my inheritance after all. Had I only gone to the trustees in the first place—"

"Of course you didn't have to—Silas already made that clear, did he not? But had you known, you would never have rescued me from my own folly—or married Grant. Perhaps it is selfish of me, but I cannot help being glad you acted as you did."

Thor supposed he must agree, though just now, still feeling somewhat betrayed, he could not bring himself to say so.

Dina looked up at him, seeming to sense his discomfort. "I am sorry. Given what we've just learned, I am willing to have our marriage annulled."

"Annulled!" Violet was clearly horrified. "But you can't. That would—" She broke off as the door to Mr. Pickering's office opened again and Mr. Moore emerged.

"Shall we go?" Thor asked, wondering how much he had heard.

The other man darted a look from Dina to Thor, frowning, then nodded. "May as well. Are we going to see the ruins? No? Then I should attend to some business at home."

During the drive back to Ashcombe, Dina was almost afraid to look at Thor, seated next to her. What must he be thinking? She had all but forced him into marriage, and now it turned out that it had not even been necessary. Her own stupidity had landed them both in this pickle, and it would not be wonderful if he never forgave her for it.

Of course, if they were to annul their marriage, she need not worry over his forgiveness. Why did that idea not give her more comfort?

Silas was not nearly so chatty on the return journey, appearing to be deep in thought, though he responded politely to Violet's occasional overtures. In fact, a pall had descended over the whole party, which Dina supposed was not surprising, under the circumstances.

"I should go speak with the vicar's wife," Dina said when they arrived back at the house. "She will be wondering why I have not called, and I need to let her know I won't be available to assist her for some time."

"And I must speak with the estate manager," Silas said. "Some, ah, changes will be necessary in the way things are run." He sent Dina a sidelong glance, and she knew he was referring to the lack of money he'd expected to be his by now.

She waited until Violet had gone upstairs to put off her bonnet, then followed her brother into his ground-floor office. "I don't want the estate to suffer by my marriage, Silas. Are the rents no longer covering our normal expenses?"

He shifted from one foot to the other, glancing over at Thor, who stood in the doorway, before answering. "I've, ah, had to borrow from the rents of late. Strictly a temporary measure, of course, but there will likely be a shortfall again this quarter."

"Again?" She didn't know why she was surprised. "How much do you need?" she asked, trying to keep any accusation from her voice. There was little to be gained by resuming the hostilities of the morning at this point.

Again he flicked a glance at Thor before replying. "Five hundred pounds should be sufficient for now."

She nodded, but before she could suggest a loan,

Thor stepped into the room and closed the door behind him. "And how much to cover your most pressing debts? No, do not deny you have them," he added when Silas began to scowl. "Just tell me how much."

For a long moment the two men faced each other, unblinking, but finally Silas looked down. "Twelve thousand pounds," he mumbled.

Dina gasped. "Silas! How on earth—?" She had never imagined it could be so much. Why, that was two-thirds of her inheritance—and he must already have gamed away his own share, nearly twenty thousand pounds. "You can't possibly believe you could ever have repaid such a sum."

He didn't meet her eyes—or Thor's. "I could have, had my luck turned. It happens all the time, you know. Fortunes are won on the turn of a die or a card."

"And lost," Thor said. "As you seem to have discovered already."

Silas shot him a look of intense dislike. "Do you mean to lecture me or to help me?" Then, turning to Dina, he smoothed his features into something that reminded her of a pleading puppy. "I dare not return to Town unless I pay at least part. Even Ashcombe is no longer a sure refuge from the circling vultures."

In spite of herself, in spite of what he'd tried to do, Dina could not resist the plea in his eyes. "Suppose I lend you half," she said, ignoring a sudden movement from Thor on the periphery of her vision. "That would help, would it not?"

He nodded. "It'd get the two most persistent fellows off me, at least. But—"

"I could provide the other six thousand—as a marriage settlement," Thor suggested.

Dina stared at him in surprise and dismay. "I—we—can't ask you to do that," she protested. For one thing, it would make an annulment nearly impossible, she was sure.

"You didn't ask," he pointed out. "I am offering. I don't want your brother continually touching us for money. I'd far rather take care of that problem at the outset, and then forget about it."

Silas was scowling again, but he apparently had enough sense to keep a check on his temper despite the insult. "That seems a fair marriage settlement," he growled. "I wouldn't want it said that I let my sister go cheaply."

Now Dina felt her own temper flare. "So you would sell me to cover your debts?"

"You already sold yourself." Silas's bluntness made her color. "If I can minimize my loss, why shouldn't I do so?"

She glanced uncertainly at Thor, who now looked dangerously close to losing his temper as well. "Silas," she said, "I should like a private word with Mr. Turpin. Perhaps we can come to a solution that will be agreeable to all of us."

For a moment Silas looked as though he might protest, but then he shrugged. Thor stepped away from the doorway and Silas left the office, shutting the door behind him.

"I . . . I thought we were going to have our marriage annulled," she said, trying to ignore her sudden nervousness at being alone with her husband for the first time since that inn room two nights before.

"Did you? I never agreed to any such thing." He smiled, his anger apparently having left with Silas. "Think how it would upset Violet."

Dina frowned in confusion. "I'm afraid I don't understand. I was certain you would leap at the chance to escape what must be a most inconvenient commitment. I'm sure we can make Violet understand. As you explained to her the day we wed, it is not as though this were a love match."

Why should those words of his still prick when they were nothing but the simple truth?

"Perhaps not," he agreed, "but that does not mean it will not work out to our advantage. Do you really believe you would be better off left to your brother's tender mercies?"

She lifted her chin defiantly. "I can take care of myself. I've done so for years."

"And look where that landed you: married to a chance-met stranger. I'd hate to think you might have to resort to such a solution again."

Again she felt herself coloring. "I wouldn't, of course. Not now that I've spoken with the trustees."

"Dina," he said gently. To her surprise, his expression was concerned—almost tender. "I can't help feeling you will be safer under my protection. If our marriage were annulled and then something, ah, happened to you, your brother would inherit all, would he not?"

She blinked. "Yes, but . . . Surely you are not suggesting that Silas would harm me—kill me—for money?"

"Perhaps not. But the idea might cost me sleep, and I'm unwilling to take that risk."

"To your sleep?" she asked skeptically. "Surely your freedom is worth the possibility of a restless night or two?"

His blue eyes were twinkling now, which she found disconcerting given the seriousness of their conversation. "I value my sleep highly—perhaps a result of too many nights without it during the war."

She couldn't understand him at all. "But suppose I prefer to have our marriage dissolved? I cannot think so ill of Silas as to believe he would intentionally hurt me."

"Perhaps not," he repeated. "However, the choice is mine to make, and I've made it. You will simply have to get used to me."

Dina swallowed, trying to summon up the anger she knew she should feel at his high-handedness instead of the insidious relief that was spreading through her. "I'm . . . I'm not sure I can," she finally said. "But if you are determined, I suppose I shall have to try."

"There's my girl. Now, why don't you make whatever calls you feel are necessary, and I'll talk with your brother and work out the particulars. Try not to be gone long, as I'm hoping we can have an early dinner and bedtime, so that we can be off at first light. No doubt you have quite a bit of packing to do."

Still struggling with her wildly conflicting feelings, Dina could only nod.

She would make her visit to the vicar's wife a brief one, then she would take a long, brisk walk and finish with a bout of calisthenics and weight lifting.

Surely that would clear her mind and allow her to come up with an argument that would convince him to annul their marriage after all. At least she hoped so.

Didn't she?

Chapter 8

Thor couldn't say he enjoyed his interview with Silas Moore, given the man's mixture of hostility and obsequiousness, but he took a grim satisfaction in laying out terms that should keep Dina safe from him forever.

"Take my advice," he said at the conclusion, "and leave off gaming entirely until you've discharged all of your debts. Perhaps you should try your hand at love, as cards don't seem to be where your luck lies."

"And maybe you should try your hand at the cards," Moore retorted, "seeing as how you're trapped in a marriage of convenience—or inconvenience, as the case may be. My sister's not exactly the biddable type, as you may have noticed already."

Thor refused to let the man ruffle him, however. "Nor is mine, so I'm used to it."

"Aye, Miss Turpin is very, ah, lively, isn't she?"

But Thor wasn't about to discuss his sister with Moore, whose interest in Violet had played a large part in his decision to leave Ashcombe so soon. "Indeed. Now, if you'll excuse me, I'd like a wash and change before dinner."

Heading upstairs, he felt he couldn't get Dina and Violet—and himself—away from Silas Moore soon enough. Something about the man grated on his nerves. It was rather depressing to realize that Moore was now his brother-in-law. Despite his efforts just now, he suspected the fellow would prove to be a continuing liability.

He still wasn't completely sure why he hadn't jumped at Dina's offer of an annulment. He didn't really believe Moore would hurt his own sister, for it was clear there was at least some small degree of affection there. He would badger her mercilessly for money if she was still living here, but sparing her that was scarcely reason enough to stay in an untenable marriage.

Of course, the relief from his mother's incessant harping about his need to marry would be considerable. And Violet seemed very happy with the match as well. A dutiful son and brother, that's what he was. The unlikely thought made him grin.

The truth was, he'd grown to *like* Dina, after only three days' acquaintance. He could search for years—hell, he'd already searched for years—and find no better prospect for a wife. Except for the fact that she was so tiny. A real shame, that, for it made him feel more protective of her at the same time it made him afraid to get too close.

That protectiveness, he realized now, had played a large part in his original decision to marry her rather than allow her to pursue the fortune hunter Plunkett. And now it made him unwilling to leave her here, to fend for herself against her mercenary brother. He only hoped that his growing attraction to her would not require protection from himself.

Dinner was a more congenial meal than breakfast had been, now that disagreements had been brought out into the open and settled. Dina still seemed quiet, Thor noticed, but Violet and Silas were loquacious enough to make up for it.

"Will you be in Town after Christmas?" Violet asked their host as the sweetmeats were served at the conclusion of the meal. "Do say you will, for I should like to know there will be at least a few friendly faces for my second attempt at a come-out."

"Second attempt?" His most pressing financial difficulties alleviated, Silas's manner was now relaxed and pleasant. "It sounds as though there may be an interesting story there."

Violet grinned, her color rising slightly. "I suppose you could say that. My aunt Philomena, who lives in Town and who offered to present me, was very strict, and I may have, ah, rebelled a bit."

"Yes, I should say that climbing out of the window and stealing Lord Hawkhurst's prime blood for a midnight gallop in Hyde Park constituted a bit of a rebellion," Thor said dryly. "Not to mention showing up at a debutante's ball in a bright red gown. Where did you manage to obtain that, by the way?"

"I wheedled it out of Mary Simpson's married sister, as she had grown too plump to wear it herself after two children. It was several years out of style, of course, but it did have the desired effect. The difficult part was keeping my cloak tightly closed until we arrived so that Aunt Philomena would not see it." She didn't sound the least bit repentant.

Silas laughed, while Dina seemed torn between amusement and horror. "And you expect me to chaperone you on your next visit? You'll have us both run out of London on a rail."

Violet waved a dismissive hand. "Oh, pooh. You'll be nothing like Aunt Philomena, so I won't feel obliged to kick against the traces. We can simply have fun together."

"I'm not at all sure I want my wife to learn your definition of fun," Thor said, though he couldn't quite manage the stern expression he'd intended. "Keep in mind that I'll be in Town myself this time, to keep you in check."

"And I'll be there, as well," Silas added. "Indeed, I wouldn't miss this for the world."

Thor was less than pleased by this news, convinced as he was that Moore had designs on Violet's fortune. Still, he said, "There, Violet. With all of us to keep an eye on you, perhaps you'll make it through an entire Season without scandal."

"Perhaps," she agreed, "though I shouldn't advise anyone to wager anything of value upon it."

They all laughed at that, and if everyone's laughter but Violet's was strained, they all pretended not to notice.

"That was certainly a brief visit, but a productive one," Violet said as their coach trundled down the main street of Ashcombe early the next morning. "How excessively pleased you must be, Dina, to discover your brother had no designs on your fortune after all. I was prepared to find him quite the villain, and was quite relieved when he proved quite the opposite. I should not have minded staying another week or two."

Dina glanced at Thor, but though he frowned slightly, he said nothing to disabuse Violet of her assumption. After a slight hesitation, therefore, she only said that she was sure Violet would have an opportunity to visit Ashcombe again sometime.

"I hope so. Still, I confess that it will be pleasant to sleep in my own bed again, Mother's inevitable scolding notwithstanding," Violet continued. "Not that the bed I slept in at your home wasn't perfectly comfortable, of course," she added hastily.

Dina smiled. "No, I understand what you mean. After so much travel, I appreciated the familiarity of my own room, if only for two nights."

It was disconcerting to think that it might be months, even years, before she returned to the only home she'd ever known—if she ever did so at all. At least she'd been able to bring along her dumbbells and exercise clothes, for they had hired a second coach to follow them, packed with most of Dina's worldly possessions, along with her maid. Her mother's jewel case she had tucked into her own valise.

She hoped that once she settled into whatever routine there might be at Plumrose, she would be able to resume her physical regimen. Its temporary cessation had proved it was far more important to her than she had realized.

"How pleased Mother must be that you have married at last," Violet said to her brother after a few moments of silence. "No doubt she will throw a grander Christmas Eve ball than ever to celebrate. Indeed, I won't be surprised if she has already sent out the announcements."

"I will," Thor replied, "considering that I did not include word of my marriage in the letter I sent."

Violet stared—as did Dina. "You didn't tell our parents?" Violet exclaimed. "But . . . why not?"

"My main concern was to inform them of your safety, and to assure Mother that you had not married Plunkett, so that she would not continue to fret. My own news, I thought, would be better delivered in person than by letter."

"I suppose," Violet said doubtfully, but then she brightened. "This will be much better, now I think on it. Mother will be so overcome by your news, she may well forget to punish me at all. How clever of you, Grant."

He arched a brow. "Believe me, mitigating the consequences of your foolishness was by no means my intent. Should Mother be distracted, you can trust me to remind her of what is due you on that head."

Violet made a face at him that Dina might have considered amusing, had she not been struggling with growing dismay. She was to meet Thor's parents, be introduced as his bride, without so much as a word to prepare them for her arrival? How awkward that would be. Nor could she help wondering why he had chosen not to tell them.

Perhaps he was not so confident of their reception as he and Violet claimed. Or perhaps she was not the only one to consider the possibility of an annulment? The thought that he might have been planning for just that, from the very moment of their marriage, was sobering. But why should he have changed his mind?

She wished she dared to ask him any of the questions now swirling in her brain, but she could not—particularly with Violet in the coach.

"The roads still seem solid," she commented, simply for something to say, when the silence began to feel strained.

"Yes," Violet agreed. "Can we reach Plumrose by tonight, Grant, do you think?"

"Not likely, though if this frost lasts and we can avoid any lengthy delays when we change horses, we should reach it by midday tomorrow," he said, glancing out the window. "It is perhaps only eighty miles from here across country, but the roads are not as direct as we could wish, making our actual journey something over one hundred miles, I would estimate."

Dina did not know whether to be glad of a day's reprieve before meeting Lord and Lady Rumble, or to dread spending another night at an inn with her new husband. The night they'd spent on the way to Ashcombe had been . . . unsettling, to say the least.

As it happened, she need not have worried. After a relatively uneventful day, they stopped for the night in Newark, a town boasting several large coaching inns. To Dina's vast relief, Violet did not protest when Thor bespoke three separate rooms at the Bunch of Grapes. She did send her brother a reproachful glance, but he ignored it—as did Dina.

With uncharacteristic discretion, Violet waited until they were alone in a private parlor, awaiting their supper, to say, "Honestly, Grant, one would never guess that the two of you are on your wedding journey."

"I've never known a gentleman to bring his sister along on his wedding journey," he replied. "I regard this trip more in the light of fetching an errant sibling home, with a wedding along the way."

"Then you do plan to take a proper wedding trip later?" She glanced from him to Dina hopefully, but sighed when neither of them gave her the least encouragement. "Sometimes I think I must be the only romantic left in the world," she grumbled.

Dina had quite a task to keep her expression neutral while her mind conjured up all manner of inappropriate fantasies in response to Violet's suggestion. What was the matter with her? Thor had given her no reason to expect a wedding trip or any other trappings of a romantic marriage. Nor did she want them.

Once she had that settled firmly in her mind, she risked a surreptitious glance at Thor. He was regarding his sister with mild amusement, proving that his mind was not engaged similarly to her own. She was just telling herself that she was grateful for that when his eyes flicked to hers.

Mortified to be caught looking at him when the conversation was on such a topic, she quickly looked away, blushing to the roots of her hair, but not before she saw something in his eyes that snatched at her breath. It was as though that quick glance stretched a fine wire from her senses to his, connecting them.

She cast about for something to say, some mundane comment on the room or the day's journey just past, anything to prove she was unaffected, but her mind was a blank. To her vast relief, the parlor door opened at that moment.

"Our supper is here," she said, as though the others couldn't see that for themselves. The grateful smile she sent the servant caused him to stumble, nearly spilling the soup.

They ate in near silence, punctuated only by occasional comments about the food or the next day's journey. Dina had no idea whether Thor felt as uncomfortably affected by her nearness as she did by his, but could only be glad when he suggested they all retire immediately after eating. Even Violet was tired enough to make no protest.

Alone in her room a short time later, Dina found it difficult to sleep, even after such a long day. Her mind kept going back to that shared glance before supper, and to that night in the Spotted Dog, then forward to her uncertain reception at Plumrose tomorrow. Finally, exasperated with herself, she climbed out of bed and sat on the—thankfully clean—floor to stretch and do a round of calisthenics.

Half an hour later, she finished with a few dozen push-up exercises and climbed back into bed. The activity had calmed her mind somewhat, and soon she drifted off to sleep.

"Almost home," Thor announced as the coach passed through the village of Rumbleton before turning onto the road leading to Plumrose. It would be his first visit home in nearly six months—the first visit in years when his mother would not be asking him several times a day why he had not yet found a bride. He smiled.

"Look, Dina," Violet said, pointing at the last large building in the village. "The Red Lion is where many of the local assemblies are held. I shall ask Mother as soon as we get home how many there will be before Christmas."

Dina obediently looked at the indicated house, though Thor thought he detected a trace of anxiety in her expression. "It . . . it seems a very well-appointed inn."

"Oh, it is. A very fine inn, with a large room upstairs that is perfect for dancing. Mother may try to forbid me from going to any balls as a punishment, but I will point out that you will not wish to go without me—and you must attend, for we'll want to introduce you to everyone as soon as may be. Won't that be fun?"

"Yes. Fun." There was no mistaking the strain in her smile now.

Thor sent his sister a quick frown. "Pray don't overwhelm her with people this first week, Vi. Dina will want to settle in, get to know the house and grounds—and Mother and Father, of course. There will be time enough for parties once she's comfortable at Plumrose."

Violet pouted, but Dina's grateful glance was all the reward he needed—indeed, it affected him far more than he cared to admit, as her very presence increasingly did. Making her smile had become a regular goal of his on this journey, for her smiles did something undeniably pleasurable to his vitals.

Dangerous ground, that.

"Parties are a fine way to get to know people," Violet pointed out, "and Mother enjoys them. I should like to keep her occupied, and I'd think you would, as well."

Thor shrugged. "I have no reason to fear her attention—not now." He gave Dina a wink that made her eyes widen. When she glanced at Violet questioningly, he tried not to feel slighted.

"I know you've heard us say that Mother has been wanting Grant to marry," Violet explained in response to Dina's unspoken question. "In fact, she has been after him so continually of late that she had driven him to distraction—and away from Plumrose entirely for months at a time. If it were not so unromantic, I would say that he married you simply to get some peace from her."

"Violet," he protested, glancing at Dina in concern, though in fact his sister's words were at least half true. "That was only one of many considerations, as I think you know by now."

Dina did not meet his eye. "It is good to think that the benefits of our marriage will not be all on one side."

"I certainly hope not," he said, wondering again whether he'd done the right thing to refuse her offer of an annulment.

How, really, did this marriage benefit Dina? It was small wonder she had suggested dissolving it on learning that her fortune was not affected, after all. He had believed she would be better off—safer—married to him, but she did not seem to agree. Was he as much a tyrant as her brother to hold her to their agreement now?

It was an unsettling thought, but luckily he did not have to dwell on it for long. Only a few minutes later they pulled to a halt on the broad gravel drive that swept through the center of Plumrose Park to end in a circle before the house. The driver opened the coach door, and Thor handed down his sister and his bride before directing the removal of Dina's trunks from the second coach.

As they all turned toward the house, the front door flew open and Lady Rumble, resplendent in a mauve day dress that made the most of her Juno-esque proportions, hurried down the broad stone steps toward them.

"Grant! Violet! Here you are at last. I've been expecting you these three days, at least, as I have been telling your father hourly. Whatever can— Oh!" Her flow of chatter stopped abruptly as she noticed Dina. "Who—? That is—"

Thor took Dina's hand in his. "Mother, I would like you to meet Dina Turpin—my wife."

His mother's mouth made a perfect O of surprise, her expression of amazement as extreme as he had hoped it would be. That, and her long, uncharacteristic silence were almost worth all the difficulties he had endured over the past several days.

He couldn't help grinning, and a glance showed that Violet was doing the same. Dina, however, looked wary.

"Is it not the most famous surprise, Mother?" Violet exclaimed. "And was Grant not the slyest thing in the world to say nothing of it in his letter?"

Dina looked from Thor's satisfied smile to Violet's, then back at Lady Rumble, just in time to see her recover from her pardonable shock. Her open mouth closed, then opened again into a smile as wide as her son's. Moving swiftly foward, she enveloped Dina in a hug that nearly smothered her.

"Married!" she all but shrieked, though to Dina, still embedded in her bosom, it was muffled. "At last, at last. Grant, you are forgiven your tardiness, most completely forgiven indeed. Married! I am delighted to make your acquaintance—Dina, was it? Oh, how I shall love introducing my daughter-in-law about the neighborhood."

Finally released, Dina sucked air into her deprived lungs before answering. "I am honored to meet you, my lady, and apologize for arriving unannounced. I only learned yesterday that Mr. Turpin had not written you about our marriage."

Lady Rumble turned fond eyes upon her son. "Oh, dear Grant has always delighted in surprising me, even as a child. Quite the prankster, our Grant. This is a surprise to cap all, however, and the happiest one I can remember.

"Oh! We must go and tell Lord Rumble. He will be

as pleased as I am, I know. Come, come, all of you."
Dragging Dina by the hand, she headed up the steps
to the house.

"See?" Violet whispered in response to the
alarmed glance Dina sent over her shoulder to be
sure that she and Thor were following.

Dina managed a dazed nod. Though she was relieved that her reception was so positive, nothing had
prepared her for the whirlwind that was Lady Rumble. Her hand felt enclosed in a lace-covered vise.

They passed through the great hall so quickly that
she was unable to identify the marble busts in al-
coves along the way, or to notice more than that the
stone floor was highly polished and the furnishings
both plentiful and fine. She was pulled inexorably
past the great staircase and into a double-doored
room on the right, which proved to be a superbly
stocked library.

"My dear Lord Rumble, only look," Lady Rumble
cried as they entered. "Grant has brought home a
bride, at last. Is it not the grandest thing?"

Lord Rumble stood up from behind a cluttered
desk to peer at Dina over a pair of half-moon specta-
cles. "A bride, say you? That's nice, my dear. And Violet home safe, too, I see." In contrast to his wife's
rapturous tones, his voice was so calm as to be almost bored.

Dina smiled politely up at the baron, noting that
he was very nearly as tall as his son, though substantially thinner. "I . . . I am honored to meet you, my
lord," she said, just as she had to Lady Rumble before. "And I apologize—"

"No apologies necessary," he replied kindly.

"Only see how happy you have made my wife. I presume you have a name?"

"Dina," she said, feeling rather foolish.

"Dina," he repeated. "I will endeavor to remember it. I must thank you, son, for bringing your sister home as I asked, and for answering your mother's fondest wish into the bargain. And now, if you will all excuse me, I was just in the middle of translating a fragment of Theagenes's defense of Homer's epic style."

They all retreated from the library, Dina feeling more overwhelmed and confused than ever.

"Don't mind him, my dear," Lady Rumble said as she led them upstairs to the drawing room. "Lord Rumble is a dedicated scholar—a genius, really. His mind is always full of Greek and Latin and mathematics and such things, but I can tell that he is nearly as delighted to have you here as I am."

Dina glanced up at Thor, and he gave her a reassuring nod and an even more reassuring squeeze of her shoulder. "She's right. It's a high honor that he intends to remember your name, for he forgets mine on a regular basis."

"Too true," Lady Rumble agreed. "Now, suppose you all tell me how this surprise wedding came about." She took a seat by the fire but then jumped back up, before any of them could answer.

"Goodness, I nearly forgot," she exclaimed. "I must speak with Mrs. Hornbuckle at once about dinner, which I'm determined will be a special one, given the occasion. And she must see to your room as well, Dina, since we had no word of your coming.

Though perhaps you would prefer to share Grant's, this evening?" She gave them both a broad wink.

Dina felt the color rushing to her cheeks. "I, ah—" she stammered, having no earthly idea how to respond in a way that would not offend her new mother-in-law.

"I'm sure Dina would like to have her own chamber," Thor said firmly, rescuing her. "It's not as though we are short on space."

"Of course not, but newlyweds, you know . . ." She trailed off with a titter. "I'll have Mrs. Hornbuckle move you into the west corner, Grant, so that Dina may have the adjoining room. Your usual room has no connection to the one next to it, and you'll want easy—and private—access to each other, I know."

Again she winked, and again Dina felt herself blushing. Finally, after a few more suggestive nods and smiles, Lady Rumble went off to find the housekeeper, leaving the new arrivals alone for a moment.

"You see, Dina, I come by my penchant for romance quite naturally," Violet said with a grin. "I am a mere dilettante compared to Mother."

"It's true," Thor agreed. "I'm afraid we are in for some embarrassment at her hands. I should have warned you, but I'd hoped she might restrain herself somewhat, at least on first meeting you."

Dina looked from one to the other. "At least you were both right that she seems happy about our marriage. But what are we to tell her about how it took place?"

"The truth, more or less," Thor replied with a

shrug. "That you helped to prevent Violet's marriage to Plunkett, and that in return I agreed to help you out of a difficult situation."

Dina nodded. "Perhaps once she knows that it was purely a marriage of expediency, she will cease making romantic allusions."

"I wouldn't count on it," Violet said. "After all, she and Father scarcely knew each other when they wed, and she never tires of telling about how it turned into a love match after all." She gave a sentimental sigh. "It may not have appeared that way in the library just now, but they really do dote upon each other. I only hope my own marriage will be as happy, when the time comes."

"There will be more chance of that if you refrain from running off with chance-met fortune hunters," her brother pointed out.

Violet made a face at him. "You're a fine one to talk, considering that I knew Mr. Plunkett rather better than you knew Dina on your wedding day."

Now they were on uncomfortable ground again, Dina felt, for she and Thor could make no particular claim to a *happy* marriage. Indeed, what they had could scarcely be called a proper marriage at all. Certainly it was no model to be emulated.

It appeared Thor's mind was similarly engaged, for he said, "Ours is a special circumstance, and well you know it, minx—especially as you were an instigator in bringing it about."

Violet only looked from one to the other of them with a mysterious smile. "Special case or no, I have a feeling that your marriage will turn out even better than Mother's and Father's. Now, if you'll excuse

me, I'd like to go up to my room and my maid to rest
and freshen up before dinner."

With a saucy wink, she flounced out of the parlor,
leaving Dina alone with her husband.

"I, ah, I'm sorry that you will be moving from your
accustomed bedchamber on my account," she said
after an awkward pause.

He shrugged. "It's no matter, really. I've not visited Plumrose more than half a dozen times over the
past two or three years, so any attachment I may
once have had to any particular room no longer ex-
ists. I'm far more familiar now with my chamber at
Ivy Lodge, in Leicestershire."

"Ivy Lodge?"

"Lord Anthony Northrup's hunting box—though
I suppose now it should be considered Rush's, as
he's leasing it from Anthony."

Dina realized afresh how little she knew about her
husband. "Leicestershire. Do you hunt with the
Quorn, then?" Like all Englishwomen, she knew
something of foxhunting, though she'd never had
opportunity to observe one.

"Aye, the Quorn, the Belvoir, the Pytchley, and
one or two others. It's fascinating to see how the different packs perform under various conditions." His
expression became more animated. "Given the
bloodlines of my newest litter, I'd wager they'll grow
up to be both fast and tenacious on the scent."

"You have your own pack of foxhounds?"

"Not quite a pack yet, but—"

"I do apologize for rushing off like that," Lady
Rumble exclaimed, reentering the parlor just then.
"But now I have dinner ordered up, and your rooms

should be ready for you as we speak, though of course we'll be adding some touches to them over the next few days. Come along up, Dina, and see whether your chamber meets with your approval."

She continued to chatter as they both followed her from the room and up the stairs. "Grant, your valet is transferring your wardrobe and other effects to your new room, but you'll need to tell him if you wish any furniture or artwork moved as well. You will share a dressing room with Dina, which I assume will present no difficulty, as that is how your father's chamber and mine are arranged, and it has worked well for us all these years."

"I'm sure it will be fine," he replied noncommittally.

Dina nodded in agreement, glad that the conversation was on a relatively impersonal topic at the moment. Foxhounds would offer another neutral subject, should they exhaust the current one.

"Here we are," Lady Rumble said then, flinging open a door near the end of the west wing. "This will be your room, Dina, and Grant's is the next one along, at the end. Your trunks and your maid are already within."

They both thanked her, and she smiled from one to the other. "Now I'll leave you two alone again, for with Violet along from the moment of your wedding, I'm sure you've had precious little privacy. You'll need plenty of that, if you're going to give me all of the grandchildren I'm counting on."

With a parting wink, she turned in a swirl of mauve and perfume and headed back down the hall, leaving them more awkwardly alone than ever.

Chapter 9

Thor cleared his throat, trying to will his color not to rise. "Why don't you see if your room is acceptable," he suggested. "I'll, ah, do the same."

"Yes. Yes, of course," Dina replied, her own face scarlet. She seemed eager to ignore the implications of his mother's parting words—though he feared they would hear more of the same, all too frequently.

He waited in the hall while Dina stepped into her room and glanced around, greeting her maid in what he thought was a tolerably composed voice, under the circumstances. After a quick survey of the chamber, she turned back to him, though she did not quite meet his eye.

"It is lovely. Please convey my thanks to Lady Rumble, if you see her again before I do."

"Of course." With a quick nod, he moved to his

own new chamber before he could give in to the temptation to join her in hers.

His mother's words had clearly not had the same effect on Dina as they'd had on him, and he felt a distinct need to be alone, to get his errant body under control before she could guess the direction of his thoughts.

Entering the corner room, he closed the door behind him and gave the chamber a cursory glance. "Quick work," he said approvingly to Spooner, his valet.

He'd sent the man here from Ivy Lodge upon setting out after Violet, knowing he'd be returning here one way or another before going back to Leicestershire.

"Thank you, sir," Spooner replied. "May I take this opportunity to offer my congratulations on your nuptials?"

Thor didn't care to think what sort of speculation must be rife in the servants' quarters over this unexpected development, and refused to add to it. "Thank you. I'll be changing for dinner in an hour or so. You're at liberty until then."

With a respectful bow, Spooner left him, and Thor crossed to the window to stare sightlessly down at the grounds, drab and gray in the fading December twilight. A faint noise next door recalled Dina's presence there—not that he was likely to forget it.

"Damn," he said aloud to the empty room. His constant awareness of his new wife's presence, not to mention his growing attraction to her, was inconvenient, to say the least.

He had hoped that once they were released from

the close confines of the traveling coach, his body's unruly reaction to her nearness would subside, but if anything the opposite had occurred. When his mother had mentioned grandchildren just now, his first, instinctive reaction had been embarrassing in the extreme. He only hoped that Dina had not noticed it.

Perhaps not. She had been embarrassed herself, though obviously not for the same reason, and so had avoided looking at him—luckily. He would have to get his physical urges under control before they went down to dinner, however, if he was not to frighten her out of her wits.

She was so small, so delicate, so . . . feminine. That must be why he felt so protective, in a way he never had with any of the healthy, strapping women he'd been with in the past. Protective was fine. This growing desire was not, and he was determined to get the better of it, as it threatened to undermine the very protection he intended.

A light tap on the dressing room door interrupted his ruminations, and he turned with a start. "Yes?"

Though he expected Dina's maid, with some question or other, it was Dina herself who entered. Her hair had been brushed out and tied with a loose ribbon that allowed the red curls to cascade down her back, he noticed, though she was still clad in the same rather fetching blue gown she'd worn on today's journey.

"I'm . . . I'm sorry to bother you," she said, taking a tentative step into the room in a way that reminded him of a doe at the edge of a field. "One of my trunks is missing, and I thought it might have been brought to your room by mistake."

"Oh." Was that the best he could do? Feeling oddly awkward—and inconveniently aroused all over again—he turned half away from her to glance around his chamber. "Is that it?" He gestured toward a small trunk that he didn't recognize, next to the clothespress.

"Yes, thank you." She moved toward the trunk, but he was there before her.

"Let me get it." Surely she didn't think she could lift it herself? He bent down, and indeed, the trunk was unusually heavy for its size. "What do you have in here, books?"

To his surprise, she colored slightly. "Er, yes. Books, among other things. Really, you don't have to—"

"It's no trouble—and far too heavy for you, in any case."

With a heave, he swung the trunk onto his shoulder in what he felt must be a rather impressive manner. Now, why should he care about impressing her? She was already his wife, after all. Besides, he'd never been given to obvious displays of strength.

Rather than looking impressed, however, Dina pursed her pink lips in an expression that looked almost peeved. "I could have dragged it," she pointed out.

He blinked. "Um, yes, I suppose so, but there was no need, as I'm here to carry it for you. Where would you like me to put it?" The trunk was getting heavy for his shoulder.

"Oh, ah, in here."

She retreated through the dressing room and into

her chamber, and he followed, turning sideways to avoid banging the trunk against the door frame. Really, it would have made more sense to simply lift it in front of him by its handles, though that would have been a less dramatic display of his strength.

Crossing her room to set the trunk in the corner she indicated, he noted in passing that this chamber suited her, with pink and ivory curtains at the windows and a matching ruffled counterpane on the four-poster bed. He caught himself staring at the bed and turned abruptly.

"Will that be all, then?"

"I . . . yes."

He turned to go, loath to leave her but knowing he needed to get away before he said or did something foolish.

"No," she said then, making him pause. "There is something else."

Reluctantly, fearing that she might somehow divine the ache she seemed to be producing within him, he turned to face her.

"What should I . . . that is, how formally does your family dress for dinner?" Her eyes—those amazing green eyes—met his, stirring him anew.

Belatedly, the meaning of her words sank in, and he frowned. He'd never paid much attention to matters of dress, leaving that sort of thing to his valet.

"Not terribly formally, as I recall," he said after a moment in an admirably detached tone of voice. "Mother did say something about a special dinner tonight, however, so I'd not be surprised if she, at least, decks herself out in her finest."

"Yes, she does seem rather determined to make an

occasion out of it." Dina sounded distinctly worried. "I'll dress accordingly—and I hope I won't do anything to embarrass you in front of your family."

Startled, Thor looked directly at her. Her eyes were now wide and concerned and incredibly alluring. "You? I've no fear of that. We can probably count on my mother saying things that will embarrass us both, however, and I'll take this opportunity to apologize in advance."

She smiled. Surely he was imagining an unspoken invitation in the curve of her lips? "You've no need to apologize. I hold you no more responsible for your mother's behavior than I hope you hold me for my brother's."

"Point taken," he replied, belatedly returning her smile. "We will both simply have to remember that words alone can do nothing to us—and try to bear up."

Now why had he used that particular phrasing? In his present mood, it took on quite another connotation than he had intended. Only for himself, of course. Dina merely nodded, showing no sign that she had read anything untoward into his words.

"You're right, of course. I will try not to let anything she says unsettle me. After all, we know how absurd her assumptions are, even if she does not yet understand that our marriage was a business arrangement rather than a love match."

"Exactly." Thor swallowed, wondering why Dina's simple reiteration of the truth should suddenly make his chest ache. "Until dinner, then."

With a crisp half bow, he turned on his heel and

disappeared through the dressing room, closing the door behind him.

Dina frowned at the door, trying to decipher the odd expression that had flitted across his face at her words. She had deliberately chosen nearly the same words he'd used on their wedding day, the ones she had not been able to forget. Her intent had been to prove that she regarded their marriage in the same light he did, that her emotions were not engaged.

It was a lie, unfortunately. Perhaps his grimace meant that he'd recognized that. Or perhaps the word "business" had made her sound so mercenary that she had disgusted him? She honestly didn't know, but suspected that she had only made her situation worse. It was done, however, for there was no recalling the words.

Letting out a breath she hadn't realized she was holding, she turned briskly to her maid. "Come, Francine, help me to unpack this trunk."

Pulling a key from her pocket, she unlocked the steel-strapped wooden box and opened it. It was a mercy, she supposed, that Thor had not asked to see the contents. At least there were two books within, so she had not—quite—been guilty of falsehood when she had verified his assumption.

Dina knelt to remove the two gowns she had carefully placed on top of the other contents against a cursory inspection and handed them to her maid. Then she reached into the trunk and pulled out three pairs of dumbbells of varying weights. She'd paid a Litchfield merchant extremely well to obtain these for her from London without her brother's knowledge, and had made excellent use of them in the three or four years since then.

"Here, Francine, put these next to the bed." She would keep them under it, as she did at home. Her maid complied, using both hands for each dumbbell. Francine was no weakling, for Dina had exhorted her to follow her example when the weights were not in use, but she did not train as diligently as her mistress, having little incentive to do so.

Next, Dina extracted a heavy leather bag filled with sawdust, which at Ashcombe had been hung in a corner of the cow byre, where Silas would never think to go. She had used it to practice the boxing moves Uncle Kendall had taught her, and to keep her reflexes quick.

"This may as well go under the bed, too, for I certainly can't use it anytime soon," she said regretfully, handing the bag to her maid.

Finally she pulled out the two books—not the novels or sermons most women would be likely to have among their possessions, but a treatise on the physical training of the ancient Greeks and *The Gentleman's Guide to Fencing and Pugilism*, rescued from among Silas's discarded texts when he had finished his schooling.

She glanced about the room, but saw no better place of concealment than behind the decorative pink bedskirt, which reached to the floor. Shrugging, she rose and tucked the books there, along with her other equipment. There. Now she could begin to feel as though she belonged here.

Directing her maid to see about having a half bath brought up, she carefully locked the dressing room door against any unexpected visit from Thor, unlikely though that seemed, stripped down to her chemise, and picked up the first set of dumbbells.

By the time Francine returned with a copper of hot water and a large basin, she had restored her equilibrium with an abbreviated session of weight lifting and some stretches. It was gratifying to discover that she had lost almost none of her strength by the interruption of her routine over the past week.

"Thank you, Francine," she said as the maid laid out basin, washcloth, and towels. "Lay out my lemon silk for me while I wash."

Half an hour later, fresh, fit, and confident that she looked as well as her limited wardrobe allowed, she opened her door to Thor's knock to accompany him down to dinner. She was determined not to be put to the blush, either by his overwhelming maleness, which affected her more than she cared to admit, or by anything Lady Rumble might say over the course of the meal.

"I see you have put your time to good use," he said, casting what could only be an appreciative glance over her ensemble, "though it might have been better to use it resting, after all of the traveling we've done of late."

"I might say the same," she replied with a slightly breathless smile, noting that he had spent no small effort on his own appearance. It was the first time she'd seen him in evening wear, and the effect of his superb physique in well-fitted coat and breeches of deep blue superfine was rather overwhelming.

He acknowledged the compliment only with a twinkle of his blue eyes before extending an arm to her. "Since we are both well armored, let us go down and face the dragon, shall we?"

Dina could not suppress a startled chuckle. "Surely you are not referring to your mother as a dragon? Really, she has been exceedingly kind to me, particularly given the circumstances."

"Perhaps 'dragon' is too strong a term, though she can be as relentless as any mythical beast on certain topics. Our task will be to evade, not to slay, of course—though that may well take even more skill and effort."

Still chuckling, Dina took his proferred arm, determinedly ignoring the shiver of awareness that went through her at the contact. A quick glance upward showed a firm jawline and handsome profile apparently unmoved by any similar awareness. As she had expected.

They descended in silence, on Dina's side because she could think of nothing to say that would not reveal her emotional state. Not only was she nervous about the coming inquisition—for such she regarded it—but she was increasingly worried that Thor would somehow divine her growing attraction to him. And that would not do at all.

"Why, how prompt you two are," Lady Rumble exclaimed when they reached the parlor. Neither Violet nor Lord Rumble was yet in evidence. "You'd have been forgiven for any tardiness this evening, you know."

Did the woman never tire of winking? Dina wondered with a trace of exasperation. At least she was able to refrain from blushing this time, steeled as she'd been for just such a comment.

"Mother, you should know that Dina and I met for the very first time on the day of our wedding," Thor said then. "We are still getting to know each other, and your continual insinuations are not precisely helping matters."

She looked back and forth between them, her eyes wide—and every bit as blue as Thor's. "You met the day you married? In Scotland? Why, how very romantic! I must hear the whole story—but not until your father arrives. Ah, Lord Rumble, here you are, and Violet, too. Let us go down to dinner at once, so that Grant and Dina can tell us what promises to be a grand tale."

Lord Rumble gave Dina a polite nod, though his gaze was slightly unfocused, making her wonder whether he'd already forgotten who she was. Violet, however, smiled brightly at her as they went downstairs to the dining room. Dina noticed that she avoided her mother's eye, which must mean the dreaded scold was yet to come.

"Now, Grant, do tell us how your marriage came about," Lady Rumble said as they all took their seats and a footman came forward with the soup. "I simply can't wait another moment to hear it. You caught up with Violet and that rascally Mr. Plunkett before they reached Gretna Green, I presume, but then what happened?"

"Actually," he said, picking up his soup spoon, "with the start they had, Violet and her fortune hunter were able to reach Scotland on Tuesday evening, while I did not arrive until Wednesday morning."

"What?" Lady Rumble fairly shrieked, turning to

stare at Violet, whose attention was riveted on her bowl of broth. "But your letter said that you had reached her in time."

"In time to prevent her marrying Plunkett," he said.

Lady Rumble stared at him incredulously. "But not in time to preserve her reputation, if she spent two nights on the road with the man and then did not marry him."

"I did not sleep with him, Mother." Finally prompted to speech, Violet spoke defensively. "I insisted on separate rooms at the first inn, and in Gretna, Dina let me share hers."

"But the world is not to know that. How *shall* we explain your absence this week past? I have avoided the neighbors, and even most of the servants, while you were gone, for fear I might say more than was wise."

"We discussed this at some length during our journey," Thor said, "and thought it might be best to claim that it was Dina and I who eloped and that Violet came along to act as chaperone before the wedding."

"Hmph. Hmph. Well." Lady Rumble continued to glare at her daughter for a long moment, then turned to her husband. "Lord Rumble, what think you? Will that serve, or must we consider our Violet ruined?"

Lord Rumble looked up mildly from his soup, which was nearly gone by now, the conversation not having affected his appetite in the least. "Ruined? Ruined for what? She looks the same to me as she ever did."

"Ruined for marriage, of course," Lady Rumble clarified. "Do you think this elopement of hers will have spoiled her chances?"

"Not if no one knows of it but ourselves," he said so practically that Dina had to hide a smile. "Reputation is all about appearances, is it not?"

His wife blinked. "Why, ah, yes, I suppose one could say that." She stopped twisting her hands together and managed a small smile. "Thank you, my dear. You always do seem to put things into perspective for me."

"I consider it one of my primary responsibilities," he replied. Then, suddenly turning an eye that was not vague in the least upon Dina, he said, "But now I confess to a great deal of curiosity about how our new daughter-in-law came to be in Scotland—alone?—and how Grant came to marry her."

Haltingly, Dina gave an abbreviated account of how she had believed her father's will required that she marry quickly, how Mr. Tallow had jilted her, and how, when Thor had expressed his gratitude for the part she had played with Violet, she had requested that he marry her as a reward of sorts. She glossed over Silas's role in the business, seeing no point in tarnishing her brother in Violet's or her new in-laws' eyes.

"I see," said Lord Rumble when she concluded, making her wonder whether he had divined everything she had left unsaid. "Grant, you found her request reasonable?" He now pinned his son with his bright gaze.

Dina, relieved to have the attention shifted from

herself, nevertheless felt some trepidation over what Thor might now say. Certainly he looked uncomfortable in the extreme, and she remembered his lofty declaration that he would not lie to his parents. Would he tell them about her intention of marrying Mr. Plunkett herself?

"I, ah, well, you know how Mother has been after me to marry," he hedged. "Besides, it seemed the only fair thing to do, especially after the service she had done our family."

Lord Rumble raised one thin brow and seemed about to ask more questions, but just then the footman returned with the next course, and he turned his attention back to his dinner. Thor waited until the servant had left them again to continue.

"Anyway, as you can see, Mother, ours was not a romantic marriage. Dina did our family a favor, and in return I did her one. Therefore, there's no need—"

"Oh, tut-tut," Lady Rumble interrupted him. "You would never have married her, or you him, my dear," she added to Dina, "if you had not felt a degree of attraction for each other. Why, I scarcely knew your father when we married—an assembly or two, and a dinner, what is that?—and see how well things have turned out for us."

She turned a fond smile on her husband, who glanced up from his fish long enough to return it.

"Besides," Violet put in, no doubt eager to keep the conversation away from herself, "you two do seem to deal very well together. And there was that night you spent together at the Spotted Dog, don't forget." Her wink, Dina thought, was irritatingly like her mother's.

Embarrassed, Dina felt moved to protest. "Only because there was no other room available. We did not . . . that is . . ."

Thor came to her aid. "Nothing happened between us. Mother, Violet, you both must understand that we went into this marriage with no romantic expectations whatsoever. Nor is that like to change."

Recalling her own turbulent feelings upstairs before dinner, Dina could only hope that he was right. Certainly she didn't *want* that to change—did she?

But Lady Rumble was looking stubborn. "Not with an attitude like that," she said. "Are you telling me that you have not so much as kissed your bride since marrying her?"

Dina felt the color rush to her face and could only be grateful that Lady Rumble's eyes were directed at her son rather than at her. Lord Rumble's were still focused on his plate. More than once since their wedding, Dina had imagined what it might be like to kiss Thor—to have him kiss her—but she had always been quick to thrust such thoughts away.

"Of course I have not," Thor replied. Though Dina did not dare to look at him just now, his voice sounded perfectly calm. "Given our circumstances, that would scarcely be appropriate."

"Appropriate? What nonsense," his mother declared roundly. "Whatever the circumstances that led to the actual wedding, you *are* married now, so you may as well make the best of it. Besides, there is the succession to consider."

Dina cringed, wishing she could disappear under the table or, better, from the entire face of the earth.

Thor had made it quite clear he had no interest in her in that way, but she would rather not hear him reiterate it before his whole family.

He did not, however, only saying blandly, "I cannot think this is a fit topic for dinner."

Seemingly undaunted, Lady Rumble snorted. "You young people are so prudish these days. Very well, I will try not to embarrass you further, but in return, you must promise me to at least kiss your bride good night."

Startled, Dina looked up—to find Thor's questioning gaze on her. "If Dina will agree, and if we may thereby have your promise to stay out of our private affairs, I am willing," he said, his eyes never leaving hers.

Though she half expected her face to burst into flame, it felt so hot, Dina managed an embarrassed nod.

"Wonderful," Lady Rumble declared, beaming back and forth between them. "That will be an excellent start. But no, I promise, I'll not say another word on the subject. Now, do try some of the turbot, for it is one of Cook's specialties."

The rest of the evening passed in a blur for Thor, so focused was he on the conclusion of it, looming ahead. As always, his father was disinclined to linger over port after dinner, instead returning to his studies. Thor, therefore, joined the ladies in the parlor, where his mother finally delivered her obligatory scold to Violet before moving on to the topic of upcoming assemblies in the neighborhood, which, as predicted, Violet was forbidden to attend, as punishment.

Dina, he noticed, took little part in the conversation, but whether because she was unfamiliar with the neighborhood or because she was similarly preoccupied with the awkward moment to come, he had no idea. If the latter, was she anticipating or dreading it?

Not that he could say which one was true for himself.

Though she held to her promise not to mention their marital relationship again, Lady Rumble declared herself ready to retire at an unusually early hour. "And you must all be tired as well, after so many days on the road," she added, with only the barest trace of a wink.

"Indeed, I am exhausted," Violet agreed with a sly glance at Thor, which he stolidly ignored. "Let's all head up to bed, shall we?"

As they stood, Dina turned to her hostess. "I must thank you again, my lady, for your extraordinary kindness to me today."

"Why, it was nothing, my dear," Lady Rumble responded. "If you can make my Grant happy, that will be more than enough thanks for me."

After that, it did not surprise him that Dina refused to meet his eye as they followed his mother and Violet upstairs. He wondered whether he could consider Lady Rumble's words breach enough of her promise to absolve him of his—but regretfully decided she had not quite crossed that line.

At the top of the stairs they parted, Violet and

Lady Rumble heading down the east wing to their bedchambers while he and Dina headed to the west wing. Determined to defuse at least some of the awkwardness between them, Thor forced himself to speak.

"I apologize again for my mother's outspokenness, but at least she seems to be trying to restrain herself now."

Dina, walking quietly at his side, nodded. "Yes, she kept her promise quite well after dinner. Again, though, no apology from you is necessary. Besides, one can hardly blame her for her feelings, however, ah, inappropriate the expression of them may have been, at times."

"You are more charitable than I," he said, "though perhaps that is because you've not been subjected to her hints and nudges for years, as I have. We can hope that her promise will hold for a few days, at least, and take what relief we can from it."

They reached the door to Dina's chamber and stopped. "I . . . I suppose we must now fulfill our promise, however," she said so softly that he had to stoop to hear her, particularly as she spoke to his shirtfront rather than to his face.

"I suppose so. Do you truly not mind?"

She gave a quick shake of her head, still looking down.

Thor felt like cursing. Over the past few days, he'd caught himself fantasizing once or twice about kissing Dina, but in those daydreams it had happened naturally, because they both wanted it to happen. This was quite different—and incredibly awkward.

But he had promised.

For a long moment he hesitated, then, steeling himself against her effect on him, he placed one finger under her chin to tilt her face up to him. Her green eyes were wide and spoke of a panic that was not precisely fear. He understood, for he felt much the same sort of panic himself.

Best to get it over, he decided. He lowered his lips to hers, intending the briefest of kisses, the minimum necessary to satisfy the bargain he'd made with his mother. The instant their lips met, however, he felt that jolt of connection he'd felt before at her touch, only far stronger this time.

Something inside him began to clamor, urging him toward her, demanding more contact, more sensation, more . . . everything. His finger slid from her chin to her jaw, tracing the delicate curve of her face. Even as reason told him it was time to end the kiss, her lips softened beneath his, and she seemed to lean into him—or was he the one leaning into her?

Either way, the heightened contact inflamed his barely banked desire, compelling him to continue. His arms went around her, seemingly of their own volition, and he gathered her to him, inhaling her fragrance, reveling in her fragile softness.

He felt her small hands against his chest and braced himself for her push, determined to release her instantly if she resisted, but instead she slipped her arms around his neck, pulling him even closer. Her lips now moved beneath his, inviting him to deepen the kiss he knew he should already have ended.

His hard-won control evaporated, and he accepted the invitation, probing her mouth with his tongue, forging a new bond between them, a white-hot bond of passion. That passion gave voice to a growl, deep in his throat, and was answered by a faint moan from Dina.

Instantly he released her. "Did . . . did I hurt you?" he panted, fear lancing through him.

Her lips were parted, slightly swollen and still incredibly inviting, as she looked up at him in dazed confusion. "Hurt—? Ah, no." Her voice was breathless, seductive.

He started to reach for her again when reason returned with a brutal crash. What on earth was he doing? Quickly he took a step backward, toward his own chamber.

"I'm sorry, Dina. I never meant—that is—good night." Sketching her a quick bow, absurdly formal under the circumstances, he escaped into his room and closed the door as quickly as he could without slamming it.

Had he gone mad? Another minute and he had no doubt that he'd have swept her up in his arms and carried her to bed—and very likely have injured her in the process. He only hoped he had stopped short of terrifying her, though he didn't doubt he'd given her a disgust of him, at the very least.

He'd come perilously close to breaking the promise he'd given her before they wed, and she must surely realize it.

"Sir?"

He whirled to find Spooner regarding him from

across the room, only the faintest trace of curiosity showing on his well-trained face.

"Pack me a trunk," he told his valet on sudden decision. "I leave for Melton-Mowbray at first light."

Chapter 10

Dina waited until Thor had disappeared into his chamber before opening the door to her own. Deeply shaken as she felt by that remarkable kiss, she wasn't about to leave the hallway if there was any chance of an encore.

After a few moments, however, she realized that would not happen and closed herself into her room with a not-unhappy sigh. Facing Thor tomorrow would be awkward after what had ignited between them just now, but in the meantime she could simply savor this evidence that he was not so indifferent to her as she had believed.

Oh, she did not harbor any illusions that he was developing a *tendre* for her, but at least that kiss showed that he found her attractive. Desirable. And that alone was enough to buoy her spirits, given what she'd just discovered about her own feelings.

For that kiss—that amazing, explosive kiss—had unleashed emotions far beyond her most worrisome imaginings. What she felt for Thor, she now knew, went far beyond mere attraction or even friendship. In fact, if she was not extremely careful, she would soon find herself head-over-ears in love with her husband.

Not good. But perhaps not quite the disaster she had feared. Turning to her waiting maid with a smile, she allowed herself to be undressed and readied for bed, certain that her dreams would be, if not sweet, then at least a great deal more interesting than usual.

Whether she was right she never knew, for when she awoke in the morning she was unable to remember any dreams at all, though she felt undeniably cheerful, despite the gloomy weather outside her pink-curtained window. She jumped out of bed for a quick round of calisthenics, then, calling her maid, she bathed and dressed with care before going downstairs for breakfast.

Not until she approached the dining room did doubts begin to assail her. Would Thor pretend that kiss had never happened? Should she do the same? Surely some awareness between them was inevitable. Would Lady Rumble divine the truth and resume her relentless hinting? Taking a deep breath, she entered the dining room—to find it empty.

Glancing around, she saw a tempting array of hot breakfast dishes on the sideboard, along with a stack of plates and serving utensils. Apparently breakfast in the Rumble household was a come-as-you-please affair. Dina shrugged and helped herself to eggs, stewed tomatoes, and a rasher of bacon.

The moment she seated herself at the long table, a footman appeared. "Would you care for coffee, tea, or chocolate, ma'am?" he inquired.

"Coffee, please." The stimulant might help her to react more quickly and appropriately to whatever mood Thor presented when he appeared.

She had taken only a bite or two when footsteps heralded the entrance of Lord and Lady Rumble, arm in arm. "Good morning," she greeted them. "I hope you don't mind that I began without you?"

"Not at all, my dear," Lady Rumble replied. "As you can see, we treat breakfast quite informally. Lord Rumble's schedule is variable, depending upon his studies, and Violet often sleeps till noon, particularly when she has been out the night before."

They both went to the sideboard to fill plates before moving to the table. Seating herself across from Dina, Lady Rumble regarded her with a concern that Dina didn't understand. "Did . . . did you sleep well, my dear?" she asked.

"Indeed, yes," Dina replied, trying not to color at the recollection of why she had done so. She almost asked what time Thor was likely to be down, but restrained herself. "My room is most comfortable," she added instead.

Lady Rumble smiled, despite the faint crease that remained between her brows. "You are surprisingly cheerful, under the circumstances. That's very brave of you, my dear."

"Circumstances?" Dina repeated. What did she mean, "brave"?

"She means Grant haring off to Melton again," Lord Rumble explained between bites of pastry. "Lady Rumble thought that your presence here would change his habits, though I warned her that might not be the case."

Dina blinked. Thor was gone? He'd said not a word last night about leaving. Before she could ask when he might return, Lady Rumble spoke again.

"I fear I am partly to blame, with my insistence on regarding your marriage as a love match, despite what you both told me. Perhaps if I hadn't extracted that promise from him last night—"

"Pray do not blame yourself, my dear," said Lord Rumble soothingly. "He likely would have gone anyway, as it's still the height of foxhunting season. When have you ever known him to stay at home during the month of December?"

Dina, however, felt sure it was not merely the lure of foxhunting that had spirited Thor away just now. That kiss last night, so much more passionate than either of them had expected . . . This must mean he regretted it, and had seized on this way of avoiding any awkwardness as a result. Her spirits, which had been so high upon awakening, plummeted through the floor.

"Did he say when he meant to return?" Lady Rumble asked Dina then—the very question Dina herself had meant to ask.

She shook her head. "I, ah, no. I don't recall that he did." Somehow she could not bring herself to admit that he had not even told her he was leaving. It was too humiliating.

"No matter. He'll be home for the Christmas Eve

ball, at the latest, and that is but a fortnight off. This will give you time to settle in here and meet the neighbors, and for Violet to take you 'round to an assembly or two." Lady Rumble spoke with rather forced cheerfulness, Dina thought.

For herself, she was finding it difficult to discover a bright side to Thor's absence. Last night they had seemed to be making progress toward a real friendship, if not more. By the time he returned, they would be strangers again—which he apparently preferred.

"That sounds like fun," she forced herself to say, though in truth the prospect of being dragged 'round the neighborhood and introduced as Thor's new bride, facing the unspoken questions about why her husband had abandoned her so quickly, sounded quite the reverse.

She had promised Thor that she would not interfere in his usual pursuits, she reminded herself sternly. She had no call to be upset simply because he'd taken her at her word. Indeed, she thought drearily, she should consider it a compliment.

Though her appetite had fled, she picked at her food while Lady Rumble's chatter flowed over her, contributing only the occasional nod or murmur of agreement when her opinion was solicited. Lord Rumble soon left them, and a few minutes later, Violet arrived at the dining room.

"I see I am the last one down, as usual," she said brightly. "Or am I? Where is Grant?"

"Gone," her mother responded mournfully. Then, glancing at Dina, she smiled again. "But as I've been telling Dina, it is no matter, for we will contrive to keep her quite busy, between us."

Violet's gaze was sympathetic, almost pitying, Dina thought.

Defiantly she lifted her chin and smiled. "Yes, Lady Rumble has been outlining all manner of plans for the next two weeks. I daresay I'll scarcely notice Th—Mr. Turpin's absence."

"I daresay you're right," Violet agreed, though her eyes searched Dina's face with disconcerting perceptiveness. "Still, I confess to a tiny bit of disappointment, for I looked forward to teasing him about that good-night kiss last night. Was it . . . romantic?"

"Violet," Lady Rumble remonstrated, but then looked curiously at Dina herself. "Was it, dear?"

Though she could feel a prickling in her cheeks, Dina did her best to appear calm and disinterested. "Not particularly," she lied. "We both regarded it as the mere fulfillment of a promise, I'm afraid, so it was rather perfunctory."

She now wished that had been true. Perhaps then Thor wouldn't have felt it necessary to leave.

Both mother and daughter seemed disappointed. "Ah, well. These things take time." Lady Rumble spoke philosophically—an attitude Dina wished she had evinced the day before. "Now, Violet, what think you of taking Dina for a fitting at Mrs. Hibble's once you've breakfasted? I'm sure she'd like a few new gowns for the assemblies."

It was with a sense of relief that Thor went up the front steps of Ivy Lodge. Once with his friends, he would no longer be alone with his thoughts—which had been unsettled in the extreme during the day's drive. The Odd Sock Club was just gathering for dinner when he walked into the parlor.

"Why, look, it's Thor," exclaimed Sir Charles Storm, better known to his intimates as Stormy, upon his entrance. "Wondered when you'd be back. You missed a fair run of the Quorn today."

Thor realized with a start that it had been exactly a week since he'd left to prevent Violet's marriage. It seemed a month or more, so much had happened since then.

"I must hope the Cottesmore tomorrow is at least as good, then," he replied.

The others came forward then with greetings and a few frank questions as to the reason for his absence. He glanced at Rush, who gave a quick shake of his head to indicate that he'd told them nothing. Just as well. To divert his thoughts from more disturbing matters, Thor had spent much of the day concocting a reasonable tale to account for both his sudden departure and his newly wedded state.

"I do apologize for leaving so abruptly last week," he began, "but a note from home forced a sudden change in my plans. You all recall, do you not, that I was engaged to marry Miss Moore, from Staffordshire?"

An outcry greeted these words, as he'd known it would, and he did his best to appear surprised and confused. "I could have sworn I told you," he said once their protests subsided.

"Shouldn't think we'd forget a thing like that," little Lord Killerby said accusingly. "All the times we talked about Anthony leaving the ranks of us confirmed bachelors, and you never said a word."

"Sorry, Killer, I never meant to be secretive, but I just never thought about it much. It was one of those long-standing arrangements—old family friends, you know—so I just assumed you all knew."

The viscount appeared somewhat mollified. "So what was in that note that necessitated you missing a week of the season? The weather's been unusually fine, too."

"I know." Not that the weather had been particularly fine up north, of course. "There was some concern that Miss Moore's brother was dipping into her funds, so the families thought it best if we go ahead and tie the knot before he could do more damage."

He'd decided it would be safest to stick as close to the truth as possible, at least when it came to those details that could easily be verified by anyone interested enough to do so.

"Then you're to be married right away?" Stormy exclaimed in horrified tones. "Sounds like a story cooked up by the girl's mother to keep you from slipping the noose, if you ask me."

"Her mother is dead—as is her father," Thor replied, effectively quenching his friend's indignation. "That's why the brother is a threat, being her guardian. As for the wedding, it's done. You see before you a married man."

He forced a grin, and in fact found himself rather enjoying their combined astonishment. Even Rush looked stunned.

"So, when do we get to meet the new Mrs.

Turpin?" his erstwhile commander asked, his eyes sharp and curious.

"I, ah, you're all welcome to visit at Plumrose. My mother is throwing her usual Christmas Eve ball."

Thor hadn't considered his friends actually meeting Dina, though he supposed it was inevitable. If not in the Shires, they would surely see her in London after the first of the year. As most of them knew his usual taste in women, they would no doubt think his choice in a wife deuced odd. Perhaps he could convince them he and Dina had been betrothed in the cradle?

Probably not.

"Perhaps we'll take you up on that, at least for a day or two," Rush said, his expression telling Thor that he had no intention of waiting that long for an explanation. "But now it appears dinner is ready. Shall we, gentlemen?"

It was a lively meal, the conversation, to Thor's relief, centering more on the day's run than on his own remarkable news. Not until the port was being passed did Killer bring it up again.

"M'mother will be sorry she missed your announcement, Thor," he said. "She only went back to Nottinghamshire two days ago. I've no doubt she'll return soon enough, though. Else I'd have to write her with the news."

"I notice you're hobbling around much better," Thor commented, as much to divert the subject as out of concern for his friend.

Killer had broken an ankle after a nasty fall from a horse some weeks since, and his mother, Lady

Killerby, had briefly taken up residence at Ivy Lodge to nurse him—and to manage all their lives. He'd been rather relieved to discover her gone, truth be told, for next to Rush, she'd have been the most likely to see through his fiction about his marriage.

"When do you expect her back?" he asked then.

"She said something about Christmas at Wheatstone, because I'm not able to comfortably travel all the way home," Killer said, "but I suspect it has more to do with Sir George's inability to travel so far than my own."

Sir George Seaton of Wheatstone was a widowed local squire, wheelchair-bound after a hunting accident some years since. He and Lady Killerby had rekindled a prior friendship during her recent visit to Ivy Lodge.

"I've promised my parents—and my new bride, of course—to return to Plumrose before Yuletide, but you can pass along my news to Lady Killerby, should I miss her." He was determined to do just that, as Killer's mother was too inquisitive by half.

Rush, however, deserved an explanation, and when they all left the dining room an hour or so later, Thor made no effort to avoid accompanying him out to the stables, ostensibly to take a look at Princess's litter.

"I confess I can come up with no likely scenario that would have you marrying to rescue your sister from a fortune hunter," Rush said without preamble as soon as they were out of earshot of the house. "Pray assuage my curiosity—or is it all a bam?"

"No, alas, it's the simple truth—except for the part

about Miss Moore having been an old family friend. I met her the very day we married."

Quickly he filled Rush in on the essentials of the past week, concluding with his mother's delight at the match.

"So you needed to get away from such maternal exultation for a bit, did you?" Rush grinned. "I'm glad Miss Moore was able to delay Miss Turpin's marriage to Plunkett until you arrived. Your sister's too much the innocent to be left in the hands of such a man."

Dina was too much an innocent as well, Thor thought, remembering that kiss last night. Surely he'd done the right thing by preventing her marrying Plunkett. He shuddered to think what might have happened had he been an hour later arriving at Gretna Green.

"I'm still a bit unclear on why you felt it necessary to marry Miss Moore, however," Rush continued. "Very gallant, of course, and it's true she'd done your sister a great favor, but still, it's quite a step."

Thor nodded. "I know, but no other solution presented itself. She did promise not to interfere in my life, so that marriage would be as small a burden as possible."

"Not interfere?" Rush laughed aloud. "That's rich. I've never in my life heard of a wife not interfering in her husband's life. You can't think she meant it?"

"Actually, I believe she did." He wasn't certain she still felt the same, but he had no real doubt she'd meant the words when she'd said them. "She even promised that I could keep any mistresses I had," he said with a grin. "Pity I don't have one at the moment."

Rush's eyes widened. "The devil, you say. I know men who'd kill for that kind of permission from their wives, sparing them all the trouble and expense of sneaking about. You should hold her to that one, Thor. It's not as though she knows you haven't a current mistress—does she?"

"No, of course not. She didn't ask and I didn't offer."

"There you go, then. Unless Miss Moore—Mrs. Turpin, I should say—has charms enough of her own to make a mistress irrelevant?"

Thor shrugged with careful nonchalance. "She's well enough, but not in my usual style. Besides, we scarcely know each other."

He would give his friend's suggestion some thought. Perhaps if he had some strapping woman on the side to slake his passions, Dina would be safe from him. Odd how important Dina's safety had become to him in only a week.

"Let's take a quick peep at the pups, then head back to the house," Rush suggested. "Though if there are any more details you'd care to share, I'm all ears."

"Nothing of any importance."

Thor hurried over to Princess's box to check on the litter—the overriding concern in his life a mere week ago. The pups had grown noticeably already, beginning to look a bit more like dogs and a bit less like rats. Princess thumped her tail when he spoke to her, and he bent down to pat her head.

"Sorry to disappear on you like that, old girl, but I'm here for the next two weeks, at least. Maybe you'd like to come to Plumrose with me for Christmas, with your brood? My sister would love to see them."

It was not Violet he was thinking of, however, but Dina.

Yes, he definitely needed a mistress—or something—to take his mind off her. Tomorrow's hunt should do the trick.

"I vow, Dina, Grant will scarcely know you when he returns," Violet exclaimed, her hands clasped before her in a rapturous pose. "What a difference that hairstyle makes. And in a few days your new gowns will be ready as well."

Dina turned from her sister-in-law to the mirror the coiffeuse held up for her inspection and nodded her agreement. Certainly the new style became her, her unruly red curls thinned and tamed so that they framed her face and trailed down her back, rather than springing wildly in all directions.

She had insisted on keeping much of the length, so that she would still be able to pull it back with a ribbon or twist it up in a bun when she exercised—not that she'd explained her reasoning to Violet or the coiffeuse, of course. Still, the change was remarkable.

"Have you something suitable to wear to tonight's assembly?" Violet asked then. Just as she'd said she would, Violet had managed to wheedle her mother out of her punishment, so that she could introduce Dina to all her friends. "Or would you like to borrow something of mine?"

Dina had to laugh. "Anything of yours would be almost a foot too long for me. I'm sure I can manage with something of my own. My lilac silk, perhaps, if I add some fresh trim?"

"Oh, yes, that would do nicely, the color is so scrumptious," Violet agreed. "Let's go to Tessey-man's to see what pipings and laces they have."

They thanked the coiffeuse again, then headed down the street to the dry goods store. As they passed the quaint shops on Alford's main street, Dina wondered whether Violet was right, that Thor would notice a change in her upon his return. And when *would* he return? He'd been gone nearly a week now, and she found herself missing him far more than she'd expected.

Not a good sign.

Between them, Violet and Lady Rumble had kept her fairly busy, what with shopping expeditions and tours of Plumrose and its grounds. She had been de-lighted to discover that the house boasted a gymna-sium and a small indoor swimming pool, both put in by Lord Rumble's father, who had apparently been as much a physical fitness enthusiast as Dina herself. Not that she'd yet had opportunity to use either one.

"This will do nicely, don't you think?" Violet held up a length of purple piping. "Sewn into the high waist and about the sleeves, it will quite bring your old lilac into fashion."

Dina agreed with her choice, and after selecting a few pairs of gloves and stockings, they were ready to head back to Plumrose for a late luncheon.

"I vow, I can't wait to see everyone's faces when I introduce you as Grant's wife at the assembly tonight," Violet said as the carriage bore them homeward. "Missy Fiskerton has been so certain this past year that he would offer for her. What a mercy he married you instead, for I should have hated having her as a sister."

"Did he, er, give her reason to think he would offer?" Dina hadn't considered any other marital prospects Thor might have had when she demanded he marry her.

Violet shrugged. "Not really, though both her mother and mine have persisted in throwing her at his head. He danced with her twice the last time he was at home, and paid her a compliment or two, but he did the same with two or three others. Come to think on it, Rose Nesbit mentioned something about expecting his addresses as well. Honestly, these country girls will get their hopes up for the slightest of reasons."

Dina tried to hide her amusement. "Do you not consider yourself a country girl?"

"In the strictest sense, I suppose I am, but I've had part of a Season in Town, which gives me a different perspective," she answered with a lofty air that made Dina chuckle in spite of herself.

After one startled glance, Violet joined in her laughter. "That did sound rather snobbish, didn't it? I'm sorry. There is nothing wrong with being a country girl, of course, so pray don't take offense at my foolishness."

Dina was able to assure her that she was not offended in the least. Indeed, it was nearly impossible for Violet to give offense, with her eager, open air. "What shall we do after luncheon?" she asked then.

"I'd thought I might go for a ride before changing for this evening. You are welcome to join me, of course. I'm certain we can find a good mount for you."

Riding was one exercise Dina had never had much opportunity to pursue. Though she hoped to remedy that lack eventually, she asked, "Is it possible to swim this time of year? I confess I've been longing to ever since you showed me that lovely pool."

"Oh, yes. Did I not tell you? The pool is built upon a natural hot spring—the reason my great-grandfather purchased this land, actually. He apparently had hopes of building a resort to rival Buxton, or even Bath, though of course that never materialized."

"Indeed?" This was news to Dina.

"Yes, he was quite the entrepreneur, I take it, but when he was made baron, he gave up all association with trade and turned his energies toward building the house instead. Then my grandfather, as I think I mentioned, extended the house over the hot spring, incorporating it into a pool, and added the gymnasium.

"Now I think on it, I believe I'll join you for a swim, for it's been quite a long time since I've done so. I hope my bathing costume still fits me. Have you one of your own?"

Dina nodded. "Not a very nice one—I only used it to swim in the pond at Ashcombe, as we've nothing like what you have here. But it should suffice."

Accordingly, after a quick meal of tea and sandwiches, they went to change, then met at the pool, on the ground floor of the west wing, next to the gymnasium. Dina couldn't resist a quick tour of the latter, admiring various pieces of equipment she'd read about but never before seen.

"Do you ever use this room?"

Violet looked startled. "No, of course not. Grant did, when he was younger, but I can't imagine Mother would have approved of my doing so—not that I ever thought to ask."

If Lady Rumble would not approve of Violet using the equipment, she would likely feel the same about Dina doing so. Still, she was determined to slip in here unnoticed on occasion—or convince Violet to ask permission for both of them to use the room, as it would no doubt do her good, as well.

"I suppose we'd best start our swim," was all she said now.

The water was remarkably warm for the season, owing to the hot spring that both heated and circulated the water. Dina was pleased to discover that Violet was nearly as strong a swimmer as she. They paddled about for a bit, then raced the length of the pool, Dina beating Violet by only a narrow margin.

"My goodness," Violet panted when they reached the end. "You must do more swimming in that pond of yours than I realized."

Dina grinned. "Only in the summer, of course, but I do walk quite a lot, and even run when I have the chance, as well as . . . other physical pursuits."

"You are quite the little Amazon, I see." Violet's admiring smile robbed her words of any taint of sarcasm. "Won't Grant—that is—"

"What?"

"Well, Grant has always been rather, ah, patronizing about women—small women, in particular. He seems to regard them as delicate flowers that will crumble at a touch. I imagine he will be quite surprised to discover you are no such thing. Pleasantly so, of course."

"Of course," Dina echoed. Was that why he'd seemed so concerned he had hurt her, his last night at home? Perhaps one reason he held himself so aloof? Interesting, if so.

"Shall we race once more before we get out?" Dina suggested.

She would prove to Thor that she was no "delicate flower." Then . . . She supposed only time would tell.

Chapter 11

～⌒◯◯⌒～

"I declare, Mrs. Turpin, you seem as fresh after a whole night of dancing as you did when you first arrived." Mr. Smallbone's glance was frankly admiring, making Dina pinken slightly.

Violet had been right that entertainments in the neighborhood of Plumrose were far livelier—and more frequent—than what she'd been accustomed to in Ashcombe. This was the second assembly they'd attended in as many weeks, in addition to several dinners and a card party.

Though such a busy social life was rather overwhelming, it was certainly far more interesting than her circumscribed existence at home had been.

"You are too kind, sir," she said now.

"Not at all. Most of the other ladies are wilting by now, but you remind me of a winter rose."

Being the object of compliments was a new experience for her as well, and one she'd do better *not* to become used to. The gentlemen were all circumspect, of course, knowing her to be Thor's wife, but their attention was flattering, nonetheless. Even Diggory Tallow had never gone beyond the polite, his compliments always seeming more perfunctory than heartfelt.

She suspected that when Thor returned—*if* he returned—the gentlemen would give her a wider berth. He was rather an intimidating man, after all. For now, though, she couldn't help enjoying the attention.

"My dance, I believe, Mrs. Turpin." Sir Albert Vaile stepped forward to take her hand from Mr. Smallbone's for the final set of the evening. She had not been without a partner all night, a triumph only one or two other ladies could boast.

Glancing down the set, she saw Violet taking her place as well. Catching Dina's eye, she grinned, and Dina returned her smile. Over the past two weeks, she and Violet had become fast friends, despite their differing temperaments.

Missy Fiskerton, beside Violet in the line, intercepted Dina's smile and sent back a syrupy-sweet one of her own. The tall girl's original hostility had given way to insincere friendliness, once she got over the first shock of Thor's unexpected marriage. Unfortunately, the same was not true of Rose Nesbit, who could still scarcely bring herself to speak to Dina.

This assembly, like the previous one, was being held at the Red Lion, Rumbleton's sole inn. Almost the entire second story was taken up by an elegant ballroom that was frequently rented out by one or another of the local gentry desirous of hosting a party larger than their own homes would accommodate. Longer than it was wide, accented by gilt chandeliers and red-figured wall coverings, this room was big enough to allow three sets of a dozen couples each to dance at once—though some care was needed to avoid collisions.

As the lively country dance began, Dina observed that Mr. Smallbone had been right—most of the ladies did appear rather wilted. Indeed, only one set had formed this time, down the center of the large room, as most of those present had retired to the sidelines by now.

As she progressed through the movements of the dance, Dina found her thoughts returning, as they too often did, to Thor. Would he return, as Lady Rumble promised, in time for his parents' Christmas Eve ball tomorrow night? That very morning over breakfast, Lady Rumble had expressed surprise that he was not yet back—then had quickly changed the subject.

Dina suppressed a sigh. She had no doubt that it was she who kept him away, and now it appeared that his mother had come to the same conclusion. That knowledge was both depressing and humiliating, but she refused to give in to either emotion. Moving on to the next gentleman in the line, she forced a brilliant smile—and found herself face to face with Thor himself.

"Oh!" she exclaimed, missing a step in her astonishment. "How did you—?"

He caught her by the elbow, steadying her until she recaptured the rhythm of the dance. "Father said I'd find you all here. I arrived just as this set began and managed to take a place at the end."

A glance showed that his partner was a smug Rose Nesbit, who had been sitting down when the set first formed. The dance moved them apart then, forcing Dina to save any other questions until after its conclusion. Still, she could not deny the sudden lift of her spirits, or the way all the candles in the room now seemed to be burning more brightly.

In vain she reminded herself that he had planned all along to return before Christmas, that his appearance here had more to do with his mother and Violet than with her. He was here, and that was enough—for now.

From his position a few places down the line, Thor glanced back at Dina, still struggling with his surprise at her changed appearance. Not that she'd been plain before, of course, but dressed in a well-fitted, fashionable gown, with that new, flattering hairstyle, she was beautiful. A beautiful stranger.

He'd been so sure that a fortnight away would break the strange spell she'd cast over him, allowing reason to return. Immersed in foxhunting and the Meltonian society, he thought it had. But now, after just one look and a few words exchanged, he was as besotted as ever. What the devil was he to do?

"Penny for your thoughts, Mr. Turpin," said Rose Nesbit as the dance brought them together again. She fluttered her eyelashes coquettishly, though she surely must know that he was married.

"Just thinking that it's nice to be home," he replied, his glance straying to Dina again. If anything, she looked more delicate than ever in that shimmering gown of pale blue-green, almost as though she were made of porcelain. That color set off her red hair and ivory skin to perfection.

"Perhaps you won't stay away so long in the future, then?"

He blinked down at Miss Nesbit, trying to remember what they'd been talking about. "Er, yes. Perhaps," he replied at random.

"Or perhaps now you'll have more reason to escape?" she suggested, looking pointedly in Dina's direction. "I make my come-out in London this spring, you know."

The dance separated them again before he could give the shameless jade the set-down she deserved for such an implication. Why, she was younger than Violet and surely had no business . . . He saw Dina moving down the line toward him and abruptly forgot whatever he'd been thinking about.

"Is this party likely to go on much longer?" he asked her the moment she was opposite him again. A vision arose of accompanying her home . . . up the stairs . . . down to the end of the west wing . . .

"I believe this is the last dance." He saw only concern in her eyes, not desire. "You must be tired after traveling all the way from Melton-Mowbray today."

Before he could assure her that he felt perfectly vigorous, they were parted again by the movements of the dance, and a few moments later it ended. The proprietor of the Red Lion and Sir Farley Goffin, the ball's host, said a few words to the assembly, and then people began milling about, exchanging farewells and last-minute bits of gossip before sending for their carriages. Thor made his way to Dina's side.

Horace Smallbone was speaking with her but looked up at his approach. "Ah, Turpin, so you've returned to Lincolnshire at last." He didn't look particularly pleased, despite his smile. "I feel I should take you to task for abandoning your lovely bride all this time, but your loss has been our gain."

"Indeed," Sir Albert Vaile agreed from Dina's other side. "I must say, if she were mine, I'd never be far from her side. Not all gentlemen are as trustworthy as we are." He smiled down at Dina as he spoke, making Thor's hackles rise.

"I must be grateful, then, that I had two such worthies as yourselves to watch over her for me." He flattered himself that he was able to keep his voice pleasant, despite a sudden desire to knock their heads together.

Still, some hint of what he was feeling must have communicated itself, for both gentlemen glanced up at him with vague alarm, then bade a quick goodnight to Dina before taking themselves off. She blinked after them in apparent confusion before turning back to Thor.

"They certainly left in a hurry," she commented, one adorable brow raised. "One might almost think they were afraid of you." Thor shrugged. "No doubt their carriages were ready. As is ours, I believe, for here come Mother and Violet. Shall we go?"

Why should he feel so nettled that other gentlemen found Dina attractive? They'd have to be blind not to. As he'd promised both her and himself to keep their marriage platonic, it would be churlish to forbid her from enjoying innocent compliments from other men. Wouldn't it?

"Grant! What a surprise," his mother exclaimed as she reached them, Violet in tow. "I've been expecting you these past few days, of course, but did not look to see you here tonight, as you'd not arrived before we left the house. You must not have left Melton till noon, at least."

Forcing down his absurd spurt of jealousy, he was able to greet his mother and sister pleasantly enough. "A bit before. I arrived a couple of hours ago, and Father told me you were all here. I had John Coachman drive me over, so that I could ride back to Plumrose with you. I'd thought to have time for more than a single dance, however." He glanced down at Dina.

"Lady Rumble is holding a ball at Plumrose tomorrow night. No doubt you will get your fill of dancing there." Was there a hint of extra color in her cheeks as she spoke? He wasn't sure.

"Indeed, Grant, I will expect you to do the pretty by as many ladies as possible, for we are likely to have a shortage of gentlemen. No escaping to the kennels, as you did last year." Lady Rumble turned to Dina with a conspiratorial smile. "I imagine your presence will induce him to behave himself."

Dina looked rather startled. "If . . . if you say so, my lady."

The baroness clicked her tongue. "Now, now, my

dear, remember what I've told you. You must begin as you mean to go on in marriage. Demand proper behavior of Grant now, and later on you'll not have to worry about him embarrassing you."

"Mother," Thor said warningly, but only earned an innocent look in return. He frowned, then shook his head. "Let's go home, shall we?"

Thanks to his mother's interference, there was again a constraint between Dina and him as he handed her into the carriage after the other two ladies. Settling into the seat beside her, he wondered uneasily how much similar advice his mother had been giving her during the past fortnight—and whether he had been unwise to leave Dina here with her for so long.

"Grant, why have you said nothing about Dina's changed appearance?" Violet asked then, breaking into his thoughts. "I am vastly pleased with what we have accomplished in such a short time—as are most of the local gentlemen, I'll have you know." She grinned mischievously at Dina, who he thought looked vaguely alarmed before she turned to gaze out of the window.

He managed to smooth his instinctive frown. Yes, leaving Dina here had definitely been a mistake. "That new hairstyle is quite fetching," he said. "I noticed it at once, of course, but had no chance of a private word with her, to say so."

"And one must never give a lady a compliment in public, of course. Honestly, Grant, I despair of you sometimes."

A sheepish glance toward Dina showed her still

staring fixedly out the window. "You really do look lovely tonight," he said to her averted profile. "I'm sorry I did not say so earlier."

"I, ah, thank you," she murmured without turning. "But pray do not think I felt slighted. You know how Violet loves to tease."

Dina couldn't remember when she'd been more embarrassed. Not until she'd found herself face to face with him had she realized just how much she'd hoped that Thor would approve of the changes in her appearance. She'd been disappointed when he hadn't seemed to notice, but now to have Violet all but force a compliment from his lips—!

For most of the evening she had felt pretty, desirable. But now she felt more like an albatross about poor Thor's neck. Not for the first time, she wondered whether he'd have been happier married to Missy Fiskerton or Rose Nesbit, who already knew his family and everyone else in the district—and doubtless knew Thor far better than she could yet claim.

"It really is most lucky you are home now, Grant," said Lady Rumble, breaking the awkward silence. "Your father has been disinclined to organize the Yule log expedition, but now you are here, you can do it."

He seemed relieved at the change of subject—a relief Dina shared. "Yes, I'll gather a few of the men and go out tomorrow morning. We'll find you something that will burn for days, never fear. And then I'll need to get the kennels in order."

"The kennels?" Violet echoed Dina's surprise. "What is wrong with the kennels?"

"Nothing, but I've brought along some additions

that need to be properly situated. Puppies, Vi, which should please you."

Violet clapped her hands and peppered him with questions, and Dina felt her own spirits lift in spite of herself at the talk of Yule logs and puppies. Perhaps having Thor back would not be as disappointing and uncomfortable as she'd begun to fear.

When they reached Plumrose a few minutes later, however, the discomfort returned in full force as she anticipated the walk down the west wing after the way their last one had ended. Not that she expected him to kiss her good night again, of course, but the memory was sure to show in her expression. Was his mind similarly engaged? A quick glance at his profile told her nothing.

"My word, I'm tired," Lady Rumble declared as they entered the house. "I'm off to bed, children. Good night."

"I'm ready for my bed as well," Violet said, turning to follow her mother up the stairs. "Are you two coming up?"

Dina braced herself, but Thor shook his head. "I need to visit the stables briefly. I'll see you all in the morning."

Though she she'd just been dreading their private walk down the corridor, Dina's fickle spirits now plummeted to her shoes. What could this be, other than an excuse to avoid being alone with her?

Numbly she accompanied Violet and Lady Rumble up the stairs, bidding them good night on the landing and traversing the memory-fraught corridor alone. "Why the devil did he come back at all?" she muttered, opening the door to her chamber.

"What was that, ma'am?" Francine greeted her, blinking blearily.

"Nothing. Here, help me out of this thing." She'd thought her new sea-green lutestring gown magnificent when she'd put it on earlier tonight, but now she couldn't get it off fast enough. Had Thor even noticed it?

Francine helped her out of gown, petticoats, and corset, and carefully laid them aside before picking up Dina's nightrail to help her into it. On sudden decision, Dina shook her head.

"No, I believe I will go down to the gymnasium for half an hour or so. Where are my pantalettes?"

Without comment, her maid fetched them from the clothespress, along with the loose-fitting gray fustian gown Dina wore when she did calisthenics. A few moments later, Dina made her way downstairs, carrying a candle in a holder, as she had done several times over the past two weeks.

Not until she reached the ground floor did it occur to her that Thor might return from the stables at any moment and see her, which could lead to awkward questions. She paused, half tempted to retreat, then shrugged. If she met him, she would simply tell him the truth. He must find out sooner or later that she was no delicate flower of a woman, and perhaps sooner would be better.

Her decision made, she walked briskly toward the gymnasium, head held high, one hand shielding the flame of her candle. Behind her, a door opened and closed. With a gasp, she ducked around the corner before she could be seen and blew out the candle, then waited breathlessly until firm, heavy footsteps went past, in the direction of the main staircase.

So much for honesty and courage, she thought with a spurt of self-disgust. What sort of Amazon was she? None at all, it seemed.

And now, because of her cowardice, she had no light—and didn't much fancy using the gymnastic equipment in the dark. With a sigh, she headed toward the stairs herself. She could always do a bit of running in place or exercise with her dumbbells before bed. Though now she thought about it, she was suddenly very tired, perhaps in reaction to her little fright. In fact, just climbing the stairs now seemed difficult.

She heard a clock downstairs chiming one as she headed down the west wing corridor for the second time that night. Really, dancing had been exercise enough for tonight, she decided, turning the handle to her chamber. All she really wanted was her bed.

"What the devil—?"

The voice came from so close beside her that she nearly cried aloud. As it was, a little squeak escaped her as she whirled, her heart in her throat, to face Thor in the dimly lit hallway.

"You . . . you startled me," she managed, once she'd caught her breath. No, she definitely didn't need any calisthenics tonight.

"Obviously." His voice was cooler than she remembered. "Perhaps you'd like to tell me where you've been? I thought you went to bed some time ago."

"I did. That is, I meant to. I . . . I needed to get

something from downstairs." Only as the words left her mouth did it occur to her that she had nothing with her that she could claim to have fetched.

He seemed to loom over her, though in fact he was almost three feet away. "And that necessitated you changing into something . . . nondescript?"

The suspicion in his voice startled her. "I didn't want to go down in my nightrail," she said, still casting about for a plausible story to explain her trip downstairs.

"And you don't own a wrapper?" His words fairly dripped sarcasm.

With a mental shrug, she decided she might as well tell him the truth, as he seemed angry with her already. "Actually, I was going to the gymnasium, but . . . changed my mind." She couldn't quite bring herself to admit she'd turned coward upon hearing his footsteps.

"The gymnasium?" If anything, he sounded more skeptical than before. "At one o'clock in the morning? Perhaps you planned to take a dip in the pool afterward, as well?"

"No, of course not. That would take too long. I simply intended to exercise on the bars for half an hour or so, then come up to bed. But once I got downstairs, I decided I was too tired." That deviated only slightly from the truth.

He stared at her in silence for a long moment, as though weighing her words. "Do you often go down to the gymnasium after the rest of the house is abed?"

"Not . . . often." Would he forbid her to do so

again? She had already come to look forward to her late-night exercise sessions.

"Then perhaps you can tell me—no, never mind. It is late. We can discuss this further in the morning. Good night, Dina." He turned on his heel and disappeared into his room, leaving her almost as startled as when he'd appeared.

His anger had seemed all out of proportion to her admission. Surely he couldn't really think she had been downstairs for any nefarious purpose? What evil could she have accomplished in less than half an hour? Her brain was too fogged with weariness to puzzle it out just then, so she entered her own chamber and this time made no protest when Francine picked up her nightclothes.

Thor paced his room, cursing himself for his cowardice. Why had he not demanded the truth there and then, after Dina's ridiculous explanation for her late-night foray? Because he'd been afraid of the answer, of course. The very fact that she'd so clearly lied to him must mean she'd been up to something, and what that something might be now tormented him.

In vain he tried to tell himself that she'd had no time to get into any real mischief. Even if her original intent had been to meet with one of her gallants from this evening's assembly—he recalled her look of alarm at Violet's teasing—she must not have actually done so. Perhaps the man in question had not come, his ardor cooled by Thor's own return home. He smiled grimly at the thought.

No, it was as well he hadn't pursued the matter

just now, given the late hour and his own state of mind. He would doubtless have said or done something regrettable. Now, though, Dina would have all night to concoct a plausible explanation for her behavior, and he already knew how convincing she could be when she put her mind to it. Was not their marriage proof of that?

He continued to pace for a few minutes, trying to anticipate what she might say in her defense and to frame his responses, but then he stopped and shook his head. If he was to think clearly in the morning, he needed to get to bed, but just now he was in no mood for sleep.

Inspired by Dina's absurd alibi, he changed into pantaloons and a comfortable linen shirt, set a candle in a holder, and headed down to the gymnasium himself.

Holding the candle high a few moments later, he observed the large room with a sense of nostalgia. For years he had been in the habit of exercising there for an hour or two every day. Now, however, it had been nearly two years since he'd so much as visited it. Some calisthenics and a vigorous session with the boxing bag would be just the thing to work off his anger and calm both mind and body enough for sleep.

Removing his shoes, he moved to the first piece of equipment, refusing to think about just why he was so angry, or what role frustration might play in that anger.

Chapter 12

$\sim\!\!\curvearrowright\!\!\curvearrowleft\!\sim$

On returning home in triumph with an enormous Yule log early the next morning, Thor congratulated himself again on his decision to visit the gymnasium the night before. Not only had he slept well as a result, but his mind was far clearer than it had been last night.

That was fortunate, for it had allowed him to formulate a plan to ferret out the truth about Dina's activities last night, while he and most of the male servants hauled back the biggest fallen trunk they could find on the estate lands.

His mother greeted them with delight, exclaiming over the size of the log, the largest in recent memory. "What a lovely addition that will be to tonight's ball. Everyone will see it blazing here in the hall before they go up to the ballroom."

Thor helped the servants to place the log in the enormous fireplace in the great hall, then his mother ushered him into the dining room, where the rest of the family was still at breakfast. Dina glanced up at his entrance with a tentative smile, but he could not bring himself to return it.

She looked more beautiful than ever in her fresh morning gown, but that only caused all his suspicions from the night before to return in full force. He had nearly convinced himself that she would have some innocent explanation for creeping about the house in the dead of night, but now . . .

Silently he filled a plate from the sideboard and contemplated his plan as he ate. The first step, of course, was to force Dina to admit that she had lied about her whereabouts and intentions, but that should be dead easy—and he knew just how to do it.

"Would you care to join me in the gymnasium?" he asked her softly as they all left the dining room half an hour later. "I thought you might show me which pieces of equipment you favor."

Dina looked startled—not surprising, as so far today they had exchanged no words at all—but she did not demur, as he had expected her to.

"I suppose so. Shall I change first, or is to be a mere matter of pointing and talking?"

Now it was his turn to be surprised. "Er, yes, now you mention it. Why do you not put on the same thing you wore for your intended visit there last night?"

Surely that would elicit a reaction of some sort, he thought. However, instead of showing the alarm or confusion natural to a woman hiding a lover from her husband, she merely nodded.

"Very well. Will you change as well, or do you mean only to observe?"

"Observe?" The very thought of watching Dina cavort in the gymnasium brought him instantly erect—not that she would actually be able to use the equipment, of course. Still, he was glad of the interruption when his mother suggested they all go into the parlor to discuss the final preparations for the ball.

"Not just now, Mother," he said. "Dina and I need to, ah, discuss something else."

Lady Rumble beamed. "Of course, of course. You two run along upstairs, then." Her wink could be construed as a breach of the promise she'd made two weeks earlier, but he ignored it.

Not until they were well out of earshot, starting down the west wing, did he answer Dina's earlier question. "I will change to appropriate attire as well. What say we meet at the top of the stairs in a quarter of an hour?"

She agreed, and they repaired to their adjoining rooms. To distract himself from the barely audible sounds of her dressing next door, Thor busied his mind with wondering just how far she meant to carry this charade. For it had to be a charade.

Stripping off his warm wool leggings, he again donned the breeches and shirt he'd worn to the gymnasium last night. Dina had never seen him in such informal clothing, even when he'd arrived in Scotland. Would she react to his changed appearance? Not that it mattered, of course. Still, he couldn't help noting in his glass that the open collar of his shirt showed a nicely tanned V of chest.

No. The point of this experiment was to prove that Dina was hiding something—though he devoutly hoped it wasn't a liaison with some other man. Still, until he knew, he should discourage any tender feelings toward her.

A few minutes later he left his room to find her already waiting in the hallway, clad in the same gray skirt and bodice she'd worn the night before. Seen in daylight, he had to admit it was an improbable outfit for meeting a lover. It looked like a servant's workdress, but less stylish. Still, on her it somehow contrived to seem quite fetching.

"Shall we go?" he suggested, determined to reserve further judgment until after they reached the gymnasium.

The room looked quite different illuminated by winter daylight flooding through the high windows instead of by a single wavering candle. Forty feet long and twenty wide, the gymnasium housed horizontal metal bars on stands, rings suspended from the ceiling, two fencing dummies, a boxing bag affixed to one wall, and several sets of barbells and dumbbells. A locked cabinet in the corner contained fencing foils and sabers, along with the equipment for various outdoor sports such as archery and croquet.

It was a man's room—so much so that he felt it slightly irreverent to bring the very feminine Dina in here at all. Really, she could not have hit upon a poorer alibi last night. Glancing around, he was struck afresh by the absurdity of it.

"What did you have in mind to do here?" she asked when he had stood several moments in silence.

He hid a grimace. "I was going to ask you the same thing. I'd like you to show me what you had planned to do last night. Before you, ah, changed your mind."

Her green eyes narrowed with dawning comprehension. "I see. Very well. I generally begin my regimen with a few stretching exercises, to loosen up my muscles. My brother's fencing master used to say that was essential before any exercise to prevent injury."

Thor blinked. "My own master said the same. Did you often listen in on your brother's lessons?"

"As often as I could without Silas's knowledge. I also managed to speak privately with his master on occasion."

Clearly she did know at least a little bit about physical training, at least as it pertained to fencing. She wouldn't be able to bluff her way through actual exercises, however.

"You were going to show me which of our paraphernalia you prefer to use," he reminded her.

She looked as though she was about to say something, then changed her mind. "Of course," she murmured instead and moved to the center of the floor.

As he watched in growing amazement, she spread her arms and twisted her torso from side to side, then bent over and touched her palms to the floor—something Thor was fairly certain he himself could not do. But women's bodies were more flexible than men's, weren't they? He thought he had read that somewhere.

Swallowing, he wondered how it was that she managed to make such simple motions seem so erotic. No, it was simply his wayward mind—and body—doing that, he decided.

After another minute or two of stretching exercises, some of which involved her actually sitting on the floor, Dina got up and fetched a wooden crate he had not noticed from a corner, then set it under one of the horizontal bars. The crate allowed tiny Dina to reach the bar, more than seven feet above the floor. Thor had to admit that the very presence of the crate here implied that she had done this at least once before. Perhaps his suspicion had been unfounded after all.

Reaching up, Dina grasped the bar, and in a smooth, controlled movement, pulled herself up until her chin reached the bar, then lowered herself, feet dangling. She repeated that exercise ten times, then dropped lightly back to the crate.

"Did you not say you were going to join me?"

Thor realized that his mouth had dropped open, and belatedly closed it. He would never have believed that a woman, particularly a small, delicate woman like Dina, could do such a thing.

"Er, yes. Of course." He moved toward the rings, telling himself that her size must make those pull-ups easier, not harder. Still, it was increasingly obvious that this was by no means her first visit to the gymnasium.

Giving only the minimum attention necessary to his own indifferent performance on the rings—he had, after all, exercised less than twelve hours ago— Thor watched as Dina moved from one piece of equipment to another, using each one with practiced ease. Some of the exercises displayed her figure to advantage, even under that loose-fitting gray gown. He couldn't seem to keep his mind from imagining what the body underneath must look like.

But that wasn't the point, he told himself firmly. He had put her to a test, and she had passed it. Finally, after a brief struggle with his pride, he walked over to the parallel bars, which she was just about to mount.

"Dina, I owe you an apology."

She raised her head, giving him a remarkably perceptive look. "Yes, I believe you do. Did you honestly think I was slipping away last night to meet some paramour? I'm sorry to think your opinion of me could be so low."

Embarrassed that his suspicions had been so transparent, Thor cleared his throat. "I realize now how foolish I was. It's just that, well, we really don't know each other very well yet, do we? Pray forgive me."

For a long moment she stared at him, tight-lipped, but then her expression softened. "Very well. You are forgiven. I'm sure my explanation did sound rather improbable, as I've taken pains to keep my activities here a secret."

"Then my parents do not know you frequent this room? Nor Violet?" That explained the late-night visits.

She shook her head. "Violet and I have used the swimming pool together on two occasions, but when I asked if she ever used the gymnasium, she seemed certain that Lady Rumble would not approve. I know I should have asked permission, but—"

"But as a newcomer to the household, you didn't want to risk it," he concluded. "I suppose I can't blame you for that. Surely you would prefer to exercise during the daytime, however?"

"Well, yes, but not at the price of your parents' opinion of me."

He suddenly realized how callous it had been for him to leave her here as he had, with only Violet to call friend. What must she have thought of his sudden disappearance—and why hadn't he thought of that before? He'd been so preoccupied with his own feelings—his feelings for Dina—that he'd given no real consideration to hers.

"Again, I apologize," he said, trying to convey his sincerity with voice and expression. "I can't imagine that my parents would think any less of you for wishing to improve your health. Indeed, my grandfather was a famous sport and gymnastic enthusiast—it's why he added this room and the swimming pool to the house."

"Yes, Violet mentioned that. But he was a man, which is rather different."

Thor couldn't deny that. Had he himself not been extremely skeptical that a woman could use this equipment at all? But now he shrugged.

"Different, yes, but not necessarily in a bad way. Tell me, how do you come to be so, ah, active? This is, as you say, an unusual pursuit for a female. Never tell me it was your brother's idea?" He couldn't imagine Silas Moore encouraging his sister in such a way.

She snorted, confirming his assumption. "Certainly not, though I suppose you could say he was the original impetus for my decision to better myself physically. He was a bit, well, a bit of a bully when we were younger—as were some of his friends."

Thor frowned. "He allowed his friends to bully you?"

"Silas has always liked to show off." Her cheeks had pinkened now, and not from her recent exercise. She stared past him at the knotted rope that hung from the ceiling. "He enjoyed demonstrating how easy it was for him to pinion both of my arms behind my back with only one of his hands. Then he and his friends thought it great fun to perch me in the big oak tree and leave me for hours, or to shut me into cupboards, because I was so small."

He couldn't imagine such a thing. While he had teased Violet as much as any brother might, he had always been extremely protective of her when it came to other boys. Nor had he ever physically bullied her. "Did your parents not intervene?"

"The boys never actually hurt me, and I didn't wish to be a tale-bearer. Besides, I became quite adept at climbing down trees and escaping from cupboards—and at being extremely difficult to catch. In a sense, I suppose they did me a favor, as those experiences made me determined to become as quick and strong as my stature and gender would allow."

Still frowning, Thor motioned for her to precede him from the gymnasium. "That's a charitable way of looking at things, but I can't help thinking of the lot of them as cowards. What schools did your brother attend?"

"Rugby and then Cambridge."

"Ah. I was at Eton and Oxford." He was glad to

know that the group of savages Dina described had not been associated with either, but now he itched to know just who they were. Doubtless he was acquainted with some of them, as the world of the *ton* was a small one.

"So, in self-defense, you began studying calisthenics and gymnastics?" he prompted when she had walked beside him in silence for some minutes.

"I also ran and swam when I could, learned as much of fencing and boxing as my uncle Kendall would teach me, and listened in on Silas's lessons in those disciplines."

"Boxing?" he echoed in disbelief. "I can't say that I've ever heard of a woman who boxed—and precious few who fence. Perhaps we'll spar sometime so that I can see what you've learned." He was joking, but the look she turned up to him was perfectly serious.

"I should like that, as I am sorely out of practice. But do you really think it wise to mention any of this to your parents?"

He smiled down at her to hide the ache he felt over what she had endured as a child. "I truly don't think they'll mind, but we needn't say anything to them if you prefer it."

"Thank you. For now, I believe I would rather not—though if I can use the gymnasium during the day without their knowledge, I should like to do that."

"That should be simple enough, as neither of them frequent that part of the house," he said as they reached the top of the stairs. "But now we had best change into more conventional clothing. I've promised to take Violet out to the kennels today to see the new pups. If you'd like to see them as well, I recommend you wear shoes that can stand up to a stable yard."

Her sudden smile hit him with the force of a blow, turning him light-headed. "I would like that very much. I love dogs."

With that, she disappeared into her room, and Thor continued on to his. The more he learned about Dina, the more he felt drawn to her—and the less he wanted to resist that draw. He tried to recall all the reasons that such an attraction was unwise, but at the moment they seemed vague and unimportant. All that really seemed to matter was getting her to smile at him again.

Dina felt almost dizzy with relief as she stripped off her gray fustian and had Francine help her into her blue day dress. She'd been so worried that Thor would be disgusted or scandalized when he learned about her physical training program, but though he was undeniably surprised, he hadn't seemed particularly upset.

She grinned, remembering the look on his face when she'd begun chinning herself on the horizontal bar. Surely that was a far cry from the liaison he'd apparently imagined her carrying on last night. Then she sobered. He'd apologized for his suspicions, but it still hurt that he could think such a thing of her.

"Ouch. Please, be careful of that shoulder, Francine. It's rather sore."

When she had realized that the visit to the gymnasium was a test of sorts, she had pushed herself to her limits to prove to Thor that she was adept on all the equipment there—and now she was paying the price. She would doubtless ache all over by tonight, which would likely hamper her dancing at the ball. Clearly, pride was not purely a masculine failing.

She doubted that Thor would suffer any such effects. Though she'd limited herself to a few surreptitious glances while he exercised on the rings, she could not help feeling a touch of awe—and nervousness—at the easy power he evinced, and the noticeable rippling of his massive muscles. The idea of sparring with him was laughable—as he clearly knew. She would hurt her fists if she punched him, and he would probably not even feel it.

And if he landed a blow on her, she would doubtless be sent flying across the room. But while Silas might do such a thing to prove his superiority, she doubted that Thor would. Still, that display of his strength had reminded her why she'd wanted their marriage to be completely platonic, even while a part of her longed to explore that magnificent physique more intimately.

Francine was just putting the finishing touches on her hair, which had been in need of extensive repair, when a tap came at her door.

"Almost ready?" Thor called.

Rising, she opened the door. "Yes, I'm ready. Where is Violet?"

"Here," came Violet's voice from the direction of the stairs. "What on earth has been keeping you two? I thought we were going to go out to see the puppies an hour ago."

Dina joined Thor in the hallway to see her sister-in-law's eyes bright with curiosity. She answered Violet's unspoken question with a quick shake of her head.

Over the past fortnight, Violet had hinted repeatedly that she expected their marriage to progress beyond the formalities once Thor returned. No doubt she'd be most disappointed to learn that they'd merely been exercising in the gymnasium—not that Dina intended to tell her. Though her intentions were always good, Violet seemed incapable of keeping a secret. Indeed, it was amazing that she'd been able to pull off an elopement.

They all trooped out to the kennels, where both girls oohed and aahed over Princess's litter. Now that they were three weeks old, the pups' eyes were open and they tumbled over one another in their eagerness to nibble on the ladies' fingers.

One of the puppies caught a claw in Dina's woven cloak and let out a series of panicked yips that brought Princess to her feet in concern.

"Oh, poor thing," Dina exclaimed. "He won't stop wiggling long enough for me to unsnag him."

Thor knelt down next to her. "Here, let me." With hands remarkably gentle for their size, he cradled the puppy, stroking its head with his thumb while deftly unhooking its claw from the cloak.

"There you go, champ." He handed the puppy back to its anxious mother, who began nosing it all over to make certain it was still in one piece.

Watching his gentle care for the pup—for all his dogs—Dina saw Thor with new eyes. She'd already known he was a good man, an honorable man, but now she realized that he was also kind and tender—and loved animals. No wonder he'd looked horrified when she'd related some of her childhood experiences. Thor was as far removed from a bully as a man could be, despite his size.

Her earlier misgivings about trusting herself to his strength in physical intimacy gave way to sudden longing. Almost as though he felt it, he looked up at her just then, an unspoken question in his eyes.

Confused, she dropped to her knees to pick up another puppy, this time taking care not to let it tangle itself in her cloak.

Violet set down the pup she'd been holding and stood, offering a welcome distraction to Dina's confused feelings. "I promised Mother I wouldn't stay out here long, but I may visit with the pups again, Grant, may I not?"

"Yes, the more they are handled the better, actually," he said. "Particularly at this age. It will make them easier to train later on."

"Oh, then I'll be out here every day—and Dina, too, I imagine."

Dina nodded, pleased at the prospect of spending time with the dogs. With a smile, Violet left them, so quickly that it was apparent she intended them to remain behind. Dina wondered whether Lady Rumble had suggested just that. Not unlikely.

"So you like dogs, do you?" Thor asked before the silence could become awkward.

"Yes, I always have, though I have only ever had one, and that briefly." She swallowed against the memory, stroking the puppy she held.

Thor gazed down at her, sensing more than she said aloud. He felt a sudden need to understand—to know as much as he could about his wife. "Why only briefly?"

"I was about fourteen at the time, and one of the local farmers' wives offered me a pup from a litter they had. I brought it home, delighted to have a pet of my own. Mother even agreed to let me keep it in my room. Unfortunately, Silas had just been sent down from school for some offense or other and was in a foul mood."

"He didn't hurt the pup, did he?" Any man, even as a schoolboy, who would—

But Dina shook her head. "No, I wouldn't let him, of course, though he did threaten to drown it, saying it looked more like a rat than a dog. Then he convinced my father to ban it from the house, claiming it would soil the carpets. I feared I couldn't keep it safe from him if it lived out in the stables, so after a few days I returned it to the farmer's family." She sighed.

"This, in addition to locking you in cupboards." The more Thor heard about Silas Moore, the more he disliked the man. "What other unpleasant things did your brother do to you?"

She carefully set the puppy down with its littermates and stood. "Mostly it was just schoolboy mischief," she said defensively. "As I said, he never really hurt me—at least not intentionally. In fact, as I grew older, he seemed quite proud of my ability to defend myself against his friends, and to outrun them. I remember he once offered any of them a kiss from me, for a shilling—if they could catch me. But none of them could."

Though Dina grinned, Thor was outraged that any brother would put his sister in such a position. "He should have been defending your honor, not trying to compromise it," he said severely. "How old were you at the time?"

Clearly startled by his tone, she sobered. "Thirteen or fourteen, I believe—and faster than any of his school chums."

"Then he would have been what, fifteen? Sixteen? Old enough to know better, certainly."

"Perhaps, but as I said, he has always felt a need to show off for his friends. No doubt that is how he ended up so deeply in debt."

But Thor was in no mood to hear excuses. Dusting off his hands, he led her out of the kennels and along the path toward the house. "And once in debt, he was again willing to sacrifice you to save his own neck. I begin to wish he had challenged me after all."

Dina glanced up at him with alarm that seemed to be tinged with amusement. "Then I suppose it is fortunate that you are not likely to see him again for some time." They had now reached the back gardens of the house.

"Fortunate indeed. If Moore were to cross my path just now, I'm not sure I could be answerable for the consequences."

Her eyes widened. "I feel moved to echo Violet's words from the morning we first met, and say, 'How medieval of you.' I thank you for your concern, but it is all in the past now."

Thor did not reply, still feeling the need to punch something—an unusual sensation, and one he did not much care for. He'd never been a violent man, but in recent weeks, it seemed that his disposition was changing—or something.

Uncomfortable thoughts, which made him just as glad when Violet appeared at the door leading out onto the back terrace—until he saw who was with her.

"Look, Dina, who has come for tonight's ball, and to spend Christmas with us," she exclaimed. "Is it not a wonderful surprise? Mother and I agreed to say nothing, though I must admit it was terribly difficult not to tell you, once he accepted our invitation."

"Happy Christmas, Dina," said Silas Moore, stepping forward to kiss his sister on the cheek. "You're looking well. Happy Christmas, Turpin."

"Happy Christmas, Moore."

Thor had to fight to keep his voice level, his expression bland, when he was itching to plant his fist in his visitor's face after what he'd just learned about him. Surely Moore wouldn't have the impudence to stay long? If he did, Thor wasn't certain he could answer for the consequences.

Chapter 13

Dina returned Silas's kiss, carefully keeping herself between him and Thor. "What a nice surprise," she said with determined cheerfulness. "And Violet, I take back what I said to you before about not being able to keep a secret, for I had no idea."

Violet preened, smiling up at Silas in a way that told Dina that surprising her was not the only reason for his invitation. A glance at Thor showed him watching his sister with a gathering frown. Apparently he'd come to the same conclusion.

"Nice place you have here, Turpin," Silas said then, seemingly oblivious to any undercurrents. "My sister's done quite well for herself."

"Thank you," Thor grated, "but it's not mine yet, nor do I wish it to be, for quite some time." Then, catching Violet's suprised stare, he forced a smile. "Welcome to Plumrose."

Dina cringed inwardly as her brother's expression changed from relaxed to wary. Silas could be exceedingly charming when in a good mood, but he could be equally unpleasant when he was not. She hoped Thor would not antagonize him into rudeness. After a tense moment, however, Silas nodded.

"Thank you. And thank you, Miss Turpin, for your hospitality. Ashcombe would have been dull indeed over Christmas, with Dina gone away. I was delighted to receive your invitation."

Violet sent Thor a warning look, then turned back to her guest with a smile. "Come, let me give you a tour of the grounds, as we are already outside. Then, when we return, I can show you the house. By then your things will have been moved into your room so that you can change if you wish."

Silas agreed, and the two went off arm in arm, Violet fairly sparkling as she chattered nonstop. The moment they were out of earshot, Thor turned to Dina.

"Perhaps you should tell Violet the same things you've told me. I'd rather she not develop a *tendre* for your brother, given everything I've learned about him."

Dina had already been considering how she could discreetly put Violet on her guard, but at Thor's censorious tone, she instinctively bristled. "All of those things happened long ago. Silas has matured since then. I can't imagine that Violet is in the least bit of danger from him."

Thor's jaw tightened visibly. "I'm not concerned that he'll shut her into a cupboard or put her up a tree. But you and I both know how poor his prospects are at present, with debts still hanging over his head and his estate still mortgaged."

"Between us, we have remedied much of that," she pointed out, though without much conviction.

"Do you really believe he doesn't want more? Violet nearly fell prey to one fortune hunter."

"And you think Silas is another." Though she suspected the same thing, having Thor put it into words was rather different. "My brother is not good enough for your sister—is that what you are saying?"

"I wasn't going to put it quite so bluntly as that, but . . . yes. I think Violet can do better, and not only with respect to fortune—which I know would never be a consideration for her."

"As it was for me?" Dina wasn't sure why she felt so angry, or so determined to defend her brother, who certainly didn't deserve it. "It could be said that I married you for money, even if it was my own."

Thor looked startled. "This isn't about you and me. You were placed in a difficult position—by your brother."

"That makes my motives no less mercenary, does it?"

"I never said—"

"You didn't have to. Your import was quite clear." She felt tears threatening, though she couldn't say why. Determined that he not see them, she turned toward the house, but he reached out and grasped her shoulder with one large hand, stopping her.

"Dina, listen to me." His voice was gentle, as was his grip, though she could feel the power behind it. "I'm angry at your brother, yes—for everything he did to you. A man who would do such things to his own sister is not a man I want spending time with mine. I won't allow him to harm Violet in any way."

She swallowed, willing her tears back to their source. What would it be like to have a brother like this, caring and protective as a matter of course? She had never had—and would never have—the kind of relationship with Silas that Violet enjoyed with Thor, she realized, painful as that was to admit.

"I don't want Violet hurt any more than you do. She has already become quite dear to me. But truly, I don't think you need worry. She is impulsive but not stupid."

"Still, I want her warned away from him. She is such a romantic that—"

"—that forbidding her to spend time with Silas may make her wish to do just that," Dina finished. "But I'll attempt to speak to her, if you think it will help."

He squeezed her shoulder, then released it. "Thank you. That would make me feel better, yes. In return, I'll promise to be civil to your brother, as far as it is within my power."

"It is a bargain. At least, as long as Silas is here, he will have no opportunity to add to his debts," she added wryly. It was the only real advantage to his visit she could think of.

"There is that, I suppose. Which only underscores why Violet must be warned away from him. If you don't do it, Dina, I will."

Dina nodded as they reentered the house, but she continued to worry. Could Thor have such a low opinion of Silas without also believing ill of her?

They had been raised in the same household, after all. And Silas's debts had already cost Thor quite a lot of money, cutting substantially into the fortune Dina had brought with her.

Perhaps that was why she'd felt a need—an unworthy need—to lash out when he seemed to be insulting Silas, and, by extension, her as Silas's only family. Never before had she felt a need to justify Silas's behavior to others.

But never before had anyone's opinion mattered so much to her.

"Well, here you are at last," Lady Rumble greeted them as they reached the front hall. "Did you see Violet when she went back outdoors?" Her eyes fairly danced with suppressed excitement.

"Yes, indeed, and my brother, too." Despite her emotional turmoil, Dina had to smile, Lady Rumble's delight was so infectious. "How clever of you both to keep his arrival a secret."

"That was Violet's idea, but I agreed with her that it would be great fun to surprise you, especially as it is nearly Christmas. I presume Violet has taken Mr. Moore on a tour of the estate, as the weather is so fine?"

Thor nodded. "She has, but I was thinking that perhaps I should go after them and play chaperone."

Lady Rumble waved away that concern with a beringed hand. "Oh, tut. He is family. No one will think anything of Violet showing her new brother-in-law about the place, I'm sure. Come up and have some tea and a bite to eat, as the rest of us have already done."

Though Dina could see that Thor would rather go after his sister, he assented, and they followed Lady Rumble upstairs to the parlor, where the remains of an unusually elegant tea were laid out—in honor of Silas's arrival, Dina presumed. Suddenly realizing that she was indeed hungry, she helped herself without protest to a few small sandwiches and a variety of biscuits.

Lady Rumble left them, and for a few minutes they ate and drank in silence. Then, glancing up, Dina found Thor watching her with a strangely intent gaze.

"What? Have I jam on my face?"

Smiling, he shook his head. "Not at all. I was just thinking how refreshing it is to see a woman evince a healthy appetite—well deserved, after so much physical activity this morning. I'm glad you don't put on those die-away airs so common to young ladies these days."

She set down the sandwich she'd just picked up with a blush, suddenly feeling awkward and unfeminine. He must think her a complete hoyden, for all he'd couched his comment as a compliment. "I'm sorry. I suppose I was rather wolfing down your mother's dainties."

"No, please don't apologize. I was quite sincere." He picked up the sandwich she'd just set down and handed it back to her. "Go ahead. Eat."

But Dina's appetite had rather abruptly deserted her. She was forcibly reminded of their discussion that day in Scotland, when he'd made it clear theirs was to be a marriage in name only. She'd accepted then that she was not the sort of woman to whom men were romantically attracted. So why should Thor's words bother her now?

"I, ah, believe I will go ask your mother whether there is anything she wishes me to do to help prepare for the ball," she said, setting the sandwich down again. "Pray excuse me."

She could only be who she was, she reminded herself. She'd never had a high opinion of women who pretended to be weaker or stupider than they actually were, simply to please men. Her mother had been a prime example, hiding her light under a bushel. Dina refused to be like that.

Already she and Thor were well on their way to becoming friends. That should be enough for her. Indeed, she suspected it would have to be.

Thor rose, ready to follow Dina, but then restrained himself. It was obvious from her distressed expression that she wished to get away from him—and no wonder. He'd never been as smooth with the ladies as some of his friends, but he couldn't remember ever bungling a compliment so badly before.

The truth was, he did find Dina's strength and energy, and yes, even her appetite, inordinately attractive. Calling attention to it so bluntly, however, had been undiplomatic in the extreme, given the standards drummed into ladies from birth. Recalling his exact words, he was not surprised she'd interpreted them as veiled criticism, especially given their recent argument over her brother.

It was as though he had no control over his tongue around Dina, simply blurting out whatever he happened to be feeling. Perhaps it was because he felt so comfortable around her, but that did not give him license to hurt her feelings. That was the last thing he wanted to do, particularly after discovering how difficult her life had been with a bullying brother and oblivious parents.

That thought brought him back to his feet. His mother's—and Dina's—protestations notwithstanding, he had no intention of leaving Violet to Silas Moore's tender mercies for the entire afternoon. Calling for his cloak, he headed back outdoors, determined to find them.

He had taken only a few steps, however, when he heard the crunch of carriage wheels on the front drive. Curious, he rounded the house to see a familiar crest on the traveling coach that was just discharging its occupants. Violet and Moore temporarily forgotten, he strode forward with a grin.

"Rush, Stormy, welcome," he called out. "So you decided to accept my invitation after all, did you? Mother will be delighted—as am I. Is Killer not with you?"

Lord Rushford gripped his outstretched hand in greeting. "No, his mother arrived only an hour or two after you left Melton and insisted he stay for Christmas at Wheatstone. We, however, found ourselves completely overcome by curiosity about your new bride. Where is she?"

"With my mother, somewhere about the house. Let's go find them." So saying, he led his friends up the front steps, absurdly pleased not only with their arrival, but with this ironclad excuse to seek out Dina again so soon.

They found the two ladies they sought in the ballroom, discussing the placement of greenery and other last-minute decorations.

"Mother, see what has turned up on our doorstep," Thor announced as they entered. As he'd expected, his mother hurried forward with a wide smile of welcome.

"Lord Rushford! Sir Charles! How delightful this is. Grant told me that he had invited you, but warned me you were not likely to come. Perhaps I'll not have a shortage of gentlemen at my ball tonight after all, what with the two of you and Mr. Moore."

Rush glanced at Thor. "Mr. Moore?"

"Yes, dear Dina's brother," Lady Rumble explained. "Oh, I suppose you will not have met Grant's new wife."

Drawing Dina forward, she made the introductions. Thor felt a glow of pride at the way Dina greeted his friends with a perfect blend of propriety and pleasantness. And that blue gown became her remarkably well. They would have to admit that he'd done quite well for himself in a wife.

And indeed, Rush and Stormy seemed both startled and charmed, each glancing back at Thor questioningly before bowing over her hand in turn.

Stormy was quicker than the earl. "I can't tell you how delighted I am to make your acquaintance, Mrs. Turpin. Or may I call you Dina?"

"Of course you may," she replied, pinkening slightly.

"And you must call me Stormy, as all of my friends do. Has this big fellow got you calling him Thor yet?"

Her color deepened further, and she avoided Thor's gaze. "Er, not exactly," she murmured.

"They are very recently wed," Rush said, gently disengaging Dina's hand from Stormy's to take it in his own. "I'm sure he wouldn't mind, though, would you, Thor?"

Now Dina did flick a glance his way, and he responded with a self-conscious smile. "Of course not."

"And you must call me Rush," the earl continued. "Dina—is that your given name or a nickname?"

"The latter," she replied with a shy smile that Thor would rather be directed at himself. "It is short for Undine."

"The water sprite? How appropriate, for one so ethereal," Rush said, and was rewarded by a chuckle.

Thor realized with a start that he had not heard her laugh since returning to Plumrose and felt suddenly irritated that Rush had been the one to elicit such a delightful sound from her lips.

"I don't believe I've ever been called 'ethereal' before," she said now. "It sounds much more pleasant than 'small' or 'puny,' I must say."

Rush looked over at Thor. "I see we must encourage your husband to pay you more compliments, then, for 'ethereal' seems a perfect way to describe you, Dina."

"Perhaps you will have more success than I have had in that area," said Lady Rumble, irritating Thor further.

It was no business of theirs whether he paid Dina compliments—though he had to confess that "ethereal" really was an apt description. He wished he'd thought of it first.

"We should go find Violet," he said, eager to change the subject—and divert his friends' attention from Dina. "She will want to know about our latest guests."

"Yes, I'm sure she will. Run along, then." Lady Rumble glanced about the spacious room. "When she's finished showing Mr. Moore about, she may wish to join us here, to have a say in the final preparations. Oh, and pray send for Mrs. Hornbuckle, Grant, so that I may consult with her about rooms for your friends."

"Of course. Gentlemen?"

His friends seemed inclined to linger, still clearly wishing to learn more about Dina, but when he headed out of the ballroom, they reluctantly fell into step behind him.

"You sly dog," Stormy said before they were properly out of earshot. "From what little you told us in Melton, I was more than half prepared to find that your new wife was an antidote. You never dropped a hint of how pretty she is."

"No indeed," Rush agreed, though at a lower volume. "In fact, I believe I understand things a good deal better, now that I've met her."

Thor glanced at him sharply, but Rush's expression reassured him that he hadn't shared the true story with anyone else. "I've never been one to brag. Besides, as I've known her for such a long time, I, ah, tend not to think of her in that way."

He hated to lie to a friend, but both Dina's honor and Violet's were at stake, and Stormy was not known for his ability to keep a secret. Still, perhaps he'd do better not to play down his attraction to Dina. He didn't want them getting ideas . . .

Not until he'd spoken with the housekeeper and sent her off to the ballroom did he finally realize that the unpleasant sensation at the pit of his stomach was pure, unadulterated jealousy—which was ridiculous.

"Now, let's see if we can find Violet and Mr. Moore," he said briskly, leading them back outdoors, glad of an excuse for some action.

It had been foolish enough to feel the stirrings of that emotion when he'd seen Dina dancing and chatting with some of the local gentry, but these were two of his very best friends. He would trust either of these men with his life.

But not with his wife? He wasn't sure he wanted to explore the implications of that.

Instead he told his friends, in general terms, of his reservations about Silas Moore as they walked toward the stable yard. It seemed likely that Violet might have taken him to see the new pups, though after Dina's story, Thor didn't want the fellow anywhere near his dogs.

"Yes, you said the brother was the reason you felt it necessary to marry so quickly," Stormy said. "I'm surprised you would have him here at all, if he's so untrustworthy."

Thor shrugged. "Mother and Violet are unaware of his failings, and they extended the invitation. And he is still Dina's brother, whatever his intentions may have been."

"All part of the marriage package," Rush commented. "It's one reason I hope to delay the inevitable as long as possible. Still, I hope you won't find Moore a continual thorn in your side. Have I ever met the fellow in Town?"

"It's possible. I had a brief run-in with him once, when he tried to bully young Heywood into playing more deeply than he could afford. Moore clearly remembered it when we met." He smiled grimly at the memory.

Rush furrowed his brow. "Big fellow? Handsome, in an obvious sort of way?"

Thor nodded.

"Ah, yes, I know who you mean. He nearly took a commission, as I recall—his father paid for it, in fact—but he apparently decided he hadn't the stomach for battle and turned around and sold it before ever reporting. Probably just as well. I certainly wouldn't have wanted him in my unit."

That fit with Thor's general impression of Moore, though he hadn't known that bit of his history. "I hear voices from the direction of the kennels. They must be there."

Rounding the corner, he saw Violet holding one of the puppies while Moore stood beside her—rather closer than was necessary, he thought. He wore an expression of mild distaste as he watched Violet touch her nose to the pup's.

"Here you are, Vi." Thor forced a joviality he didn't feel into his voice. "Look who have come to boost the numbers for Mother's ball."

Delight spread across her face when she saw Rush and Stormy. Not bothering to set down the puppy she held, she hurried forward to greet them.

"Why, Lord Rushford, Sir Charles," she exclaimed. "How delightful. I haven't seen either of you for an age."

Moore, Thor noticed, looked considerably less delighted, though he quickly hid the grimace that had crossed his features as he turned and converted it to an insincere smile. He greeted the two men with perfect politeness, though Thor thought he detected a certain wariness in his eyes.

Once the introductions were completed, Rush and Stormy turned back to Violet with twin expressions of disbelief.

"I would never have believed a few short years could work such a change," Stormy declared, bending over her hand. "You have grown up with a vengeance, Miss Turpin."

"May I take that as a compliment?" Violet asked with a saucy smile.

Thor determined to keep a much closer eye on his sister in the future. When had she become such a flirt?

"You may indeed," Stormy replied.

"Then you will both dance with me at the ball tonight?" She looked from Stormy to Rush, her face becomingly flushed and her eyes twinkling.

Stormy agreed with alacrity, and Rush nodded as well, though he seemed more amused than eager.

Silas Moore seemed less than pleased by this development. "Don't forget that you have promised two dances to me already," he reminded Violet.

"Of course I will not forget." She smiled up at him so warmly that Thor's earlier concerns returned in full force. Surely she could see that Moore was inferior to either of his friends?

"That reminds me," Thor said now. "Mother and Dina are in the ballroom, up to their elbows in decorations. I would have thought you would want a say in the final decisions."

As he'd hoped, that pulled her attention away from Moore. "Indeed I do. I'll see you all at dinner tonight, if not before." Handing the puppy unceremoniously to Thor, she turned and hurried toward the house.

Stormy, never known for his tact, turned to Moore. "So, did this wedding between your sister and Thor here take you as much by surprise as it did us? Could have knocked me over with a feather when Thor showed up in Melton a fortnight ago and told us he was married."

"Melton?" Moore repeated, glancing at Thor. "Your sister mentioned that you had just returned home last night, Turpin, but not that you'd been gone a whole fortnight."

"I'd already missed a full week of the foxhunting season, and the weather becomes unpredictable after Christmas." Thor knew he sounded defensive, so he forced a grin. "Can't have my new bride thinking I'll give up my favorite pastime just because I'm married, can I?"

Rush and Stormy both chuckled and expressed agreement, lightening the moment—until Moore spoke again.

"To answer your question, Sir Charles, I expect I was even more surprised than you were by the wedding." He flicked another glance toward Thor. "But then I suppose elopements generally catch people by surprise."

"They eloped?" Stormy exclaimed, turning to regard Thor with renewed interest. "For some reason, Thor kept that small detail to himself."

This was dangerous ground, as Moore had no idea about the story Thor had told in Melton to account for his sudden marriage, to include the fictitious long-standing connection between their families. And Lady Rumble, he knew, had been putting about the tale of Violet playing chaperone to his own supposed elopement, which Moore presumably didn't know, either.

"It, ah, seemed the most expedient solution," he improvised, setting the puppy down with its mother to hide his sudden alarm. "As I said, I didn't wish to miss any more of the hunting season than necessary."

"Of course." Moore's eyes narrowed speculatively, but he didn't ask any more awkward questions, to Thor's relief.

He would have to say something to Moore before tonight's ball, he realized, though he dreaded giving the man any sort of leverage. Otherwise a slip might put Violet's reputation at risk. To do that, though, he needed to get the fellow alone.

"Why don't I show you to your rooms," he suggested on sudden inspiration. "You'll want to change your shoes, at least, before touring the house itself. After that, perhaps we can play a few games of billiards to while away the afternoon. That should keep us well clear of my mother's preparations for tonight."

On reentering the house, he inquired of a maidservant which rooms had been assigned to the new arrivals and was told that Mr. Moore was in the east wing, while both of his friends were in the west wing. Perfect, for his purposes.

"You've both been here before, so I'm sure you can find your rooms," he said to his friends when they reached the landing between the two wings. "They'll be the first doors you reach after the turning, across the hall from each other. Come, Moore, I'll show you where you'll be staying."

He waited until they had turned a corner before saying, "As you may have guessed, my family thought it prudent to, ah, change a few details before making the story of my marriage public—primarily for my sister's sake."

"So I gathered. Hushing up her aborted elopement by making it yours, or something like that?" There was a gleam in his eye that Thor didn't care for at all.

"My mother has accounted for her absence by saying that she came along to preserve propriety until Dina and I were able to marry. I'm sure you wouldn't want to compromise my sister's reputation by implying otherwise?"

Moore raised a brow at the implied threat. "Of course I would not want Miss Turpin's name sullied. I regard her as . . . family. Now, which will be my room?"

"Here, on the right." Should he warn Moore away from Violet now, or would the fellow see that as a challenge of sorts?

"I hope you'll excuse me from billiards this afternoon," Moore said before he could decide. "I'd thought to ride into Alford. I've never visited it, so wanted to have a look about, buy a few things I forgot to pack, that sort of thing."

Though more than a little bit suspicious, Thor was too relieved at the prospect of having Moore out of the house—and away from Violet—to question him. "Very well. Will we see you at dinner, before the ball?"

"Of course," he replied with a smile that was nearer a smirk. "I wouldn't miss it for the world."

Chapter 14

Silas waited until he had turned from Plumrose's long drive onto the lane leading to Alford to give vent to his feelings, cursing loud and long.

What foul luck to have Lord Rushford and that other fellow show up just now, when he'd been making such good progress with Violet Turpin. He was confident of his ability to compete with any local suitors she might have, but an earl—particularly a Meltonian, who had served with distinction in the army—was another matter.

A few discreet inquiries in the village of Rumbleton on his way in had revealed that Miss Turpin was universally liked and, more importantly, that she would come into a considerable fortune one day. A fortune he sorely needed, as he'd already managed to gamble away nearly all the money Dina and

Turpin had promised him, in an effort to increase it before paying his debts.

The invitation to Plumrose had been welcome indeed, as he was finding it increasingly difficult to dodge his creditors. London was essentially closed to him now, nor would it be wise even to return to Ashcombe without something to pacify the most insistent of them.

Winning Miss Turpin might not be as easy as he'd thought, however, with this new competition. He needed a drink and some time to think—and to plan how he might put this latest information on the doctored elopement story to good use.

Half an hour later, he was well into his second mug of ale at the Half Moon tavern but no closer to a plan.

He'd first thought to persuade Violet Turpin with the threat of exposing her folly, but that might only worsen his chances of marrying the chit, particularly if her brother found out. There was always a risk that Turpin might take more permanent measures to silence him, if he believed his sister's name threatened. So desperate was his need that Silas would even have considered more direct measures, but for a conviction that he could never carry off an abduction unaided.

Morosely he surveyed the handful of farmers chatting about spring planting prospects in the corner near the fireplace. Maybe coming here hadn't been such a good idea after all.

The door opened again, and he glanced up without much interest, expecting yet another farmer, but was surprised to see a smartly dressed gentleman who appeared to be about his own age. The man appeared to be familiar with the place, for he moved without hesitation toward a table near the window, calling out for a drink over his shoulder.

"Excuse me," Silas said, standing to get his attention as the man passed his table.

The gentleman glanced his way, started violently, paled, and turned toward the door. But then, glancing back at Silas again, he stared for a moment, then relaxed as suddenly as he had panicked.

"Sorry," he said rather breathlessly. "Thought you were someone else for a moment there. Not many fellows your size hereabouts, you see. Did . . . did you want something?"

"I was going to suggest you join me. You're the first man I've seen since I arrived who looks like he can carry on a conversation about something other than drainage and seed starts."

Silas waited until the other man had taken a chair across from him and been served his own mug before saying, "The man you mistook me for a moment ago—that wouldn't have been a Mr. Turpin, would it?"

The stranger looked suddenly wary again. "Why? Is he a friend of yours?"

"Not exactly." Silas chuckled. "But as you said, how many men of my size can there be in this district? It seemed an obvious guess. I'm Silas Moore, by the way." He extended his hand.

"Gregory Plunkett," responded the other man, taking the proferred hand in an indifferent grip. "Moore, did you say? Well, ain't that an odd coincidence."

The name Plunkett niggled at Silas's memory, but he could not quite place it. "Coincidence? How so?"

"I nearly married a Miss Moore in Scotland a few weeks since, before Turpin intervened. It's rather an odd, long story."

Silas sat back in his chair and took a long pull from his mug. "I'm in no hurry. I'd very much like to hear it."

Dina turned this way and that before the long pier glass mounted between the windows of her bedchamber. Perhaps it was simply an illusion created by the shimmering, emerald green silk ball gown and the waning daylight, but her reflection showed a woman who was almost beautiful—and very feminine.

The gown, cut low and gathered high beneath her breasts, made the most of her modest bosom, while the deep green of the silk made her hair seem a richer red by contrast and accentuated the creaminess of her skin.

She had allowed Francine to apply just the slightest hint of color to her cheeks and lips for this special occasion, and had to admit that it enhanced her appearance. The green silk ribbon and tiny white flowers woven through her red curls completed the Christmas effect.

It was a pity she did not feel as festive as she looked. She had not seen Thor since early afternoon, as he'd chosen to spend the day with his friends instead of with her. Friends he'd left in Melton-Mowbray only the morning before—friends to whom he had apparently spoken disparagingly of her, judging by the comment she had overheard Sir Charles make as they left the ballroom.

Glancing at the mirror again, she forced a bright smile in response to her maid's questioning glance. "You have outdone yourself, Francine. Thank you."

Dina reminded herself that she had no right to pout simply because Thor was living his life as he chose—as she'd promised he could do. No, she would dance and be all that was charming tonight, and if Thor did not notice how pretty she looked, other gentlemen would. Perhaps, if he noticed them noticing . . .

A tap sounded at her door, and an instant later Violet swept into the room, a welcome interruption to such wistful thoughts. "Oh, Dina, you look simply gorgeous," she exclaimed, giving her confidence a needed boost. "I knew that color would flatter you, but I had no idea how much."

"Thank you, Violet. You are a perfect vision of loveliness yourself, you know."

It was true. Dressed in clouds of white gauze threaded with the narrowest of red ribbon at hem, waist, and neckline, Violet looked like a Christmas angel.

Violet dimpled at the compliment and twirled before the glass. "It is pretty, if a bit childish. I would far rather wear dramatic colors than insipid white, to tell you the truth. Married women have all the fun."

Something in Dina's expression must have hinted at her disagreement with that statement, for Violet suddenly frowned at her, then motioned for Francine to leave them. As soon as the maid was gone, she sat on the bed—carefully lifting her confection of skirts to avoid creasing them—and re-garded Dina with serious eyes.

"What is it, Dina? Are you and Grant at odds with each other? I thought, or at least hoped, when I saw you together this morning, that you had finally come to a new understanding."

Dina bit her lip, then released it before she could chew off the tinting Francine had applied. "I wouldn't say that we are at odds, exactly. It's more that we don't . . . He doesn't . . ."

"He doesn't treat you like his wife?"

With a sigh, Dina nodded. "I shouldn't complain, truly, for we agreed before we married that there would be no real, ah, intimacy between us. And that's what I thought I wanted—then."

"But now?" Violet prompted gently.

"Now . . . Oh, I don't know." Dina turned away to gaze out the window, refusing to give in to the prickling she felt behind her eyelids. "I've . . . I've grown to like him quite a lot," she finally con-fessed when Violet remained uncharacteristically silent.

"But that's wonderful," Violet exclaimed, bound-ing up from the bed to hug her. "Is it because of that kiss Mother insisted upon, or did you two not go through with it? I could see Grant didn't care to be forced like that."

"We, ah, we went through with it."

Violet put a hand to her heart, her expression dreamy. "And was it wonderful? Do say it was wonderful."

"It was actually quite nice," Dina said, "or at least I thought so. But then he left for Melton-Mowbray the very next morning, so perhaps he wouldn't agree."

"Then that is all that has happened between you? That one kiss?" She was clearly disappointed.

Dina could only nod, trying not to show her own disappointment.

Then Violet caught her completely off-guard by asking, "Do you think you're in love with him?"

"I don't know," Dina whispered. Then, in a stronger voice, "I suppose I should hope I am not, if he does not feel the same."

Violet looked thoughtful for a moment. "I suppose that's true. Sometimes I think . . . But that's neither here nor there. It's completely unthinkable that Grant can see you tonight, looking as you do, and not fall prostrate at your feet, head over ears in love. You'll see—one look at you and he will sweep you off upstairs for a night of passionate romance."

Dina had to laugh at her sister-in-law's unquenchable optimism. "I take leave to doubt that, but if he indeed falls to the floor—or sweeps me upstairs— you may say you told me so." She had no expectation of hearing Violet say those words, however.

Still, when the two of them went downstairs a few minutes later to join the family and houseguests in the parlor before dinner, she had to admit that the expressions on all the gentlemen's faces were quite gratifying. Even Lord Rumble, who tended to ignore formalities, rose to his feet and bowed.

"I don't know that I've ever seen such lovely ladies," he said, coming forward to take Violet's hands and kiss her cheek, then turning to do the same with Dina. "The two of you, with Lady Rumble, put me in mind of the three Graces."

Dina murmured her thanks and glanced at her mother-in-law, who blushed nearly as pink as the brocaded silk ball gown she wore.

"Why, Lord Rumble," she exclaimed. "I'd nearly forgotten what a pretty way you have with compliments."

Thor's voice came from just above Dina's shoulder. "Indeed, such beauty would inspire any man to eloquence." She turned, startled, then caught her breath at the look in his eyes. Violet, just beyond him, winked and nodded.

"Thank you," Dina said, sure that she was blushing just as deeply as Lady Rumble had done. "You look very fine yourself."

She was forcibly reminded of their first night at Plumrose, when she'd seen him formally dressed for the first time. When he'd kissed her for the first time—the only time. If anything, he looked even more handsome now, in tails and knee breeches that showed off his muscular calves to advantage.

"We gentlemen in our dull finery can't compete. We must content ourselves with complementing—and complimenting—our partners." Thor extended an arm, and Dina, slightly dazed, placed her hand on it so that he could lead her to the sofa near the fireplace.

"I must say, you clean up very nicely, Dina," Silas agreed from the other side of the room. "But Miss Turpin, you fairly take my breath away. I regret now that I only bespoke two dances, for I'm certain that once the other gentlemen get a look at you, there'll be no chance of any more."

Dina felt Thor's arm tense under her hand, the brief spell between them broken. Guiltily she realized that she should have taken the opportunity upstairs to speak with Violet about her brother, instead of the details of her own marriage.

"Moore is quite right, Miss Turpin," Sir Charles chimed in after what Dina was almost sure had been a slight nod from Thor, beside her. "In fact, I'd like to take this opportunity to solicit a second dance myself, if you'll grant it."

Violet laughed delightedly. "You gentlemen will quite turn my head, if I let you, but yes, Sir Charles, you may have another dance, if you insist."

She glanced at Lord Rushford, clearly expecting him to make a similar request, but at that moment the butler announced that dinner was ready.

Silas was the first to Violet's side, forestalling the other two gentlemen. "You will do me the honor of allowing me to lead you to table, Miss Turpin, will you not?"

"Violet, you should allow Lord Rushford to lead you in, as he holds the highest rank here," Lady Rumble protested.

For the merest moment Violet hesitated, with another glance at the earl, but when he did not immediately step forward, she took Silas's arm with a smile. "Nonsense, Mother," she said. "Silas is family, and this is a family dinner."

Again Dina wished she had spoken with Violet about Silas earlier, but then Thor drew her to her feet, and she no longer had any thought to spare for her sister-in-law, so affected was she by his nearness, by the firm feel of his arm beneath her hand. What was wrong with her? She had hoped to bewitch him tonight, not fall even further under the spell he'd already cast on her.

"I hope you will like what we have done to the ballroom," she said as they descended the stairs to the dining room, mainly for the sake of saying something.

He smiled down at her, making her heart accelerate just as though she'd been doing calisthenics. "I'm certain I will, for you will be decoration enough, with nothing else necessary."

She felt her eyes widen at this, his second compliment to her within five minutes. Perhaps Violet had not been entirely wrong after all. "You are very kind," she said in all sincerity.

At that, however, he seemed to withdraw, his expression going blank as he turned his eyes forward. "Not at all."

"You'll notice that I've ordered only a light dinner tonight, as there will be a nice hot supper during the ball," Lady Rumble told them all as they arranged themselves around the table. "We mustn't linger at table too long, as guests will begin arriving in just over an hour."

"That's just as well," Violet said, "for I'd not want to be too full to dance." Silas and Sir Charles, sitting on either side of her, both hastened to agree with her.

Dina glanced from one to the other, wondering a bit wistfully what it would be like to have gentlemen vying for her attention. It was something she'd never experienced, and wasn't ever like to, now she was married.

Lord Rushford, on her right, startled her by saying, "Mrs. Turpin—Dina—I have neglected to ask if you would honor me with a dance tonight. Will you?"

"Oh. Of . . . of course," she stammered, wondering in embarrassment whether her thoughts had shown on her face. His expression was merely pleasant, however, not pitying.

"I reserve the supper dance." Thor, on her other side, spoke coolly. "As well as the first dance, of course."

"And all waltzes?" Lord Rushford looked amused, though more at Thor than at her, Dina thought.

Thor frowned at his friend for a moment, but then shrugged. "You may waltz with her, if you wish."

The illusion that they were competing for her attention vanished. Clearly Thor meant only to observe the proprieties. No doubt that had been the motivation behind his compliments as well, keeping up appearances before his friends and family. And Lord Rushford was merely being polite—and perhaps teasing his friend a bit.

She sighed and picked up her spoon.

With one last, warning glance at Rush, Thor turned his attention to his soup as well. It was already taking every ounce of his control to resist Dina's charms without his friend baiting him like that. At least now that he realized what Rush was doing, he would not fall into that trap again.

He sneaked a sidelong glance at Dina while she was focused on her dish, still stunned by her appearance tonight. Lately it seemed as though each time he saw her, she was still more beautiful than the time before. It couldn't be just the gown, though that was lovely, for he'd thought the same even when she wore that old gray thing to the gymnasium that morning. He was rapidly becoming obsessed with his wife, he realized. But what was he to do about it?

Running away to Melton for two weeks hadn't helped in the least, and now he was back, he could scarcely avoid her, particularly tonight. Not only would it looked dashed odd, it would give every gentleman in the district an open field to dance and flirt with her. The way she looked tonight—he sneaked another glance—they would be falling at her feet, unless he was at her side to prevent them.

For the remainder of the meal, he tried to distract himself by keeping an eye on Silas Moore and his conversation with Violet, with some small success. That afternoon, in the billiards room, he had enlisted the help of his friends to keep them apart, and Stormy, at least, had risen to the task. Still, Violet and Moore were chatting together more than Thor would prefer.

"Goodness, look at the time," Lady Rumble exclaimed, just as his thoughts were drifting back to Dina for the dozenth time. "We must hurry to our places before the first guests arrive."

A startled glance at his plate showed that Thor had indeed finished all his dinner, though he could not now name a single dish he'd eaten. Dina, he noticed, had eaten far more lightly. But then she was small and had eaten well that afternoon.

As there was now no time for the gentlemen to linger over port and cigars, they all rose, the gentlemen helping the ladies to their feet. This time, Thor noted with approval, Stormy had been quicker than Moore and was the one to lead Violet from the room. Then Dina placed her tiny hand on his arm, and he was unable—again—to think of anything but her. Her hair. Her skin. Her scent. Her feminine daintiness.

It was that last thought that stopped him on the verge of paying her another compliment. Swallowing, he instead said, "I believe Mother wants us to stand just beyond her and Father in the receiving line."

His voice was more brusque than he'd intended, and Dina responded with a questioning glance. Afraid of what his own eyes might reveal, he stared stolidly ahead. He simply had to get his emotions under control. There was a whole evening to get through. He didn't dare even think of what would follow, going upstairs to their adjoining rooms, bidding Dina good night in the hall . . .

It was a relief when the guests began arriving, but the distraction was short-lived, as every one of them made a point of congratulating him on his new bride.

"Such a delight, our new Mrs. Turpin," gushed Lady Vaile, Sir Albert's mother. "Do you know, Mr. Turpin, that she and Miss Turpin helped me deliver food baskets to some of our elderly tenants last week? I doubt I could have managed on my own, with this gouty toe of mine."

Thor glanced down at Dina, who smiled at the older woman. "It was a pleasure to do so, Lady Vaile, and a wonderful way to learn more of the district. Please let us know when you need help again."

"You are generosity itself," said Sir Albert, coming along the line behind his mother. "And I'm hoping that generosity will extend to granting me a dance tonight. Will it?"

Dina's smile was identical to the one she'd given Lady Vaile, but for some reason it bothered Thor this time. "Of course, Sir Albert."

A few minutes later, she promised a dance to Horace Smallbone as well, then another to Jeremy Nesbit, Rose's brother. Thor almost said something about making sure she left a few dances for him, but then thought better of it. Dancing with Dina was likely to be pure torture, so the fewer the better . . . he supposed.

After what seemed an eternity of jealous twinges followed by Thor chiding himself for those twinges, they were released from the receiving line to mingle with the guests. To distract himself from the heady sensation of Dina's hand on his arm, Thor looked around for Violet. She was already talking with Moore again.

"I take it you've had no chance to speak to Violet about your brother?" he murmured to Dina.

Following his gaze, she shook her head. "We only had a few minutes in private before coming down for dinner, and discussed . . . other matters."

Her constraint made him wonder whether she had deliberately avoided the topic. She had promised, however, so he would not badger her about it. Irrelevantly, he noticed that he could see well down

her cleavage. He frowned. None of her other partners would be as tall as himself, but they were still all
much taller than Dina, which meant—

"—overdo the greenery?"

"I beg your pardon?" Thor felt his ears reddening.
He had been so preoccupied by her bosom that he'd
missed her question.

"I was just wondering whether we were too lavish
with the decorations. With all of the candles lit, it
looks rather different than it did in daylight."

Belatedly he gazed around the room, really seeing
the decorations for the first time. Evergreens and
holly festooned the walls, with extra candle sconces
cunningly nestled amid the greenery.

In addition, numerous kissing boughs had been
hung in every archway and from each chandelier as
well. His mother's innovation, no doubt. Nervously
he glanced up and was relieved to find that they did
not happen to be standing directly under one at the
moment.

"I think it's very festive," he assured her. "It is
Christmas Eve, after all. Would you care for a glass
of something before the dancing begins?" That
would give him a chance to get his emotions under
better control—and also to memorize the location of
every kissing bough, so that he could avoid them
without it seeming obvious that he was doing so.

"Yes, thank you."

Perversely nettled that she seemed as willing to
have him leave her side as he was eager to leave
hers—if only for a moment—he gave her a terse nod
and headed toward the refreshment table. Passing

close to Violet and Silas Moore, he frowned at the latter, only to have the man surprise him with a broad smile.

"Grant, did we not do a nice job with the decorations?" Violet asked him, glancing around.

"Indeed," he all but growled, reassuring himself that the pair before him were not too close to any of the kissing boughs, either. "Whose idea—?"

"I fear I can take little credit, for Mother and Dina had all but finished the arrangements by the time I joined them. However, the red velvet bows on all of the sconces were my suggestion. A nice holiday touch, don't you think?"

"A lovely touch," Moore agreed before Thor could reply. "You have a skilled eye, Miss Turpin."

She dimpled up at him. "Now, Silas, you know I have asked you to call me Violet. We are family, after all."

"Of course—Violet."

Thor caught the smugness in the fellow's tone and decided he could not afford to wait for Dina to speak with Violet about him. "A word, if you don't mind, Moore?"

Though his brows rose, Moore did not hesitate. "Of course. If you will excuse us, Violet?"

Drawing him off to the side where they could not be overheard, Thor turned to his brother-in-law. "You seem to be spending a great deal of time with my sister," he said without preamble.

"Yes, well, she is quite a fetching thing, and extremely sociable." His tone was bland, giving nothing away, which irritated Thor further.

"I know what you are about, Moore. Don't think I'll stand idly by while you attempt to take advantage of my sister's good nature."

Again Moore surprised him by smiling. "Are you telling me to stay away from her? That would look rather odd, would it not?"

"Don't play the fool with me, or I may believe you are one," Thor said warningly.

"Oh, no." Suddenly Moore was quite serious. "Far from being a fool, I'm awake on all fronts. It would be awkward, however, if everyone in the neighborhood—and in London—were to learn the truth about sweet Violet's elopement, would it not?"

Thor narrowed his eyes. "Are you threatening me, Moore?" he asked softly. After all Dina had told him today, he was itching for an excuse to thrash the man.

"Of course not. But it seems imprudent of you to antagonize a man who knows not only about your sister's indiscretion, but that you were my own dear sister's third choice of a husband in as many days. That must be rather galling to you, I would imagine, and even more so should it become common knowledge."

"How—?" Surely Dina would not have shared those details with her brother?

Moore's smile widened. "I met a most interesting fellow recently—a man by the name of Plunkett. The tale he had to tell was quite, ah, enlightening."

Damn. "And just where is Plunkett?" He should have killed the fellow when he had the chance.

"You can't think I would betray the man after he was so forthcoming with helpful information? To tell you his whereabouts would be to play accessory to murder, from the look on your face."

With an effort, Thor forced himself to relax. It would do him no good to give anything away to Silas Moore. "So you would ruin the reputations of both our sisters? That would seem counterproductive, as you seem set on wooing mine."

"I would rather not, of course," Moore said with a shrug. "The dissolution of your marriage would be a palatable alternative to courting sweet Violet, though less enjoyable."

"An annulment, do you mean? A bit late for that, wouldn't you say?"

"Is it?"

Awareness of his surroundings stopped Thor just in time from forcibly removing the smirk from Moore's face. Even so, his involuntary movement made the other man take a step back. How the devil could he know—?

Though it had slipped for a moment, Moore's smirk was now back in place. "Of course, I can't really blame you, if you are the, ah, reticent one. My sister is such a little dab of a thing, not in your usual style at all."

"Be careful, Moore," Thor warned.

The other man's eyes narrowed, though the smile never left his lips. "I might say the same to you, you know, with respect to Dina. I shouldn't like to learn that you had injured her in any way. Best not to take the chance, wouldn't you say?"

It was disconcerting to have a man like Silas Moore echoing Thor's own concerns. Did that mean they were unfounded, or so obvious that anyone of intelligence would think the same? He didn't know.

When Thor did not answer, Moore shrugged. "Still, it must rankle to have played the gallant rescuer and then be denied the just rewards of heroism. I trust those rewards are not being bestowed elsewhere? I did hear some rumors . . ." He let his voice trail off suggestively.

Again Thor was nearly moved to violence, but this time he managed not to show it. "I strongly recommend you keep any such insinuations to yourself. The intimate details of my marriage are of no concern to you."

"In this particular circumstance, I must beg to differ. But I see that the first set is about to form, so I will say no more—for now. No doubt you are as eager to join your partner as I am to join mine." He glanced over to where Violet waited. "An observant—and talkative—girl." With a parting smile, Moore sauntered back to Violet's side.

So that was how he'd discovered the state of Thor's marriage. And now the blackguard offered him the choice of annulling it, or allowing him to marry Violet, or having both ladies' reputations destroyed. Or Thor could just kill the fellow, and hope, in time, that Dina would forgive him—assuming he wasn't hanged for it.

Chapter 15

Dina spent the first five minutes of the opening minuet wondering whether she should ask Thor about his conversation with her brother. It had been clear, from both men's expressions, that it was no friendly chat. And now, though he strove to conceal it, she could see that Thor was in an extremely foul temper.

Not that she could blame him. Silas often had that effect on her as well. Still, she was exceedingly curious to know what had occurred between them to put Thor in such a towering rage.

Whatever it was, it would be best for all concerned if she could smooth his ruffled feathers. She was far too fond of Lady Rumble by now to wish her embarrassed by any kind of scene at her Christmas Eve ball.

"How is it that you dance so well, after so many years spent soldiering and hunting?" Dina asked him when the movements of the dance allowed for speech.

Thor blinked, distracted for at least a moment from his black mood. "Do I? Wellington did insist that all of his officers master the art, but I can't recall anyone complimenting my dancing before. Thank you."

They moved apart, but a few moments later they were face to face again. "You are quite skilled at the dance yourself," he told her now, "particularly as you have lived so retired."

"I had the benefit of a master when younger," she replied, dipping and curtsying as the dance demanded. "Until these past two weeks afforded me some much-needed practice, however, I would hardly have been a fit partner for you."

That, apparently, had been the wrong thing to say, judging by his sudden frown. "Now I am here, perhaps you'll not feel so great a need to *practice* with other partners."

Again, she wondered what Silas had said to him, but with people on every side, this was hardly the place to ask. If Thor only knew how very much she preferred dancing with him, talking with him, spending time with him . . . But surely it was better that he did not. Less mortifying, at any rate.

"Perhaps," she responded, just before they were separated again. There. Let him wonder what she meant by that.

The dance ended before they had another opportunity for conversation, and then Sir Charles Storm came forward at once to claim her for the next. Thor bowed stiffly and moved off to partner Miss Nesbit in the lively country dance that followed.

"Guess I'd better be careful to keep you away from all of these kissing boughs, judging by the look Thor just gave me," Sir Charles commented as they took their places. "What have you done to put him in such a pucker?"

"Nothing." Dina sighed. "I believe it was my brother."

"Ah, yes. Some definite friction there." The dance began then, saving them both from pursuing that uncomfortable topic.

Sir Charles's mention of the kissing boughs reminded Dina that she still needed to have a word with Violet about Silas—which led her to wonder whether Violet might have been the cause of this latest disagreement between Thor and her brother.

Glancing around, she was relieved to see that Violet was now dancing with Sir Albert, whom Dina was fairly certain would never have the courage to steal a kiss. She knew perfectly well that it was because of her and Thor that Lady Rumble had insisted on hanging so many kissing boughs, but at the moment it seemed unlikely in the extreme that any would be put to their hostess's intended use. She stifled another sigh.

The next dance was a waltz. Dina had deliberately left her waltzes free, hoping to share them with Thor, but it was Silas and not her husband who stepped to her side as the music began.

"I'm quite certain your husband would not approve of my waltzing with his sister, but surely he can have no objection if I partner mine," he said, leading her onto the floor.

Though disappointed, Dina realized this was a perfect opportunity to relieve her curiosity. "What were you and he discussing earlier?" she asked before she could change her mind. "Just before the first dance, I mean."

Silas guided her through the opening steps of the waltz before replying. He was a competent dancer, though he lacked Thor's flair. "We discussed several things. His disapproval of my admiration for Miss Violet, for one."

"Can you really blame him for that? He knows your financial situation, after all. It's not surprising he should want the best for his sister." Dina couldn't quite keep the irony from her tone.

Silas didn't seem to notice. "Which I'm not, eh? Fine sense of family loyalty you have there, Dee."

"Oh, please. I could say the same of you, Silas, and well you know it." Now she made no effort to conceal her bitterness.

He maneuvered her past two other couples before replying. "Aye, I admit I haven't always put your interests first, and I'm sorry for that. Maybe if I had, we wouldn't find ourselves in this fix." He sounded contrite, but she wasn't fooled.

"What fix? Between us, Thor—Mr. Turpin—and I have settled most of your debts. And, as you said earlier today, I've done quite well for myself in my marriage."

The look he turned on her was openly pitying.

"Have you, then? Can you honestly say you are happy in your marriage?"

Dina dropped her gaze, suddenly confused and unwilling to let Silas see it. *Was* she happy? She could be. She could be very happy, if only . . . "I . . . yes, I'm happy," she finally said, telling herself it wasn't precisely a lie.

"Even knowing that you're not the sort of woman your husband prefers?" He lowered his voice so that there was no possibility of being overheard. "Everyone knows that he has always gone for tall, buxom wenches: Margot Fowles, Belle Bonnet—opera dancers he cavorted with in London," he clarified. "No wonder most folks around here thought he'd marry someone like Miss Fiskerton."

Unwillingly, Dina followed his gaze and saw Thor waltzing with Missy Fiskerton, who indeed was of noble proportions, and nearly a full head taller than Dina herself.

"Why, I wouldn't be surprised if he can barely bring himself to touch a puny thing like you," Silas continued, "though of course that isn't your fault. I've no doubt some men quite prefer smaller women."

But not Thor, Dina thought dejectedly. Hadn't Violet said something about him regarding small women as too delicate to touch? She'd thought to show him she wasn't delicate at all, but there was nothing she could do about her size. No wonder he held himself so aloof from her.

"We will simply have to make the best of it, I suppose."

Silas's dark eyes reflected only sympathy and concern. "Dina. Wouldn't it be fairer—to both of you—to renounce this sham of a marriage, so that you each might have a chance to find a better match?"

Suddenly she understood. "An annulment would be very convenient for you, would it not? It would be as though my marriage had never taken place. But then you would have to pay back that generous settlement, you know. Or did you already offer to do that? Was that something else you and Mr. Turpin discussed?"

"We didn't get so far as such details, but yes, he did say something about an annulment, I confess."

Dina tried to stifle a gasp, shock causing tears to start to her eyes. "No," she whispered.

"Now, now, Dee, would that be such a bad thing? As I said, it might well benefit you as much as it would him. You're not so very old yet. You may still have time to find a man who likes you for yourself, who will give you a . . . *proper* marriage."

Stricken, Dina wondered if it was obvious to everyone that she and Thor had not yet consummated their union. Clearly Silas assumed it. But then her pride reasserted itself, and she lifted her chin to stare defiantly at her brother.

"I'm sorry, Silas, but you seem to be laboring under a misapprehension. I assure you that matters have progressed between myself and Mr. Turpin to an extent that would make an annulment quite impossible. In fact, I may already carry his heir."

The stunned outrage on her brother's face was almost worth committing such a flagrant falsehood. Indeed, she might have laughed if her heart had not been so full of pain from his earlier words.

"But . . . but . . ." he stammered. "Miss Turpin said—"

So that was how he knew. "Violet and I have become quite close, but there are some things that are rather too private to discuss," Dina said.

The waltz ended then, before he could question her further. With a perfunctory curtsy, she turned to look for her next partner, relieved at her escape. She was not at all certain she could play her part convincingly much longer, when all she really wanted to do was cry.

"—don't you agree, Mr. Turpin?"

Thor reluctantly pulled his gaze away from Dina, waltzing with her brother on the opposite side of the floor. "I beg your pardon, Miss Fiskerton?"

His partner pouted in a way he had once thought rather fetching but now found contrived and vaguely irritating. "I was saying that Lady Rumble has outdone herself with the decorations, but I can see your attention is elsewhere."

"Er, yes, of course," he responded vaguely. What the devil was Moore saying to make Dina look so unhappy? Perhaps he should have drawn the fellow's cork earlier, after all.

"Ah, the dance is ended, and for once I can't say I'm sorry." Miss Fiskerton tossed her blond curls. "Really, sir, I think you do the ladies a disservice tonight to dance with anyone but your wife. Ah, here comes Rose for the next one. With so many kissing boughs about, you'd best watch your step with her, Mr. Turpin."

With another toss of her head, she flounced away,

and Thor realized she was right—his obsession with
Dina was making him rude to his mother's guests.
Determined to do better, he turned to greet his next
partner with a smile.

"Ah, Miss Nesbit. You look very . . . festive tonight." Nearly as tall as Miss Fiskerton, Rose Nesbit
had festooned her gown with sprigs of holly and red
bows, making her look rather like a vertical Yule log.

It was clear she could not divine his thoughts, for
she curtsied and dimpled flirtatiously. "Why thank
you, Mr. Turpin," she simpered. "Or may I call you
Thor, as your friends from Melton do? After all,
we've known each other simply forever. I must say, I
think it a fitting nickname for an imposing gentleman like yourself." Her giggle grated on his nerves.

"Call me whatever you wish," he said shortly, noting that Dina was moving to stand opposite Jeremy
Nesbit, his partner's brother, for the reel that was
forming. He debated hurrying across the room to
join the same set, but the music began, trapping him
where he was.

He went through the motions of the dance mechanically, his eyes more often turned to Dina's set
than his own until a misstep forced him to pay better
attention.

"Really, sir, I had thought you a better dancer than
this," Miss Nesbit remarked as he executed a belated
allemande with her. "Has all that foxhunting put
you out of practice?"

Thor murmured an apology and strove to do better for the remainder of the reel. He didn't need the
whole room gossiping that he couldn't keep his eyes
off his wife, as Miss Fiskerton had already remarked.

Accordingly, he made a point of smiling at Miss Nesbit every time he faced her, and giving cordial nods to the other ladies and gentlemen he passed as they went through the dance. His partner preened at the attention, showing that she, at least, had no suspicion that his real thoughts were elsewhere.

As the dance concluded, Thor decided to partner Dina for the next one. Perhaps a few words with her would allow him to put her from his thoughts for a while—long enough to avoid insulting the other guests, at least. When he started to move away, however, Miss Nesbit clung to his arm.

"Oh, look," she exclaimed with a coy titter.

Following her gaze upward, he felt his heart sink. They were standing directly under one of those damnable kissing boughs. Blast his inattention.

"I suppose we must abide by tradition," she said. Sending him a suggestive glance through her lowered lashes, she tilted her face up to his.

Thor flicked a panicked glance across the room and saw Dina watching him, her expression unreadable.

"Er, excuse me," he said to Miss Nesbit's expectant face. With a crisp bow, he turned on his heel and walked away, ignoring her outraged exclamation behind him.

He had just been inexcusably rude, but he didn't care. There was no way in hell he was going to encourage that hussy by so much as a kiss on the cheek—especially while there was the least chance that he might hurt Dina by doing so. On sudden inspiration, he detoured past the orchestra.

"Another waltz," he ordered, even as they were

bringing their instruments up to play whatever tune they'd intended next. "Now."

The conductor hesitated only an instant, then turned to the others. "Right, then," he said. "A waltz." They all began shuffling through their sheets of music, and Thor continued on his way.

He reached Dina just as Horace Smallbone took her by the hand to lead her to the next set. "Excuse me," Thor said, "but I believe this dance is mine."

Both of them regarded him with surprise. "You must be mistaken," Mr. Smallbone protested. "When I first arrived tonight, Mrs. Turpin promised the Boulanger—" He broke off as the opening strains of a waltz were played. "Oh. Ah, my mistake." With a bow, he took himself off, casting one last, puzzled glance over his shoulder.

"Shall we?" Thor asked, as though it was the most natural thing in the world—as though his heart was not pounding furiously at the prospect of having Dina so close to him for a whole quarter of an hour.

Still looking confused and a bit embarrassed, she placed her hand in his and allowed him to place his other hand at her waist. "I thought—" she began.

"I know. But I felt a waltz was called for just now, and persuaded the orchestra to my opinion."

He swept her into the dance then, before she could question him further. To his surprise, their difference in height did not make waltzing awkward in the least, as he had assumed it must. She moved easily to the music, matching his steps without hesitation, seeming to float across the floor. Nymphlike,

indeed. By comparison, waltzing with Missy Fiskerton had been like trundling a handcart about.

"You especially requested a waltz?" she asked,
breaking the silence that had stretched between
them. "Why?"

"I wished to speak with you, and this seemed the
easiest way." That shimmery gown made her eyes
seem even greener in the candlelight—almost impossibly green. He didn't realize he had lapsed into
silence once more until she spoke again.

"What . . . what did you wish to say?" She
seemed nervous, almost fearful. And delicate. He
was able to span her waist with one hand, she was
so delicate.

Pulled back from his musings, he frowned. "Your
brother. What was he saying to you earlier?"

Dina stumbled, but he caught her easily, supporting almost her entire weight—such as it was—until
she caught the rhythm of the dance again. "I . . . I
don't remember." Her heightened complexion be-
lied her words.

"I rather doubt that, as it seemed to upset you. Did
he threaten you in any way?" Perhaps Moore had
tried to pressure Dina as well into annulling their
marriage? She had been in favor of that from the
first, Thor recalled with a pang.

She shook her head. "No, Silas did not threaten
me. He was rather put out that you disapproved of
his courtship of Violet, and even more put out when I
told him that I agreed with you. I . . . I take it that is
what you and he were talking about earlier, when
you looked so angry?"

"Among other things," he replied, then wished he hadn't. There were some parts of that conversation he would not repeat to Dina for the world.

"What other things?" she asked, just as he'd known she would.

Instead of answering, he twirled her, marveling at how well she responded, how gracefully she danced. "You waltz extremely well," he said, anxious to change the subject. "Perhaps I should have engaged you for every one tonight after all."

She smiled at the compliment, though her eyes were still shadowed. "Each time I dance it, it becomes easier."

Though she surely didn't intend it as such, her words were another unwelcome reminder of all of the men she'd danced with while he had been away at Ivy Lodge. Her brother's comment about being her third choice echoed unpleasantly in his ears.

"Then you have danced many waltzes in the past fortnight?" His voice came out more accusatory than he'd intended.

"Of course I did," she replied, her chin coming up defiantly. "If you did not wish me to waltz with others, you should have forbidden it before you disappeared to go foxhunting."

"I didn't realize—then—that it would be necessary," he shot back, her unexpected display of temper sparking his own—even as it inexplicably aroused him.

Her green eyes narrowed. "So you do not trust me after all. What of your apology this morning?"

"That was before I learned that your behavior has

given rise to rumors." As soon as the words were out, he regretted them.

All he had was Moore's word that any such rumors existed, and he certainly didn't consider the man a reliable source. What was it about Dina that made him blurt out whatever was in his head? That had never been a particular problem of his before.

But now the damage was done. She stared up at him with anger—and perhaps a hint of tears— sparkling in her eyes.

"Rumors? What rumors? I've done nothing to cause the least talk—unlike you, with your tall, buxom opera dancers."

Thor stared. "My what?"

She snatched her hand from his shoulder to cover her mouth. "I . . . I'm sorry. I should not have said that. I did promise before we married that if you had mistresses you could keep them. I have no right to berate you for them now."

Dumbly, Thor shook his head. Who would have told her about his past mistresses? And they were well past, as he'd not had one for more than a year. No one in his family knew, or would say anything if they did, nor would he have thought any of the local folk would—

"Did your brother tell you this?" he demanded.

She nodded silently, her face averted, her gaze apparently fixed on their feet, amazingly still flawlessly performing the steps of the waltz.

"Dina, look at me."

With obvious reluctance, she raised her eyes to his—tear-drenched eyes that tore at his heart.

"There are no opera dancers, and have not been

for quite some time—nor are there like to be in the future. I've had no desire for any other woman since meeting you."

She raised one brow skeptically, then smoothed her face into a mask of unconcern. "That is very kind of you," she said without expression.

"It's the truth."

He wanted to say more, to reassure her that he found her more alluring than any other woman he'd ever known, but he was afraid that if he gave voice to his feelings, he might commit himself to a course that could end in his harming her—and that he would not do, particularly after his talk with her brother.

They finished the waltz in silence, giving him further opportunity to admire Dina's grace and skill at the dance. It seemed that every hour in her presence, he found something new to admire about her. How could her own brother hold her in such low esteem? He clenched his teeth, anger surging through him anew at Silas Moore's insinuations.

The moment the dance ended, Violet accosted them. "Why, I've never seen a couple waltz so divinely," she exclaimed. "Everyone was commenting upon it. Is that what you two were doing this morning? Practicing together?"

Thor and Dina exchanged glances. "In a manner of speaking," he said, his body hardening unexpectedly at the memory of Dina exercising in the gymnasium.

"Then that explains your improvement, Dina, for I'll swear you did not waltz so well at the assemblies, on the one or two occasions when I convinced you to waltz at all."

"A good partner makes a big difference," Dina replied, though she was again avoiding Thor's eye.

"And a big partner makes a good difference," Violet joked. "Oh, here comes Sir Albert to dance with me again. A pity he has such a long nose—and that I've known him since we were children. That is the problem with dances here in Lincolnshire. No new faces. I cannot wait until we go to London!"

She turned to greet her partner with a brilliant smile that gave no hint of her feelings. A moment later, Horace Smallbone came forward to claim Dina.

"Now this, surely, is my dance?" he said, with a nervous glance at Thor.

Thor managed a pleasant nod. "It is. I will speak with you later, my sweet," he added to Dina, and saw her eyes widen with surprise at the endearment as he turned away.

Though he was tempted to escape the ballroom for a while, he knew his mother would ring a peal over him, so instead he solicited Miss Drinkpin, Miss Fiskerton's maiden aunt, for the set just forming. Though she must have been near forty, the lady was clearly delighted at the attention, making him glad he had made the effort.

At the conclusion of the dance he cast about for a likely partner for the next, though his mind was already on the supper dance—surely another waltz?—when he could again dance with Dina. Somehow he must make her understand just how desirable she was without breaking his promise to keep their marriage a platonic one. It was simply a matter of finding the right words.

So preoccupied was he that the music began for the next set before he had approached any of the ladies in need of partners. Shrugging, he moved to the edge of the floor, relieved to see Dina dancing with Rush this time. But then his attention sharpened as he noticed Violet paired with Silas Moore in the same set.

Frowning, he walked over to the buffet table, where Stormy was sampling the canapes. "I thought you were going to keep my sister away from Moore tonight?"

Stormy looked up from his plate in surprise. "Should I have brought a pistol to the ball? I can scarcely stand up with her for every dance, you know. As Rush pointed out to me, if I pay her too much attention, I could end up raising expectations toward myself. And sorry, old chap, but fetching as Miss Turpin has become, I'm not ready for that sort of commitment."

Thor nodded reluctantly. "I see your point. I suppose it wouldn't do to have you break her heart in the course of protecting her fortune. Just . . . keep an eye out, will you?"

"I have been." Stormy looked wounded. "And so has Rush. Rest assured, we won't let her do anything foolish like leave the room with him. I think your talking to him earlier had an effect, however, for I notice he has not so much as attempted a waltz."

"Ah. Well. Good." Thor nodded again and moved off. Moore was only biding his time, he suspected, waiting to see whether Thor would accede to his blackmail before pressing his suit with Violet any further. This dance was just to keep his oar in the water.

When the music ended again, he was startled to hear the supper dance announced. Where had the evening gone? There was some milling about, as gentlemen sought out their favorite ladies for this dance, as they would lead their partners in to supper at its conclusion.

"Well, Mr. Turpin, here we are again," exclaimed Rose Nesbit as he moved past her. "Dance with me, and I may forgive your rudeness earlier."

"My apologies, Miss Nesbit," he said with a scrupulously polite bow, "but I have already promised this dance to my wife."

To his surprise, she giggled. "Oh, you need not worry about her. My brother will be happy to take her in to supper."

Thor turned to see Jeremy Nesbit looming over Dina, a dozen feet away. She shook her head, but instead of moving off, Nesbit stepped even closer to her.

Without even bothering to excuse himself to Rose this time, Thor headed in their direction. If that whelp would not take a dismissal from Dina, he would most assuredly take one from himself. As Thor came up behind him, Mr. Nesbit glanced up at yet another of those ubiquitous kissing boughs and plucked a berry from the mistletoe.

"I presume you know what this means, Mrs. Turpin?" he said playfully, holding the berry aloft.

Thor plucked it from between his fingers. "It

means *someone* must kiss her." Nesbit turned with a start, his face paling visibly as he looked up at the much larger man. "Fortunately, I am here to relieve you of any . . . obligation."

With a wild glance from Thor to Dina and back, Nesbit mumbled some sort of incoherent excuse and scurried off. Thor watched him for a moment, then turned back to Dina, who was frowning.

"Was it really necessary to frighten the poor lad out of his wits like that? I would have evaded any attempt he made to kiss me without your aid, I assure you."

"I don't doubt it." Thor gazed down at her, struck anew by the strength and spirit housed in her small but delectable frame.

"Nor do you need to feel any *obligation* to kiss me, simply because Mr. Nesbit unwisely picked a berry off one of the decorations." She glanced away, but not before he saw the glitter of tears in her eyes.

He cursed himself for his choice of words to Nesbit. Instead of reassuring Dina that she was indeed desirable, he had done just the reverse.

"Dina," he said softly, and she turned her face bravely up to him, clearly refusing to give in to her threatening tears. Without giving himself time to think, to tell himself how very unwise this was, he bent down to touch her alluringly rosy lips with his own.

And was instantly lost. All the emotions he had been struggling to hold in check all evening crashed through him, demanding that he take possession of this woman who had somehow become the very focus of his being.

Grasping her shoulders, he pulled her closer,

deepening the kiss, oblivious to the guests around them. Dina responded without hesitation, her arms going about his neck, her head thrown back so that her curls cascaded seductively across his hands.

Yes, this was just what he'd been wanting, needing. He slid his hands down her arms, caressing, exploring—but then the opening strains of a waltz broke the silence, and he abruptly remembered where they were. Lifting his head, he stared at her dazedly, dimly aware that all around them people were laughing and murmuring.

"Would you . . . care to dance?" he asked.

Chapter 16

$\sim\!\!\sim\!\!\sim\!\!\sim\!\!\sim$

Dina blinked, clearing the warm, red haze from her vision. "Of . . . of course," she murmured. How could she have so completely forgotten where she was?

Before a sea of interested eyes, they converted their embrace into the proper stance that the waltz demanded. After that kiss, the loose clasp of hands and light touch at shoulder and waist seemed both too intimate and not intimate enough. Moving mechanically to the music, Dina had to exert every bit of her willpower to keep from flinging herself back into Thor's embrace.

As the dance progressed, her perspective slowly returned. She told herself that he had had no choice but to kiss her. It would have seemed odd if he had not, after chasing away young Jeremy Nesbit. He'd likely intended only a quick kiss, a fulfilling of tradition, but then she had turned it into something quite different.

Suddenly overcome by embarrassment, she kept her eyes averted from Thor's. What must he think of her, now that she had revealed her feelings so blatantly? Gazing off to the side, she encountered the stares of their fellow dancers, some amused, some curious. Rose Nesbit, waltzing with her brother, shot her a look of pure venom. Dina redirected her gaze to Thor's shirtfront.

His very broad shirtfront. What would the chest beneath it look like, feel like . . . taste like? No, she mustn't think of such things, or she would never make it through the evening without embarrassing herself even further.

"How late is the ball like to go?" she asked, simply for the sake of saying something.

Thor gave a slight shrug that made his muscles ripple under her hand on his shoulder. "There will be more dancing after supper. Knowing my mother, she will have the musicians play for as long as anyone is willing to stay."

His voice sounded odd, husky. Dina risked a quick peek up at him and found him watching her intently, no trace of censure in his expression. She managed a tentative smile. "I will try not to put you in such an awkward situation again."

One corner of his mouth tilted up, charmingly, she thought. "I felt no awkwardness until it was over. And the fault was Nesbit's, not yours."

Did he mean to ignore her immodest response to his kiss, then? She breathed a sigh of relief before it occurred to her that perhaps he hadn't even noticed it—that the passion she'd felt crackling between them was purely on her side.

"Of . . . of course." Whether that was the case or not, she couldn't seem to bank the flames that had been ignited. Her whole body seemed scorched by his touch, his nearness, and there was no escape while this waltz lasted.

"I hope I have not spoiled your evening," he said.

Shocked, she wondered if he could read her thoughts. "Spoiled—? Of course not." Turned it into sweet torture, perhaps, but spoiled? No, certainly not that.

"I'm glad. Please believe that your happiness is exceedingly important to me."

Was it her imagination, or had his grip on her hand tightened as he said that? Glancing away again, she saw Lady Rumble waltzing nearby with her husband. She smiled and nodded encouragingly, but Dina pretended not to see, as she could not bring herself to smile back. At least she was reassured to know that the baroness was not put out that their kiss had gone somewhat beyond the bounds of propriety.

"I did not have a chance before to apologize for what I said." His voice was still low, serious.

Startled, she looked up at him again. "What you said?"

"About those supposed rumors. Your brother mentioned them, but I should have known he was not telling the truth. I begin to realize that he is more skilled in deception than I'd given him credit for."

That forced a sour laugh from her. "Yes, Silas has

never had much use for the truth, unless it suited his purposes."

Her brother had always been very quick to discover the fears and weaknesses of others and then play upon them, she recalled, which was doubtless why he had mentioned Thor's mistresses, even though he must have known none was current.

"I wish to apologize as well. Knowing my brother as I do, I had even less cause to believe him."

Thor guided her past the buffet table, now laden with more substantial fare for supper. "You already apologized," he reminded her.

"For throwing your supposed mistresses in your face, but not for believing you still kept them," she clarified. "You have given me no cause to . . . to complain."

That wasn't exactly what she meant, but how could she tell him that the better she came to know him, the more she felt certain that her future, her happiness, was safe in his keeping, whether he ever grew to desire her or not?

"And I will endeavor never to give you such cause," he said seriously.

Striving to lighten the mood between them, for fear she might reveal more than was wise, she forced a smile.

"As you are only human, I will try not to hold you to such an impossible standard. I've no doubt I will give you reasons to complain upon occasion as well, for we are neither of us perfect." She had to admit that he was as close to perfect as any man she'd ever met, however.

As she'd hoped, he responded with a chuckle. "Fair enough. But enough of apologies and regrets. Are you enjoying the ball thus far?"

Enjoying? Her emotions had been in too much turmoil for true enjoyment, but Dina did feel happier than she had for a fortnight—since Thor had disappeared to the Shires after their last kiss. She devoutly hoped he wouldn't do so again.

"It has been a most . . . stimulating evening," she was able to respond truthfully.

"It certainly has." Something in his tone made her glance up, and the intensity in his blue eyes, the suggestiveness of his smile, suddenly convinced her that she was not the only one who had been affected by that kiss.

Hesitantly, she smiled back, but could think of nothing to say that would not take them into dangerous territory. Thankfully, before the silence between them could become awkward again, the music ended and supper was announced.

"I declare, I could watch the two of you waltz forever, you are so well matched," Lady Rumble exclaimed, hurrying over to them as they headed toward the supper tables. "I was just telling Lord Rumble so, wasn't I, dear?"

The baron inclined his head, his eyes twinkling. "You were indeed, though I was so entranced by your dancing, my dear, that I scarcely noticed."

"Flatterer." She gave her husband a playful tap with her fan. "But come, you two, you must sit at our table for supper and tell me what you think of my little party."

There was no question of refusing, though Dina

worried that she would not be able to conceal her preoccupation—no, obsession—with Thor and worried what her enterprising mother-in-law might say if she noticed. Her trepidation only increased when Lady Rumble waved Violet and Silas over to join them.

"Now, this is a nice family party, is it not?" Their hostess beamed about the small table at her companions. "Do tell me that you are having a nice time this evening."

They all assured her that they were, and Violet added, "Mother, you must know that this will be the most talked-of ball in the district for months—perhaps years—to come. Everyone is saying so. Your kissing boughs, in particular, have attracted quite a lot of attention."

"Yes, that was a happy inspiration of mine, was it not? Lady Vaile tells me there may be at least one betrothal in the neighborhood as a result." Lady Rumble tittered. "Not to mention a few married couples who have taken advantage of them." She winked at Dina and Thor.

Dina felt heat rushing to her face and had no idea where to look. Her darting eyes fell upon Silas for a moment, to find him glowering at her—which, paradoxically, lightened her mood enough to mitigate her embarrassment somewhat. Clearly he had witnessed Thor kissing her, and that, she decided, was no bad thing.

"I only hope, my dear, that no scandals will arise that can be attributed to your decor," Lord Rumble said blandly before applying himself to his roast beef.

But his wife seemed unconcerned. "Scandals,

pfft. A few little kisses are scarcely like to lead to scandal. Though you, missy," she added to Violet, "will keep well away from the things, as I told you this afternoon."

"Of course, Mother." Though Violet's voice was meekness itself, there was an amusement in her eyes that made Dina glance at Silas. To her relief, however, he appeared more petulant than smug.

"You need not worry about Miss Turpin, Lady Rumble," he said then. "Between her brother and his friends, I can't imagine that she will have the least opportunity to get into any sort of trouble tonight."

"Yes, they've all been most attentive," Violet agreed with a sigh. "Despite their efforts, however, I can't claim the evening has been dull."

Dina had to agree with that sentiment. Beside her, Thor began to eat, and she was almost painfully aware of every bite he took. The way his hand held his fork, the motion of lifting it to his lips, the way he opened and closed his mouth, all struck her as unbearably erotic. How could the others not notice?

Belatedly she turned her attention to her own plate and realized that she was indeed hungry after hours of dancing. Still, remembering Thor's comment about her appetite that afternoon, she was careful not to eat too quickly. Besides, the longer she could occupy herself with her food, the longer she could distract herself from Thor's most distracting nearness.

His thigh was separated from hers by several inches, but she could still feel the warmth of him radiating toward her. Her thoughts went back to that morning in the gymnasium and the way those thighs had flexed and straightened as he worked on the rings. The way the muscles of his arms had rippled and swelled. She set down her fork and took a long draught of lemonade.

"Dancing is hot work, is it not?" Violet asked brightly from across the table. "I vow, it makes me thirsty as well."

But Dina was fairly certain it was not the dancing alone that had made her hot. Surely, in that case, she would be feeling cooler by now, rather than the reverse?

"You two seem unusually quiet," Silas remarked a few moments later. "I hope nothing is wrong?"

Dina met his falsely solicitous gaze with a deliberate smile. "Of course not, Silas. Why should you think so?"

"Indeed," Lady Rumble commented, "from what I observed, I should say things are finally coming right. In fact, the two of you can consider your social obligation fulfilled, if you should wish to retire early. I will be glad to make your excuses and will take not the tiniest bit of offense, I assure you."

This was unforeseen, though Dina realized it should not have been, given Lady Rumble's prior machinations. If she or Thor now made excuses to stay, it would only give Silas further evidence that their marriage was not as it should be. But if they went upstairs together . . .

A delightful, fearful shiver went through her, though she strove to conceal it.

Beside her, Thor cleared his throat. "That is very kind of you, Mother, but—"

"—but we hesitated to suggest it, for fear it would

put too great a burden upon you and Violet for the remainder of the evening," Dina broke in, conscious of her brother's eye on her. "If you are certain that will not be the case, however . . . ?"

"No, no, not in the least," Lady Rumble protested. "Now supper is served, I've nothing left to do but make certain our guests get into their proper carriages and accept their compliments for the evening. That, I assure you, I can well manage without your help."

"And if she does need help, I will be here," Violet added, not bothering to hide her delight at this development.

Thor opened his mouth, no doubt to form another protest, but Dina caught his eye and gave a quick shake of her head. She would explain her reasons as soon as they were alone. Meanwhile, he looked distinctly alarmed—though not as alarmed as Silas did.

"My lady, are you certain—" Silas began, only to have Violet punch him in the side.

"If you say anything to keep them here, I'll never speak to you again," she whispered, but so audibly that Dina had no doubt that everyone at the table— and perhaps the nearby ones as well—could hear her.

Embarrassed but determined, Dina rose. "I believe we will take advantage of your generous offer, Lady Rumble, and bid you all a good night."

She had told Silas outright that she and Thor had consummated their marriage and now refused to give him any indication that she had lied. Indeed, if Thor had the least spark of desire for her, she was determined that by morning her falsehood would be truth.

* * *

Mechanically, wondering whether he had gone mad—or if Dina had—Thor accompanied her from the ballroom. The past hour of waltzing and then dining with Dina had been sweet torture. Already his resolve was weakening, here among his mother's guests. Alone with Dina, his tenuous control might well snap completely.

Or not. Surely her intent was simply to escape the crowd and go early to bed? That would free him from her maddening presence, from fantasies he could never allow to become reality, for her sake. For tonight. Tomorrow the torture would begin again.

"I'm not surprised you are tired," he said as soon as they had left the crowded ballroom behind, the musicians already tuning their instruments for the resumption of dancing. "You have had a long and exhausting—but productive—day."

"Tired?" she echoed, slanting a glance up at him. "I am not tired. Did you really think that was why I seized upon your mother's suggestion?"

He was suddenly aware of her hand on his arm, of how isolated they were as they traversed the passageway, all the servants busy with the ball. "Er, wasn't it?"

Dina shook her head, the little curls about her face swaying in an impossibly fetching manner. "It . . . it was Silas," she said, "or at least partly Silas. He taunted me earlier, saying that ours was not . . . not a proper marriage. I, ah, told him he was wrong."

They had reached the stairs leading up to the next floor—to their bedchambers. Thor paused at their foot, forcing Dina to do the same. Her averted face was pink—understandably so, for he shared her embarrassment.

"You told your brother that I . . . that we . . ."

"That we had consummated our marriage." Her voice was so faint that he had to stoop slightly to catch it.

Thor wasn't sure whether to laugh or curse. What a blow that news must have been to Moore's plan to regain Dina's fortune. But would he now fulfill his threat to ruin Violet's—and Dina's—reputations? Perhaps not.

"I, ah, may have implied the opposite when I spoke with him," he felt obliged to confess.

Dina looked up at him, clearly startled, her face now paling. After a long moment of silence, however, a sickly laugh escaped her. "No wonder he seemed so stunned by my assertion. I thought it was only Violet who had—that is—"

Belatedly, Thor realized that this was hardly the place for such a conversation. "Come, let's go upstairs." Not until she sent him a questioning glance did it occur to him that his suggestion might be misconstrued.

With every step, he was more and more aware of her nearness, her allure, his every fiber straining toward her though he continued implacably forward, their only point of contact her light touch on his arm. As they turned down the west wing, he forced himself to speak again.

"I did not actually tell your brother anything, but it was clear he considered my lack of response to his impertinent questions a sort of admission."

"So you did not precisely make me out a liar? I

suppose I must be glad of that, at least." He thought he detected a shimmer of unshed tears in her eyes.

He tried to think of some way to reassure her, but when they reached the door of her chamber, she spoke again.

"Pray do not think that I was trying to force you to do anything you do not wish to do. I was merely goaded beyond prudence by Silas's taunts. It was wrong of me, for I know that you do not—that is—"

Thor could not help himself. She looked so sorrowful, so beautiful . . . He grasped her shoulders and pulled her to him, covering her mouth with his own.

As before, the connection was instant, searing, robbing him of the ability to think. Gathering her slight frame against him, he intensified the kiss, striving to prove to her how very desirable she was—how very much he desired her.

As she had beneath the kissing bough, Dina responded at once, seeming to submit herself wholeheartedly to his kiss. Parting her lips, she invited him to plunder her sweetness, even as her hands stroked his shoulders, then pulled him yet closer.

After a long, ecstatic moment out of time, he reluctantly released her, dimly aware that if he waited any longer, he would be unable to do so.

"As you can see, it is by no means a question of my not wanting a 'proper marriage,' as you called it," he said, his voice rough with passion barely held in check. "Quite the reverse."

She gazed up at him, her rosy, swollen lips erotically parted, her eyes shining. "Truly, Thor?"

It was the first time she'd called him by that nickname. On her lips it took on a new meaning, one he longed to fulfill. She made him feel more powerful than he ever had before—a heady feeling. And a frightening one.

"I can't deny that I want you, Dina, more than I've ever wanted a woman. You . . . you intoxicate me. But—I promised."

"I release you from your promise," she responded promptly, her eyes still shining. "I want this, too." She reached behind her and opened her chamber door so that he could see her bed, the counterpane turned down invitingly. There was no sign of her maid.

A shudder went through him, so strong was the urge to carry her to that bed, to release his overwhelming need into her. She reached up and touched his cheek with one small, smooth hand, inflaming him further.

"Thor?" Her use of his nickname was incredibly erotic, making him feel like the Norse god himself, capable of anything.

Including injuring her.

"I . . . I can't, Dina. I could so easily hurt you. Perhaps your brother is right and an annulment would be best after all, for your sake. I'd never forgive myself if—"

She silenced him by pulling his mouth down to hers for another long, scorching kiss. "You won't hurt me," she whispered against his lips. "Don't you know by now that I am no fragile flower?"

He swallowed, his heart pounding with the rhythm of his desire, his erection straining powerfully against his tight, formal knee breeches. He allowed her to lead him into her chamber and close the door, too preoccupied with fighting the strongest temptation of his life to protest. Not until she began to unbutton his coat did reason reassert itself.

"What—what are you doing?" he asked hoarsely.

"What we both want." Her voice was as breathless as his. The knowledge that she desired him nearly put him over the edge again.

"Wants are not always safe," he forced himself to say. "The risks—"

"I promise to be gentle with you," she teased, kissing him again. His buttons undone, she now pushed his coat off his shoulders and went to work on his cravat.

With a groan, he caught her to him and returned her kiss, losing himself in her sweetness once again. He wanted this. She wanted this. They were man and wife. Perhaps if he supported his weight—

His weight. That was the problem. But—"I have an idea," he said, suddenly smiling. "Come."

Pulling his cravat the rest of the way off, he tossed it over the foot of her bed and opened her chamber door. A quick glance showed the hallway still deserted—as was every part of the house, no doubt, except the ballroom and the kitchens.

"Where are we going?" There was a trace of frustration in her voice, but if his plan worked, it would not be there for long.

"You'll see." With an arm about her slender shoulders, he picked up a candle and led her down the back stairs, all the way to the ground floor, then turned left.

"You're taking me to the gymnasium?" she asked incredulously.

"Not exactly."

His heart pounding with anticipation, hoping desperately that his idea would work, he led her through the gymnasium and down the stairs to the long room housing the swimming pool. He then pulled closed the double doors—doors that had never been closed in his memory—and locked them.

"We're, ah, not exactly dressed for swimming," Dina said, looking down at her lovely, emerald-green ball gown.

Thor smiled. "Not yet."

Setting the candle on a small table, he pulled his shirt over his head and draped it over one of the wooden chairs near the wall. He turned back to Dina, whose eyes were wide—but not frightened.

"Now, why don't you let me help you out of your things," he suggested.

Chapter 17

~~~ ⚬⚬ ~~~

Dina swallowed, her eyes tracing the broad lines of Thor's bare chest in the flickering light of the single candle. She'd been right. It—he—was a most impressive sight, indeed. The muscles she'd only been able to guess at that morning were now revealed in all their sleek, rippling glory. She swallowed again.

"Dina?" His voice was soft, smooth—as smooth as the golden flesh that riveted her gaze.

Blinking, she glanced up. "I, ah, yes. Yes, of course. My clothes." She felt her skin heating with anticipation, now that she knew what he had in mind. The moment she'd known for certain that he desired her, in the hallway upstairs, her insecurities, her hesitation, had vanished. She would not draw back now.

"If you can just unfasten these hooks down the back—?"

"Of course."

She held her breath as he moved behind her, tensing slightly for the first touch of his hands. When it came, his fingers brushing the nape of her neck, tiny shivers ran down her spine, her arms, the backs of her legs. Was it possible for every nerve in one's body to feel at once?

As he undid hook after hook, the heat where he touched her was followed by coolness as the gown parted down the back. Delicious coolness, she thought, a taste of what the water would feel like when they entered it. Warmth suddenly rushed to her cheeks, making her glad he could not see her face just at that moment.

"I don't want to sully your gown," he murmured when he reached the last hook, just below her waist. "Can you—?"

Not trusting her voice, she nodded. Carefully stepping out of the dress, she turned—not quite facing him—to drape it next to his shirt.

"I see your corset laces down the back, as well."

Again she nodded mutely. He apparently understood it for the invitation it was, for he moved close behind her and set to work at once unlacing it. This time the chill as it opened was more pronounced—and even more welcome. She wasn't certain her body would not burst into flames before the pool could quench them.

When he'd laid her corset aside, leaving her clad only in her shift, she finally turned to look at him, and the delicious power of his naked torso struck her anew. "Now what?"

His smile was slow, seductive. "We won't want to get our undergarments wet, either, so it seems wisest to remove those as well."

She glanced back at the locked doors, then around the room to reassure herself that there was not some other entrance she had never noticed before.

"All . . . all of them?" Her voice squeaked slightly on the second "all," and she suddenly felt foolish. Of course they would have to have their clothes off to . . . to . . . Wouldn't they?

"Unless you'd rather not." His voice was so gentle she nearly melted on the spot.

"No, I'd rather. I'd definitely rather." To prove her words, she bent down and took off her dancing slippers, then lifted the hem of her shift to untie her garters. The first came undone easily enough, but the second caught and knotted.

Swiftly, as though it was the most natural thing in the world, Thor knelt at her feet. "Here, let me."

She caught her breath and willed herself to stillness as he slid his hands up her calf to the garter, tied just above her knee. His fingers fumbled with the knot, sending streaks of flame up her leg to the juncture of her thighs.

"Hard to believe these little bits of lace can hold a lady's stockings up for a whole evening of dancing." She'd have thought he was commenting about the weather, if not for the slight tremor in his voice. "There. I hope I haven't ruined it."

She took the garter from him and glanced at it.

"No, it . . . it seems fine," she said, with no idea whether it was true or not. What the devil did she care about a garter at a time like this?

"Good," he said, just as though it mattered. With a single, smooth movement, he was back on his feet, towering over her, his bare chest so close that she could touch it—if only she dared.

Where was her earlier boldness now? Dina lifted a tentative hand, then hesitated. "You don't intend to swim in your shoes and breeches, do you?" There. That was bold enough—for now.

His slow smile made her wonder whether he guessed her thoughts—and her cowardice.

"You're right." Bending from the waist, he unbuckled his shoes and kicked them over to the chair that held their clothing. Next he removed his hose, revealing calves as muscular as the rest of him. Then, straightening, he began to unfasten his breeches.

Suddenly Dina didn't know what to do with her eyes. It seemed as awkward and cowardly to look elsewhere as it seemed forward and immodest to watch. She compromised by focusing on his face—until he glanced up and captured her gaze with his own.

"You don't intend to swim in your shift, do you?" he asked, echoing her question to him.

Belatedly she realized she did have something to do other than stare. Turning half away to hide her embarrassment, she untied the ribbons at the front of her shift, loosening the low neckline. Then, her face still averted, she pushed it from her shoulders and past her waist and stepped out of it, as she had her gown.

It felt exceedingly strange to be completely naked, a state she'd only experienced before when stepping into or out of a bath. According to legend, Atalanta had raced this way, but Dina realized she was no Atalanta. It took every ounce of her courage simply to turn around, heart hammering in her chest, and face her husband.

While her back had been turned, he had also finished divesting himself of the last of his clothing. He now stood between her and the pool, looking like a magnificent Greek sculpture, though of smooth, golden flesh instead of marble.

For a long moment, she drank in the glorious sight of him, too overcome to remember her own awkwardness. His broad chest tapered down to a relatively narrow waist, slim hips, and powerful thighs. And—goodness! None of the drawings of Greek statues she had seen had given any hint of the size of his . . . his . . . No fig leaf would ever cover that!

Startled, her gaze flicked to his face, to find him watching her. "Well?" he asked, one brow arching in wary amusement.

"I . . . I never . . . that is . . ."

"I hope you're not disappointed?"

She gave her head a fervent shake. "Quite the reverse. I'd tried to imagine, but—"

Not until she saw the relief in his sudden smile did she realize that he'd actually been worried she might recoil from the sight of his unclad body.

"I've done a lot of imagining myself," he confided then, "and I must say that the reality far eclipses fantasy."

How much better he put it than she had, she

thought, then belatedly remembered that she was as naked as he, exposed to his gaze—which, to her own relief, was frankly admiring.

"I . . . I'm glad," she stammered, resisting a strong urge to cover herself with her hands. "What do you suggest we do now?"

He grinned. "I thought that was obvious."

Confused, she dropped her gaze. "I mean, do we get into the pool, or—?" She couldn't resist peering through her lashes at that most amazing portion of his anatomy. How could it possibly—?

"Yes, that was my idea. Here." He took one step forward and put a large, warm arm about her shoulders, guiding her toward the steps leading down into the shallow end of the small pool. "Violet tells me you can swim?"

She nodded. "Yes, of course, but that wasn't what you had in mind tonight. Er, was it?"

"We can begin with a swim. No need to rush anything, as we have all night." He stepped into the water, drawing her with him.

The water deliciously engulfed her ankles, her calves, noticeably warmer than the surrounding air, its mineral tang sharp in her nostrils. The hot spring, she knew, was at the deeper end, continuously circulating the water, keeping it at the perfect temperature, neither too hot nor too cold.

"This pool is an engineering marvel," she commented, mainly for something to say, and to distract herself from what lay ahead. "Your grandfather was a very clever man."

"He had the vision, yes, but he also had the funds to employ the finest engineers of his time to help him realize it. I confess, having grown up with this pool in the house, I've tended to take it for granted, but it is likely unique."

"I've certainly never heard of anything like it."

Together they stepped deeper and deeper into the water until it lapped against Dina's breasts and Thor's waist, hiding that most fascinating part of him—not that she'd actually been looking, of course.

When the water reached her shoulders and was midway up his chest, he said, "Shall we paddle around a bit? I used to sneak down here and swim nude on occasion as a young boy, but I've not done so in nearly twenty years."

In answer, Dina lifted her feet and stroked forward, keeping her head above the water, mindful of her elaborately upswept hair. The water swirling against her breasts, between her legs, felt like a caress—indescribably erotic. She hoped he did not mean them to simply swim for long.

"I see Violet was right." His voice, right beside her, made her start guiltily. "You are quite an adept swimmer." He matched her pace with no apparent effort.

"As are you." Her voice was breathless, but not from exertion.

His grin was only a flash of teeth in the dim light, as they were now some distance from the candle. "Did we not compliment each other's dancing similarly? It seems we are well matched in more ways than I had realized."

They reached the far end of the pool, which Dina knew was six or seven feet deep, then turned and headed back. They had gone only a few strokes, however, when Thor stopped.

"Come here, Dina."

She turned toward him, putting one leg down, only to discover that she was still well out of her depth, though Thor was standing, the water lapping his shoulders. She took the hand he held out to her, and he drew her to him through the water, releasing her just before her bare breasts would have grazed his chest.

For a moment she treaded water, but that made her bob foolishly about him. Gathering her courage, she put her hands on his shoulders, allowing him to be her anchor, her face on a level with his, for once.

"See? Now I don't have to stoop," he said, echoing her thought, just before he put one firm hand behind her back and pulled her against him for a kiss.

There were almost more new sensations than Dina could take in at once—the roughness of the hair on his chest against her sensitive breasts, the feel of his hands on her bare back, the dreamlike sensation of floating, effortlessly, in his embrace. And his kiss, which flamed her desires more intensely than ever before, abetted by the rest.

She pressed herself more tightly against him, her arms now around his neck, her legs instinctively coming up to twine themselves around his waist. She gave a small gasp, shocked at herself, for that movement put her feminine cleft only inches above his rampant maleness. Indeed, she could feel its tip grazing the back of her thigh.

"Oh! I didn't mean—" She started to pull away, but he clasped her to him.

"It's all right, you didn't hurt me. You're being as gentle as you promised," he murmured. "We merely need to make a small, ah, adjustment."

Kissing her again, he moved forward, up the sloping floor of the pool. As he did so, she felt herself sliding downward against him, her breasts, her opened cleft, rubbing against his chest and stomach, sending a new surge of desire through her.

She clung to him, unsure of what she was supposed to do, but then his hands slid down her back to cup her buttocks, both supporting and guiding her until his shaft teased at the very spot that most hungered for his touch. Slowly, gently, he lowered her onto it, then, just as she was bracing herself for the inevitable thrust, he lifted her again.

Her mouth still fastened to his, she whimpered at the loss of contact. Surely—? Yes, now he was lowering her again, further this time, until she could feel the size of him invading her, stretching her. And then, once more, he raised her higher, depriving her of that glorious sensation.

Only for a moment. Again he let her drift downward, onto his impossibly hard erection, then lifted her, then lowered her again, each time deeper, quicker, until they were locked in a rhythm that drove them both inexorably toward a goal she couldn't quite fathom. She only knew that she would die if she did not reach it.

The water made his hands, his body, as slick and smooth as butter, but the sheer size of him provided friction enough to push her nearer and nearer to that crisis she craved. As she began to think her body might ignite, turning all the pool to steam, he slid one hand under her thigh to touch her sensitive nubbin, even as he continued his primal rhythm within her.

With a cry that echoed through the long room, Dina threw her head back and let herself fall, impaling herself on him more deeply yet. The water, the world, seemed to shatter around her, or perhaps her body itself turned to water, flowing out in all directions in waves of pure pleasure.

Dimly, echoing through what little awareness she had left of anything beyond her own ecstasy, she heard Thor give a loud groan. She wrapped her arms and legs tightly about him as he surged up into her, over and over, until he paused, his muscles as hard and taut as tempered steel, while she felt him pulsing, pulsing within her.

As they both spiraled down, gradually relaxing, Dina recalled vaguely that she'd heard there would be pain the first time. But there had been no pain at all. Only pleasure. More pleasure than she'd imagined could exist in any one time and place.

Slowly, gently, Thor raised her up again, to kiss her lingeringly on the lips. Then he pulled back to examine her face with tender concern. "I hope I didn't—"

"May we do that again, please?" she asked before he could finish. "Now?"

He blinked. "What?"

She knew she sounded wanton, but she didn't care. "I've never enjoyed anything so much in my life. I had no idea—that is—thank you. Will it always be like this?"

Thor felt relief explode through him almost as strongly as his passion had a few moments earlier. He hadn't hurt her. Hadn't given her a disgust or, worse, a fear of him. The sudden release of anxiety made him chuckle.

"Did I say something funny?" she asked, pushing against his chest as though to escape his embrace.

Still chuckling, he caught her to him again, running his hands over her back, her buttocks, her lovely curves. His. His own tiny Venus, perfect in every way.

"Not funny, no—just unexpected," he finally answered when she was beginning to frown. "I'm more delighted than I can express that you found this pleasurable."

She was still frowning. "Didn't you? I thought—"

"More than anything I've ever experienced. My thanks to you, as well. As for whether it will always be like this, I suppose only time will tell us that."

He realized, almost with surprise, that he had not exaggerated in the least. No woman had ever brought him to such bliss, an ecstasy that left every other encounter far behind. Perhaps he and Dina really were formed for each other. It seemed the only explanation.

Or maybe it was the water. He'd never before—

"So, may we?"

She was serious, he realized. She was also shivering. "You're cold."

"Not cold. Perhaps not as hot as I was before— well, maybe a little bit cold," she admitted, shivering again. "I've never spent so long in the pool before.

But if we can do that again, I'm sure I will warm up at once." She pulled herself tight against him again and kissed his jaw.

Already Thor felt himself responding, so it was with genuine regret that he shook his head. "No, we need to get you out of the water, not deplete your energy further."

He caught her about the waist and knees, cradling her as he walked toward the steps, hoping she would not catch a serious chill. She was so delicate, for all she was more passionate than any woman he'd ever known.

"I can walk, you know," she protested, half laughingly, as he carried her up the broad steps. "Though I'd rather . . . you know." She rubbed her cheek against his chest, catlike.

Chuckling, he set her down—and her knees buckled. He caught her easily before she could fall, but now he regarded her with sharpened concern. "Are you certain you are all right?"

"I'm fine, I'm fine," she insisted, stepping away from his embrace to prove her words. To his relief, she did not stumble. "I became too accustomed to the water, that is all."

Seemingly embarrassed, she walked over to the niche in the wall that held a stack of rough linen towels. Though still somewhat worried, he couldn't help appreciating her shapely backside as she moved across the room. She wrapped a towel about her torso and brought another back for him.

"You're still shivering," he pointed out, draping the second towel about her shoulders instead of using it himself. "Let's get you dried off and dressed."

"Then we're not going to—?" She looked genuinely disappointed. And impossibly seductive, gazing up at him with her lips parted, still swollen from his kisses, and the towel dipping down to reveal the tops of her breasts.

"Not now," he said firmly, as much to himself as to her. "Besides, it must be nearly three, and tomorrow—or, rather, today—is Christmas Day."

"Christmas! Goodness, I'd nearly forgotten."

He fetched another towel and wrapped it around his waist, then returned to help her dry off thoroughly before drying himself. Amazingly, her hair was barely damp, which he considered a mercy. She'd be that much less likely to catch a chill.

Quickly, efficiently, giving himself no time to savor the touch of her body, he helped her into her shift, stockings, corset, and gown. Not until she was fully clothed and tying up her shoes did he begin dressing himself.

He kept glancing at her as he fastened his breeches and buckled his shoes, alert for any more signs that he had overtaxed her strength. Guilt assailed him. What if he had caused her some lasting harm, simply to sate his own desires? Looking up, she caught his eyes on her.

"I'm perfectly all right. Don't you believe me?"

"I believe that you believe it," he hedged. "As your husband, it's my responsibility—"

She turned to face him fully, her expression exasperated. "Honestly, Thor, I'm twenty-five years old, not a child, and I'm as healthy as a horse. Half an hour in comfortably cool water is not going to injure me in any way."

"Perhaps not, but I'd prefer not to take any unnecessary risks." Was he being overprotective? Almost from the moment he'd met her, she had brought out his protective instincts, but now that he'd made her truly his, they seemed to have increased tenfold. "Come, let's go up to bed."

He draped the wet towels over the rack set up for that purpose, picked up the candle, and went to unlock the doors, trying to decide whether making love with Dina in the pool had really been the perfect solution he'd first thought it.

As they approached the center of the house, he could hear the faint hum of voices still emanating from the direction of the ballroom, though the musicians seemed to have stopped playing. No doubt the last of the guests were saying their good-byes and calling for their carriages.

To lessen the chance that they might encounter anyone, he again headed for the back stairs. Dina walked at his side, silent, making him wonder what she was thinking. Was she beginning to have regrets for what they had done? At least she had stopped shivering, he noted with relief.

Not until they again stood outside their chamber doors did she speak. "Will you join me in my room, or would you like me to sleep in yours?"

He frowned, startled. "I'm not sure either would be wise." In a bed, he could not so easily avoid hurting her, and he had no illusions that he would be able to resist her charms. Not now.

She looked confused. "But now that we—that is—

we don't need the pool for our enjoyment, surely?"

"I think it safest," he replied, trying to blot out the enticing image of her in his bed, sleeping with his body against her, feeling—

"Safest. For me, do you mean?"

He nodded. "Once the weather is warmer, you will be less likely to become chilled." He wouldn't risk her health any more than he would risk injuring her.

"But we may not even be at Plumrose then. Are we not to take Violet to London next month? I can't imagine there will be a convenient body of water inside your aunt's town house."

That reminded him of Silas Moore's veiled threats that evening. Now that an annulment was completely out of the question, would he attempt to carry out either or both of them? He'd been so bewitched by Dina that he hadn't given it any thought until now.

"You're frowning again. Are you plotting to convince your aunt to build a pool, perhaps?" She took his hand in hers. "Come, let me prove to you that's not necessary."

He was tempted to let her do just that—so powerfully tempted, in fact, that it frightened him. Gently, trying not to hurt her feelings, he disengaged his hand. "Much as I would like that, this is not the time. It has been a long day—and night—and you need your sleep."

"But—"

"Good night, Dina." Bending down, he cut off her protest with a kiss—a mere touch of the lips that still almost stirred him to madness—then turned away and escaped into his room before he could reconsider. Taking a deep breath, he stepped forward to allow his valet to help him out of his things.

He simply had to find a way to control himself around Dina. If he did not, how long would it be before he hurt her? Not just by allowing her to become chilled in the pool, but truly hurt her? And now he had less confidence than ever in his ability to hold himself back.

For far from slaking his appetite for Dina, as he'd half hoped it would, tonight's encounter had only whetted it. Indeed, he now doubted he would ever have enough of her, even if they visited the pool every night for the rest of their lives.

He should have insisted on an annulment when there was still time.

Chapter 18

❧❧❧

Dina stared at Thor's closed door in stunned disbelief. She had all but begged him to take her to his bed, and he had rejected her. Though he claimed it was for her sake, she wondered. Surely, if he had enjoyed their lovemaking as much as she had, he would not have been able to resist another opportunity for pleasure, given so much encouragement from her.

A sudden rush of embarrassment heated her cheeks. In her inexperience, had she done something wrong? Perhaps he had merely been polite when he said she brought him the most pleasure he'd ever experienced. If that were the case, his resistance to her invitation was no strange thing after all.

But . . . could that truly be the case? She relived those ecstatic moments in the pool, remembering how he had clasped her to him, how he had groaned with pleasure at his release. How delighted he had seemed at her own enjoyment.

Certainly she had not exaggerated that in the least. Never, in her most erotic dreams, had she imagined how wonderful the physical side of marriage could be. How foolish that she had once dreaded it.

Perhaps, even now, she could convince him—

She took a step toward his door, her hand outstretched to knock, then hesitated, desire battling with pride. Suddenly weariness washed over her, making her sway where she stood. Dimly, she heard a clock somewhere downstairs chiming three.

Yawning, she turned back to her own chamber. She would figure out what to do, how to feel, tomorrow. Thor was right that it had been an extremely full day and evening. Calisthenics in the gymnasium in the morning, Silas' arrival in the afternoon, helping with the decorations after that, and the ball itself in the evening. Hours of dancing, and then . . .

Despite her wounded pride, she smiled as she opened the door to her chamber.

"Is the ball finally over, then, ma'am?" Francine greeted her sleepily, rising from the chair where she'd been dozing. "Here, let me help you out of your things. Ma'am?" she prompted, when Dina continued to gaze dreamily into space, reliving her memories yet again. "Are you all right?"

"What? Oh, yes. Yes, of course. I am beyond tired, that is all."

But that wasn't all. She was a woman now, in every sense of the word. She yawned again. Tomorrow she would figure out exactly what that meant.

* * *

Dina awoke to bright, wintry sunlight streaming across her bed. Startled, she sat up. "Goodness. What time is it?" she said aloud.

At the sound of her own voice, all the memories from last night came flooding back—the sweet as well as the bitter—followed by a sudden fear. Would Thor have disappeared again, as he had after their first kiss?

"It's half past eleven, ma'am." Francine popped into the room as she answered Dina's question. "Mr. Turpin said I wasn't to wake you, but I figured you'd want to go down right away whenever you did wake up."

"Mr. Turpin is downstairs, then?"

Francine nodded.

Dina's spirits lifted at the removal of that fear, which she now realized, on reflection, had been rather absurd. Of course he would not have left on Christmas Day. That did not necessarily mean he had not wanted to, however.

"Have all the rest of the household been up for hours?" Dina asked then, with a belated sense of guilt. How terrible to oversleep on Christmas of all days.

"Oh, no, ma'am. Everyone is getting what you might call a late start today, what with the ball last night and all. Mr. Turpin and his two gentlemen friends were up earlier, but the others are just now going downstairs."

Relieved, Dina hurried to wash and dress, skipping her morning calisthenics routine. As she left the room, she found herself breathlessly impatient to see Thor again. She strove to subdue her excitement, reminding herself that she had no idea how he might act toward her today.

A buzz of voices led her to the dining room, but she hesitated just outside the door. What if Thor acted as though nothing had happened at all? She wasn't sure she could bear it. If he did not, however, if he greeted her tenderly, would everyone else guess what they had done last night? She didn't know if she could face that embarrassment, either.

"Dina! Do wait a moment, won't you?" came Violet's voice from behind her. "If we go in together, Mother can't scold me for being the last one down."

Dina waited gladly enough, for she had no more desire to enter the room alone than did Violet. Still, she could not subdue a flutter of nervousness as all eyes turned toward them from the table. Her gaze went at once to Thor, to find him watching her as well—though his expression seemed more worried than doting. Swallowing, she returned his nod, still unsure of his feelings.

"Happy Christmas, Violet, happy Christmas, Dina," Lady Rumble greeted them from her place at table. "Help yourselves to some breakfast, do, and then we will all go up to the parlor and sing carols before attending the midday Christmas service."

The two young women obediently went to the sideboard, at which point Violet took the opportunity to whisper to Dina, "Well? Was I right about last night? May I say, 'I told you so'?"

Caught off-guard, Dina felt herself blushing deeply and was grateful her back was to the rest of the group. She shot Violet a quick, sidelong glance and gave her a quick nod.

Any hope that Violet would be discreet was dashed when her sister-in-law set down her plate to clap her hands. "I knew it. I knew Grant would not be able to resist you," she whispered excitedly.

"Pray be quiet," Dina breathed, alarmed. She should have been more guarded, particularly after what Violet had apparently let slip to Silas last night. What if Thor was intending to act as though they hadn't—?

"I would much prefer you not discuss such things before the whole family—or any guests," she added.

Violet glanced over her shoulder. "No one is listening, but I suppose you are right. We can talk later." With a wink and a grin, she finished filling her plate and moved to the table.

Dina took her time filling her own plate, waiting for her color to return to normal before turning around. She saw that the only empty chair was next to Thor and wondered whether that was by his design or his mother's. Either way, she had no choice but to take it—not that she was reluctant, exactly.

Still, she wasn't sure where—or how—to look as she took her seat between Thor and Lord Rushford. Lord Rushford murmured a greeting, which she returned, and then Thor spoke for the first time since she'd entered the room.

"Good morning. Are you . . . quite well today?" His voice was as full of concern as his glance had been when she entered.

Taking a deep breath, she met his gaze with a determinedly cheerful smile. "Perfectly well. And you?"

To her surprise and secret delight, he colored slightly. "Er, yes, quite well. Happy Christmas, by the way."

Violet, seated across the table between Sir Charles and Silas, winked. "Yes, happy Christmas to you both. A most happy Christmas indeed, I should think."

"And to you all," Dina said, sending her sister-in-law a speaking glance that resulted only in a slight shrug and another grin.

Silas, Dina noticed, was frowning. "You'll want to eat up, if we're not to be late for the service," he snapped when she caught his eye.

Violet glanced at him in surprise, and he quickly smoothed his frown into a solicitous smile. "Do be sure to wrap up warmly when we leave the house, Miss Turpin, for it's quite cold today and I would hate for you to take a chill."

His words reminded Dina forcibly of Thor's concern for her last night, in the pool. She dared a quick glance at him, to find him watching her intently.

"I'm glad you took no chill yourself," he said, so softly that not even Lord Rushford, on Dina's other side, could have heard him.

She smiled shyly up at her husband, her earlier fears fading somewhat. "I told you I would not. You needn't have worried."

"No, I suppose not." Slowly his lips curved into a smile, reminding her vividly how those lips had felt against hers, how his hands had caressed her body.

Suddenly embarrassed, she dropped her gaze to her still-untouched plate and picked up her fork.

Across the table, she heard Violet telling Silas that there was no hurry and that while she appreciated his concern, she felt sure she could walk to the church and back without ill effect. He muttered an apology and a compliment, though Dina thought both lacked sincerity. Had Violet noticed? Sometime today, she really must attempt to speak with her about Silas.

Lady Rumble took control of the conversation then, laying out her plans for the rest of the day. Dina, however, found it difficult to concentrate on anything but Thor's nearness, and the moment when they might once more be alone together. When she might finally discover how he felt about what they had done last night.

When they all rose from the table a short time later, she was rather surprised to discover her plate was empty, for she could not remember eating a single thing.

Taking Thor's arm, she felt a stronger sense of awareness than ever, again reminded irresistibly of last night's intimacy. How, she wondered, did married women manage to deal with such mundane matters as correspondence and ordering a household? All she wanted to do right now was closet herself with her husband and continue what they had begun the night before.

"You are positively glowing this morning, Mrs. Turpin," Sir Charles commented as they gathered in the parlor. "Christmas must agree with you."

Violet giggled. "I think it is marriage that agrees

with her—with both of them, in fact." Not until she spoke did Dina notice that Violet had come upstairs on Sir Charles's arm rather than Silas's.

"Yes, I rather think it does," Thor responded, smiling down at Dina in a way that warmed her to her toes. "Not that it is any of your business, Miss Impudence."

Violet's eyes went wide and innocent. "I am merely pleased to see you both so happy. That is not impudent, is it?"

Her words were loud enough for all to hear, and everyone laughed—except Silas. Luckily, Lady Rumble launched them into a rousing chorus of "Good King Wenceslas" before anyone but Dina—she hoped—could notice his sullenness. She prayed that his temper would not mar the day for anyone else.

Half an hour later they all left for the village church, where they found that nearly everyone who had attended last night's ball had opted for this later service. Sitting beside Thor in the family pew at the front, Dina felt that all eyes were on her, that it must somehow be obvious to everyone what had transpired after she and Thor left the ball last night.

The sermon was mercifully brief, the vicar no doubt eager for his own Christmas dinner. After the service, everyone gathered in front of the church for a few minutes to exchange holiday well-wishes. Dina chatted with the neighbors, her hand tucked through the crook of Thor's arm, just like all the other married ladies—though she still didn't quite feel like one of them. She supposed she wouldn't, until things were finally settled between Thor and her.

Still, it was a pleasant preview of what village life here could be like, if her wishes became reality.

Though the sun was bright, the wind was bitter, and it soon drove everyone off to their homes for their Christmas dinners. Dina found the walk back exhilarating, but both Lady Rumble and Violet—this time on Silas's arm—were shivering by the time they reached the house. When Lord Rumble suggested a bowl of hot rum punch, everyone enthusiastically agreed.

As the others headed upstairs to the parlor, Thor hung back. "If you are not too cold—and I confess, you do not appear to be—there is something I should like to show you outdoors."

"So you are finally realizing that I am no delicate flower?" Dina asked teasingly, though she knew her cheeks were pink from more than the brisk walk home. "Whatever it is, I should like to see it," she added, before he could reply.

Putting a hand atop hers, still nestled in the crook of his arm, he squeezed it, and she could feel the warmth of his touch even through her glove and his. "I am realizing that you are even more courageous than I'd thought. And, yes, that you do not take a chill easily."

It wasn't quite the concession she'd hoped for, but it was something, so she did not argue the point further as she accompanied him through the house and out the back, through the gardens and along the path toward the outbuildings.

"Are we going to the kennels again?" Dina asked in surprise.

He nodded but did not speak, only smiling in a way that increased her curiosity.

"The cold snap won't have hurt the puppies?" she asked in sudden concern.

"They should be fine, with all of the straw I've packed 'round them. Who is overprotective now?" he teased.

Dina had to laugh, partly in relief that he had all but admitted that he had been overprotective of her earlier. That boded well, she hoped, for more of what she so desperately wanted.

"Happy Christmas, Princess," Thor greeted his foxhound when they entered the kennel a moment later. "I've brought you a present." Reaching into his pocket, he pulled out a bit of sausage from breakfast, wrapped in a handkerchief.

"You had that in your pocket all through the service?" Dina didn't try to hide her amusement.

"If you didn't notice the smell, I doubt anyone else did." He held the meat out to Princess, who took it daintily between her teeth, then swallowed it whole. "There. Now I've paid properly for *your* present," he said, smiling back at Dina.

"My present?"

In answer, he picked up one of the sleeping balls of fur and handed it to her. "I decided yesterday, after hearing the story of the dog you did not keep, that you needed another."

Dina stared down at the tiny creature, which now opened its eyes and blinked up at her. "He's mine?"

"She, actually. I've found that the females tend to make better pets."

"But . . . won't you want to train all of these pups

to hunt?" The puppy sniffed at her thumb, then nibbled at it, charming her completely.

"All but this one," he said. "She has a more important job to do."

Dina looked up to find him regarding her tenderly and felt her heart turn over. "Being mine, you mean?"

He nodded. "Happy Christmas, Dina. But now I suppose we should get back to the house. You can decide later what you'd like to name her."

Charmed anew at the thought of naming her very own dog, Dina grinned up at him, then touched her nose to the puppy's. "Thank you," she said. "I wish I had something as wonderful to give to you."

Gently he took the pup from her arms and set it down with its littermates, then helped her to her feet. "You already have," he told her.

"Oh." Dina looked away in sudden embarrassment. "But that wasn't—I mean—I enjoyed that as much as you did, so I'm not certain it can count as a gift."

"Certainly it can." He sounded amused. "But I was talking about something else."

She looked up at him questioningly.

"Your friendship. It's been a delight to discover how many interests we have in common, and I've no doubt we will discover many more. You have become a good friend to Violet, as well."

Dina felt her heart drop to her stomach with an almost audible thud. Friendship? Was that still all he wanted from her, even after last night? She must have been right, then, that he hadn't enjoyed their time together nearly as much as she had.

She struggled for an appropriate response, one that would not reveal how his words had hurt her, as that had clearly not been his intent. Before she found one, however, Silas's voice rang out from behind her.

"So the old housekeeper was right. You are out here."

Dina turned to see her brother bearing down on them, Violet just behind him. "What are you doing out here, Silas? I thought you had all gone up to the parlor for some punch."

"We went up, but then you two were suddenly nowhere to be seen. I became . . . concerned."

"I told you there was no need to track them down," Violet exclaimed in evident irritation. "I can't imagine why you thought it necessary."

Dina could guess, given what Silas had suspected about her marriage last night, but saw no reason to speak her suspicions aloud. Instead she bent and lifted up her Christmas present. "Look, Violet. Thor, er, Grant has given her to me, to be my very own."

"Why, Grant, how sweet," Violet said, stroking the puppy's soft fur. "And how unlike you. How many times have you told me that your foxhounds are working dogs, not pets?"

Thor shrugged, though Dina thought he looked a bit sheepish. "Occasionally it's necessary to make an exception. This was one of those occasions." He shot an accusatory glance toward Silas, who appeared not to notice.

Instead he was looking at the puppy in Dina's hands, his lip curled in a sneer that was all too familiar to her. "No doubt something is wrong with this one, making it unsuitable for the hunt," he said. "In which case, you'd have done better to drown it, Turpin, rather than let my sister pamper it into old age."

Dina clutched the little thing to her chest, remembering all too vividly the threats he had made against her only other pet, years ago. Before she could speak her mind to her brother, however, Violet did so.

"What a dreadful thing to say," she exclaimed. "I'm glad you do not breed foxhounds, or anything else, Mr. Moore, if that is how you feel."

Silas clearly realized he had blundered badly. "It was a jest," he said quickly. "Surely you cannot think that I would really—"

"No, I don't think it was a jest," Violet retorted, hands on her hips. "You have said more than one thing since your arrival yesterday that has struck me as rather mean-spirited. I have tried to give you the benefit of the doubt, Mr. Moore, but I begin to believe that everything Dina said about you is true after all."

Now Silas turned on Dina with a ferocity that made her step back, out of long habit. "And just what lies have you been telling her about me?" he demanded. "What gives you the right—?"

With a single step, Thor placed himself in front of her, facing Silas. "You no longer have the right to bully my wife, Moore," he said with deadly softness. "If you cannot keep a civil tongue in your head, you would do better to leave before I am moved to guarantee you can never bully anyone again."

Silas's eyes blazed, and he made a move as though to sidestep Thor to get to Dina. Then, so suddenly that Dina did not quite see what had happened, her brother was on the ground, rubbing his jaw and blinking up at Thor.

"I—I must say, that was uncalled for," he stammered. Then, to Violet, "Miss Turpin, surely you do not wish me to leave? I assure you, I never intended the least harm."

Violet hesitated, her expression one of mingled pity and repugnance. "I suppose you must stay for Christmas dinner. You are Dina's brother, after all. But . . . perhaps it would be better if you did not stay for the whole of the holidays. It seems your continued presence here is likely to cause more friction than happiness."

For a long moment, Silas glared at all three of them from his awkward position on the ground. Then, with a snort of disgust, he scrambled to his feet.

"In that case, I beg you will make my excuses to Lord and Lady Rumble. I'll get my things and clear out at once, as I've no wish to cause anyone unhappiness—particularly you, Miss Turpin. I'm sure I can find a room in Alford. They're not likely to be full up on Christmas Day."

With that, he slammed his hat back onto his head and turned on his heel to stalk toward the house without a backward glance.

"Oh, dear," Violet sighed. "He didn't take that well at all."

Dina put an arm about her shoulders, just as glad to have something to focus on other than Thor's last words to her before Silas's interruption.

"Pray don't blame yourself, Violet. Silas has always had a vile temper. It was only a matter of time before something set him off."

Violet glanced again at Silas's retreating back. "Perhaps. But he was so charming, so attentive, last night at the ball. He did seem somewhat distracted after supper, but I was able to tease him back into a cheerful mood."

"Good riddance, if you ask me," Thor snapped. "I'm sorry, Dina," he added in a conciliatory tone, "but he really did seem to be trying to stir up trouble in one way or another."

Dina nodded, though it rankled a bit to have Thor's opinion of Silas proved right. Still, she couldn't help feeling a guilty relief that Violet had taken his measure without any overt warning from her.

"Yes, it's as well he is leaving. I only wish, well, that things might have turned out differently." She had so hoped that with his debts paid, Silas would accept her marriage and change for the better.

"I'm still cold," Violet declared suddenly. "Let's go back inside and have some of that hot rum punch, shall we?"

To this, Dina and Thor readily agreed. Once again, Dina put her puppy back with its mother, then turned to accompany the others to the house. Violet chattered all the way back, as though determined to smooth over the awkwardness of Silas's leaving.

"And tomorrow is Boxing Day," she concluded as they reached the gardens. "We always have a wonderful time with the tenants and villagers, don't we, Grant?"

Thor nodded. "Where is the party to be held this year?"

"At Farmer Kibble's. He and Farmer Puckridge

have the largest barns," she explained to Dina, "so they generally take turns hosting the St. Stephen's dance."

Dina tried to keep the wistfulness out of her smile. Her father, and Silas after him, had never cared for the Boxing Day tradition, honoring it only by giving most of the servants the day off and allowing Dina's mother—and later Dina—to distribute a bit of extra food among their poorest tenants. How much happier her childhood might have been with parents like Lord and Lady Rumble.

But there was no point in regretting what was long past—or what was recently past—she supposed. Even though Thor had made it clear he still regarded her as friend, not lover, she could not regret what they had done last night. It was an experience she would treasure for the rest of her life.

She would not, however, humiliate herself again by begging for a resumption of such intimacies. She could have a good life here, if she did not spoil it with vain wishes. And that, she was determined, was just what she would have.

In fact, with Silas gone, perhaps she could recapture a bit of the youthful sense of Christmas she had missed as a child. Secure in the knowledge that Silas had finally given up all hope of ever marrying Violet, she could simply enjoy the rest of the Yuletide season.

It should be possible, she told herself, as long as she did not allow herself to dwell on the knowledge that Thor would never love her as she loved him.

Chapter 19

❝I'll take Violet Turpin to wife one way or another if it kills me," Silas muttered as he drove into Alford an hour later.

Now that Dina's fortune was well and truly lost to him, marrying Violet seemed the only option remaining to keep him out of debtors' prison. Whatever Dina had said to turn her against him, Silas would undo the damage. He'd charmed women enough in the past to be confident he could do so now, when it mattered far more than ever before.

But . . . what of the unlikely possibility that he could not? He suddenly recalled when he'd believed Dina had been kidnapped for ransom. Yes, that could always be his last-ditch option.

On sudden decision, he passed by the Half Moon, where he'd planned to bespeak a room, and drove instead to the house at the end of the street, where Plunkett had told him he lived. He stared at the weathered cottage with some distaste. Plunkett had told him he'd inherited the place from an uncle, but clearly he hadn't received any money to pay for its upkeep.

Still, Plunkett was familiar with both the area and those who populated it, and his financial straits, apparently even worse than Silas's, would make his help that much easier to purchase. Telling his man to bring his trunk, Silas jumped down from the box and went to knock at the door, a plan beginning to form.

Yes, one way or another, he was determined that Violet Turpin's fortune would be his before New Year's Day.

Thor accepted another mug of beer from Farmer Kibble with a perfunctory smile before resuming his frown as he watched the dancers in the middle of the barn floor. Dina seemed to be enjoying herself, dancing a reel with the estimable Mr. Kibble's eldest son, but he was almost certain she wasn't really happy.

He didn't see how she could be, after the distant way she had behaved toward him this morning and, even more noticeably, last night.

When they had gone upstairs to their chambers after a protracted evening of Christmas festivities, he'd already had his arguments prepared against the inevitable moment when she would again insist that they share a bed. He was tired, she was tired, there had been too much emotional turmoil that day with her brother leaving, and, of course, his concern about hurting her.

But none of those reasons had been required.

Upon reaching the end of the west wing, she had murmured a polite good-night and stepped into her chamber, leaving him blinking in the hallway. And today she had treated him with the same studied politeness, smiling more sincerely at Rush and Stormy as they took their leave this morning than she had smiled at Thor himself—her husband.

Though he could not claim that she had precisely avoided him, Dina had given him not the least hint that she desired any repetition of the intimacies that had both thrilled and frightened him on Christmas Eve. Far from cajoling him, as she'd done that night, she seemed willing to pretend it had never happened. It was exactly what he'd hoped for.

And it was driving him mad.

The reel ended, and Thor quickly set down his mug and stood up from the bale of straw where he'd been sitting, determined to claim Dina for the next dance before some other farmer could do so. He was a moment too late, however, for as soon as she turned from exchanging thanks with young Bill Kibble, old Mr. Inker stepped forward and seized her hand.

Thor sighed and headed back to his straw bale, but was intercepted by blowsy Mrs. Puckridge, who'd clearly had a drop more ale than was good for her, though it was not yet noon.

"Hi, now, Mr. Turpin, why for b'an't you dancin'?" she demanded. "Yon Tim Bumble is fiddling better than I ever heard him. Come on, then, and show me how the fine Lunnon gents hop to a reel, won't you?"

He could hardly refuse without insulting her, so reluctantly followed her to the set, where she took a place only two down from Dina. Thor nodded to his wife and received a stiff, cordial smile in return. The music began, a lively jig of a tune, and he tried to throw himself into the dance as enthusiastically as everyone else seemed to be doing, though his attention was almost wholly on Dina, diagonally across from him.

Her blue dimity gown fit her curves exceedingly well, and as she skipped along to the movements of the dance, its full skirts occasionally flipped up high enough to reveal her ankles and even, once, one shapely calf. Thor swallowed and looked away, fighting an absurd but almost overwhelming impulse to snatch her away from so many common, admiring eyes and have her all to himself in some corner.

"My compliments," he said as the movements of the dance brought them briefly together. "You dance as well on a dirt floor as you do on polished oak."

Though her green eyes widened slightly as though in surprise, she responded with only a small, polite smile and a perfunctory thank-you before moving on.

A few minutes later, Violet moved past him down the line, partnered by a sturdy farm lad. "What have you done to upset Dina?" she asked accusingly as Thor swung her about as the dance demanded. "You two have scarce spoken today."

"Nothing," he replied, but she moved on down the line before he could ask whether Violet had any theories. All he could think was that Dina was angry about the way he had sent her brother packing the day before, though she'd said nothing about it.

When the reel ended, he thanked Mrs. Puckridge, declining her offer of dalliance with feigned regret before hurrying to Dina's side. "Might I have this next dance?" he asked, forestalling young Rufus Eubanks, who had clearly been about to ask the same thing.

Dina hesitated long enough to cost him a pang, but then she nodded. "Of course." She did not sound eager, however.

"Or we could sit it out," he suggested, trying not to show how her reluctance hurt him. "I'm beginning to think we need to talk."

"If that is what you would prefer," she said, sounding as though it did not matter in the least, one way or another.

He glanced around the gaily festooned barn and assured himself that Violet and both of his parents were happily occupied: Violet lining up for the next dance, his father deep in a discussion of crops with Farmer Kibble, and his mother chatting about childbirth with half a dozen village women.

"Over here." He indicated a stack of hay bales piled near the ladder to the loft.

She followed him without protest, but when he seated himself on a bale, she remained standing rather than sit down beside him. "What did you wish to say?" she asked. "I did promise Eb Bullfinch I would teach him the quadrille."

Thor felt somewhat at a loss in the face of her cool

politeness, but forced himself to speak, now that he had the chance. "I can't help feeling I've done something to upset you, Dina, and I wish you would tell me what it is."

She gave a slight shrug. "I am not upset."

"Is it your brother? Perhaps I was harsher than necessary, but when he tried to threaten you—"

"Silas behaved poorly. You were well within your rights to ask him to leave." Still, she showed no real emotion, nor did she meet his eyes, her gaze straying instead to the dancers in the middle of the barn floor.

"But perhaps I did not consider your feelings as I ought," he persisted, reaching out to place a hand on her arm. "Dina, please believe that the last thing I wanted to do was to upset you."

She moved away from his touch, but so casually that he could not quite call it a rejection. "I told you, I am not upset. I'm sorry if I have done anything to give you that impression."

Frustrated, Thor stood, since she would not sit. "Of course you are giving me that impression. Since your brother left, you have treated me almost like a stranger, when before, you—we—"

Finally she looked him in the eye. "Not a stranger, surely. I thought I was treating you as a friend."

"A friend?" He blinked at her, confused.

"Is that not what you wanted?"

"Er, yes, but—" How to explain to her that he wanted far more than that, especially when he'd insisted both to her and himself that he did not? When he knew friendship was the best, safest thing for both of them?

"Then where is the problem?" she asked lightly. "Ah, I believe the quadrille is next, and I did promise Eb. If you will excuse me?"

Turning, she walked away, neither quickly nor slowly, leaving him to frown after her. He was no closer to understanding the change in Dina's attitude than he had been before. And he had never desired her more.

It was all Dina could do to keep from glancing over her shoulder as she deliberately walked away from Thor. Had she imagined that pleading in his eyes? Most likely, since it was what she most wanted to see there. She would not allow her romantic fancies to pull her back into foolish dreams or embarrassing displays of affection that would not be returned.

Still, she could not quite subdue a flutter of hope as she recalled his words and, more, his expressions both during the last dance and just now, by the loft. If anything, however, it only firmed her resolve to continue on her present course, waiting for him to make the next move. If he did, she would respond willingly enough. And if he did not, well, at least she would not have humiliated herself again.

"Are you ready to learn the quadrille, Eb?" she asked the ruddy-cheeked farm lad waiting eagerly near the rough stage where three of his fellows plied fiddle, tin whistle, and drum.

"Oh, aye, Miz Turpin," he exclaimed, brushing a straw-colored shock of hair out of his eyes. "Once't I learn a fancy Lunnon dance like that, Daisy Gill will be sure to pay me more mind, don't you think?"

"You'll charm stars into her eyes," Dina assured

him, hoping she was not raising the lad's hopes too high. She knew all too well how that felt.

When the music started a moment later, Dina did her best to walk clumsy Eb through the figures of the popular quadrille, pointing out to him where it differed from the familiar cotillion. He needed a lot of coaching, which was just as well, since Thor had joined the same set just as the dance began. If she was frequently tempted to watch him as he partnered little Becky Spinet, she was careful not to show it.

It was a novel experience, teaching someone a dance she'd only learned earlier that year, to the inexpert tune scratched out by the country musicians. Dina did her best to savor that novelty, telling herself that life held many such small pleasures and that she would be a fool to overlook them while pining after the ones she could not have.

By the time the dance ended, she could truthfully compliment Eb on his improvement, as he'd learned at least two of the five figures. Beaming, he pumped her hand in thanks, then went off to find his Daisy. Dina could not help grinning as she watched him go, but her grin abruptly faded when she turned to find Thor at her elbow, a serious, searching expression in his eyes.

"This time, let's actually dance," he said before she could come up with some excuse to hurry off. "You deserve a reward after that good deed." He nodded after Eb.

"Very well," she replied airily, determined that he not see what his nearness did to her. All the dances so far had been reels and square, figured dances, which meant there would be little contact between them, and almost no chance for conversation.

Safer, surely, than not dancing, all things considered.

Then, to her great surprise, old Tim Bumble scraped out the opening strains to a waltz on his battered fiddle, and balding Mr. Mallet joined in with his tin whistle.

"Did you—?" she started to ask, before noticing that Thor looked as surprised as she did. Then she saw Violet hurrying away from the musicians, a mischievous smile on her face. When she caught Dina's eye, she sent her a conspiratorial wink.

"My sister has clearly spent too much time in my mother's company of late," Thor commented with a shake of his head.

Dina would have to have a talk with Violet, let her know that now, with things standing as they did with Thor, Violet was doing her no favors by such machinations. At the moment, however, she simply had to get through this waltz without embarrassing herself.

"I think it is commendable that your father sponsors something on this scale for his tenants every year," she said, trying very hard to ignore the thrill that went through her at the touch of Thor's hand on her back, the feel of her own hand in his.

"It's not pure virtue, for he always enjoys himself immensely at these things, but I do think the tenants and villagers appreciate it."

Dina followed his gaze to where Lord Rumble

stood, mug of beer in hand, laughing heartily with a group of farmers. He seemed nothing like the studious baron she had met upon her arrival at Plumrose, but she knew him well enough now to realize that such egalitarianism was by no means out of character.

"I wish my own father had been willing to mingle more with our tenants—or even our neighbors. Perhaps he'd have been a happier man." Not until she glanced up to see Thor regarding her with sympathy did she realize she'd spoken the thought aloud.

"Was he very harsh, your father?" he asked then.

Though it felt disloyal to do so, she nodded. "It was as though, having no joy in his own life, it angered him to see it in anyone else's. My mother, Silas, and I all rebelled in our own ways, I suppose, but I can't say ours was a happy family."

"Perhaps I have not been thankful enough for mine," Thor said. "But I hope in future you will find some of the joy you missed as a child here at Plumrose."

She blinked up at him, startled by how closely his words paralleled her earlier thoughts. His expression was tender. Pitying? Confused, she cast about for another topic. "The Kibbles have done nicely with their decorations, don't you think?"

Looking about at the greenery hanging from the rough rafters of the barn, he nodded. "I'm glad to see they did not neglect the most important decorations, at least."

Before she knew what he was about, he maneuvered her backward, then glanced up, significantly. Her heart in her throat, knowing what she would see, she followed his gaze to the kissing bough above their heads.

"But I thought—"

He cut off her protest with a kiss that melted her worries into a pool of warmth and left her in no doubt about his feelings. This was not the kiss of a mere "friend."

Though the music played on, the two of them stopped dancing, suspended in a world of their own, a world out of time. Dina felt Thor's arms come around her, enclosing her, cherishing her, as he deepened the kiss. Rising up on her toes, she put her own arms around his neck, abandoning herself to his lips, losing herself in the wonderful relief of knowing that he still desired her.

Finally, a particularly strident note on the tin whistle recalled them at least partially to their surroundings. Thor's lips released hers, though he still clasped her in his arms. For a long moment they stood, their lips only inches apart, gazing into each other's eyes. Then from all around them came cheers and applause.

Blinking, Dina realized that the ground was still beneath her feet—she had not soared up into the rafters, as she had seemed to do during that amazing kiss. Thor grinned down at her, then lifted a hand to wave at the jubilant crowd, which resulted in another round of cheers. Though she knew she was blushing crimson, Dina was far more happy than she was embarrassed.

"Does . . . does this mean you want to be more than friends after all?" she asked under cover of the noise around them. After spending more than a day in miserable uncertainty, she wanted no more misunderstandings—if she *had* misunderstood.

Thor looked genuinely startled. "I thought we already were. Is that what has been worrying you?"

She nodded, fighting down a sudden fit of shyness. "Yesterday you acted almost as though we had never—and then, when you gave me the puppy, you talked about friendship. Only friendship."

Despite all the interested eyes in the barn, he bent his head and kissed her again, to a new burst of applause. "Dina, I've wanted you as more than a friend since the day we met. True, I worried—still worry—that a, er, physical relationship may have risks for you, but I never intended to hurt you emotionally instead."

Dina smiled up at him, happier than she'd been since climbing out of the pool on Christmas Eve. Everything would be all right now, she was sure of it.

Suddenly she chuckled. At Thor's questioning glance, she explained, "I was going to scold Violet for arranging this waltz, when I was doing my best to accede to what I thought were your wishes. Now I suppose I shall have to thank her instead."

He nodded, grinning. "Let's both go thank her, shall we? Now, where did she get to?" He scanned the room, an easy task, given his height. Suddenly his happy expression changed to one of outrage.

With a sense of foreboding, Dina peered through the crowd and finally saw what Thor had seen. Violet, sitting on the straw bales near the loft, smiling and chatting . . . with Silas.

* * *

"So you see, Miss Turpin—or may I still call you Violet?" Silas asked with a humble show of deference.

"Of course," she replied warmly. "You are family."

"Thank you. As I was saying, Violet, my temper has always been my besetting sin. When it gets the better of me, I too often do or say things I regret almost immediately afterward." He hung his head in mock contrition.

"Believe me," he continued, "by the time I reached Alford, I realized how poorly I had behaved. I came back to apologize, not only for arguing with your brother, but for leaving without even a farewell to your parents or their guests. I haven't noticed Lord Rushford or Sir Charles here, however."

"No, they left this morning," Violet told him, to his great satisfaction. That made his path easier.

"I'm sorry to hear that. Still, I can convey my apologies to the others—if you think they will speak to me, after my behavior yesterday."

"I'm certain they will. Indeed, my brother and Dina seem to be in excellent spirits just now. If you'd arrived a moment or two earlier, you'd have seen—" She broke off to frown up at him uncertainly. "Well, that is neither here nor there. Since you know that your temper is a problem, why do you not endeavor to control it better?"

This was the prompt he'd been waiting for. "I have been trying for years, but I now realize it is too great a task to accomplish alone. I need someone to help me—to hold me accountable. Someone willing to speak up when I show the first signs of anger."

"I could help you," she offered. "Perhaps we could arrange some sort of signal that I could give you when I see you beginning to frown, or hear you say something you oughtn't. I could put my finger to my chin, perhaps, like so." She demonstrated.

"You are as generous as you are lovely," Silas told her gravely. "With your help, I am sure that I would be able to overcome my affliction. But . . . I fear we may not see each other often enough for your plan to work."

"Of course we will. You promised to come to London when I make my come-out next month, did you not? And I'm certain my brother will not mind if you remain here until we leave."

Silas was certain of no such thing, nor did he intend to gamble on it. Glancing up, he saw Turpin and Dina headed their way, and neither looked in a particularly forgiving mood. Pasting his most cordial smile on his face, reminding himself that it would all pay off in the end, he stood.

Jumping to her feet, Violet stepped forward. "Grant, Dina, look who has come back. And you mustn't scold, for he has returned to apologize for yesterday."

"Yes," said Silas, extending a hand and forcing down an instinctive surge of resentment. "My behavior yesterday was inexcusable, but I pray you will all forgive me anyway."

Turpin was still frowning, so Silas turned to Dina. "I should not have spoken as I did, Dina. I'm sorry. The cold made me snappish, but I would hate to be the cause of a breach between us, as you are my only family, now."

"Not your only family, Silas," Violet assured him.

"By virtue of Dina's marriage, you now have all of us, as well."

"You are far too kind," he murmured with a grateful glance intended to convey more than his words. He was rewarded by an understanding smile.

Then Violet turned back to her brother. "You will forgive him, Grant, will you not? He has promised to work at controlling his temper in the future."

Turpin regarded Silas through narrowed eyes, as though trying to judge his sincerity. Silas realized, given his current plans, he'd have done much better not to make those insinuations and veiled threats at the start of the ball on Christmas Eve.

Seeming to become aware of both women's eyes upon him, Turpin finally nodded and shook Silas's proferred hand. "Very well, Moore. Apology accepted. Acknowledgment of one's faults and a desire to eradicate them is admirable, and should not go unrewarded."

"I have offered to help him—as a sister," Violet said then. "We were just discussing ways I might do that, in fact, and then he means to apologize to Father and Mother."

Turpin gave another terse nod. "Very well. I've promised my wife another dance." With a hand on Dina's elbow, he led her away, clearly having no desire to spend any more time in Silas's company than necessary, despite the lip service he gave to forgiveness.

Silas was careful to let none of his cynicism show in his expression as he turned back to Violet. "That was very clever, throwing in that bit about being my sister," he said. "I think it was just what your brother wished to hear."

"I didn't say it to be clever." She smiled up at him guilelessly. "I truly do regard you as my brother now. And, as such, I very much want to help you so that we can all be comfortable as a family."

Though that was not exactly what he'd hoped to hear, Silas nodded gravely. "You are far kinder to me than I deserve." Then, glancing around at the crowd of revelers, he said, "It is quite noisy in here, is it not? What do you say we go outside so that we can hear each other better, while discussing the plan you spoke of?"

Violet's ready agreement showed she had no suspicion yet of his own plan. Fetching her cloak from the pile near the door, she accompanied him out into the barnyard, where his coach was parked near Lord and Lady Rumble's. A quick glance showed his manservant waiting, as instructed, just behind his coach.

Draping an arm across Violet's shoulders, he said, "Why do we not sit in my coach to talk? I would not wish you to become chilled on my account."

She glanced up at him with a slight frown and stepped out from under his arm. Realizing that he was overplaying his hand, Silas shrugged. "Or we can stand out here, if you prefer it. I don't mind the cold, particularly."

A well-timed blast of icy wind swept through the barnyard, making both of them clutch their cloaks more tightly about them.

"Yes, of course you are right. Let's sit in the coach," Violet said with an apologetic little smile.

Being careful not to touch her, Silas moved to the

coach, opened the door, and put down the steps so that she could easily climb inside without his assistance. Once she was in, he got in after her and closed the door.

"I confess, I did have hopes that you might regard me as more than a brother," he said, settling himself into the seat across from her. From the corner of his eye, he saw Jefferson, who was acting as both valet and driver on this visit, moving to the front of the coach.

"My brother told me I was a shameless flirt, and I fear he was right. I'm so sorry, Silas, if I have led you to believe I am romantically interested in you, but I really don't think we should suit in that way. Surely we can both be content to be brother and sister—and friends?"

He sent her his most melting look, the one that had enticed more than one ostensibly virtuous woman into his bed. "Have I no chance at all of eventually persuading you to become my wife?" This would be far easier if Violet was willing.

Unfortunately, she shook her head. "I'm afraid not." Her voice, like her expression, was regretful but firm.

"Pity," he said, and rapped on the roof of the coach. With a lurch, it started forward, then quickly gathered speed.

Chapter 20

ﾟﾟﾟﾟﾟﾟ◞◠◡◠◞ﾟﾟﾟﾟﾟﾟ

66**W**hat—? Where are we going?" At the moment, Violet sounded more curious than concerned, though Silas imagined that would soon change.

"Just taking a little drive," he told her with careful casualness. "Don't like to leave the horses standing too long in weather like this, you know."

She frowned. "That's all very well, but I think I had better go back inside before my parents wonder where I've got to. Stop the coach, please."

He shooke his head with mock regret. "I'm sorry, Violet, but I can't do that."

"What do you mean?" The first signs of real alarm sounded in her voice. "Of course you can stop."

"Not if I'm going to mend my fortune—and you are going to help me to do just that. You now have

two options: to marry me, or to be held for ransom—
though that option will doubtless ruin your reputation beyond recall."

With a strangled exclamation, she lunged for the
door of the coach, but he easily stopped her, then
moved to the seat opposite, between her and the door.

"To think I believed you sincere in wanting to
change," she exclaimed angrily. "You will never get
away with this, you know. Grant and Dina will have
noticed I left with you, and they know what your
coach looks like. We'll be stopped before we've gone
three miles."

Silas shrugged. "They looked pretty wrapped up
in each other, to me. I doubt they'll notice anything
at all for quite some time." He couldn't quite conceal
his bitterness, as that relationship was what had
driven him to this step. "As for my coach, I had already considered that detail."

They rounded a bend, and a moment later the
coach stopped by a stand of trees only a few yards
from the road into Alford. There, another coach was
waiting—a brown, nondescript traveling coach that
looked nothing like Silas's green landau. Even the
horses were a different color.

Keeping a firm grip on Violet's arm, Silas opened
the door. "I may need some help getting her inside,"
he called to the cloaked figure waiting by the new
coach.

"Couldn't get her to agree, eh?" he asked, moving
forward.

Violet stopped struggling to stare at the man.
"Gregory? What on earth are you doing here?"
Then, without waiting for him to answer, "You must

help, me, please! Mr. Moore is trying to kidnap me—to force me into marriage."

Plunkett shrugged. "That was the plan—or, well, the backup plan, if he couldn't get you to come willingly."

"And you're helping him?" she demanded disbelievingly. "Why?"

"Money, m'dear, what else? Since our elopement went awry, I've found myself increasingly in need of funds. Moore offered to help me out if I would help him out."

Silas was growing impatient. At any moment Violet's absence might be noticed and the pursuit begin. "C'mon, c'mon, enough chatter. We need to be on our way."

Suddenly Violet wrenched her arm from his grasp and turned to run back the way they'd come. With a curse, Silas went after her, but Plunkett reached her first. She threw a wild punch at him, but missed. Pinning her arms to her sides to prevent her trying again, he thrust her toward Silas.

"I begin to think it's as well we didn't marry, my dear, given your violent tendencies. Good luck with her, Moore."

Violet turned and spat toward Plunkett. "You're a bounder and a cur, Gregory Plunkett. And a plagiarist, as well, for I discovered you did not write those poems you sent me. You'll get your comeuppance eventually, you'll see."

Plunkett laughed, but Silas was increasingly agitated. Glancing back up the road, he forced Violet into the brown carriage and climbed in after her.

"Get my coach off the road and hide it, if you want

the rest of what I promised you," he barked to Plunkett. "Remember, if you're questioned, you haven't seen me since Christmas Eve." Slamming the door, he pounded on the roof of the coach, and Jefferson whipped the horses to a fast trot. Silas just hoped it was fast enough.

"You don't believe him, do you?" Dina asked as soon as they were out of earshot from Violet and Moore.

Thor shrugged, unwilling to damage the new understanding that they had reached before Moore's arrival. "I would like to."

"So would I," she said with a sigh, "but I've heard him say similar things too many times in the past to hold out much hope. He is uncannily adept at saying whatever he thinks people wish to hear, if he thinks it will benefit him in some way."

Thor glanced back at Moore and Violet, who were again talking together. "Have you told Violet that?"

"Not in so many words, but surely you cannot think her in any danger from him now, after what happened yesterday? It seems clear that she has no romantic interest in Silas."

"I suppose not," he agreed. "Still, a word to her about his powers of deception might not be amiss. Just now, however, I would like to sit out a dance with my wife in some secluded corner and forget such worries for a while."

"Far be it from me to fault such a plan." Tucking her hand through his arm, she accompanied him to the far end of the barn, where all the farming implements had been moved to make room for the dancing.

Glancing back to be sure they were no longer being watched by the crowd, he drew her behind a partially disassembled threshing machine, then gently cupped her face between his hands. "Now, are you finally convinced that I find you desirable in every way, or do you need further proof?"

Dina's green eyes sparkled up at him. "Given a choice like that, what can I say? Proof, please, sir."

Chuckling, he bent down to capture her lips with his own, wishing he could spirit them both back to Plumrose, to the swimming pool. For now, though, this would have to suffice. Her lips were soft and pliable beneath his, promising him more delights later.

"Mmm," she murmured when they finally parted. "Now perhaps you need some proof of your own?"

"I believe I've received it already, but I'm more than willing to have more."

Smiling a most seductive smile, she twined her arms around his neck and pulled his mouth down to hers again.

When they finally parted, he straightened up with a sigh. "Much as I would prefer to spend the rest of the afternoon here with you, we both have a responsibility to help my parents in their duties."

"Goodness," Dina exclaimed guiltily. "I had nearly forgotten. I've promised dances to half a dozen lads, and I've no doubt all of the lasses are hoping for a dance with you as well."

"I think our delay will be forgiven, but we'd best go back." They headed back to the lively end of the barn. "We can resume where we left off later tonight. I trust you will have no objection to another visit to the pool?"

"Of course not, although—" She broke off as Lady Rumble hurried toward them, her expression concerned.

"Is something wrong?" Thor asked, half expecting his mother to chide them for their brief disappearance.

She looked from him to Dina, then peered behind them. "Is Violet not with you?"

He shook his head, as did Dina. "I last saw her over there, speaking with Silas." Dina pointed toward the loft.

"Silas? Your brother returned?" Lady Rumble asked in surprise, which surprised Thor in turn.

"Yes, not half an hour ago. Did he not speak with you and Father?" His earlier suspicions revived. "He said he came back to apologize for leaving so precipitately yesterday."

Lady Rumble looked relieved. "No, we have not seen him yet, but perhaps he and Violet stepped outside to talk, as it is so noisy in here."

Glancing at Dina, however, Thor detected an alarm in her eyes that echoed his own. "We'll go look for them," she offered. "They must be nearby."

"Very well," Lady Rumble said, "though if she is with Silas, I've no doubt she is perfectly safe."

Thor wished he shared his mother's certainty. Together, he and Dina first circled the large barn, then checked the loft. Once assured that Violet and Silas were nowhere inside, they retrieved their cloaks and stepped out into the yard.

"I don't see any sign of them," Thor said, more grimly than he'd intended.

Dina glanced up at him. "Surely you don't think that they—that Silas—"

"You tell me. Is your brother the sort of man who would persuade an innocent like my sister into a tryst—or an elopement?" He couldn't help remembering Moore's threat on Christmas Eve.

Though she paled slightly, Dina did not flinch. "If he thought to profit by it, then yes. I fear Silas is indeed capable of such a thing. I cannot believe that Violet would agree, however. She may be romantic, but she is by no means stupid."

"No, she is not, but that did not prevent her from eloping with Plunkett. You, there," he called to a farm lad just returning to the barn, most likely after answering a call of nature. "Did you happen to see Miss Turpin out here?"

The lad approached them, blinking. "Oh, aye, sir, she were out here just a bit ago, with a gent near as tall as yourself. They was talking, private-like, so I hurried off, so's not to seem to be eavesdropping."

"Did you see where they went after that?"

"Nay, but they was headed toward that green coach what's gone now, so like as not they drove off in it. Mayhap he took her back to Plumrose."

Thor nodded and thanked the lad, who tugged his forelock and went back into the barn. "I suppose we'd better make certain that's where they went," he said to Dina.

For all their sakes, he hoped they had.

"Why don't you go back inside while I ride up to Plumrose? There's no need for both of us to miss more of the party."

Dina shook her head. "I'm coming with you."

"No. If I don't find them at the house, I'll be heading off in pursuit at once. You don't—"

"Yes, I do," she interrupted. "You are looking decidedly murderous, and I'm not about to let you become a criminal over any idiocy Silas may have committed."

Thor snorted. "Nor, I suppose, do you want your precious brother killed."

"That, too," Dina conceded, realizing guiltily that hadn't been her first concern. "I can also act as chaperone to Violet if it turns out they have eloped—or something." She still couldn't believe Violet would be quite that foolish.

"Come on, then," he snapped, veering away from the stables to the barouche the family had driven here and shouting for the coachman. When the man finally appeared, he was clearly very much the worse for drink, so Thor waved him back into the barn and climbed onto the box to take the ribbons himself.

Dina scrambled inside without a word, praying that they would indeed find Silas and Violet at Plumrose.

Unfortunately, her prayer went unanswered, for there was no sign of them at the house, or of Silas's coach or horses.

"If I set out at once on horseback, I'll have a better chance of catching them," Thor said after he finished cursing.

"Or of getting drenched and frozen," Dina retorted, looking pointedly at the lowering sky. As if in response to her words, a thin, icy rain began to fall.

Thor cursed again. "But you'll want to pack, and every minute of delay plays into their hands."

"I won't be five minutes," Dina promised. "And I'll bring a few things for Violet, as well, since she can't possibly have planned this in advance. Against the very slight chance that we don't catch them at once," she added hastily, when he began to glower again. "Meanwhile, why don't you arrange for whatever carriage is the fastest?"

Not waiting for his answer, she hurried into the house, then raced up the stairs to her chamber. Dragging out her valise, she began flinging into it the barest necessities for a night on the road—necessities she prayed she would not need. Then she ran down to the east wing and burst into Violet's room, startling her poor maid half to death.

"Never mind," she said in response to the woman's questions. "Miss Turpin can explain when she gets home. Run down to the kitchens and get some of those pasties left over from breakfast and meet me in the front hall with them."

The confused maid hurried to comply, and Dina threw a change of underthings and some sturdy shoes of Violet's into the valise, then headed back downstairs. She had just reached the hall when Violet's breathless maid appeared with a cloth-wrapped parcel. Dina thanked her as she snatched it from her hands, then ran out the door and down the front steps.

Thor was just rounding the corner of the house in a covered curricle, pulled by a pair of restive bays. He appeared startled to see her.

"You did mean five minutes, didn't you?" he said as she climbed up beside him under the awning. "This should be faster than your brother's landau, unless he's got a crack coachman."

"He doesn't," she said. "He usually drives himself. When old Jefferson, his manservant, drives, he tends to slow down whenever Silas isn't shouting at him to hurry."

Wasting no more time on conversation, Thor whipped up the bays and they were off, back to the Kibble farm to pick up whatever trail there might be. There was still no sign of Silas's green landau anywhere about, so Thor turned the horses to head down the only other track leading away from the barn.

"They'll have reached the road by now," he muttered savagely. "I should have ridden in the direction of Alford the moment we saw they were gone."

"No, we had every reason to think they had gone back to Plumrose," Dina reminded him gently. She knew from long experience that men in a temper were never reasonable, so she braced herself for the tongue-lashing that was sure to follow.

It did not come, however. "Yes, yes, you're right of course," Thor said in a calmer voice after a short pause. "I'm sorry, Dina. I should not take my anger out on you, when I'm as much at fault as anyone."

Amazed and gratified, she put a hand on his arm. "Silas is the one at fault, not you. If we are to apportion blame to all and sundry, surely I should have my share as well, since I never did specifically warn Violet against him."

Thor seemed to relax a fraction. "I believe I'm glad after all that you're along," he said. "You have a remarkable way of putting things into perspective."

"Like your father?" she teased, hoping to lighten his mood further. The less angry he was when they caught up with Silas and Violet, the better—for everyone.

"Rather like that, yes—though I hope the implication doesn't follow that I'm like my mother, always flying into a tizzy over something."

Dina scooted closer to him on the seat, tucking her hands around his arm. "Somehow, I can't imagine you in a tizzy. In fact, you are the most levelheaded man I've ever known—not that I've known so very many men, of course."

Instead of laughing, as she'd hoped, he nodded soberly. "From what you've told me, the men you've known best haven't been particularly fair-minded. I'm glad to know they weren't able to sour you on the whole of my sex."

"In truth, I had become quite cynical about men in general before I made your acquaintance," Dina confessed. "I must thank you for showing me that there are kind, trustworthy men in the world."

"That means a lot to me, Dina. Thank you."

She wanted to say more—to tell him that he'd won not only her respect and admiration, but her love—but the words would not come. Not yet.

Then they rounded the corner from the track onto the road, and they both had other things to think of, for there, only a short distance ahead, was Silas's green landau, headed toward Alford at a leisurely trot. With a shout, Thor urged the horses faster, and in minutes they drew even with the other coach.

"You, there," Thor called to the coachman. "Stop—I want a word with your master."

Instead of stopping, however, the man on the box sent one panicked look their way and whipped

Silas's grays to a startled trot. The coachman's hat was pulled low over his eyes, but Dina could see at a glance that he was neither Silas nor Jefferson. In fact, he looked surprisingly like—

"Plunkett? Thor, I believe that is Mr. Plunkett driving Silas's coach," she exclaimed. "How on earth—?"

But Thor was too busy goading his own pair to greater speed to reply. Though the landau had leaped ahead again, the curricle was lighter and their horses presumably fresher, so well before they reached Alford they had caught up again.

This time, Thor did not slow until he had moved well ahead of the landau. Then, with a maneuver that brought Dina's heart to her mouth, he turned the curricle to block the narrow road, leaving Plunkett with no choice but to stop or to drive right into them. For a moment she thought he intended to do just that, but at the last minute he swerved onto the verge, as though to go around them.

Unfortunately he had not reckoned on the shallow ditch that ran along the road, all but obscured by dead, overgrown grass. The landau lurched, then tilted, finally coming to a halt with two of its wheels in the air, turning idly. Mr. Plunkett scrambled off the box and turned to run, even as Thor leaped to the ground and lunged toward him.

"Check the coach," he called to Dina over his shoulder. "Make certain Violet is uninjured."

Dina hurried to comply, and by the time she reached the door of the landau, Plunkett was on the ground with Thor standing over him. "You won't escape me so easily this time, Plunkett," he was saying. "I don't know how Moore inveigled you into helping him, but—"

"It's empty." Dina stared into the interior of Silas's coach in disbelief. "They're not here."

"What?" Placing a booted foot on Plunkett's chest, Thor turned toward her. "How—? They must have switched vehicles. So that was your role in this enterprise, was it, Plunkett? What is Moore driving now?"

The man on the ground looked up at him fearfully. "I . . . I don't know what you mean," he stammered. "I bought this coach from Silas Moore fair and square two days ago and haven't seen him since."

Dina came toward him now, anger and heightened concern for Violet warring in her breast. "Then how did Silas come to be driving it less than an hour ago?" she demanded.

"I don't—that is—please, ma'am, you won't let him hurt me, will you? Back in Gretna, you and I were . . . were friends, were we not?"

"Hardly that. I knew the moment I met you that you were a weak-willed, opportunistic fortune hunter, but now I see I gave you more credit than you deserved. If you do not tell us where Silas has taken Miss Turpin, along with a complete description of the coach they are in, I will not only allow Mr. Turpin to hurt you, I will assist him in doing so." Picking up the whip he had dropped, she moved closer.

Plunkett's eyes widened, and he looked frantically from Dina to Thor and back before finally capitulating. "Very well. I doubt Moore intended to pay me the rest of what he owes me anyway. Let me up, and I'll tell you all I know."

Removing his foot from Plunkett's chest, Thor heaved him into a sitting position. "Well?"

Plunkett glanced at Dina, who continued to finger the whip, half hoping he would give her an excuse to use it—not that she actually knew how. "I . . . I don't actually know much. It was just last night he told me what he had in mind, though he seemed to think Miss Turpin would be going with him willingly."

"But she did not?"

The steel in Thor's voice made him flinch visibly, then he shook his head.

"She was mad as a hornet. I . . . I should have backed out of the plan then, but the money . . . Besides, she tried to hit me."

"Good for her," Dina said, proud of Violet. "Hard, I hope." She hadn't convinced Violet to learn any boxing, but perhaps her example had helped somewhat.

Plunkett shrugged. "It showed spirit, I'll give her that. If Moore gives her the least chance, she'll most likely manage to escape from him. As it was, she delayed him long enough that—"

"That we were able to catch you," Thor finished. "How much of a start do they have? And what are they driving?"

"A quarter of an hour or so. Brown coach, no markings. A mismatched pair, one black, one sorrel. They were the best I could find on short notice, with the money Moore gave me."

"Which direction did they go? Were they heading for Scotland?" Dina asked.

When Plunkett did not answer immediately, Thor took a step toward him, fist raised.

"Yes, yes, I think that was the plan, though Moore wasn't specific. They took this road, at any rate—they'd have to, wouldn't they? As for their lead, the more time you spend here with me, the longer it gets."

Thor cursed. "He's right, damn it. Let's go." He turned back toward the curricle, but Dina hesitated.

"We're not going to just let him go, are we? Shouldn't he be . . . arrested or something? Surely assisting in a kidnapping is a crime."

"It is. But taking him to the magistrate—even finding the magistrate, on Boxing Day—could cost us hours."

Dina had to admit he was right, though she didn't like it. "Suppose we tie him up, then tell someone in Alford to come collect him?"

"But it's freezing out here," Mr. Plunkett protested. "Besides, if you get the law involved, it will be difficult to keep this whole thing quiet—as you seem to have managed the last time. You won't want Miss Turpin's name sullied for something that isn't even her fault, will you? If you let me go, I promise never to breathe a word of it, on my honor."

"Your honor doesn't particularly impress me, Plunkett," Thor said. "How's this? If I ever learn you've said a word against my sister, I will hunt you down and kill you."

Mr. Plunkett paled visibly, and Dina felt a bit of

color leaving her own cheeks. Thor sounded deadly serious—not that she blamed him.

"Actually," Thor continued, "you may wish to consider leaving England entirely to make certain that can't happen."

Plunkett scrambled shakily to his feet and began dusting off his clothes. "Leave—? I, well, yes, I may just do that." He glanced from Thor to Dina and back, with what Dina thought was a calculating expression.

"Now I think on it, I'm sure there are things you'd prefer I keep to myself about your little wife, as well." He smiled, regaining a degree of his earlier swagger. "Of course, I'd be able to leave the country sooner if you could spot me enough to pay my passage . . ."

Thor took a step toward Plunkett, but Dina was closer. Almost without thinking, enraged by his impudence, and even more by the phrase "little wife," she took two quick steps and drove her left fist into Plunkett's stomach. He doubled over with a startled *oof*, bringing his head down to her level, allowing her to throw a right punch straight from the shoulder into his nose.

Plunkett crumpled to the ground, clutching at his face, blood flowing freely down his chin. "What—? How—?" he mumbled, his eyes wide with shock.

"Remember that if you think again to bargain or bully—or to take advantage of any woman," Dina told him severely. "Breathe a word about Violet—or me—and you'll find more than your nose broken."

She then turned her back on him to face Thor, whose eyes were as wide as Plunkett's. He stared from her to Plunkett and back, his mouth opening and closing without any words escaping.

"Let's go," Dina said, her anger subsiding, to be replaced with renewed concern for Violet. "We shall have to hurry if we are to catch up to Silas after this delay."

Without a backward glance, she walked to the waiting curricle, leaving a flabbergasted Thor to follow or not.

Chapter 21

❧◦◦◦◦

Blinking, Thor forced his feet to move. Still stunned by the masterful way Dina had dispatched Plunkett, he hurried to her side, opened the door, and handed her into the vehicle—not, he realized, that she really needed his help. He then climbed inside himself and took up the reins.

One last look at Plunkett showed him still sprawled on the ground, making no attempt whatsoever to rise. No doubt he was as astounded by what had just happened as Thor was.

Not until he had turned the curricle and whipped up the horses to continue the pursuit did Thor find his voice. "Good show," he finally managed. "How, er, where did you learn to fight like that?"

When Dina did not reply at once, he glanced

down to find her regarding him warily. "Are you angry with me?" she asked.

"Angry? Of course not. A bit startled, perhaps." That was a monumental understatement. "I mean, I knew you were quite fit for your, ah, size, but—"

"I did tell you that I had learned to box," she reminded him.

Again he blinked. "Yes. Yes, you did." He had not quite believed her at the time, but clearly she had not exaggerated in the least. "I apologize for doubting you," he said now.

"Apology accepted," she replied, the worry leaving her eyes, her lips curving into a tentative smile.

They reached Alford then, and Thor stopped long enough to discover that Moore had gone south rather than north, as expected, no doubt to throw off pursuit.

He also penned a quick message to his father and let someone know about the disabled coach on the road behind. "For the horses' sake," he explained to Dina as he climbed back into the curricle. "Plunkett can rot, for all of me, but those poor beasts don't deserve to freeze out there."

She was looking pensive. "You don't think he'll retaliate for what I did by spreading stories, do you?"

He shook his head without hesitation. "Plunkett is a coward before anything else. Now he'll be afraid not only of what I'll do to him, but of you as well." Suddenly he chuckled. "I would imagine he's thanking his stars right now that he didn't end up marrying you after all."

"Why, what an ungallant thing to say," Dina exclaimed, but there was laughter in her voice as well. Then, after a moment, "I must confess that one reason I thought marriage to him would be safe was my belief that I could, ah, control him."

"A reasonable belief, I should say. But then you ended up with me instead. Clearly I have not been treading as carefully around you as I ought." He was only half joking, still slightly shaken by what he'd seen her do to Plunkett.

She sobered. "That's exactly why I was so reluctant to marry you. I could see at once that you would not be nearly so . . . tractable as Mr. Plunkett."

"I am a bit larger," he conceded.

"That, too. But I doubt I could overpower even Mr. Plunkett without surprise on my side. No, I was referring to your strength of character, more than your physical strength."

"Indeed?"

Dina nodded. "Within moments of meeting you, I could tell that you were a man of conviction, who would not be persuaded from any course he felt to be the right one. A man who could not be bought."

"I am flattered. But I'm also curious as to what it was that gave you that impression. From other things you have told me, I gather that you have not known many such men."

"Very few," she agreed, "and none well. Our vicar, I suppose, and perhaps one or two others." She fell silent for a moment, thinking. "I believe it was your concern for Violet, as well as, paradoxically, your initial distrust of me."

He had to smile. "I did subject you to quite the inquisition before agreeing, as I recall. It never occurred to me that you would find that admirable, however."

"Your approach showed both honesty and intelligence." She smiled tentatively back at him. "Qualities I have come to appreciate even more as I've become better acquainted with you."

Thor felt a rush of tenderness for Dina, not tempered in the least by the knowledge that she could box as well as many men. "I hope that in time you will discover more about me that you will approve—just as I am discovering about you."

In answer, she moved closer and again folded her hands over his arm, leaning her head against his shoulder.

They fairly flew along the road, Thor pushing the horses as fast as he dared, but still there was no sign of a brown coach. At Spilsby they learned that Moore was still nearly half an hour ahead of them, and still headed south. At Boston they were forced to change horses, as the bays were nearly spent.

"A brown coach, with two passengers," Thor prompted the hostler as he unhitched the pair. "A large man and a dark-haired woman."

"Aye, they was here, changing horses like yourself. The young lady seemed a might agitated, wanted to go into the inn, but the gent wouldn't hear of it. In a terrible hurry, he was. They left not twenty minutes since, headed toward Sleaford with our fastest pair."

Thor pulled out half a crown and flashed it.

"Oh, aye, sir," the hostler said before he could even speak, eyeing the coin in Thor's hand. "I c'n have you on your way in half a moment, with our next best."

True to the man's word, only a minute or two later they were thundering along the road again, this time headed east. "They can't be far ahead now," Thor muttered.

"How much faster do you think their horses are?" Dina asked anxiously.

He shrugged. "There's no way to tell, but they're driving a heavier coach, which has to count for something. With any luck, we'll catch up to them before they reach Sleaford."

But luck seemed to be conspiring against them. Halfway to Sleaford, some blasted shepherd chose just the wrong moment to drive his flock across the road. By the time the last stragglers were out of the way and Thor was able to set the team back in motion, they had lost nearly ten minutes.

"Why the devil wasn't that fellow out celebrating Boxing Day like other decent people?" Thor muttered savagely.

Dina patted his arm. "We'll catch them. No harm will come to Violet, I'm sure of it."

Thor wished he could share her confidence. What if Moore had other confederates besides Plunkett and had switched coaches again? They could even now be pursuing the wrong one while Moore and Violet were headed straight to Scotland. He did not speak his fear aloud, however, merely nodding as though reassured.

At Sleaford they changed horses again, but again Moore had taken the best the village had to offer. At least Thor was reassured to discover they were still on the right road, and that they had cut Moore's lead to a mere ten minutes. As they neared the much larger town of Grantham, on the Great North Road, they began to encounter other vehicles on the road. Twice they had their hopes raised and then dashed as they overtook brown coaches that proved not to be the one they sought.

Finally, not five miles out of Grantham, with the daylight nearly gone, Thor sighted another coach up ahead that looked to be brown. Dina, at his side, leaned forward.

"Please, please, let it be them," she chanted.

It was. That became obvious as soon as they drew near and the other coach suddenly picked up speed. With a shout of triumph, Thor urged his pair to a canter, and the lighter curricle began gaining on the larger coach.

They had nearly caught up when Moore's head appeared in the window of the coach, shouting directions at the driver, who moved to the center of the road, preventing Thor from passing. "That tactic can only work for so long," Thor said grimly. "Eventually another carriage—ah."

Even as he spoke, a traveling coach with a team of four horses rounded the bend up ahead, coming toward them at a placid trot. Moore's coach held the center of the road for another dozen yards or so, then the driver swung his pair over to the side.

Thor was ready. "Hold on," he cried to Dina. The moment there was enough space to pass, he plied his whip, startling his own pair to a burst of speed that sent the curricle hurtling past the brown coach, then deftly swerved to the side with only a few feet to spare before the chaise and four lumbered past, its driver shaking his fist and swearing something about "damned holiday drunkards."

Now that he was in front of Moore's coach, Thor moved his own vehicle to the center of the road, blocking the other from passing as he gradually slowed, forcing the larger coach to do the same. Glancing ahead, he saw that the road would soon widen slightly. Deciding they had slowed enough for safety, he executed the same maneuver he'd used to stop Plunkett, turning the curricle to block the road completely.

A better driver, or even one driving a familiar team rather than a hired one, might have managed to get around the curricle, but Moore's driver didn't even try. When his pair shied, he pulled the coach to a halt. At once Moore slammed out of the coach with a curse.

"Damn it, man, I knew I should have driven myself. Spineless wastrel, you should have tried—" He broke off as Thor leaped down from the curricle and advanced on him.

"You had to know you would never get away with this, Moore."

The other man wheeled to face him, his face red with fury. "That's all you know, Turpin. If I'd been driving—"

"But you weren't." Thor kept his voice calm, knowing instinctively that would infuriate Moore more than anger would. Any moment now, the fellow would give him an excuse to thrash him.

"Grant?" Violet's voice came from the coach, and

an instant later she was clambering out. "Thank heaven!"

"Get back in the coach," Moore shouted over his shoulder. "I'll deal with this, and then—"

"No, Silas, you won't." It was Dina this time, speaking from behind Thor. "Violet, go around the other side of the coach and get into our curricle."

Moore's eyes bulged with fury as he glared past Thor's shoulder. "You! You conniving, disloyal, whoring little—"

That was enough for Thor. With intense satisfaction, he sent his fist crashing into Moore's jaw, effectively silencing him. Moore was no Plunkett, however, but a powerful man nearly as large as Thor himself. Though he staggered and went to one knee, in a moment he was up again and charging, head lowered.

Thor barely had time to get into a defensive stance before Moore crashed into him, fists flying. He caught one in the stomach and another in the side, then came back with a blow to Moore's ribs that made the other man grunt.

"Stop it," Dina cried from behind him. "This will solve nothing. Silas, please!"

From the corner of his eye, Thor saw Dina moving past him to make a grab for her brother's right arm. To Thor's horror, before he could prevent him, Moore swung a fist at her. Though she tried to side-step, the blow caught her shoulder with enough force to send her flying back several feet to land in a crumpled heap on the road. Somewhere behind him, he heard Violet screaming.

With a roar of fury, Thor launched himself at Moore, bearing him to the ground beneath him. Straddling his chest, he rained blow after blow on his enemy's face, a red haze all but obscuring his vision. He'd never been so angry in his life. Beneath him, Moore struggled and gasped, trying to ward off the blows with his hands, but Thor was like a man possessed.

Dimly he became aware of voices, then felt small hands tugging at his shoulders.

"Thor, don't! You'll kill him." Incredibly it was Dina. Startled and relieved, he turned from his victim to see her standing there, dusty but not visibly hurt.

"Yes, Grant, please stop. He's not going anywhere," came Violet's voice from his other side. "If he tries, I . . . I have a pistol." Indeed, she was gingerly brandishing the weapon he'd brought along, then left in the curricle in his eagerness to engage Moore physically.

The red haze receded, and Thor glanced down at his adversary, whose left eye was beginning to swell shut. He rose and took the pistol from Violet, then aimed it at Moore. "He deserves to die for what he did. He could have killed Dina just now—"

"But he didn't," Dina said, putting both hands over the one that held the gun, forcing him to lower it. "I'm barely bruised."

Thor frowned down at her, anxiously raking her from head to toe with his gaze. "Are you sure? I thought—"

"I'm sure. I won't deny that Silas deserves punishment—severe punishment—for kidnapping

Violet and putting her through such an ordeal, but I doubt she wants you to become a murderer any more than I do. He's not worth it."

"No, Grant, he's not. We won't let you do it." Violet moved to his other side. "Let the authorities deal with him instead."

His anger ebbed away, to be replaced by relief at Dina's safety—and Violet's. Thor heaved a great sigh. "Very well. But I should warn you both that what he's done will almost certainly result in his hanging."

Both women gasped.

Moore, still prostrate on the ground, made a choking sound of protest. "Dina," he whispered. "Please. You can't allow—"

"Is there no other alternative?" Violet asked when Dina made no response. "Dina, you won't want the notoriety that would come with a trial, will you?"

"I . . . I suppose not," she conceded, frowning down at her brother. "But I'd far rather that, than for Thor himself to get into any trouble with the law."

Thor glanced from Violet's pleading face to Dina's troubled one and made a sudden decision. "Very well. Let's get him into the coach. You there," he called to the dumbstruck driver, who had watched the entire proceeding from the box of the coach. "Drive my curricle into Grantham. We'll meet you at the Black Boar."

He darted a frightened glance at Dina, who nodded. "It is all right, Jefferson. If you cooperate, I'll see that you are not implicated in my brother's crimes, for I know you were merely following his orders."

Nodding, he scrambled down from the box. "D'ye need help gettin' Mr. Moore into the coach?"

Though conscious, Moore seemed unable to stand on his own, and it took both Thor and the coachman, with a bit of help from Dina, to hoist him to his feet and bundle him into the coach. Even though Moore looked helpless at the moment, Thor took a length of spare rein and tied his hands behind his back as a precaution, then handed the pistol to Dina.

"Do you know how to use this?" He wasn't particularly surprised when she nodded. "I need to drive, so it will be up to you and Violet to see that he doesn't escape—not that he looks in any condition to try it just now."

"Are we going back to Plumrose?" Violet asked. "It's nearly dark."

Thor shook his head. "We'll leave the curricle in Grantham, then head to Melton-Mowbray. With fresh horses, we should reach Ivy Lodge in less than three hours."

He waited until the curricle had started off, then climbed onto the box of the coach and flicked the reins, hoping he had done the right thing by sparing Moore's life. Of course, killing him might well have alienated Dina forever. Still, he very much hoped that Rush could advise him on his remaining options for dealing with Moore.

Inside the coach, Dina settled herself in the backward-facing seat beside Violet, since neither of them cared to sit next to Silas. As her brother was both tied and nearly unconscious, she did not bother to keep the pistol trained on him, but kept it on her lap, where she could bring it into play if necessary. She did not think she would hesitate to use it if she had to, for she was nearly as angry with Silas as Thor had been.

After all that Thor had done for him—that she had done for him—to help him out of debt, only to have him betray their trust in such a way . . . She'd never had a high opinion of her brother's ethics, but she would not have guessed he would stoop to something like this. Clearly she had been blinded by family loyalty, but no more.

"What do you think Grant means to do?" Violet asked after they had driven in silence for several minutes.

"I don't know. He spends a lot of time in Melton-Mowbray, so perhaps there is a magistrate in the area he wishes to consult."

At that, Silas stirred. "Don't let him take me to a magistrate, Dina," he mumbled through thickened lips. "You heard what he said. Kidnapping is a hanging offense."

"You should have thought of that before you committed it, then," she told him sharply. "Honestly, Silas, I don't know what you could have been thinking to do something so stupid—so vile."

He flinched at the tone of her voice, but then struggled to sit up straighter. "It's your own fault," he said, his voice a bit clearer as his senses returned. "You drove me to it, with this accursed marriage of yours. I had no choice."

"Of course you had a choice," she snapped.

"You've always had the choice of living within your means, of giving up the gaming. Of treating others with respect. It's simply not the way you choose to live, and now you are likely to pay for that."

They arrived at the Black Boar then, and Dina was just as glad, for there were things she wished to say to Silas that were not fit for Violet's ears. She would strive to get her temper under better control before they continued on to Ivy Lodge.

"Everything all right?" Thor asked her, opening the door to the coach. Though he glanced at Silas, the concern in his eyes was for her alone.

"He's revived enough to attempt bargaining, but yes, we are all fine." Reaching up, she touched his bruised cheek. "I'm sorry he was able to hurt you before you subdued him."

Thor seemed to start at her words. "Me? I was afraid he had killed you with that blow. I've never been so relieved in my life as when I saw you standing next to me." He helped her down from the coach, then pulled her to him, only to release her abruptly. "I'm sorry. I didn't hurt you, did I?"

Dina had to laugh. "I'm fine. Didn't I just say so? Perhaps a bruise or two, but nothing worse. When will you believe—"

"I hate to interrupt, but . . . may I get out of the coach?" asked Violet, leaning out of the door. "I've been in it for hours, except for our altercation on the road."

Thor turned to help his sister to the ground, then took the pistol from Dina while the ladies went inside the inn to use the necessary. By the time they returned, the horses had been changed and old Jefferson put up at the inn for the night.

A few minutes later, they were on their way again. To Dina's relief, Silas did not renew his whining, contenting himself instead with glaring across at her in sullen silence. Violet, understandably exhausted by her ordeal, soon fell asleep. Dina was tired as well, but dared not close her eyes with Silas in his present mood. Instead she passed the time by wondering what Thor meant to do with her brother—and by occasionally stroking the pistol in her lap.

It must have been nine o'clock when the coach finally stopped again. Dina blinked, realizing that she must have dozed after all. Luckily Silas had fallen asleep as well. Now he sat up again, as did Violet, both blinking bleared eyes.

"Where are we?" Silas asked groggily.

"Ivy Lodge," Thor replied, opening the door of the coach just as Silas spoke. "Ladies?"

As he helped them from the coach, Dina saw the door to the ivy-covered house open and two or three figures emerge.

"Rush, is that you?" Thor called. When Lord Rushford's voice answered in the affirmative, Thor beckoned him over. "I need your assistance here—and Stormy's, too."

Dina and Violet stepped back and watched while the three friends hauled Silas bodily from the coach. He was now able to stand on his own, though his hands were still tied behind him.

Lord Rushford looked from the ladies to Silas to the coach, then said, "I confess, I am all agog to hear the story of what brings such an unlikely group here at such an unlikely time."

"Let's all get indoors," Thor suggested. "Once I tell you everything, perhaps you can put your vaunted capacity for strategy to good use and advise me on my next course."

An hour later, Dina found herself in the comfortable parlor of Ivy Lodge, surrounded by several members of the Odd Sock Hunt Club, which seemed to comprise Thor's best and most trusted friends. The travelers had been fed, Silas's hands untied so that he could eat. He now sat near the fireplace with everyone else in a semicircle around him, looking very much like a prisoner on trial.

"I agree he deserves the hangman's noose," Lord Rushford was saying, "but I understand your inclination to spare him." He glanced at Dina. "Still, he's proved himself completely without principle, so I can't see allowing him to simply go his own way."

"Certainly not," exclaimed Lady Killerby, a handsome, middle-aged dowager who had been visiting her son at Ivy Lodge and who seemed to have installed herself as a matriarch of sorts. "Such impudence cannot go unpunished. What have you to say for yourself, young man?"

Silas blinked, for it was the first time in the discussion that someone had addressed him directly. "Er . . . that I'm very sorry, my lady, and will never do any such thing again."

Dina was startled when Lady Killerby snorted rudely. "Pretty words are easy enough to say. I don't believe them for a moment. What made you think you could carry off such a scheme as eloping with an unwilling lady?" She gestured toward Violet, who appeared to be struggling to stay awake.

"It was a foolish impulse." Silas looked contrite, but Dina didn't believe it any more than Lady Killerby did. "When she refused my offer, I was so distraught that I fear I was not thinking clearly."

"It was a remarkably well-planned impulse," Thor said dryly, "as you had clearly already arranged with Plunkett to exchange vehicles to put off pursuit."

Silas's eyes darted around the room, his composure slipping. "It, ah, it was Plunkett's idea. I should have guessed he would put you on my trail. He's as guilty as I, believe me."

"Perhaps not quite, but it may comfort you to know he did not escape unscathed." Thor looked over at Dina with a half smile that sent a pleasurable tingle down her spine, despite the seriousness of the current proceedings. "In fact, he may well be leaving England soon to avoid further consequences."

"Perhaps that would be the best solution for Silas as well," said Dina on sudden inspiration. "We have an uncle in America. Silas could take ship and join him there."

"Uncle Kendall?" Silas asked, clearly alarmed. "But he doesn't even like me."

Dina smiled, liking her plan more and more. "Because he could always see right through your little schemes. He won't allow you to impose upon him, that's true. But as you are his nephew, he won't turn you away, either."

"I . . . I suppose not," Silas conceded. "But—"

"An excellent solution," Lord Rushford declared. "What say you, Moore? You have the choice of starting over in America or relying on the tender mercies of the English judiciary."

Silas flinched, but Dina could not find it in her to feel sorry for him. "Very well. I'll go to Uncle Kendall."

"Good choice," said Thor. "But before you leave, I believe it would be best if you signed over your share of Ashcombe to your sister, as you will not be in any position to care for it. In return, I'm sure she will be willing to pay your passage and advance you a small sum to set yourself up in some trade or other across the Atlantic."

For a moment, Dina thought Silas would refuse. But then she could see him working through his options and realizing that he had none. Reluctantly he nodded.

"I suppose I can trust her to see the estate don't come to ruin," he said grudgingly. "What do I need to do?"

Lord Rushford, who seemed to have some expertise in such matters, began outlining what documents would need to be written up, signed, and witnessed, while Dina listened in growing disbelief. Ashcombe was to be hers! With Silas no longer draining away its income, she had no doubt that she could turn it back into the productive estate it once had been—with Thor's help.

She looked over at her husband with a grateful smile, to find him watching her.

"You approve?" he asked quietly.

Dina nodded, her mind flooding with possibilities.

"Then I propose we leave for Ashcombe in the morning."

Chapter 22

In fact, their departure was delayed until Saturday, for it took all of the next day to make the arrangements that would change the course of more than one life. With the help of a local solicitor, the necessary papers were drawn up to transfer full ownership of Ashcombe to Dina and Thor.

Lord Rushford was persuaded to escort Violet back to Plumrose, under the chaperonage of Lady Killerby, who claimed she was longing to see Lady Rumble again. Viscount Killerby, her son, offered to come along as well, as he was still unable to hunt as a result of an injury he had sustained early in the season.

And Sir Charles and Lord Uppingwood, another member of the Odd Sock Hunt Club, offered to escort Silas to Bristol, where Lord Uppingwood had family, from which port Silas would be able to take ship to New York, in America, where Uncle Kendall lived.

Dina's only disappointment, among so many satisfactory developments, was that she and Thor had yet to share a bed. While at Ivy Lodge, Lady Killerby had insisted that Dina share a chamber with Violet to preserve propriety in such an overwhelmingly male establishment.

"Though no fault of her own, this incident is of just the sort that is likely to cause talk," Lady Killerby affirmed. "Should that occur, it will be as well if we can all say that there was never the least opportunity for Miss Turpin to have been visited in private by any gentleman during her absence from home."

She could not disagree with Lady Killerby's reasoning, Dina supposed, however it might frustrate her personal plans.

Finally, however, all was settled, and three carriages stood in the yard before Ivy Lodge, ready to leave for their various destinations.

"Good-bye, Silas," Dina said to her brother. "Please believe that I wish you the very best in your new life in America. Give Uncle Kendall my love."

Silas gave a terse nod. "Take care of yourself, Dina. And you, Turpin, treat her properly, won't you?"

"You have my word on it," Thor promised, one hand on Dina's shoulder.

As he climbed into the coach beside Lord Uppingwood, Dina could not suppress a last twinge of wistfulness for what might have been. Perhaps, someday, in the distant future—

"Grant, you and Dina will be returning to Plumrose soon, will you not?" Violet asked as Lord Uppingwood's coach started off, interrupting Dina's melancholy thoughts.

"I'm not certain," Thor replied, glancing down at Dina. "There may be much to do at Ashcombe before we can safely leave it in the hands of the steward. We won't know how much until we get there and look things over."

Violet started to pout, but then seemed to remember something and grinned conspiratorially at Dina. "Well, take your time, then. Just don't forget about my come-out next month. I am counting on you both to rescue me from Aunt Philomena."

She hugged and kissed them both, then turned expectantly to Lord Rushford to help her into Lady Killerby's coach. However, little Lord Killerby was quicker, despite his limp, and stepped forward to hand her up beside his mother.

"Keep an eye on her, won't you, Killer, Rush?" Thor called as the gentlemen climbed into the coach after her. "The girl's already eloped twice, so there's no knowing what she might attempt next."

Violet's indignant protest was cut off when Lord Rushford closed the coach door and the coachman whipped up the team.

"And now it's just us." Thor smiled down at Dina with an expression that made her heart pound. "Shall we?"

He opened the door of the last coach, the same brown one Silas had used for his kidnapping, though with a far superior pair of horses. Dina allowed him to help her inside, fighting down an absurd flutter of nervousness as he seated himself beside her and closed the door.

"If all goes well," Thor said as the coach started off, "we should reach Ashcombe by dinnertime. What is the first thing you'd like to do once we get there?"

"Decide which bedchamber we will occupy for our stay," she replied daringly.

Thor chuckled and pulled her against his side. "I was going to suggest beginning the construction of a swimming pool."

Though she laughed along with him, Dina felt a stab of irritation. Did he still believe that they could only safely be intimate with such a precaution? She was determined to prove him wrong—and before morning. Here in the coach was hardly the place to start, however, so she turned the conversation to her hopes and tentative plans for the estate.

With just one stop at midday for luncheon and a change of horses, they were able to reach Ashcombe before nightfall. Thor helped Dina from the carriage with a renewed sense of relief that the problem that was Silas Moore had been solved so neatly. He only wished the same could be true of his remaining problem—that of achieving the kind of marriage he and Dina both desired.

Though he supposed he should feel reassured that she was tougher than he'd assumed, the events of the past few days had served to make him feel more protective of Dina than ever. That moment on the road when she had crumpled after a blow from her brother's fist still haunted him.

"Good evening, Purseglove," Dina greeted the startled butler when he opened to Thor's knock. "Will you please gather all of the staff here in the hall as quickly as possible? I have an announcement to make to them."

Though the man's brow furrowed with apprehension, he only said, "Of course, ma'am. I'll have a footman bring in your luggage."

"Er, we don't have any," Thor said, hoping the Ashcombe servants were not overly given to gossip. "It will be arriving in a day or two, however."

"Very good, sir." His eyes bright with curiosity and concern, Purseglove left to carry out Dina's order.

A few minutes later, some dozen or so servants were collected in the entry hall, their faces all reflecting their anxiety at such an unprecedented event. Thor stood off to one side, letting Dina handle this, as they had agreed.

"Thank you for coming so quickly," she began. "I have something to tell you that will undoubtedly come as a surprise."

"Please, mum, are we all to be sacked?" blurted out one young housemaid, apparently unable to contain her worries. Though the housekeeper quickly shushed her, the older woman's expression was just as distraught.

"Sacked?" Dina repeated, looking around at them all. "Certainly not. Why should you think such a thing?"

"Er, well, ma'am, we know money has been tight," the housekeeper, Mrs. Macready, explained, twisting her apron between her hands. "And Mr. Moore has threatened to let every one of us go, at one time or another." She peered past Dina toward the front door, as though expecting him to come bursting in at any moment.

Dina smiled around at all the anxious faces. "You no longer need to fear anything my brother might have threatened, for he will not be returning to Ashcombe for quite some time—perhaps ever. He has decided to take an extended trip to New York, in America, to visit our uncle there, and has left the management of the house and estate to me—and to Mr. Turpin." She nodded toward Thor.

A few of the junior servants broke into a spontaneous cheer before the butler and housekeeper frowned them into better decorum. Purseglove then turned to Dina with the first smile Thor had seen on his face. "That . . . that is welcome news, ma'am, if I may say so."

"You may indeed. Over the next few days, Mr. Turpin will be going over the books with the steward, and if any of your wages are in arrears, they will be paid up. I hope that together we can all make Ashcombe a more pleasant place to live and work."

This time the senior staff made no effort to quiet the younger ones when they cheered, instead joining in the general air of celebration.

"But now, ma'am, sir, do let us freshen up your rooms," said Mrs. Macready, beckoning to two of the housemaids. "And I don't doubt that Cook will want to put together something extra special for your dinner, as soon as may be. Shall I put Mr. Turpin in Mr. Moore's old chambers, next to your own, ma'am?"

Dina nodded. "And have the door between the

two chambers unlocked, if you please. We'll wait in the parlor until everything is ready."

The servants all bustled off, and Thor followed Dina to the parlor. "You handled that admirably," he told her once they were alone. "Not that I doubted for a moment that you would." He was beginning to wonder if there was any area in which Dina could not impress him with her competence.

"I've known most of the servants for years. Some, all of my life." She smiled a bit wistfully. "I confess, I have missed them—and my home—more than I ever expected to when I first left here a month ago."

"Not surprising, as you've lived your whole life here, even if some of your memories are less than pleasant."

"Some, yes," she conceded. "But I have many happy ones as well: of my mother when she was alive, of my uncle Kendall's visits and the lessons he gave me, my rambles about the countryside, swimming in the pond—" She stopped, coloring slightly.

Thor felt his body responding to the same memory. "Perhaps tomorrow you can show me the pond—though just now it is likely iced over. I would like to learn all I can about Ashcombe."

"Yes, the better you know it, the better you will be able to advise me on how we might turn it back into a profitable estate."

"That, too. But I find myself wanting to see all of the places you haunted as a girl, to share in your favorite memories of the place. Will you show me?"

Her face lit up with delight. "Truly? I should love to do that. Tomorrow, after services, we can start with

the house and grounds, then traipse about the countryside. I'll . . . I'll show you all my secret retreats."

Thor was touched more than he could express by
the trust that promise implied. He prayed he would
never do anything to violate it.

Dinner was announced then, and they repaired to
the dining room. The servants, clearly delighted at
the change of regime, were assiduous in their atten-
tions during the meal, frequently expressing their
pleasure at having Dina home. As a result, Thor and
Dina were forced to keep their conversation to
household and estate matters, since they never had
the room to themselves.

As the last plates were cleared away, Thor rose, feeling no particular desire to linger alone with a cigar or
brandy. "Would you care to return to the parlor?"

But Dina shook her head. "Why do we not see if
our bedchambers are ready? You will not have seen
yours yet, and will want to make some changes, I
know."

"Tonight, all I care about is having clean linens to
sleep on, after so much travel," Thor said, though in
fact his thoughts were straying to other possibilities.
Dina had not suggested any such thing, however,
and he was not about to press for anything that
might cause her discomfort.

"Come, then," she said, getting up and tucking
her hand through his arm.

As they mounted the stairs, Thor fought to subdue
his body's eagerness for something that almost certainly would not take place tonight. Dina was tired.
He was tired. Or so he kept telling himself.

"This is my room, as you may recall," she said, opening a door on the right to reveal a pleasant chamber boasting a large four-poster hung in yellow and green, and a wide stone fireplace, in which a cheerful fire already crackled.

"Yours will now be the next one along—the best bedroom, by the bye, or it will be once you've arranged it to your liking." Closing the door to her chamber, she opened the one to his.

Though he felt rather uncomfortable at the idea of sleeping in the room her brother had occupied, Thor could not deny that it was a handsome chamber of noble proportions, with wide, double windows, heavy, well-made furniture, and beautifully carved woodwork. The colors were a bit somber for his taste, but that would be easy enough to remedy.

"I take it these were your parents' rooms, when they were alive?"

Dina nodded. "They are so much larger and nicer than the others that Silas and I moved into them after a year or so."

Remembering the shabby guest chamber he had occupied on his previous visit to Ashcombe, Thor could not fault their decision. "I'm sure we can make the other rooms more pleasant as well, with some work, against the day that they might be needed for visitors."

"An excellent idea," she agreed, stepping into the room to pull the window curtains closed. "You have candles on the mantel and desk, and an oil lamp on the bedside table," she pointed out. "Until our things arrive in a few days, I fear you will have to make do with some of Silas's clothes, though they will doubtless be a bit small."

Was it his imagination, or did she seem nervous? "I'm certain I can manage," he said. "If necessary, we can drive into Litchfield on Monday and purchase a few things."

"Yes. Of . . . of course." She was definitely nervous. "This door leads to a dressing room," she said, opening it, "beyond which is another, then my chamber." She tried the handle of the door linking the dressing rooms, and it turned under her hand. Clearly the housekeeper had unlocked it, as she had requested.

Blushing, she turned back to him. "Ah, as my maid is still at Plumrose, I thought—that is—would you mind helping me change for bed?" She asked the question in a rush, as though determined to get it out before she could lose her courage.

Thor felt his throat drying at the thought of undressing her. Surely that would not be a good idea? Safer for one of the housemaids to—

"Certainly," he heard himself saying. "As my valet is not here, either, I could use some assistance as well."

That was not true, for he could easily disrobe without her help, but it seemed the . . . polite thing to say.

"Of course. Let's, ah, go into my room, shall we?"

Thor could understand her reluctance to undress, to . . . do anything else . . . in the room that had so recently been her brother's. He would make some changes to the chamber tomorrow, he decided, though he didn't examine why that seemed so important.

Wordlessly he followed her through the two dressing rooms to her chamber, trying to keep his eyes from the inviting four-poster as she led him to a spot right next to it. She had only asked for help with her clothing, he reminded himself. Besides—

Without warning, Dina turned, put her hands on his shoulders, and pulled him down for a kiss. After one startled instant, Thor responded, gathering her slight body to him, delighting in the taste of her lips, the firm lushness of her curves. She was everything he wanted—everything he could ever imagine wanting.

Just before the capacity for rational thought left him entirely, however, he remembered the possible danger they were courting. Gently he disengaged himself from her kiss to look down at her tenderly. Not for the world would he have her believe he did not want this.

"Dina," he whispered huskily, "you know I don't want to hurt you. Wouldn't it be better—"

"No." Her voice startled him with its firmness. "It would not be better to wait. I'd hoped, after what you've learned of me over the past few days, you would realize I am not nearly so breakable as you had feared. Let me prove it to you."

She looked up at him, her lips slightly parted, wet and swollen from his kisses. A shudder of overwhelming desire went through him, but still he tried to protest.

"Not breakable, no. But you must be sore, bruised—"

"Do I act as though I'm sore?" she asked, pressing against him again. "If Silas's deliberate attempt to hurt me did no real damage, can you honestly think you are likely to harm me by accident?"

He did not answer, so torn was he between his need of her and his determination to protect her. While he hesitated, she untied the simple knot of his cravat, then began unbuttoning his shirt.

"You won't hurt me, Thor," she whispered. "I won't let you. And you must tell me if I hurt you, for I don't promise to be gentle this time."

So saying, she pushed him backward with a force that took him completely unaware, given their disparity in size. The edge of the bed hit him behind the knees, and he found himself falling back onto the soft mattress. Before he could push himself upright, Dina clambered atop him.

"This would be much easier if we already had our clothes off," she told him, undoing the last of his shirt buttons. "Luckily this gown fastens down the front." Not until she began unbuttoning her dress did Thor suddenly realize she had not needed his help at all.

"Here, let me do that," he said. With that push onto the bed, she had finally convinced him that she was indeed strong enough to withstand his love-making, if he was careful. His decision made, he was eager—more than eager—to begin. Deftly he released her from her bodice, then sat up just enough to pull his shirt off over his head.

"Can I get up for a moment?" she asked. "Do I have you properly subdued?"

He grinned up at her, wondering how he ever could have doubted that Dina was the perfect woman for him. He loved her with all his being. "You have indeed. I promise not to run away."

"Good." Standing up, she quickly struggled out of her gown, then unlaced her corset and discarded that as well. Thor watched her with hungry eyes before belatedly remembering that he was still half clad as well.

When she bent to remove her shoes and stockings, he sat up and took off his own, then hurriedly undid his breeches. When he started to stand to pull them off, however, she pushed him back to the bed. "No, you don't. Promise or no, I'm not letting you off this bed until I get what I want from you," she said teasingly.

She tugged at his breeches, and he obligingly lifted his hips to assist her in their removal. When he finally sprang free of them, he saw her eyes widen with desire. With a fluid movement, she pulled her shift off over her head. For a moment she stood there, gloriously naked. He drank in the sight of her, feeling ready to explode already.

He started to sit up again, to reach for her. At once, she flung herself at the bed, straddling him as she had before, but this time with nothing separating them. Exultantly he ran his hands up and down her sides, exploring her curves, then pulled her face down to his for a long, deep kiss that was a mere taste of what was to come.

Her mysterious cleft was just brushing his shaft, and now he slid his hands down to her waist to move her along it, much as he'd done in the pool. She gasped, and he could feel that already she was slick and ready for him.

Still he took his time, sliding her hips back and forth, back and forth, rubbing her sensitive nubbin along the length of him, holding himself back until he felt her body tense with the beginning of her climax. Then, lifting her with both hands, he impaled her, driving upward into her glorious depths.

Throwing back her head so that her hair streamed down her back, she cried out, but he had no fear that it was a cry of pain. She began contracting around him, and he lost the capacity for thought, burying himself deeper and deeper within her, in that age-old rhythm of ecstasy.

Above him, she rocked, faster and faster, then cried out again, just as he reached his own peak, emptying himself into her in an exquisite rush. He heard himself chanting her name, over and over, as their rhythm slowed.

Finally she collapsed atop him, her body slick with sweat, her breathing still fast and shallow. He cradled her against him, the most precious being in the world.

Dina had never imagined her experience in the pool could be repeated, much less exceeded. She had to admit, however, that it had. It seemed incredible that she could survive so much pleasure.

"I didn't hurt you, did I?" she murmured sleepily, her head nestled in the hollow of his throat.

He chuckled, a lovely rumble in his chest beneath her cheek. "Not at all. And I won't even ask, because I know you'd have told me if I had."

"Mmm. Exactly. I'd never keep a secret like that from someone I—that is—" She broke off in confusion, panicked by how nearly she had told him she loved him. She had sworn to herself she would not burden him with that knowledge, not until she was sure—

"Dina?" he said softly. "Dare I hope you were going to say, 'someone I love'?"

Embarrassed, she nodded into his neck.

His arms tightened around her. "I'm glad to know that, because I've been longing to tell you for days that I love you, but feared you might not be ready to hear it."

She lifted her head to stare at him. "Truly, Thor?"

He nodded, a smile playing about his perfect lips. "Truly, Dina. I love you more than I ever thought it possible to love anyone."

Leaning forward, she kissed him. "I love you, too—so, so much. But I was afraid—"

"Shh. No more fears—for either of us. And no more waiting until we have a body of water handy."

They both chuckled, and for a long moment, she lay contentedly in his arms. Then she lifted her head again to regard him quizzically. "I hope that doesn't mean we can't, ah, visit the pool again, when we return to Plumrose?"

"Not at all. I believe I'll always have a special fondness for that swimming pool now," he said with a smile. "But we may not be back there for some time."

"What do you mean?" She'd assumed he would want to go home as soon as they had things in order here at Ashcombe.

"It occurs to me that living with my parents may not be the best way for us to begin our new lives together, nor have I spent enough time at Plumrose in recent years for it to feel much like home to me. Not the way I know Ashcombe feels like home to you."

Sudden delight welled up in her breast. "Do you mean we can live here? Stay to oversee all of the improvements we have discussed? I should like that above all things."

"That's exactly what I mean—assuming we survive Violet's come-out in London next month." They both laughed, and then he continued, "Living here will give me a chance to learn a bit about estate management before the time comes that I will have to manage my own. Besides, newlyweds should have a place to call their own, don't you think?"

She nodded happily, a beautiful vision of the future opening up to her imagination. "I do believe that running off to Scotland was the best decision I ever made."

Summer nights are hotter than ever thanks to these July releases from Avon Romance . . .

The Marriage Bed by Laura Lee Guhrke

An Avon Romantic Treasure

Everyone in society knows that the marriage of Lord and Lady Hammond is an unhappy one. But all that is about to change, when John, Lord Hammond, begins to see what a beautiful woman he is married to. Now he prays it's not too late to win back the love of his very own wife.

The Hunter by Gennita Low

An Avon Contemporary Romance

In order for Hawk McMillan, SEAL commander, to succeed in his latest lone mission, he needs a tracker, and the best woman for that job is CIA contact agent Amber Hutchens. But when their mission requires Hawk and Amber to risk everything, they've got too much at stake to stay far away from danger . . . or from their passion.

More Than a Scandal by Sari Robins

An Avon Romance

Lovely Catherine Miller has always been timid—until the treachery of unscrupulous cousins threatens her childhood home. To save it, she steals the identity of the notorious "Thief of Robinson Square" who, years ago, preyed on pompous society to help the poor.

The Daring Twin by Donna Fletcher

An Avon Romance

When Fiona of the MacElder clan is told that she must wed Tarr of Hellewyk so the two clans can unite, she is furious. Fortunately, Fiona's identical twin sister Aliss is on her side. The two boldly concoct an outlandish scheme—to make it impossible to tell who is who—and it works. The only trouble is, one of the twins accidentally falls in love with the would-be groom!

REL 0605

Knaur®

Benoîte Groult

(65043)

(60205)

(65040)

(65044)

(2997)

(3113)